SILENT SIN

E.J. RUSSELL

Published by Reality Optional Press

Cover art: Natasha Snow Designs, http://natashasnow.com
Edited by Liz Fitzgerald

ISBN: 978-1-947033-09-2

First edition
March, 2020

Contact information:
ejr@ejrussell.com

SILENT SIN

E.J. RUSSELL

For silent Hollywood's lost stars—faded, fallen, or forgotten, your legacy nevertheless endures.

TABLE OF
CONTENTS

CHAPTER ONE

July 28, 1921

Robbie slid the last crate of fruit out of Mr. Samson's truck and only wobbled a little as he handed it off to a grocer's assistant on the dusty Bakersfield road. He took off his battered straw hat, wiped the sweat off his forehead with the side of his arm, and settled the hat back on his head. Not that it kept out much sun—it was more holes than straw by this time.

Mr. Samson, the orange grower Robbie had been helping for the last two days, strolled out of the little store, tucking a wallet into his back pocket. Robbie snatched his hat off his head again.

"Will there be anything else, sir?"

"Not here." Samson's gaze slid away from his. "Don't have the cash to pay you anything now, but I might have something for you back home at the groves." He nodded at the truck. "I'll give you a lift."

Robbie's empty belly sank toward his toes, but he forced a smile. He'd learned in the last six weeks that the promise of a job rarely translated into money in his pocket, even if he actually did the work. A lift with the promise of work at the end of the ride—anything that got him farther from Idaho, really—

was more than he could hope for. "Thank you, sir." He stumbled toward the truck cab.

"Hold on, you. Not up front." Samson jerked his thumb toward the truck bed. "Back there. But give us a crank first."

Robbie nodded and scuffed through the dirt, where a pebble worked its way through the hole in the bottom of his right boot. He waited for Samson to get behind the wheel and then gave the handle a practiced crank. The engine caught, and the truck belched exhaust. Robbie hurried to the rear before Samson could change his mind about the lift too.

As he was about to scramble over the tailgate, he spotted half a dozen discarded half-squashed fruits—a lemon and five oranges—almost beneath the wheels. He scrabbled them out of the dust, rolled them into the truck bed, and heaved himself in after them. The jerk when Samson put the truck in gear nearly sent Robbie over backward, but he grabbed on to one of the rough slats that bracketed the bed to save himself, driving a sliver into his thumb.

He crawled forward, herding his contraband in front of him until he could sit with his back to the cab. As the truck jounced along, raising clouds of dust in its wake, Robbie gathered the precious fruit in his lap and hunched over his knees. Fingers trembling, he tore into the skin of the first orange and dropped the peel through the slats. He shoved the first section into his mouth and moaned as the tart juice hit his parched mouth and throat. *Squashed or not, this is pure heaven. How wonderful that people can grow something this marvelous, let alone make a living at it.*

His last meal was nothing but a hazy memory, so he ate one fruit after another—even the lemon, so sour it made his eyes water—as the string of discarded peels fell behind, a trail of gold dimmed by dust.

After he polished off the last orange, he licked his fingers. Then he picked at the sliver in this thumb as he tried to dodge puddles of fermenting juice whenever Mr. Samson took a corner too sharply. The exhaustion of weeks of rough travel, most of it on foot, caught up with him, and he fell into a fitful doze.

With a bone-rattling thump, the truck pulled to a stop. Robbie blinked, disoriented, and peered around in the glare of the setting sun. *Where are we?* His heart sank when he took in the sturdy buildings lining both sides of the road. *A good-sized town.* He tried to keep to open country whenever he could—less chance of getting work, but easier to find a stream for a drink and a wash or a secluded barn where he could catch enough shut-eye to go on the next day.

Mr. Samson slapped the side of the truck. "End of the line, kid."

Robbie scrambled to his feet and wiped his hands on his trousers, not that it did much good. His pants were as sticky as the truck bed.

He hopped down onto the road and caught the tailgate when a wave of dizziness threatened to take him down for the count. "Thanks for the lift. I appreciate it."

Mr. Samson tilted his cowboy hat back and scratched his forehead. "No skin off my nose. You were a good worker. But turns out, now I think about it, I don't need any help on the farm." He shrugged. "Sorry."

"I understand. Thanks anyway." He wished he hadn't fallen asleep on the ride. He had no idea where he was. "Does this road lead to Mexico?"

Mr. Samson hitched his dungarees up under his prosperous paunch. "Whatta you want to go there for? Nothing you can get there that you can't get here."

"Where's here?"

He jerked his thumb over his shoulder. "Hollywood."

Robbie shaded his eyes with one hand and scanned the storefronts across the road. Hollywood Dry Goods. Hollywood Haberdashers. Hollywood Drug Store. "I guess it is."

With a touch of his hat brim, Mr. Samson climbed into his truck. "Give us another crank, will you?"

Robbie complied and then backed away as the truck rattled off up a side street.

What the heck can I do in a place like this? Robbie doubted his years of scratching out a living on a potato farm would qualify him for work in some other grower's orange grove. There weren't any factories that he could see, and Hollywood Haberdashers wouldn't hire somebody with only one set of clothes—and those almost too worn to be decent.

Mexico still seemed like the best bet, but suddenly he couldn't muster the energy to take the next step or cadge the next lift or scrounge the next dime.

So he shoved his hands in his empty pockets, forced his back straight, and strode down the sidewalk as though he truly had someplace to go, as though he wasn't adrift or as castaway as his namesake—*Robinson Crusoe Goodman*. He shook his head as he followed the route Mr. Samson's truck had taken, away from the main street and up a slight hill. *Ma sure had some odd notions when it came to naming her sons.* Eddie had been lucky. At least Pa had put his foot down over Oedipus.

At the back of Mr. Samson's orange grove, Robbie found a wooden shack worthy of his old man's farm and secured with nothing but a two-by-four across its door. He slipped inside and blinked until his eyes adjusted to the gloom after the brightness of the westering sun. The dirt floor was littered with arm-long sections of metal pipe as big around as his head, and a stack of broken crates leaned against the wall like a rummy who'd never heard of the Volstead Act—not the most comfortable flop but better than he had any right to expect.

He curled up on the floor with his back to the wall, arms wrapped across his belly, and begged sleep to take him before he cried.

"I'm not working with Boyd Brody again, Sid. I can't." Martin Brentwood met his own gaze in the mirror over the drink cart in his living room. God, he looked like ten miles of bad road. "He tried to drown me."

Sid Howard, Martin's manager, emerged from the kitchen, drying his hands on a dish towel. "Come on, Marty. He was just kidding. Giving you the business, same as he does with any actor. You can't take this personal."

"I damn well do take it personally. He'd never try that shit with Fairbanks."

"Shite."

Martin frowned at Sid. "What?"

"A baronet's son from Hertfordshire wouldn't say 'shit.'"

"But I'm not a baronet's son from Hertfordshire." Martin sloshed more gin into his glass. "That would be you. Me? I'm only a tailor's apprentice from Flushing."

Sid tossed the towel on top of the piano and pried the glass out of Martin's grip. "No. That would be me. And don't forget it, even when we're alone. Even in your own head. It's easier to remember the lies if you live 'em full-time." Sid sniffed the contents of the tumbler and made a face. "And don't drink this shit. You'll go blind."

"I'll have you know this gin was brewed in Barstow's finest bathtubs." Martin shuffled to the davenport and flopped down on the cushions. "But you're right." He bared his teeth. "It's *shite*."

"That's more like it." Sid settled in the wingback chair across from Martin. "So. I met with Jacob Schlossberg today."

"Better you than me," Martin muttered. "I loathe the bastard, and the feeling is decidedly mutual."

"Maybe. But the reasons for the hate are different. You hate him because he's—"

"A pontificating blowhard with delusions of grandeur and the morals of a weasel?"

"*Because*," Sid raised his voice over Martin's, "he's the one who controls your career."

"He's not the only one. Ira owns half the studio."

"Yeah, but Ira's the talent-facing brother. Jacob's got his sausage-like finger on the studio's financial pulse. And when it comes down to it, at Citadel Motion Pictures, money'll trump talent every time."

Martin snorted. "So much for art."

"Pictures aren't art, Marty. They're business. *Big* business. And if nobody pays to see your picture, it don't matter if it's as arty as the Russian crown-fucking jewels."

"Really, Sid," Martin murmured. "Your language."

Sid grinned. "Unlike some, *I* don't forget who I'm supposed to be." Sid folded his hands on his knee, and no matter how much he might be able to ape a working-class stiff from Queens, if anybody in Hollywood paid attention, his hands would give him away. Tailor's apprentices didn't have the kind of practiced grace that had been drilled into Sid when he was busy getting kicked out of every prep school in England.

"As I said, I met with Jacob today."

"And?"

Sid's heavy brows drew together. "He and Ira are split on whether they want to re-up your contract. Ira's liked you since he brought you in from Inceville and put you in a suit instead of a cowboy hat. He thinks you're the best bet the studio has to counter Valentino. But Jacob… well…."

"I know, I know. He hates queers."

"Nobody knows for sure that you're queer, Marty." Sid's scowl said, "And keep it that way" louder than words could. "Anyway, Jacob may hate queers personally, but he depends on them too, as long as they're in their place."

Martin's snort was a low-class sound, but nobody could hear him except Sid, who already knew the truth. Sid had invented Martin's backstory. Hell, Sid had *lived* Martin's backstory and he'd traded it with Martin's when it became obvious which one of them could make a go of it in pictures.

"Right. In wardrobe. In the art department. Where the public never sees."

"It's not the invisibility that he cares about. He covets their taste. He knows he's got none. He's a stevedore's son from the Bronx. He craves sophistication, so you'll keep delivering it, because the only thing Jacob really hates is a threat to his profits. You can be as queer as Dick's bloody hatband and he wouldn't care as long as your pictures make money. But they won't make money if your fans turn away. Remember what happened to Jack Kerrigan."

"Kerrigan's popularity dropped because he made that asinine comment about being too good to go to war, not because he's queer."

"Exactly. But with the Hollywood press in their back pocket, the studio didn't lift a finger to save him. He'd become a liability with all his talk about no woman measuring up to Mother, and his lover tucked cozily away downstairs, masquerading as his secretary. You don't want to be in that position."

Martin pinched his eyes closed. "If it's not because they suspect I'm in the life, then what is it? The cocaine? Because I told you, I'm never taking that stuff again, no matter how much the studio doctor prescribes."

"No. It's because of your last driver. What was his name? Homer?"

"Vernon, actually."

"Right. Well, they don't like that you fired him."

"I fired him because he was a manipulative son of a bitch who saw driving a studio car as a sure way to stardom, provided he could fuck the right people."

"Swive."

"What? Are you telling me a baronet's son wouldn't say *fuck*?"

"Baronets' sons definitely do, especially when imprisoned at boarding school with dozens of other baronets' sons. But Martin Brentwood, leading man and one of Hollywood's finest gentlemen, does not."

Martin leaned his head on the cushions. "Jesus, Sid. Don't you ever get tired of the act?"

"I'll keep up with the act as long as it pays the bills. And so will you." Sid crossed his legs. "I met with Ira too. He needs you back in to do retakes on that pro-Prohibition picture you wrapped last week."

Martin groaned. "Good lord. Must we pander to the temperance unions and morality clubs even more? Wasn't it enough that I died horribly in the gutter at the end?" Martin should have gotten a clue about where his career was headed when he was cast as the drunken lout instead of the fellow who heroically takes an axe to the kegs of evil whiskey.

"It has nothing to do with your performance. There were light flares in some of the scenes, and the cutter can't fix it."

"Very well. I'll return tomorrow to die again."

"Good. They expect you at ten."

"Ten." Martin cracked open an eye. "That's a civilized hour, but how am I supposed to get there? No chauffeur, remember? The studio still won't let me drive, and you refuse to learn how. I'd take the streetcar, but—"

"No. The last time you tried that, you nearly caused a riot." Sid stood up and collected his briefcase from the ormolu side table. "I'll contact the studio. They'll assign you a driver, although you may have to share." He lifted one perfectly straight eyebrow. "You're not Valentino, after all. Yet."

"Isn't it grand that I don't want to be, then?"

Sid sighed. "Marty, you need to think about your image. The studio'll only protect you as long as you're an asset, and you'll only be an asset if—"

"If I make Jacob enough money."

"If you don't make their job harder. Having a car at your disposal twenty-four hours a day is more of a temptation than you need right now."

Martin pushed himself upright with clenched fists. "What's that supposed to mean?"

"Lay off the steak and pinochle parties with Bill Taylor and George Hopkins. Stay away from Pershing Square. The only reason Homer—"

"Vernon," Martin murmured.

"—was a real threat was because he suspected what was really going on there. If one of those jokers decides to spill to the press—"

"They wouldn't. Nobody who's in the life would ever give me away. We don't do that to one other. Not ever."

"That's what everyone says until the first time. If anyone suspects the truth—"

"Truth? This is Hollywood, Sid. Truth is what the fan rags print, and the studios have all of them in their back pockets, cheek by jowl with their string of crooked cops."

"Maybe. But you can't depend on that lasting forever. Remember Kerrigan." Sid settled his straw boater on his head. "A studio driver'll pick you up tomorrow by nine thirty. I'll take care of it."

Martin heaved himself to his feet to walk Sid to the door. "Thanks, Sid."

"And next time? If you're gonna fire your driver, at least make sure you wait until he takes you home."

"Yeah, yeah."

Sid grabbed Martin's wrist, his dark eyes serious. "I mean it, Marty. Be careful. This may be your last chance at Citadel, but if you pick the wrong man, you may not have another chance at anything."

Martin opened his mouth to argue, but Sid walked out before he could gather his thoughts. He stood in the doorway as Sid strode down the sidewalk, the July sun beating down on the dusty boxwood hedges that lined the bungalow court.

Damn it, he's right.

The places where it was safe to be a man who preferred men were few—New York, San Francisco, Hollywood. And even there, security was an illusion. The only thing that shielded them was the total obliviousness of most of the country. Hell, they didn't even have a word for it.

In the life. A nice, nondescript phrase that could mean anything. But to the men and women who sought their partners from their own gender, its very blandness was the only thing that stood between them and ruin, scandal, imprisonment... worse. With sodomy laws on the books in every state, the punishment for a conviction could be positively medieval.

Martin shuddered, and as he wandered back to the drink cart, the streetcar bell clanged on Alvarado. *I've still got some of my costumes from my vaudeville days. I could take the trolley to Pershing Square. Just for a little while.* If he dressed in the rough clothes of a dockworker or the cheap suit of a salesman, nobody would know him for Martin Brentwood, movie star.

He leaned his forehead against the wall, excitement warring with shame in his belly. *One last time. Without a driver, nobody would know.*

So much of being a star was in *behaving* like one. Presenting yourself like a person who would prompt people in middle America to shell out their dough for the privilege of watching you caper around on a screen for an hour or two. Hell, he'd heard United Artists was going to charge a *two-dollar* admission for Fairbanks's next picture.

It was nuts.

It was nuts, but Sid was right. It paid the bills—his *and* Sid's. He owed it to them both not to destroy his career, not to destroy his *life*. Because the sailors in Pershing Square might be thrillingly rough, but you never knew where they'd been. The last thing he needed was a case of the clap. Sid was right about that too.

Martin wandered over to his desk. He had a pile of fan mail that needed answering. He probably should do that—he had few enough fans left. He'd best keep the faithful remnants happy.

With one last sorrowful glance at the gin bottle, he sat down and picked up his fountain pen.

CHAPTER TWO

Dawn was pinking the sky when Robbie slipped out of the shack the next morning. His mouth tasted foul, and he was desperately thirsty. Yesterday's juice stains were stiff and sticky on his seat and knees, and his trousers had picked up another layer of grime from the floor, but in town he'd find no convenient stream to bathe in, wash his clothes, or slake his thirst.

In front of him, orange trees marched down the gentle slope and globes of fruit peeped out between dusty leaves. Robbie's belly rumbled and clenched, and he remembered the bright, sharp taste of the oranges he'd scavenged yesterday. Nobody could see him up here on the edge of the grove. He could snag half a dozen and be gone with no one the wiser.

Mouth watering, he crept under the nearest tree, reached up, and closed his fingers around one perfect orange.

Then his belly roiled and he snatched his hand away to stumble toward the road. It was one thing to help himself to something nobody wanted—scavenging and making do was part of the hardscrabble life on a farm at the edge of the Bitterroots—but this was someone else's livelihood. While he'd taken the discarded fruit yesterday in exchange for work he hadn't been paid for, he couldn't outright steal.

He shoved his trembling hands in his pockets. As he walked down the hill, the ranks of trees gave way to neat bungalows tucked back from the road. Ramshackle structures, some nearly as disreputable as Samson's shed, were plopped in the middle of several lawns for no reason that Robbie could see. As he passed one, a man stepped out its sagging door, dressed in full Western regalia, complete with boots, spurs, chaps, and hat.

Robbie blinked, sure his hunger had finally sent him over the edge into delirium. But the cowboy touched a finger to the brim of his hat.

"Morning."

"Uh… morning."

The cowboy tilted his head and surveyed Robbie's sorry appearance. "Pump next to the house, if you want to wash up."

"Th-thanks."

"Don't mention it." The cowboy walked off down the road in a chink of spurs.

Robbie scurried over to the pump, afraid that at any minute somebody inside the house would throw up a window and tell him to scram. So he quickly ducked his head under the cold stream until it gave him a headache. Although a shaggy bush screened the pump from the street, it wasn't *private*, so he shed his jacket but didn't dare take off his shirt. His ma would have a fit if she knew he'd been half-naked where somebody could see.

She won't see. Nobody I know will ever see me here. Nobody he knew would ever see him again. *Frank….*

Robbie set his jaw and stripped off his shirt because to heck with it. He splashed water on his chest, under his arms, and over his shoulders, shivering with the chill even though it was already promising to be another scorcher of a day. His pants got soaked, but in this heat, they'd dry off, just like his skin and hair would. He crouched on the pump pad and guzzled straight from the spout, but he lost his balance and water went up his nose. He fell backward, coughing wildly and afraid the water was about to come back up. He put his head on his knees, and his back twitched as water trickled down his spine.

At the scrape and slide of a window sash behind him, he jumped to his feet and snatched his shirt to hold in front of his chest. A woman in a flowered wrapper glared at him from between lace curtains.

"I don't allow you movies to loiter. You've had your shot at the pump. Now you git."

Movies? What's that mean? But since she probably wouldn't tell him even if he asked, Robbie dipped his chin in an apologetic bob. "Yes, ma'am. Sorry, ma'am."

She gave him what Frank called the once-over. "I don't hold with pictures about low-class people. You tell them that when you get to work. More pictures like *Daddy-Long-Legs* or *Pollyanna*. Tell them."

"Yes, ma'am. I surely will." Robbie struggled into his shirt, the grimy fabric catching on his still-damp skin. There wasn't any point telling her he didn't know what she was talking about. She wouldn't listen to him. Nobody ever did. Only Frank.

Except for once.

Robbie picked up his threadbare jacket, but his head swam when he straightened up. He steadied himself on the pump handle, but since the woman was still watching him from behind her curtains, he clapped his hat on his head, touched the brim, and headed back down the road.

Pretty soon the bungalows and lawns gave way to sidewalks and businesses, and he reached the spot Samson had dropped him off the day before. There was some kind of commotion going on at the corner, so Robbie slowed down to see what it was.

Another cowboy was grinning fit to beat the band, holding his hat upside down in his hands. *How many cowboys are there in Hollywood? The place doesn't have any cows.*

"Whoo-eee! Got myself a part in Bill Hart's next picture!" He pulled something out of the crown of his hat—wrapped peppermints, the kind Robbie's ma used to give out to her students when they'd done well on their lessons—and passed one to a man in a business suit, another to a little girl in a pinafore, and one to her mother. Robbie's mouth watered, and he wandered closer. "Everyone have a peppermint. I'm celebratin'!"

Robbie held out his hand, and the cowboy dropped the candy into his palm. Even through the cellophane wrapper, the scent of peppermint was strong enough to nearly send Robbie to his knees. "Thank you, sir."

The cowboy cackled. "I ain't a sir. Not yet." He tossed a handful of mints into the group, and the little crowd that had gathered grabbed them out of the air. "But someday I might be. This is just the beginning. You mark my words." Then he clapped his hat on his head and sauntered off around the corner. Robbie gaped after him until he heard a sharp cry from behind him. He spun—a mistake, since his head wanted to keep spinning—to see a hollow-cheeked young woman, her hair coming loose from its pins, steal a peppermint from a little boy in short pants.

"Hey!" the boy hollered. "That was mine."

She tore off the wrapper and shoved the candy in her mouth. From his spot a few feet away, Robbie heard her whimper.

He glanced down at his own mint and up at the girl. Then he sighed and held it out to her. "Here. You can have mine if you want it."

For an instant she gazed at him with eyes like the feral barn cats back home. Then she snatched the mint off his palm and scuttled away.

Oh, well. Wouldn't have been much of a meal anyway.

But if a cowboy could find a job without a horse or cow in sight, surely Robbie could find *something*. After all, he wasn't afraid of hard work. But to find it, he'd have to look, so he started toward the busy street a couple of blocks away.

"Hold on there, young feller."

Robbie didn't stop, but then someone tapped him on the shoulder.

"I said hold on there."

Robbie flinched and glanced behind him. A white-haired man was peering up at him from under a pair of eyebrows that would give woolly-bear caterpillars a run for their money. He was wearing some kind of uniform—high-collared jacket, dark trousers, and a peaked cap. A uniform meant *authority*, and Robbie had been running from authority for six weeks. *Guess I can't run forever.*

"Yessir?"

"I been watching you."

Robbie's empty belly dropped to his boots. Had the man seen him emerge from Samson's shed or wash off at the pump? Jehoshaphat, had he seen Robbie without a shirt? In *public*?

Thank goodness I didn't steal that orange. They couldn't pin theft on him. But vagrancy was a definite possibility. He'd almost been picked up for that in Bakersfield before he offered to help Samson with his deliveries. For that alone, Robbie was willing to forgive the lack of wages and the failed promise of work at the end of the line.

Robbie snatched off his hat and twisted it in his hands as he ducked his head. "I'm sorry, sir. I didn't mean to—"

"Don't worry." The man patted him on the arm. "You done nothin' bad." He nodded toward the dispersing crowd, where the boy was still loudly complaining to his mother about the girl who stole his peppermint. "You done something real good. I can tell you need food just as bad as that little gal. But you gave up what I'll wager is the only thing other than water down your gullet for days."

"Not days," Robbie mumbled. "Had a couple of oranges yesterday." His gaze flew to the man's face. "I didn't steal them.

Honest. They were squashed. Discards. I helped a grower load his truck, and—"

"Now, now. I ain't accusing you of anything. Just pointing out that you've got a good heart. And that's something I can appreciate. You come on along with me."

The man turned and walked up the road. Robbie stared after him, swaying a little on his feet. What could he want? He said he didn't think Robbie was a thief. At least, that's what it seemed like. Robbie rubbed his forehead. If only his head weren't so muzzy.

The man got to the corner and turned. He raised his eyebrows when he saw Robbie hadn't followed. "You comin'?"

"I don't know. Where are we going? And who are you?"

The man chuckled. "You can call me Pops. And I'm treatin' you to breakfast. Unless of course you'd rather take your chances on another peppermint."

Robbie's belly rumbled so loudly that a man in a business suit shot a startled look at him and moved pointedly aside. Robbie shook his head—*mistake*—and hurried to catch up with Pops.

"You don't have to do this. I can manage. That girl—"

"She's long gone." Pops sighed and pointed down a side street. "Thisaway." When Robbie fell into step with him, Pops glanced up from under his eyebrow thicket. "There's more of her kind every day. They come to town, sure they'll hit it big, but instead they end up stealing candy from little kids." His expression darkened. "I've heard hundreds starve every year. Or worse."

"Worse?" What could be worse than starving? "So why not offer her breakfast, if it'd keep her from… from worse?"

"Because I can't give her or any of those young gals what they want. I'm just a gatekeeper. I'm not a producer."

Producer of what? But the question died on Robbie's tongue when Pops opened the door to a diner. The aroma of bacon and coffee drifted out and nearly knocked Robbie on his behind. His mouth watered so much that he had to swallow twice to keep from drooling on the sidewalk.

Pops gave him a crooked smile. "Comin' in? Or are you gonna stand out here and watch through the window?"

Robbie scooted through the door, half expecting the motherly waitress in her crisp pink uniform to order him out again, given that he looked like something scraped off the bottom of one of those cowboys' boots. But Pops raised a hand in greeting, and the woman smiled back, nodding toward two red leather stools at the corner of the long counter.

Pops sat on one and patted the one kitty-corner from him. "Sit. You like coffee?" Robbie nodded, still not trusting himself to open his mouth. Pops held up two fingers, and the waitress brought over two heavy ceramic mugs, almost blindingly white. She filled them up, and Robbie nearly fell face-first into his, overwhelmed by the aroma curling out of the cup.

"Bacon and eggs for us both, Earlene, but give us a couple of them doughnuts while we wait." Pops chuckled and poked Robbie's arm with one finger. "Not sure my friend here'll survive otherwise."

"You got it, Pops."

Robbie watched Earlene's every move as she lifted the lid off an oversized cake stand and used a wedge-shaped spatula to transfer chocolate-frosted doughnuts onto two plates.

She plonked them down in front of Robbie and Pops. "How do you all want your eggs?"

Pops slid his plate closer. "Over easy." Mesmerized by the doughnut with its glistening frosting, Robbie didn't answer. "Make it two." As Earlene bustled away, Pops picked up his cup and blew on it. "You gonna eat or just stare at it all day?"

"I'll eat. Thank you. Nobody's done anything this nice for me… well, in a while. I shouldn't accept, since I can't repay you, but—" He smiled shakily. "Not like I can afford pride anymore."

Pops shrugged. "Way I figure it, I'll do somethin' nice for you, and down the road, you'll do the same for someone else." He grabbed the sugar dispenser and measured two teaspoons into his cup. "You never told me your name."

"Oh. Robbie. Robbie Goodman."

Pops chuckled. "Fittin' name for you, I'd say. Your name Robert?"

Robbie wrinkled his nose. "Nothing so normal. Robinson. Robinson Crusoe Goodman." He shrugged. "My ma was a fan of the book. Sometimes I think she felt like she was marooned on our farm." *Same as me.*

Robbie cradled the steaming cup in his hands and inhaled deeply and slowly. The dark aroma of the coffee sent him nearly dizzy with anticipation. *Wait. Make it last. Who knows when you'll get more?*

He kept one hand curled around the cup and picked up the doughnut. It wouldn't do to wolf the whole thing down. After three days with nothing but a stray orange or two, he'd probably upchuck the whole megillah.

He took a tiny bite. The chocolate frosting melted on his tongue, and he couldn't help it. He moaned. "I think that's the best thing I ever tasted in my whole entire life."

"Wait'll you taste the eggs." Pops slurped his coffee. "This place ain't fancy, but it's good, plain food. You'll see. Everything in Hollywood's better'n anything anywhere else."

Robbie dared a sip from his own cup and fought another moan as a jalopy, as battered and dusty as his old man's, putt-putted along the road outside the diner. "I don't know about that. Hollywood doesn't seem that different from most other places." *Except there are a lot of cowboys around for a place with no cows.* "It's just a town. Bigger than some, but smaller than San Francisco." He gestured to the street and its sparse traffic. "In Boise, I—" His mouth dropped open, and he fumbled the doughnut. "Jee-*hoshaphat*. Is that car *purple*?"

The sleek automobile, with its white tires and silver grill gleaming in the morning sun, was as different from the Model T ahead of it as Robbie—scruffy, scrawny, and almost indecently threadbare—was from the man behind its wheel.

Pops cackled. "Yep. That's Fatty's car."

Robbie eyed the driver. His light hair was slicked back on a round head and his natty gray jacket covered a body that had clearly had larger and more regular meals in the past months than Robbie'd had. But still. "Fatty? Kinda mean, isn't it? He's not that big."

The old man's grizzled eyebrows rose up his forehead. "Where you been, boy, that you never heard of Fatty Arbuckle? He's one of the top film stars in the country."

Robbie shrugged and hoped the sunburn on his face and neck hid his blush. "Idaho." He leaned over to steal a last glimpse of the car as it disappeared down the road and caught himself before he slid off the slick leather stool. "Besides, my pa doesn't hold with the flickers. Says they're low."

Pops shook his head. "I hope you're plenty smart, then, young feller," he said around a huge bite of doughnut, "because you've got one hell of a lot to learn."

"I know." Robbie hunched his shoulders and took comfort from the warmth of his cooling coffee mug. "I've known that for a while."

But I know a lot more now than I knew six weeks ago. Like how guilt could twist your guts, even when your belly was full. Like how a wide smile and a handshake could mask the soul of a snake. *Like how you could abandon your best friend so you could save your own worthless hide.* He sighed and set his doughnut down, his appetite suddenly gone.

Pops nudged Robbie with a bony elbow. "You talk pretty good for a rube."

"My mother was a teacher."

"She pass on?"

"No. Just stopped teaching after—Well, she stopped."
Stopped doing most things, other than staring out the window,
waiting for someone who'd never come home again. *Wonder if
she's noticed I'm gone yet?* His pa might, but only because he'd
expect Robbie to help with the chores. It had taken Robbie a
good two weeks on the road before he'd stopped looking over
his shoulder, terrified that Pa would have somehow tracked him
down to drag him back to the dreary life on the farm. On the
other hand, Pa might think *good riddance.* He'd never had much
use for Robbie. All his hopes had been pinned on Eddie. In a
way, Pa was nearly as bereft as Ma, but he showed it with his
fists and his temper instead of tears and pining. Robbie didn't
want to think about that, so he raised his cup to his lips.

"What are you running from, son?"

Robbie spluttered and sprayed coffee across the counter.
"Me? I'm not—" He grabbed a couple of napkins out of the
dispenser and mopped up the spill. "I mean, does it matter?"

"Nope. Not in Hollywood, anyway. Everybody here's got
something they'd rather forget."

"Do you?"

"Me? I'm different. I was born out here. Watched the picture
people come in and stake their claim." He jerked his thumb
toward the window. "But there's some folks out there, folks who
founded the town or lived here before the studios started
sprouting up like jimsonweed, who can't see what's in front of
their noses."

Robbie dared another bite of doughnut. "What's in front of
their noses, Pops?"

His laugh sounded like a creaky hinge. "The future. Those
fools wanna believe everyone in the country'll get tired of the
pictures and go back to Bible study, but they're wrong.
Someone'll be making pictures after every one of those orange
trees on the hill are dead and gone. They'll last longer than all of
us. So I figure it's smarter to work *for* 'em than *against* 'em.

Because that's one fight nobody can win. Pictures are here to stay. You mark my words."

Robbie blinked. "Um…. All right?"

"Another thing. The problem with running? Sooner or later, you're bound to run out of road."

"I know that too." *I've got a feeling I just did.*

"Speaking of roads, you know how to drive?"

"Sure. But I never drove anything like Fatty's car."

"Don't matter. You come along with me, young feller. Prove I'm not wrong. Prove you're not a bum."

Earlene returned with a couple of plates that held perfectly cooked eggs, flanked by crisp bacon and thick brown toast. Robbie turned wide eyes on Pops. "For a meal like this, I'll do whatever you want. But how?"

Pops grinned as he slathered strawberry jam on his toast. "You're gonna take a job."

CHAPTER THREE

The studio had a bathroom. With a bathtub. With running water. With *hot* running water. For the first time in his life, Robbie was able to bathe without first hauling the water and heating it on the woodstove. *It's the first time I've had hot water at all for weeks.*

When you were on the run, you didn't have a lot of options. The biggest vessel he'd had was a tin cup, and someone had stolen *that* outside Sacramento.

Pops said the studio didn't stint on the plumbing or the hot water because some of the actors got so dirty while they were filming. "The comedians use it on the regular," he'd told Robbie as he handed him a towel, "just to wrangle the custard-pie mess."

Robbie swiped the steam off the mirror and used his snaggletoothed comb to slick back his wet hair. He desperately needed a haircut, but not much he could do about that now. Then he steadied himself on the sink. *What do I know about desperation?* Shaggy hair was nothing. Less than nothing.

Would Frank have hot water? Did they let you wash in private in prison? If they didn't.... Robbie gulped. He didn't want to think about that. Didn't want to think about Frank being hurt or forced, not after he'd explained to Robbie that the way they felt, the things they wanted, weren't *wrong*. That they weren't hurting anyone. That they—

"You fall in, Robbie?"

Robbie jerked upright and smoothed his undershirt over his belly. "No, Pops. I'll be right out." As well as the dandy uniform hanging on the back of the door, Pops had given Robbie a couple of sets of underdrawers and some street clothes. Those weren't new by any stretch and probably weren't that fancy when they were, but anything beat what Robbie had been wearing for the last six weeks.

He slipped into the cotton shirt. It didn't have a collar, but the uniform jacket had one of those high-buttoned numbers that hid it anyway. The pants were ridiculous—jodhpurs, like some fancy horseman's outfit. The knee-high boots that went along with them fit all right, although they squeaked with every step he took.

He fingered the jacket sleeve. *Whipcord.* It was going to be murder in the July heat, but Pops said the car he'd be driving was closed. The studio didn't want the actors to be exposed, in case the fans got too excited and tried to mob them, so at least the sun wouldn't be beating down on him.

Don't complain. You've got *clothes, not to mention a job and a full belly.* Although Robbie was starting to regret eating so heartily at the diner, because his eggs and bacon weren't sitting so well.

He took a mouthful of water out of the faucet, ordered his queasy stomach to settle down, and then tucked his change of clothes into the satchel that was another gift from Pops. With a last glance around the room to make sure he'd tidied up after himself, he stepped out into the hallway. "I really appreciate what you've done for me, Pops—the clothes, the job, the chow. Everything."

Pops waved one gnarled hand. "Bah. That ain't nothin'. The costume folks've got stuff down there from years' worth of pictures. Most actors—the men anyway, not so much the ladies

—wear their own duds for the modern pictures. But sometimes they need spares."

"Still, when I can pay you back—"

"It's not my money. It's the studio's leavings, and since you're one of us now, it makes sense for you not to look like a hobo. Now come on. You need to pick up Mr. Brentwood in half an hour."

Robbie fell into step next to Pops. "Mr. Brentwood? Who's he?"

Pops stopped to face Robbie and gave him what Ma would call the stink-eye. "If you know what's good for you, you'll never ask who someone is, not to their face. Mr. Brentwood, he probably wouldn't mind. A nicer gentleman you wouldn't want to meet. But some of 'em...." Pops rolled his eyes. "Let's say if you wasn't to recognize Gilbert Flint or Aurelia Arthur? Your name would be mud faster'n you could say *snap*."

"But I *don't* know them." Robbie's belly roiled again. "Not any of them. What if I—"

"There now." Pops patted his shoulder. "After you bring Mr. Brentwood back here for his meeting, I'll show you the gallery."

"Gallery?"

"Photographs of all of Citadel's stars. Hope you've got a good memory."

"If I don't, I'll get one."

"Good. Come along."

Robbie followed Pops out of the building and tried not to gape at the *size* of everything. The studio had over a dozen buildings inside its walls, some of them as big as the airplane hangars Robbie had seen in the airfields outside San Francisco. Some were regular three- or four-story buildings that didn't look much different from the joints in downtown Boise. But one of 'em—the one to the left of the giant wrought iron gates with the fancy curlicued C in the middle—looked almost like the pictures of the White House Robbie had seen. Or maybe one of those fancy plantation mansions down south, but bigger.

Pops's station was a little glassed-in booth right inside the gates. He stopped in the doorway and pointed to a square of pavement twenty or so yards away. "Car's parked outside the main shooting stage. It's the only Dixie Flyer in the lot. You can't miss it."

Robbie swallowed and sweat beaded his brow under his hatband. "Um, Pops? I can drive the car, no problem, but *where* am I supposed to drive it? I've been in town for less than a day. How am I supposed to drive some big shot around? He'll know I'm a phony."

"It ain't hard. Town ain't that big. Least not the part you need to worry about. Here."

Pops ducked into the booth and pulled a used envelope out of a trash bin. He sketched a sparse grid on it with the stub of a pencil. "Mr. Brentwood lives at 412A Alvarado. It's not far. Nice little bungalow court. Pull up on Alvarado and wait there. He'll be expecting you."

"I don't go to the door?"

Pops glanced up from his map, his woolly-bear eyebrows drawn together over his nose. "You stay put in that car. Only time you get out is to open the door for Mr. Brentwood. Understand?"

"Sure. But how'll he know I'm there?"

"He'll come out when he's ready. It's your job to be there when he does."

"Right."

Pops laughed and shook his head. "You look like you're about to faint dead away. Mr. Brentwood ain't gonna eat you." He took Robbie's arm and led him to the car.

The Dixie Flyer was black and its tires plain—nothing like as fancy as Fatty's car, which Pops had told him was a custom Pierce Arrow—but it beat the heck out of Pa's Model T. Robbie slid behind the wheel and tried to look as though he saw such vehicles every day. Judging by the twitch of Pops's lips, he wasn't successful.

Pops slapped the roof and waited for Robbie to start the car. *At least I don't have to crank it.* "Remember. Park on the street and —"

"Stay put. I got it. Thanks, Pops. I won't let you down. I promise."

The telephone rang as Martin was coming downstairs, adjusting the knot in his tie. He strode over to it, picked it up by its stem, and lifted the receiver. *The blasted thing looks like a daffodil dressed for a funeral.*

"Hello?"

"Marty, it's me." Sid's voice was scratchy over the line. Martin imagined the operators all listening in, although what they expected to hear was more than he could figure out. "Have your new driver swing by my office and pick me up. We can talk in the car on the way to the studio."

"Talk about what?"

"Your career. What else? I've got a meeting with the studio brass, and there's some stuff you need to know."

"All right. You're sure the studio'll send a new driver?"

"Positive. I talked to Pops about it last night."

"Well, in that case…." The studio's gate man was the most responsible person on the lot.

"Whatever you do, don't fire the new fellow before he gets you to the studio. All right?"

Martin counted to ten. "The decision to get rid of Vernon wasn't spur-of-the-moment, you know."

"I know. Just don't be late. This is important."

Sid hung up. Never one to waste time, that was Sid, which was one of the reasons he'd been popular with the directors of the two-bit musicals they'd done in New York. He never missed an entrance, and he made sure whatever chorus girl he was partnering got onstage on time too.

Martin didn't have the same reputation. If it hadn't been for pictures, he'd be back in the tailor's shop by now, measuring portly businessmen for second-rate suits.

He pulled his watch out of his waistcoat pocket. If Pops had indeed come through, his driver ought to be waiting for him by now. He put on his boater, checked its angle in the mirror by the door, and stepped outside.

The gardeners were busy trimming the boxwood hedge, and a crew of workmen were erecting a gazebo at the east end of the court near Bill Taylor's place. Martin strolled toward the street, touching his hat brim to a neighbor out walking her dog.

When he emerged onto Alvarado, the studio's lone Dixie Flyer was stationed at the curb. Martin sighed. *Of course they wouldn't waste a Rolls on me.* But as soon as Martin set foot on the sidewalk, the driver jumped out and raced around to open the rear door for him.

Ye gods, was the fellow ever young—young and fresh-faced and clearly nothing but trouble, at least as far as Martin was concerned.

Under his peaked chauffeur's cap, he was tan—not as brown as Fairbanks, but then who was?—but otherwise his complexion would give Pickford a run for her money. There was only one reason for a man that pretty to be driving an actor around Hollywood—he wanted to make it in pictures himself. That had been Vernon's angle, and he thought he'd found his leverage when he saw Martin lighting Antonio Moreno's cigarette.

This boy's blond hair brushed his uniform collar and curled a little bit there and on his forehead, where a lock had escaped his hat brim. His speedwell blue eyes were wide and seemed guileless, but Martin knew better than to trust the appearance of innocence.

Martin was an actor, after all. His stock in trade was pretending to be other than what he was. He wasn't about to let another ambitious nobody, be he ever so beautiful, get under his skin.

"Good morning, Mr. Brentwood, sir. I'm Robbie. Pops sent me to—"

"Yes. Just get on with it." He nodded curtly and climbed into the car. But as he settled himself in his seat, he noticed how the boy's open face fell, as if he'd been kicked when he hadn't expected it.

Actors, remember. I could pull off the same look on cue.

But guilt threaded through him, nevertheless. So many stars were rude to their servants or employees, to people they'd decided were beneath them, even though they'd *been* them in the not too distant past. Hell, when Martin was a tailor's apprentice, he'd have considered a chauffeur in a uniform to be so far above him as to be untouchable.

We were all shop girls or apprentices or butcher's boys once. If I don't treat this man with respect, I'm no better than Gilbert Flint.

So when the boy—when *Robbie*—climbed behind the wheel, Martin relented.

"I'm pleased to meet you, Robbie. Please convey my thanks to Pops, since I was convinced I'd have to hike all the way to the studio this morning."

Robbie turned to look at him, a smile—*nice, even teeth; he'd photograph well*—lighting his face. "Thank you, sir. I'll let him know. But you wouldn't have to worry about walking. The studio treats their folks really well. Did you know they've got bathrooms with real bathtubs? And hot water?"

Martin's lips twitched, but he kept his smile contained. "Yes. I had heard something of the sort."

Pink suffused Robbie's face under his tan. "Of course you do. You know way more about Hollywood than I do. I bet—"

"Perhaps we could go now? They expect me on set sometime this morning."

"Oh. Yes. I'm sorry." Robbie turned in his seat, settled his cap, and started the car.

"Oh, by the way, we'll need to pick up my manager on the way. His office is on Melrose."

"M-M-Melrose?"

"Yes. It's on the way."

"Um…."

Martin raised his eyebrows. "You *do* know where Melrose is?"

Robbie's shoulders rose until they were in the vicinity of his ears. "I'm sorry, but I only got to town yesterday. I never really heard of Hollywood before. I mean, sure, I've *heard* of it…."

"I assume you've come here to get into pictures?"

"Me?" Robbie's laugh was a free and open sound that made Martin sorry, if the fellow truly *was* an aspiring actor, that pictures were silent. "No. This is just as far as my ride took me. I was thinking of heading down to Mexico, but then I met Pops. Thing is, I only know how to get from here to the studio one way. Pops gave me a map. But as for anyplace else? I've got no more idea than a cat."

Despite his reservations, Martin was charmed. *Nobody could be* that *green.* "Head up Alvarado and then take Beverly over to Western. Turn right and then a left on Melrose. His office is on the right. 5625."

Relief spread over Robbie's face. "*Thank* you. I'll have it all figured out by tomorrow, I promise."

"I believe you will," Martin murmured.

He was fully prepared for Robbie to continue to chat all the way to Sid's office, but instead, he paid almost obsessive attention to his driving. Martin recognized that kind of focus. *He's memorizing the route. He really will have it figured out by tomorrow.* Or if not, then quite soon.

They pulled up in front of Sid's office to find him standing on the sidewalk, glaring at his pocket watch.

"Jehoshaphat," Robbie muttered. "I hope he hasn't been waiting long."

Martin chuckled. "Don't mind Sid. He anticipates everyone being late, so he likes to have his disapprobation fired up and ready. We're right on time."

Robbie turned off the car, but before he could get out, Martin tapped his shoulder. "After you let Sid in, turn right on Vine. That'll take you back to Sunset. You know what to do from there?"

Robbie flashed a grin, and Martin was hit with an unexpected spear of *want*. "Yes, sir. Thank you, sir."

Martin took the opportunity of Robbie ushering Sid into the car to remind himself that he, Martin Brentwood, formerly Marvin Gottschalk, was not *stupid*. *No infants. No greenhorns. And* definitely *no chauffeurs.* He was a grown man. He could control his urges, even though very few people in pictures bothered to do so.

Sid slid inside and balanced his briefcase on his knees. "New driver seems a little young."

"Perhaps. But Pops vouches for him, apparently."

"Hmmph." Sid popped the latches of his case and took out a sheaf of papers as Robbie eased the car into traffic. "Here's the scoop, Marty. The Prohibition picture wraps today, tomorrow tops, and then we're hitting your image like gangbusters."

"My image? Which one are you referring to? The image of me firing my chauffeur in front of the Hollywood Hotel—" From the corner of his eye, Martin saw Robbie flinch. "—or the image of me perishing in the gutter from Demon Rum?"

"We're talking about your *next* picture. Well, maybe not the next one, because I've got some work to do, a couple of directors to talk to, a scenarist or two to bring onboard. But when I've got that squared away, we'll be flying high."

"Really, Sid," Martin murmured, "if your father could hear the way you talk…."

Sid barked a laugh. "If only. But never mind that. You need something different. Something that shows you're still the guy who did all his own stunts back in those Western two-reelers, not just some gigolo who knows how to light a woman's cigarette while gazing soulfully into her eyes."

"I doubt anyone remembers me in the two-reelers. I rarely did anything but ride into town and ride out again, and then only if the Gower Street cowboys would stop laughing long enough for me to do it." The men who played cowboys up in Inceville had been actual working cowboys until ranch and Wild West Show work started to dry up. They had a great respect for horses, but not much for actors. Martin had finally gotten on their good side by putting himself entirely in their hands, learning to care for his horse himself, and taking riding lessons—with the accompanying ribbing—from the men.

"Doesn't matter if the *audience* remembers. By the time I'm done, the studio heads'll remember. So will the directors. And *then* the fans'll take notice because we'll get Herbert Howe over at *Photoplay* to make sure they do."

"Howe?" Martin slid a glance at the back of Robbie's head, but once again, he seemed focused on his driving. Everyone knew Howe was smitten with Ramón Novarro, even though he wasn't part of the motion picture fraternity of men who were in the life. "You realize he's—"

"Yeah, I know. That's why getting him to do this story'll be a cinch."

"You're being unrealistic, Sid. People don't transfer affect— *appreciation* from one man—one *person* to another so easily."

"Maybe not. But reporters want stories, and that's what we'll give them. We're gonna make you Valentino crossed with Bill Hart. Fairbanks plus sex. But you've gotta *be* that. It's not like theater, where the audience knows the set on the stage isn't real. The picture-going public believes what they see on the screen, and if you don't live up to it, in their eyes, you've betrayed them. Lied."

"Yes." Once again, Jack Kerrigan was a salutary lesson. "And you really think a single article in a fan magazine will make them believers?"

"No. That's only part of it, and it won't work unless we can find the right property, but I've got some ideas, and there's a scenarist—Well, never mind. Time enough to discuss it if things work out the way I want."

The car pulled up to the Citadel gates, and Pops trotted over to open them. He touched the brim of his hat to Martin as Robbie drove through.

Martin straightened his tie, which had suddenly become too tight. "All right. Am I to join you in this momentous meeting?"

"Not yet. Just get over to the shooting stage and get those retakes done. We'll talk later." Sid slapped the front seat. "Let me out here."

"Yes, sir." Robbie obligingly stopped the car and trotted around to open the door.

Sid eyed him suspiciously. "Watch out for this kid. I don't like the look of him."

Martin raised his brows. "What do you mean? He's a fresh-faced kid who fell off the turnip truck about ten minutes ago. Completely green and eager to please."

"Yeah," Sid said darkly. "That's what I'm afraid of. Keep your nose clean, Marty. Otherwise nothing I do will make any difference."

Martin opened his mouth to argue, to promise he had no intentions, evil or otherwise, toward Robbie, but when Robbie smiled in the face of Sid's glower and then grinned sunnily at Martin, he wasn't so sure he could keep his promise or, for that matter, what the promise should be.

Robbie hopped back behind the wheel. "Where can I drop you, Mr. Brentwood?"

"The back of the lot, please. The building on the left."

"Yessir."

As Robbie navigated the studio alleyways, Martin studied the back of his head. Really, those blond curls on his collar were far too enticing. He forced himself to look away. Even if Robbie was amenable to a bit of petting, he was Martin's… well, not employee. He was technically employed by the studio. But

Martin was in a position of power and authority over him, and he had no intention of abusing that power.

Good God, I'm actually starting to think *like Sid wants me to speak.*

He frowned out the window at a girl who couldn't be more than sixteen—picture hat on her golden curls, lace collar on her organdy dress—being escorted toward the discreet back entrance to Jacob Schlossberg's office. Martin had no illusions about what Jacob might require of that girl in exchange for the chance at a contract.

Every actor in Hollywood owed their bread to the producers, and the producers took advantage of it in any way that suited them. It was worse for women. Martin admired the ones who persevered despite having the deck stacked against them. He got a certain satisfaction every time one of Marion Davies's pictures was a hit, because he knew it stuck in Louis B. Mayer's craw that W.R. Hearst had more power in his own studio than he did.

The public didn't know about Marion's relationship with Hearst, of course, but everyone in the film industry did. You didn't mess with Hearst, with all his money and the power of his newspaper empire behind him, and that meant you didn't mess with Marion. Luckily, Marion was lovely and Martin was fortunate to count her as a friend. That might be the only reason Jacob hadn't already fired him.

"Mr. Brentwood? Is this the place?"

Martin blinked and shook himself out of his reverie at the sound of Robbie's voice. "Yes. Thank you."

Robbie turned off the car and raced around to open the door for Martin to climb out. "When shall I pick you up?"

"I'm not at all sure. It will depend on when shooting completes. I'll send a message to Pops when I'm ready." He reached into the inner pocket of his jacket and drew out his wallet. "I appreciate your work today, Robbie. I hope you weren't offended by my manner at first."

"Oh no, Mr. Brentwood. You're the boss."

"Actually, the Mr. Schlossbergs are the boss, er, bosses." He drew out a five-spot, folded it, and held it out. "But I appreciate the sentiment."

To his surprise, instead of discreetly accepting the hand-off, Robbie put his hands behind his back. "Oh no, Mr. Brentwood. I couldn't accept that."

Charming. Martin smiled and tucked the bill into Robbie's pocket. Was that a bit forward? Yes, but he didn't have time to convince Robbie to accept the money, and he was determined that Robbie have it. "Nonsense. Welcome to Hollywood."

Martin left Robbie gaping, and strolled, whistling, into the studio. For some reason, facing that dreadful pro-Prohibition picture didn't seem quite so appalling anymore.

CHAPTER FOUR

"Mr. Brentwood *tipped* me. Five whole dollars." Robbie held the bill out to Pops. "That can't be right."

Pops pushed Robbie's hand away. "That money's yours, son. It means you did your job right."

But he hadn't. Not really. Mr. Brentwood had had to tell *him* where to go. More than once.

"You got a place to stay yet?" When Robbie shook his head, Pops tapped his chin and pursed his lips. "Hmmm. Then here's what you do. Take that five-spot over to Levy's on Hollywood. They'll rent you an upstairs room for three dollars a week if you give 'em my name and tell 'em you're working for the studio. It ain't much, but it'll do until you get paid."

Robbie wadded the money in his fist. "Pops, I don't like to ask. I don't want to be ungrateful, but what *am* I getting paid?"

Pops's eyebrows shot up. "Didn't I tell you? Guess not. Last feller was gettin' twenty dollars a week and not doin' diddly for it, so I expect you'll get the same." He pointed to the bill Robbie was still clutching in his sweaty hand. "Plus any tips, a' course."

Robbie's jaw dropped. *Twenty dollars a week?* "Are you *sure*?" His voice came out on a squeak.

"Why? That not enough? It's less'n the extras make. They get five dollars a day with a box lunch thrown in, so I can ask—"

"No, no. I mean, Jehoshaphat, Pops, that's a *fortune*!"

Pops cackled again. "This is Hollywood, Rob. And you'll earn every penny by the time you're done, even if it don't feel like it at the time. You're Mr. Brentwood's driver, whenever he wants you. So you make sure you're always there, whenever that is and *wherever* that is. Sometimes, it'll mean waiting on a set or at a location for hours, but you *wait*, because that's your job now."

"Yessir." For twenty dollars a week, Robbie'd stand on his head in the corner all day, if that's what Mr. Brentwood wanted.

"Now, for vittles, you can have lunch in the studio commissary for free. As long as you don't get fancy, the two dollars you've got left from Mr. Brentwood's tip should feed you for the rest of the week."

"I've never had fancy. I don't need fancy."

Pops cackled. "Didn't figure you would. That diner we ate at this morning? Fifteen cents'll get you a chicken sandwich. Couple of doughnuts costs a dime. Same for a cup of coffee." He jerked his head down in a nod. "You'll get by. If you get into trouble, you come to me." He waggled a finger under Robbie's nose. "Now mind, I don't hold with any gallivantin'. You stay out of the speakeasies."

Robbie shook his head. "I wouldn't. My ma would—" Truthfully, these days Ma probably wouldn't notice if he danced on a table with a lampshade on his head, but he remembered the days when she would've. "Anyway, that's not my style."

Pops patted his shoulder. "I knew you was a good boy. Could tell the minute I saw you. Mr. Brentwood say when he wants you back?"

"No. He said he'd send you a message."

Pops nodded. "Good. You can take time to get the lay of the land here. I'll draw you a map. You can start—"

"You, there! Boy!" The voice, deep, harsh, and a little nasal, made Robbie jump. *It could almost be Pa.* That's how he'd referred to Robbie most of his life, with the same tone of annoyance edged with disgust.

Robbie shoved the money in his pants pocket as he turned. Then he snatched his hat off his head. "Yessir?"

A man stood outside Pops's little booth, his feet planted wide on the pavement and his arms folded across his barrel chest. He was wearing dungarees and an open-necked shirt, same as a fellow at home might do if he was heading out to the fields on a hot day. But those boots…. Nobody in Pierce would set foot in the dirt and mud of a potato field in boots that shiny. *Maybe they're new and he hasn't broken them in yet.*

But the soles weren't heavy enough to stand farm work. They looked like a fancier version of the ones Robbie was wearing with his uniform.

The man crooked a finger, and Robbie started forward, only to have Pops catch his arm.

"What can we do for you, Mr. Flint?" Pops's voice was affable but neutral, without the friendliness Robbie had come to expect.

Mr. Flint scowled and his dark brows descended over his nose—Robbie's ma would have called that nose Roman. Robbie just called it long and straight. "I need your boy here to run me out to Inceville. I've got a meeting with Hart."

"Robbie here is assigned to Mr. Brentwood. Arnold's your driver. Do you need me to find him for you?"

Flint's scowl deepened. "I know where he is. I sent him out to Santa Monica on an errand."

"Now, Mr. Flint, you wouldn't ask Arnold to do anything illegal, would you? Not on studio time."

Robbie glanced sideways at Pops. Jehoshaphat, if anybody'd used that tone of voice on *him*, Robbie would have headed for the hills. But it seemed Mr. Flint was a tougher nut.

"I need to get to Inceville now."

From the way Pops's eyes narrowed, he hadn't missed that Mr. Flint didn't answer the question. "I'd be happy to call you a taxicab. Or—" Pops's face took on the blandest expression Robbie had ever seen on his seamed face. "—you could always take the streetcar."

"I don't take the fucking streetcar." The venom in Mr. Flint's voice made Robbie take a step backward. "He's a driver, assuming that uniform means anything. He can drive me."

"You know the rules, Mr. Flint. He has to wait for Mr. Brentwood."

Mr. Flint's scowl deepened, something Robbie hadn't thought was possible. "To hell with you, old man. The studio doesn't pay him to stand around."

Pops scratched his chin, his face screwed up as though he were trying to solve some tricky problem. "They pay him to be where he's told, same as they pay me and same as they pay you."

"And *I'm* telling him—"

"Sorry, Mr. Flint, but *you* ain't the studio."

Flint seemed to expand like a balloon about to pop, which reminded Robbie even more of his pa. "Jacob will hear about this. You mark my words." He turned on the heel of his shiny boots and stalked into the building across the way, slamming the door behind him.

Robbie glanced down at Pops, who was hiding a small smirk. "I don't want you to get in trouble, Pops. I wouldn't have minded driving him somewhere, especially if it was close. I can't imagine Mr. Brentwood could be finished in ten minutes."

"Nah. What I said was the truth. You're Mr. Brentwood's driver. Exclusive, unless *he* says so. Besides, you give Gilbert Flint an inch, and he'll take the whole damn country."

"Who is he, anyway?"

Pops shook a finger at him. "What did I tell you about asking who somebody is?"

"I didn't ask *him*. I'm asking you."

"He's one of the studio's stars, although he don't shine as bright as he did once. He's the rough-and-tumble type. Used to star in those Western two-reelers up in Inceville, same as Mr. Brentwood, but he got blackballed by the cowboys because of the way he treated the horses."

"That's another thing. I keep seeing cowboys on the street around here, but where are the cows?"

Pops stared at Robbie for a moment. Then he slapped his knee and wheezed with laughter. "You are a caution, young feller, and no mistake. Them cowboys aren't real cowboys. They're actors. Extras, hoping to get day work at the studios. They show up at the casting office in their outfits, hoping that one of the films being shot needs a cowboy or two to fill out the crowd."

"What if nobody wants cowboys that day?"

Pops shrugged. "Then they don't work."

His uniform suddenly took on a new meaning for Robbie. It meant he had *steady* work. He didn't have to worry about showing up every day and hoping they needed him. He polished one of the black buttons on his jacket. "But doesn't the studio have other clothes for them to wear if they need something other than cowboys?" Pops had given him underdrawers, for goodness' sake.

"Depends. For the drawing-room stuff, the modern-day pictures, men mostly wear their own suits. The big Biblicals, or the historical pictures, that's different. But extras mostly have to come ready to walk on the set, just as they are. The smart ones find out what pictures are shooting and pick out their clothes to match. They can get pretty steady work that way."

"For five dollars a day plus lunch."

"Yep."

Only yesterday, Robbie would have jumped at the chance—not that anyone would have hired him in his threadbare shirt and trousers, not unless they needed a bunch of hobos in the picture. From what he'd heard from his pa, who was always going on about how the pictures showed nothing but high-class folks pretending they were better than the average Joe, Robbie didn't imagine there'd be much call for that.

But I'm making twenty dollars a week, with a uniform thrown in and tips on the side.

The telephone inside Pops's booth rang with two shrill bursts. Pops ducked inside to answer it. "Front gate." He took a pencil stub from behind his ear and jotted something on a pad of paper. "Yessir. I'll see he gets it right away. Thank you." He hung up the phone and ripped the paper off the pad. Then he stepped out to hand it to Robbie.

"What'd I tell you? This here's a message for Mr. Brentwood from Mr. Ira Schlossberg." Pops dipped his chin and peered at Robbie from under his eyebrows. "Vice president in charge of production."

Robbie reverently took the note. "I guess he's an important person?"

"Since Mr. Ira and Mr. Jacob Schlossberg own Citadel Motion Pictures, you could say so. If I'd let you take Gilbert Flint over to Inceville, you wouldn't have been here to do your job." He waggled a knobby finger under Robbie's nose. "Let that be a lesson to you."

Robbie grinned. "That Pops always knows best?"

Pops cackled and patted Robbie's shoulder. "You do learn quick, don't you?" He pointed toward the back of the lot, toward the building where Robbie had dropped off Mr. Brentwood. "Take this over to stage two. Find the unit that's shooting Mr. Brentwood's picture, wait until there's a break, and then give this to him."

"Unit?"

Pops shook his head. "Good thing you're quick, because you've got a lot to learn. There are a dozen, maybe more, units filming inside that big barracks of a place. You'll need to wander around until you find Mr. Brentwood's."

Robbie nodded. At least he'd know Mr. Brentwood anywhere. *Those eyes.* He shivered. "I'll be quiet."

Pops cackled again. "You don't need to be quiet. The building'll be plenty noisy. Stay out of the way of the cameras and don't run into the scenery and you'll be fine. In fact, after you've delivered the message, hang around and watch for a bit. Get a notion of what making a picture is all about."

"Right." Robbie turned to go, but Pops caught his arm.

"And Robbie? You stay away from Gilbert Flint. That feller gives a rattlesnake a good name."

The message Robbie delivered, written in Pops's block printing, was extremely sparse—*Report to Mr. Ira's office.* But Martin had a bad feeling about it. If it was good news, wouldn't Ira have written the note himself? Or at least had his secretary do it on Ira's personal stationery?

Nevertheless, after he'd expired for the third time in a gutter flowing with beer—under Robbie's wide-eyed gaze—he showed the note to the director. No fool, the director immediately shooed Martin away to get cleaned up. Ira might be slighter and less of a blowhard than his beefier brother, Jacob, but he was still head of production and he still had an uncomfortably shrewd head on his shoulders. He approved all the scenarios, all the directors, all the casting choices for every picture Citadel produced.

After Martin washed off the fake beer and dressed in his own suit again—the script called for him to wear an artfully shredded number from the costume department—he emerged from the bathroom to find Robbie waiting for him, hat in hand.

"Do you need me to take you somewhere, Mr. Brentwood?"

Martin smiled at the boy—man, really. He should definitely stop thinking about Robbie as a boy. "Thank you, but no. I'm only going across to the production office, nothing more than a short stroll. I'll return here when I'm done, so you can continue to watch if you like. Otherwise I'll send word to Pops when I'm ready for you. I assume he'll know where to find you?"

"Yessir. Thank you, sir."

Martin nodded and strode off, pretending a confidence he didn't feel. For some reason, having that ingenuous young man call him "sir" made him feel more like a phony than usual. *What's with all this self-doubt? I'm an actor, for God's sake. I fake things for a living.*

And he'd had a lot of practice, considering his entire life was a fake—fake name, fake accent, fake backstory. What would it be like to have something, just one thing, that was real?

He certainly wouldn't find it behind the wide, colonnaded porch of Citadel's main office. For some reason, half the studio heads in Hollywood had decided that Greek revival architecture lent them class and grandeur. But from Martin's perspective, it was nothing more than another pathetic pretense.

Maybe those morality groups and temperance societies have it right. We're not the new nobility. We're nothing but overindulged, out-of-control commoners, all desperate to believe we're better than we are, yet making no attempt to be *better.*

On the other hand, as Sid said, it paid the bills.

Martin tugged on his waistcoat, straightened his tie, assumed the slightly knowing smile that was his trademark, and walked through the vast double doors.

"Good afternoon, Mr. Brentwood," the receptionist said. "Please go right up. Mr. Schlossberg is expecting you, but he's running a bit late."

"Thank you, Jenny. I don't mind waiting." After all, it kept him out of a beer-drenched gutter for a while.

The rise of the marble steps that led to the second-floor offices was shorter than that of a normal staircase. Someone—Martin couldn't remember who—had told him it was so actresses wearing wide-skirted crinolines could descend them regally without tripping. Martin suspected it was more to put people off-kilter, since the muscle memory for climbing regulation stairs was so deeply ingrained. Or perhaps it was to give ample time for visitors to gawk at the photographs of Citadel's stars that marched up either side of the staircase.

Martin automatically glanced at the spot where his own portrait hung, three treads from the top. His breath caught and he nearly missed the next step.

There was nothing there, nothing but an empty rectangle, paler than the walls around it.

A workman in overalls was whistling through his teeth as he lifted a picture of someone Martin didn't recognize and hung it where Martin's had been.

It's over. That's what this meeting is about. They're not renewing my contract.

When the workman stopped midwhistle and glanced over his shoulder, Martin forced his most urbane smile, straightened his shoulders, and glided, unhurried, to the landing.

He turned right and strolled into the antechamber of Ira's office. The inner door was closed, but Frederick, Ira's secretary, looked up from his typewriter.

"Good afternoon, Mr. Brentwood. I'm afraid Mr. Schlossberg is running a bit late."

"So Jenny told me."

"May I get you something while you wait?"

"A glass of water, if you would be so kind." Perhaps it would combat his dry mouth, although he suspected that nothing would fix that. *At least I no longer have to worry about the impure thoughts I'm having about my chauffeur.* At this rate, Robbie wouldn't remain his driver for a full twenty-four hours.

Maybe afterward we could—No. Even if Martin were convinced that Robbie was in the life, that he'd accept advances from someone at least a decade older and not nearly as appealing, he'd promised Sid he'd be discreet.

And if the studio let him go, he would no longer have their power behind him as proof against the press and the police.

He settled on the crimson velvet chesterfield across from Frederick's desk and accepted the water from him with a nod and a smile. He fully expected to have to refill it several times while he waited, since producers never hurried for the convenience of actors they were about to fire, but he'd barely soothed his parched mouth before the telephone jangled on Frederick's desk.

"Yes, Mr. Schlossberg. He's here. Very well."

Frederick hung up and rose. "Mr. Schlossberg will see you now." He opened the inner door and stood aside for Martin to enter.

For a moment he was blinded by the westering sun that streamed in through the tall windows on the far wall. When he tilted his head to avoid the glare, he was surprised that Ira wasn't sitting behind his massive oak desk.

"Over here, Martin."

Martin turned toward Ira's voice. He was sitting in a leather wingback chair next to the fireplace—a fireplace in Hollywood, for the love of God. At least no fire burned in the grate today. A breeze from the open windows fluttered the gauze curtains, and a trio of ceiling fans circled lazily above.

Across from Ira, one arm draped along the back of a brocade love seat, sat Evelyn Trent, cool and sophisticated as usual in a deep red dress, her dark hair upswept and a double strand of pearls around her throat.

"Darling," she said as she held out her hand. "So lovely of you to join us."

Martin strode across the room, took her hand, and raised it to his lips. "An unexpected pleasure." Evelyn was one of his closest friends. What was she doing here? Surely Ira wouldn't fire Martin in front of her. That wasn't his style. Now Jacob... Jacob would do it and grin around his cigar the whole time.

Both of the Schlossbergs had been sniffing around Evelyn for years, ever since she'd joined the studio as a dewy-eyed ingenue. She was their answer to Lillian Gish and she'd aged into a devastatingly beautiful woman whose understated sex appeal on-screen had the class that Jacob was always aiming for.

"I know, darling." She patted the seat next to her. "I would have warned you, but once Ira and I hit on our brilliant plan, I didn't want to wait."

"Plan?" Martin lowered himself to the overstuffed cushion.

"Yes. I'm doing yet another one of those dreary drawing-room pictures—"

"They're not dreary, Evelyn," Ira protested. "They're extremely popular. Our distributors love them because they pull in men *and* women."

"Yes, Ira dear, I'm aware that the audiences love them. I meant that they're dreary *for me*." She lowered her eyelashes and glanced sidelong at Martin. "Unless I have the perfect leading man to make the time pass more agreeably."

Martin nearly laughed. Evelyn was no more interested in men than he was in women, but she liked to use him to keep the Schlossbergs at bay. They were too busy vying with each other to take Martin seriously as a contender for Evelyn's affections, but that could backfire at any moment. If either Jacob or Ira thought Martin was about to land the prize, they could fire him just to remove him from the field. Evelyn always held her cards close to her chest. Martin hoped she didn't overplay her hand.

"What co-star did you have in mind?"

She widened her eyes. "Why you, darling, naturally. As I told Ira, I simply cannot play opposite Wendell Orton anymore. He *slavers*, darling. It's really too off-putting. This script calls for subtlety, sophistication, sex appeal."

"And you think I'm the man for the job?"

Another practiced flutter of her lashes. "But of course. You know the value of a slow smolder better than anyone. You'll make the women in the audience swoon for the chance to tip you over the edge into flames."

Martin couldn't help his laugh this time. "I think you overestimate my charms."

"Darling, how can you think so? I'm a woman, after all. Who are you going to believe? Me, or your own modesty?"

Martin inclined his head, although his insides were in a whirl. *I've still got a job.* "I would never contradict a lady."

"Then it's settled." Her tone turned businesslike. "Ira, dear, you'll take care of it, won't you?"

"Of course, Evelyn."

"Excellent. We start filming next week. You're bound to be finished with retakes on that ridiculous pro-Volstead picture by then, aren't you?"

"I devoutly hope so. I've had my fill of dying in gutters."

"Not a gutter in sight in this one, darling. Divans, cocktails, and evening clothes. Perhaps an indignant slap on the face—me to you, of course—but our love will triumph in the end. Now." All trace of languid grace vanished from the set of her spine. "We'll discuss the details, and then you can drive me home."

"But, Evelyn," Ira said. "I thought maybe you and I could have a drink?"

"Not tonight, dear. I have close-ups tomorrow on that dreadful picture of Boyd's, and if I drink anything but mineral water after noon, I look positively *haggard.*"

Martin leaned back and let Evelyn do what she did better than anyone in the business—twist producers around her graceful fingers until they gave her precisely what she wanted.

Martin was just thankful that this time, for whatever reason, she wanted *him.*

CHAPTER FIVE

Robbie prowled through the vast building. A shooting stage, Pops called it, although it didn't really have any one place that looked like a stage to Robbie. He picked his way around the cables that snaked across the floor every which way, and the two-by-fours that propped up the flimsy walls of a dozen different.... What did Pops call them? Units.

He passed by an Old West saloon, where two cowboys were fighting over an unconcerned dancehall girl. The next one was a restaurant with a half dozen tables with red-checked tablecloths, and as he passed, two of the patrons began flinging spaghetti at each other, egged on by a fellow with a bullhorn who was standing behind another fellow cranking a camera. *Director and cameraman.* Robbie at least knew *that* much.

In the corner, separated a bit from the rest of the chaos, a violinist and a pianist played "Hearts and Flowers" next to what looked like a throne room, where a woman in an elaborate hooped dress sobbed over a man in a long, curled wig and a satin suit. The man had apparently been felled by the arrow sticking out of his chest, although as Robbie watched, the arrow slowly toppled over. As the man sat up, his wig snagged on the woman's huge jeweled brooch and got knocked cattywampus, covering one of his eyes.

The director called, "Cut!" Then he swore at the actress, using words that would have earned Robbie a thrashing from Pa if he'd said even one of them to a man, let alone to a woman.

But to his astonishment, she gave as good as she got… until she noticed Robbie standing behind the camera. "What are *you* starin' at, ya big lummox?"

"Sorry." Robbie backed away. *I ought to get out of here before I do something stupid.* He could wait for Mr. Brentwood at Pops's booth.

He skirted the stage, hugging the wall, but halfway to the exit, he had to clamber over some of those two-by-four braces. There was a square opening halfway up the fake wall, so he ducked underneath it, remembering Pops's warning not to run into the scenery. Judging by the ruckus coming from the other side of the cutout, a fight was either in progress or about to start.

Someone yelled, "Get out of the way! It's going over!"

To Robbie's horror, the wall started to topple forward. *Jehoshaphat! Did I do that?*

He grabbed one of the braces, which wasn't attached to the floor, and hauled on it. The contraption wasn't light—although the wall itself was made of canvas, it was cross-braced with two-by-fours, and Robbie strained to hold it. *If I can slow it down, maybe everybody can get out of the way.*

He set his teeth, his muscles straining, as his slick-soled boots slid over the floor.

"Cut! Cut! What the hell is going on? Why isn't that wall falling?"

Suddenly someone was at Robbie's elbow. "Come with me. Quick."

He glanced down into the face of a girl, her expression a mixture of alarm and amusement. "But if the wall falls down, someone could get hurt."

"The only one who'll get hurt is you, if Boyd finds out you ruined this shot. They've spent all morning setting up for it."

"But—"

"Just let go. The other side is clear, and the grips'll catch it now."

Jumping nimbly over struts and cables, she towed Robbie away and dragged him into a corner room. Then she shut the door behind them, collapsed against it, and burst into laughter. "My stars, if you could have *seen* Boyd's face. And Harold Wynn. Both of 'em were fit to be tied."

Robbie peered at her in the dim room. "I don't understand. If that wall had fallen on somebody, they could have been hurt or killed."

"Did you see that window cutout?"

"The hole in the wall? Yes."

"Well, Harold was standing on the set, positioned so that the wall could come down around him with him standing in the window."

Robbie scrubbed a hand through his hair and realized he'd lost his cap. His belly rolled over. "I think I dropped my hat back there. Will they fire me once they figure out I'm responsible?"

"Nope. Because they're not going to know. I'll say you were here with me."

"But I wasn't."

"So?" She cocked her head and grinned up at him. "You and me have got an advantage. You're a driver and I'm a girl. So people don't *see* you—they only see the uniform. They don't see me because I'm not a star, and around here, those are the only girls who matter."

"Really?"

She nodded emphatically, her frizzy brown bob bouncing. "Yep. But not for long. Not if I can help it."

"Er, can you? Help it? I mean, who *are* you?"

She chuckled and held out her hand for him to shake. "I'm Dorothy Dashwood, but everybody calls me Dottie. I'm a cutter."

"A cutter?"

"Yeah. You think pictures just magically show up on the screen with everything in order, all the title cards in place?"

"I wouldn't know. I've never seen a picture."

Dottie gaped at him. "*Never*? Where have you been hiding? Under a rock?"

"Almost." Robbie shrugged apologetically. "Idaho."

"So what? There are picture palaces and nickelodeons everywhere. Even Idaho, I imagine."

"Not where I lived."

She grinned. "Well, you live in Hollywood now, so you've got no excuse." She tugged on his sleeve. "Come here. I'll show you."

She led the way across the cluttered room to a long wooden table. Next to it, narrow strips of what looked like dark, mottled cellophane hung from a line, illuminated from the back by lights behind frosted glass panels. She pointed at the strips. "Know what those are?" Robbie shook his head. "That, my friend, is a moving picture."

Robbie narrowed his eyes. "They look pretty unmoving to me."

She guffawed and poked him with her elbow. "Good one. That's the developed film. Pieces of it anyway. For it to move on the screen, somebody"—she pointed to herself—"has to put it all together and then print it out and load it onto reels so it can move through a projector and show up on a screen."

Robbie blinked. "That sounds like an important job."

"It is. A bad cutter can ruin a picture, no matter how good the actors or director or cameraman might be. In fact…." She leaned forward and lowered her voice. "I know some cutters who've done that on purpose, because of a grudge."

"Really?"

"Yep." Her expression darkened. "We've got our standards. There was a picture a while ago. A stunt went wrong, and the stunter got killed. The director wanted to keep the shot in the picture, but the cutter refused. She said it was wrong."

Robbie's stomach tried to retreat. *People could die making pictures?* "Did they... did they make her do it anyway?"

"Nope. Because the stunters backed her up and so did the star of the picture."

Robbie squinted at the narrow strips lined up like so many dark-uniformed soldiers. "Don't take this the wrong way, but I didn't know they let girls do things like this."

Dottie sniffed. "This is Hollywood. Things are different here. Women can do lots of things that they can't do in Peoria or Poughkeepsie. Or Idaho, apparently."

"I didn't mean any offense," Robbie said humbly.

"I know. Most men wouldn't bother to ask."

"So how do you do it?"

Dottie pulled on a pair of thin white gloves, probably cotton, since they didn't look to be leather or kid. Then she unhooked one of the film strips from the line and held it up to the light. "See this? This is the negative, the film the way it comes out of the camera, before we make the print. This is a scene from that awful pro-Prohibition picture they made Martin Brentwood do."

Robbie shifted uneasily. Should he be listening to other people talk about Mr. Brentwood? On the other hand, Pops had told him to learn about the actors, about the people who worked at Citadel. Dottie seemed willing to spill the beans, and he hadn't *asked* her to bring up the subject. "Didn't he want to do it?"

"Please," she scoffed. "*Nobody* would've wanted to do that picture. For one thing, nobody in Hollywood pays any attention to Prohibition. There are more blind pigs around than you can shake a stick at."

Blind pigs? Now Robbie was really confused. "I haven't seen any livestock. How were the pigs injured?" And what did maimed livestock have to do with the Volstead Act?

Dottie stared at him. "Can you really be *that* green? A blind pig is a speakeasy, a secret saloon, someplace you can only get into if you know the right people and they know you."

"So why would Mr. Brentwood make the picture?"

"Because he's an actor under contract with this studio, and they told him to."

"They?"

"The Schlossbergs—Ira and Jacob. Although"—she squinched her turned-up nose—"it sounds more like something Jacob would do, even though Ira's the VP in charge of production. Jacob hates Martin."

Robbie frowned. How could anyone hate Mr. Brentwood? "Why? Mr. Brentwood seems like a real nice fellow. A gentleman. Anyone can see that."

Dottie stared at him, her expression neutral. "I guess you really *can* be that green. What's your name again?"

"Robbie. Robbie Goodman."

"Well, Robbie Goodman, you've got a lot to learn."

He sighed. "That's what everyone keeps telling me."

She punched him in the arm, none too gently. "Lucky for you I know everything about everybody. So anytime you've got a spare minute, come visit me here in the cutting room. You'll be in the know in no time."

"Thanks, Dottie. I appreciate that."

"One thing I'll tell you right off—there's some people you want to steer clear of. First one? Jacob Schlossberg." She ticked them off on her fingers. "Second, Gilbert Flint."

"Pops told me about him. Said he's mean as a snake."

"Snakes are cuddlier than kittens compared to Gilbert. Next, Boyd Brody."

"Who's he? Whoops." Robbie clapped his hand over his mouth. "Pops said I wasn't supposed to ask that question, ever," he mumbled from behind his hand. "That folks might not take it so well."

"He's not wrong. But you're in luck again." She strode over to a bookshelf in the corner of the room, took down a massive loose-leaf binder, and thrust it into his arms. "I've got the scoop on this place right here, starting with stills from all of Citadel's pictures for the last seven years. So saddle up, partner. You're about to get a crash course in Hollywood."

CHAPTER SIX

The next month was eye-opening for Robbie in a dozen different ways. He often felt as though his head was like to explode, he'd had to learn so much in so little time.

He was still living at the same rooming house Pops had steered him to that first day. It suited him. It was clean and quiet. He could get breakfast for an extra dollar a week. His landlady, Mrs. McGuire, liked him and took care of his laundry in exchange for him doing odd jobs. She was so happy with the flowers he planted next to the house that she added extra starch to his underdrawers by mistake. He was chafed for a week because he didn't want to upset her by mentioning it.

The place was also convenient, only a quick streetcar ride away from the studio, where he reported every morning to sign out the Flyer and drive over to Alvarado to pick up Mr. Brentwood.

But more than anything, Robbie was determined to justify Pops's confidence in him, so he buckled down and *studied*. When Mr. Brentwood was filming, as he had been for the last three weeks, Robbie spent at least an hour or two every day with Pops, learning the faces of the studio folks who passed through the gates and listening to Pops's praise or warnings about each one.

He'd gotten a map—a real one, not just one jotted on the back of an envelope—and memorized streets and intersections and routes. Mr. Brentwood never had to give him directions again as he had on that first mortifying yet exhilarating day. Of course Robbie would never presume to borrow the studio automobile to motor around town for his own benefit, but he spent his weekends riding the streetcar. He'd been all the way to the end of every line and could get pretty much anywhere he needed to go.

When Mr. Brentwood didn't need him in the evenings, he went to the pictures with Dottie. Mostly they stuck to small theaters near her place in Venice, but a couple of times, they went into downtown Los Angeles, to Mr. Grauman's Million Dollar Theater.

Jehoshaphat. That place was fancier than anyplace Robbie had ever seen, with its gigantic pipe organ and fancy carpets and murals in more colors than the rainbow. Some of the walls were actually gold. *Real* gold. Well, gold leaf, anyway. And huge? Dottie said there were three thousand seats in the place. There weren't three thousand *people* in Pierce. Yet the theater had been full, or near as. He and Dottie sat in the top of the balcony, so far away from the screen that the actors' faces looked almost normal life-sized.

During the day, when he wasn't with Pops, Robbie spent most of his time in the dim cutting room with Dottie. Sometimes she showed him bits of the film she was working on, but once Robbie realized how painstaking her job was, he did his best not to distract her.

That was easy because of the *photographs*—book after looseleaf book of them, stills from Citadel's history captured in black and white, the light and shadow sometimes so beautiful on the actors' faces that Robbie's heart threatened to break.

And at no point was that more likely to happen than when he was looking at pictures of the man who was supposed to be his job.

Martin Brentwood was beautiful. In the rough clothes of a dock worker, slumped against a crate. On horseback in full cowboy regalia, backlit by a setting sun. In evening dress, his face half in shadow, a cigarette dangling from his fingers—although by this time, Robbie had learned that, unlike almost everybody else in Hollywood, Mr. Brentwood didn't smoke.

Yes, Martin Brentwood was beautiful in photographs. Unfortunately he was even more beautiful in person, and Robbie had to see that person every day, a person who stirred unwanted feelings in Robbie's chest.

He'd fled from those feelings, long and hard, only to smash into them again at the end of his journey. *Guess there's no escaping yourself, no matter how far you run.*

That last night Frank had explained to Robbie that feelings like those, like both of them shared, weren't wrong, even if they were illegal. *"I'll prove it to you, Rob. It'll be fine. I promise."*

But it hadn't been fine—not for Robbie and especially not for Frank.

Now here he was again, with nowhere else to run. But at least he'd learned something since that horrible night—*don't say anything.* Don't admit those shameful feelings, and for God's sake, don't *do* anything about 'em.

Not that he'd ever do or say anything to Mr. Brentwood. Lord, no! Not only was he Robbie's boss, even if it was Mr. Jacob who signed his paycheck, but he had *class*, Mr. Brentwood did. He was as far above Robbie as one of those fancy golden walls was above a dirt clod.

So he gazed at photographs or sat spellbound in the darkness while all the beautiful people played out their stories on the silver screen.

And he dreamed.

Martin paused to straighten his already impeccable white tie in the mirror next to the door. His fingers trembled slightly, setting the tie askew. *Ridiculous.* He had no reason for nerves, for the love of God. Tonight wasn't about *him*—although in a way it was. The reaction to Fairbanks's picture had Ira all fired up. If the public ate up swashbucklers like that—which were really nothing more than Westerns with fancier costumes—then Sid was right. Martin's days of lighting women's cigarettes were numbered, even if the woman in question was Evelyn. And numbered days meant no paydays on the horizon.

What would I do if I wasn't an actor anymore? He could hardly apprentice again at the advanced age of thirty. The tailor he'd worked for, while grudgingly complimentary of Martin's fabric and style choices, had told him his seams were barely passable.

He pushed the thought aside. *I'll think of that when the time comes.* Tonight, he had fans to face. Presenting his aloof, sophisticated image to them was second nature. Maintaining the same urbane elegance in front of his chauffeur was another story altogether.

Over the last weeks, the best part of Martin's day was his time in the back seat of the Dixie Flyer, where Robbie's sunny presence lightened the gloom of Martin's career worries.

Martin had been tempted—so tempted—to arrange longer trips out of town for no reason other than to spend more time with the ingenuous young man, to see the wonder in his face the first time he watched the waves crash on the beach along the Pacific Coast Highway, to see his excitement bloom at the mad chaos of the amusement rides on the Pickering Pier.

But he'd resisted, in part because he simply *liked* the man. Robbie was courteous, genuine, always cheerful, and unfailingly kind and deferential to Martin. He truly lived up to his name—he was a sincerely *good* man.

And Martin knew he'd be tempted to take things further than simple outings, which was out of the question since he'd had no indication that Robbie suspected a relationship between two men was even possible. So many people in America's heartland had no idea, had no *name* for it other than the Biblical, and even that was inaccurate and never spoken of outside of fire-and-brimstone revival tents. Or, for the very unlucky, the courtroom.

Was it wrong that he craved the admiration in Robbie's eyes when Robbie shyly admitted to looking at stills from Martin's pictures? Or that Martin took extra care when shaving and choosing his suits, simply because he delighted in the way Robbie's habitual open-the-car-door-trot hitched at his first sight of Martin each morning?

But sometimes that direct, unwavering gaze was disconcerting, because Robbie wasn't only *nice*. He was intelligent. Witness how quickly he'd found his feet in Hollywood. Anyone that sharp was bound to see through Martin's facade, given enough time.

"Be careful, *Marvin*. Remember all you have to lose," he murmured to his reflection. Nevertheless, his belly fluttered as he locked his front door behind him. This would be the first time Robbie had seen him in full evening dress, other than in those stills from old Citadel pictures. If Martin was wrong to hope for a reaction—not that Robbie would fall at his feet, precisely—then Martin would do penance later. *I'll even endure sitting next to Boyd or Gilbert or, God forbid, Aurelia Arthur's mother.*

When he realized he was almost sprinting away from his door, he slowed his pace. *Aloof, sophisticated men do not careen along the pavement, particularly when wearing evening clothes.*

So he sauntered out of the bungalow court and struck a deliberately casual pose as though he were checking for his watch. But his masterful entrance was completely wasted.

Robbie wasn't watching for him.

Instead he was frowning at a newspaper in his lap, squinting in the failing light.

Burying his disappointment, Martin approached the automobile. Robbie must have caught the movement out of the corner of his eye, because his head jerked up and he tossed the paper aside.

"Jehoshaphat!" He leaped out of the car and hurried to the curb. "I'm so sorr—" His voice died away and his steps slowed as his gaze traveled from Martin's head to his shoes and back again. "Wow."

Martin's mood instantly lightened. He held out his arms and revolved slowly. "You think I'll pass muster, then?"

"Are you kidding? I didn't think anything could look better than you did in those pictures, but in the flesh?" The flush on Robbie's cheeks rivaled Lillian Gish at her demure, blushing-rose best. "I—I mean in person. Because of course you're not—"

Martin chuckled. "It's all right, Robbie. I know what you mean. And thank you. One likes to know one hasn't entirely lost one's touch."

Robbie held the car door for Martin to climb in and then rushed back to slip behind the wheel. "Nobody'll compare with you tonight."

"Trust me. If Valentino has graced the evening with his presence, no one will favor me with a second glance."

"If you say so."

Robbie's obvious disbelief was balm to Martin's soul. He settled into the leather seat with a much lighter heart than he'd had since Evelyn rescued his career—or at least granted it a stay of execution—by insisting on him as her co-star in *The Imaginary Husband*.

"Will Miss Trent be there tonight?"

Martin smiled. Robbie couldn't see him, of course, since he always paid strict attention to the road whenever Martin was in the car. But they'd abandoned formality weeks ago, with Martin encouraging Robbie to ask questions about Hollywood or to regale Martin with breathless tales of his latest discovery. "Yes, I believe so."

"Don't you usually arrive in her car? It's a sight fancier than this one."

Martin frowned, struck by the notion. Since the studio was already starting to publicize *The Imaginary Husband*, having him arrive with Evelyn would have made sense. They always liked to hint at a romance between leading lady and leading man, provided both were single. They thought it made the audience more predisposed to accept the on-screen relationship. If Citadel wasn't bothering to promote the relationship as well as the picture….

How had he missed that danger sign? *Because I've been so preoccupied with my chauffeur that I forget about my leading lady unless we're on set together.*

A shard of ice lodged under Martin's heart. "Perhaps one of the Schlossbergs is escorting her." As soon as the words were out, he realized they were mere wishful thinking. Evelyn would have begged him to rescue her from Ira's—or God forbid—Jacob's company if that had been the case.

"But Dottie said that neither of the Schlossbergs are coming to the party tonight. She *said*—but you have to understand that Dottie's a kidder, right? She doesn't mean anything by what she says."

"Of course," Martin said dryly. "What *doesn't* she mean about the Schlossbergs?"

"That, um, they don't want to make it look like they think Mr. Fairbanks's picture is important. So they're letting the head of the publicity department handle the Citadel presence. That'd be Leo McCorkle. Have I got that right?"

The ice spread, heavy in Martin's chest. "You do. Well done." He gazed out the window. "Perhaps Evelyn has found an excuse to escape the premiere tedium after all."

"Would she want to? Dottie made it sound like a big deal."

"It's a big deal for United Artists, since *Three Musketeers* is their picture. But Evelyn and I are under contract with Citadel. Consequently, we're there merely to remind everyone that we exist."

"Nobody could ever forget that," Robbie murmured.

The ice receded a tiny bit. "Thank you, Robbie. You're very good for my ego."

65

"It's only the truth."

Martin wanted more than anything to ask whether Robbie was referring to Martin alone or to Martin and Evelyn as a couple, but since Robbie was negotiating the traffic leading to Broadway, it wasn't an opportune time to distract him.

The newspaper, discarded on the seat next to Robbie, caught Martin's eye. He leaned forward, snagged the edge of it, and pulled it into his lap.

"What had your attention so riveted earlier?"

"Oh!" Robbie swerved a little and then corrected, his hand gripping the steering wheel. "That's just—I didn't mean—I'm sorry I didn't—"

"Relax, Robbie. I don't expect you to hang on my every word and movement." *Although I wouldn't mind if you did.* "I'm simply curious."

"It's only the Boise paper."

"Ah. Keeping up with news from home, are you?"

"Sort of. I come from farther north, up near the Bitterroots, but our town isn't big enough to have its own paper."

"Is Boise the closest town with a paper, then?"

"N-n-no. That'd be Coeur d'Alene, I expect, or Moscow, although neither of them is as big."

"Then why—"

"If it's all right with you, Mr. Brentwood, I'd as soon not talk about it." Robbie's voice trembled. *Why, Robbie? What is it about Boise that frightens you so?*

If Martin persisted with his questions and pressed the issue, he doubted Robbie would refuse to answer. And that would be an abuse of his own rather negligible authority.

But he itched with the need to *know*. Robbie rarely volunteered any information about himself. Martin had chalked that up to Robbie's innate courtesy and deference, but it looked as though there might be another reason.

"You know, Robbie," Martin said slowly, "you don't have to be ashamed if there's something in your past you're trying to forget. Nearly everyone in Hollywood has something they'd prefer to hide." *Some of us more than others.*

"Thank you for being so nice about it, Mr. Brentwood, but I really think—"

"For instance, take Doug Fairbanks, the star of tonight's picture. He got expelled from high school for cutting the wires on the school piano."

Robbie laughed and his shoulders relaxed a trifle, lowering from their position by his ears. "Really?"

"You have my word for it. It doesn't play very well to his image, does it?"

"I suppose not."

"And the absolute *last* thing he'd want the public to know was that his father abandoned his family when Doug was only five. Because that might lead people to pity him, and no one that robust and successful can survive being *pitied*."

"But it's a shame, isn't it? For a father to abandon his family?"

"Perhaps. But in this town, it's a story that's not remarkable in any way. Half of Hollywood's got disappearing fathers."

"The other half comes from good homes?"

Martin grinned at Robbie's hopeful tone. "The other half *are* the disappearing fathers. Besides, just because a home has a father in it, doesn't make it good."

"I'll say," Robbie muttered. "My home would have been a whole lot better if my father *had* disappeared."

"Cheer up, my friend. It could still happen. After all, in Hollywood, anything is possible."

The street in front of the Million Dollar Theater wasn't as packed with cars as it usually was for a film opening, possibly because the official premiere had been in New York three days earlier. Robbie was able to pull up to the curb several yards from the glittering marquee.

"When should I come back for you, Mr. Brentwood?"

Martin scanned the sidewalk. The red carpet was empty, although some people still milled around behind the velvet ropes. "It doesn't look as busy as I expected, although we are a bit behind schedule."

"I'm sorry—"

"That was my fault, Robbie. Ah, there's Leo. He'll have my ticket. Shall I see if there's an extra balcony seat for you?" He leaned forward and patted Robbie's shoulder. "Wouldn't you like to see the latest in Hollywood adventures while it's still a novelty? Because before the end of next week, I promise you every studio in town will be scouring the library for the classics and cranking out period melodramas. Maybe they'll try your namesake."

Robbie's snort was oddly endearing. "That'd be a right boring picture. Some fellow in raggedy trousers wandering around on a beach by himself. At least until he meets Friday."

Two men alone on an island. Martin could think of worse fates, particularly if one of the men was Robbie and the other was Martin himself.

"Well, I'll just check, shall I? Wait here for a moment or two."

After Robbie raced around to open the door with his usual athletic grace—really, Doug Fairbanks had nothing on this man—Martin emerged with his movie-star persona firmly in place. You never knew where a photographer might be lurking, ready to catch an unflattering shot, or where a disgruntled fan might be waiting to prove actors weren't nearly as glamorous in real life as they were on-screen.

Martin nodded his thanks to Robbie and strolled down the sidewalk to where Leo was standing under the marquee, directly in front of *The Three Musketeers* poster, and scowling at a list in his hand. A coincidence that Leo was blocking Doug's image? *I think not.*

"Good evening, Leo. I'm sorry I'm a trifle late."

Leo's scowl didn't disappear when he glanced up at Martin, but it included an element of surprise. "Martin. I didn't—"

"Do you happen to know if there's an extra balcony seat going begging? I'd like my driver to get in to see the picture."

"Your driver?" Leo peered over Martin's shoulder to where Robbie was standing next to the automobile. "Oh, him. Sorry, Martin, but the place is sold out."

"Ah. I see. No standing room even?"

Leo snorted, not nearly as endearingly as Robbie. "They don't allow that in picture palaces the way they do in vaudeville houses."

"Very well. I'll let him know." Martin smiled, permitting a hint of displeasure to show in the set of his jaw. "I trust you haven't placed me next to Gilbert Flint."

Leo blinked, for an instant looking a trifle panic-stricken. "I, ah…. Thing is, Martin, we're sold out."

"Yes. You said that."

"I mean, sold out as in there's no ticket for *you*."

Martin's stomach plummeted to his shoes. "No ticket. But there's always a ticket for me. I've attended the Los Angeles premiere of every major picture since I first signed with Citadel."

Leo shrugged. "Not this time. Somebody must've dropped the ball when it came to letting you know."

Martin pasted on his best ingratiating smile. "Think nothing of it. I'm sure there's a message waiting for me somewhere that I simply missed." He inclined his head. "Good evening. I hope the picture is as well-received by Los Angeles audiences as it was in New York." He made himself wink. "Or as well-received as Jacob and Ira—as friendly competitors, of course—would like."

"Martin—"

But Martin turned and strolled back toward the automobile, keeping his attention fixed firmly on Robbie's face, which was creased in concern. He didn't want to give Leo the chance to offer him the sop of attending the reception afterward, even though he'd been excluded from the main event.

Thank goodness the press has all decamped. The last thing he needed was photographic evidence of his humiliation—proof of exactly how little he was worth to the studio.

CHAPTER SEVEN

Something's wrong.

The lights chasing around the marquee lit up Mr. McCorkle's smirk, although Mr. Brentwood's face was shadowed as he strode toward Robbie.

"Shall we go?" Mr. Brentwood was close enough now for Robbie to see him clearly in the yellow glow of the streetlamp. Jehoshaphat, there'd been more emotion in those still photographs than in his expression now.

"Go?" Robbie glanced between his shuttered face and Mr. McCorkle's smirk. "If it's because they don't have a ticket for me, I don't mind. I can come back—"

"Apparently there was a miscommunication somewhere." Mr. Brentwood's tone was languid, almost bored. "I find I don't wish to see this picture tonight after all."

But Robbie had absorbed more in Dottie's cutting room than just the mechanics of motion pictures. She'd given him his first lessons in studio politics too. Mr. Brentwood's stoic expression, Mr. McCorkle's smirk, the lack of fans clamoring for their favorite stars told the story.

They didn't expect him.

Robbie would give a lot to know whether Martin had been excluded on purpose, but studio gossip and intrigue weren't

Robbie's business. Taking care of Mr. Brentwood, though? Robbie might only be the driver, and a new one at that, but he'd *make* Mr. Brentwood's welfare his business. *Somebody* needed to, and the studio was sure making a hash of it.

He tightened his grip on the door handle so he wouldn't be tempted to touch Mr. Brentwood's sleeve. "I know you're not exactly dressed for it, but if you don't have any other plans, how would you like me to take you to my favorite diner? You'd definitely class up the place, and they've got the best doughnuts in town. My treat."

Mr. Brentwood brushed the back of Robbie's hand with the tips of his fingers, his smile a little sad. "That's incredibly sweet of you, Robbie, however—"

"Of course." Robbie dropped his gaze to stare at the reflection of the marquee in the Flyer's window. "I'm sorry. I shouldn't have overstepped. I'll take you—"

"What I was going to say is that I'm incredibly flattered by the invitation, but"—he leaned closer and lowered his voice—"I can pay for my own doughnut."

Robbie jerked his chin up in time to catch Mr. Brentwood's more heartfelt smile. And was that an actual twinkle in his eye? *Don't be stupid. It's probably just more reflections from the marquee chaser lights.* "You mean it? You'll come with me?"

"I'd be honored."

"Hot dog! I mean, very good, sir."

Mr. Brentwood threw back his head and laughed. "Oh, don't start 'sir-ing' me now. In fact, since we're about to share Hollywood's finest doughnuts, I think you should call me Martin, don't you?"

A thrill spiraled up Robbie's spine. He'd been using Martin's given name in his secret thoughts for weeks, but he never imagined he might be able to actually *say* it. "M-Martin, then. The place is near the studio. We should be able to get there—"

"Let me in, damn you!"

The shout, strident yet slurred, startled both of them. Directly under the marquee, a young man in evening dress, his tie askew and his hair flopping across his forehead, was swaying in front of Leo, poking his chest with a finger.

"Shite," Martin murmured. "Wesley."

"Mr. Thornhill?" Robbie looked closer. Yes, it was him, all right, but in all the stills Robbie had seen of Wesley in his college-boy adventures, he'd never looked so... debauched.

"I'm the biggest star this studio's got," Wesley shouted. "I wanna go see this piece of shit Fairbanks thinks is so damn wonderful. I can do the same stunts he does. I *have* done 'em. You show me what he's doing in this one, and I'll do the same thing by next Tuesday."

"I'm afraid the doughnuts will have to wait for another time," Martin said. "We'd better get Wesley out of here before he does any more damage."

Robbie kept pace with Martin as he strode down the sidewalk. "You think he'll hit Mr. McCorkle?"

"I meant damage to himself, to his reputation. He's supposed to be a clean-cut American college boy, not somebody who's clearly spent the last few hours in a speakeasy. Thank goodness the press has either left or gone inside."

Martin lunged the last two steps and caught Wesley's cocked elbow before he could throw a punch at Mr. McCorkle. "Wesley, my boy. Just the man I wanted to see. Come along with me, there's a good chap, lest you forget yourself."

"Leggo." Wesley jerked his arm out of Martin's grip. "I don't forget *me*. I don't forget *you*. I don't forget *nothing*. You think they'll"—he swung his arm wide and nearly smacked Robbie in the chest—"stand behind you if you don't do what they want? They won't. In fact...." Wesley's grimace turned sly. "They're doing it already, aren't they? That's why you're out here instead of in there."

"That's enough. Robbie, if you wouldn't mind taking Wesley's other arm." Martin nodded to Mr. McCorkle. "We'll straighten him out."

Leo snorted. "Good luck with that."

"Wait! I wanna see the picture!" Wesley struggled in their grip, but Robbie had been plowing fields and pitching hay his whole life, and Martin was apparently stronger than he looked. Wesley was no match for the two of them.

But as they marched him toward the car, a flash popped in their faces. Wesley shrieked, attempting to cover his eyes with his hands.

"Drat," Martin muttered. "Get the door, please, Robbie."

Robbie sprang forward to obey, and they managed to wrestle Wesley into the back seat. He tried to scramble out again, which the photographer also caught, but Martin shoved him inside and climbed in next to him.

Robbie raced around the car, fully expecting he'd have to chase Wesley down the street if he escaped out the other door. But by the time Robbie slid behind the wheel, Wesley was slumped in the corner, weeping quietly.

"Where to, Mart—Mr. Brentwood?"

Martin sighed and smoothed his own hair, which had gotten rumpled in the struggle. "We'd best take him to my place and pour a gallon or two of coffee into him. Let us fervently hope he doesn't spew all over the automobile before we get there."

Robbie was tempted to push the Flyer harder than usual, not because he was worried about the upchucking—he'd cleaned up worse messes back home after Pa'd slaughtered a pig—but Wesley was worrying him. By the time they left downtown Los Angeles, he had stopped crying, but he'd started a rhythmic tapping against the window, coupled with low-voiced swearing that made the hairs on Robbie's neck stand up. He couldn't get to Alvarado fast enough.

When he pulled up along the curb in his usual spot, Martin said, "Not here. Turn right up ahead and circle around to the garage in back. It's empty since my car... well, it's empty."

"But Pops told me never to—"

"I'm going to need your help, Robbie. It'll be easier to get Wesley in and out discreetly from back there than if we're enacting this farce in full view of traffic, not to mention passengers disembarking from the streetcar."

"Yessir."

In and *out?* Robbie's belly flopped like a landed trout. *I'm going to be* inside *Martin's home. Maybe for a while.* Robbie wasn't sure how to feel. It seemed... intimate, somehow, even though Wesley would be there too. Sure, Martin had invited Robbie to use his given name tonight, but to invite him into his home.... *Jehoshaphat. I need to get hold of myself. It doesn't mean anything.* Martin was just being a gentleman. And a friend.

A friend to *Wesley*.

Robbie stopped the car in front of the garage and jumped out to open the big double doors. The place was empty, like Martin had said. Cobwebs festooned the corners and dust danced in the headlights. Robbie got back in, eased the automobile forward, and turned off the engine.

Martin didn't wait for Robbie to open the door for him, and together, both of them helped Wesley out the other side. Wesley was twitchy, but he didn't fight them again, which was lucky because they passed a couple of Martin's neighbors on their way to his place.

"Good evening, Douglas, Faith. Lovely evening."

The couple murmured a greeting and then passed on, though the woman glanced at Wesley with a slight frown. Wesley craned his neck to watch her.

"Bloody hell," Martin muttered. "Try for a little discretion, Wesley. Do you *want* to advertise your condition to representatives of every studio in town?"

Wesley jerked his arm out of Martin's grip. "There's nothing wrong with me. If anyone says there's something wrong with me, I'll—"

"Stow it, you imbecile." Martin caught Wesley's arm again and dragged him up the sidewalk to one of the neat, two-story bungalows. "Hold him while I find my keys, Robbie."

"He doesn't need to hold me. I can hold myself. I can hold my liquor. I can hold my—"

"You'll be holding your bollocks in a minute because I'm about to punch you there just to shut you up. Ah, finally." Martin unlocked his door and dragged Wesley inside.

"Should I, uh, go?" Robbie asked.

"Good God, no. I need your support. Then I'll need you to drive him home." Martin seemed to catch himself. "That is, you don't mind, do you, Rob?"

A little warmth twined around his heart at Martin's use of a nickname. *He thinks of me as somebody who deserves a nickname.* Not that Robbie wasn't a nickname already, but still. "No, I don't mind."

"Why should he mind?" Wesley said as he flopped onto the long leather sofa in Martin's tidy living room. "It's what he's paid for, isn't it?"

"He's not paid to keep you from assaulting Leo in full view of the press. What were you thinking, Wes?"

Wes. Maybe Martin was just a person who gave people nicknames all the time. Or maybe he'd run so short of patience that saying everyone's full name was too much trouble.

Wesley's expression turned sullen. "Nothing."

"That's obvious." Martin heaved a sigh and sat down on the edge of the sofa. "Talk to me, Wes. I thought you were drunk at first, but you don't smell of hooch, and you're twitchy as hell. Are you on it? The pick-me-up?" Martin flicked a glance at Robbie. "Cocaine?"

Robbie sucked in a breath. *Cocaine?* He'd heard about it, but he'd never…. And Martin seemed to know all about it.

For a moment Robbie didn't think Wesley would answer. Then his face crumpled. "I can't help it. After that stunt went wrong on my last picture, my back was so banged up that they put me on opium. You know, for the pain? But that makes me sleepy, so I use the coke to keep going."

"That stuff'll kill you, Wes, and I should know."

Robbie put out a hand to steady himself on the edge of an upright piano. *Martin? Does he...? Has he...?*

Wesley blinked. "That's right. You wrecked your car. That's why they won't let you drive yourself anymore. Do you still—"

"No. I don't." Martin's voice was sharp. "And you shouldn't either. Why not simply rest and recover?"

Wesley slumped against the sofa cushions. "I can't. My contract has a nonperformance clause. If I don't show up, they can fire me." He raised his woebegone face to Martin. "And if they fire me, nobody else'll hire me either. If I can't work, what will I do, Martin? This is the only thing I know. If I can't work, I might as well be dead."

The next morning, Martin wasn't at all surprised when the morning newspaper included a touching story of how upset Wesley Thornhill had been about the sudden illness and death of his beloved grandfather. The studio publicity machine was nothing if not efficient—not to say ruthless—and the press danced to their tune on a regular basis.

Martin tried not to resent Wesley. The man had enough problems between his injury and his apparent drug dependency. But if Wesley hadn't staged his scene last night, Martin might have had a chance to spend time with Robbie in a way completely unrelated to the studio.

A diner. Doughnuts.

Damn Wesley anyway.

The telephone shrilled as Martin was shrugging into his suit coat. He tucked the newspaper under his arm and crossed the room to answer it.

"Martin Brentwood."

"Hey, Marty, it's me."

"Roscoe. How are you?" Roscoe Arbuckle, who loathed the nickname Fatty that branded his pictures, had been the first big star to be kind to Martin when he and Sid first arrived in Hollywood.

"Can't complain. Say, I looked for you at the premiere last night but must have missed you in the crowd."

A ghost of last night's shame curled in Martin's chest. "Ah, well. I couldn't make it. But I understand your fans are eating up *Gasoline Gus* and *Crazy to Marry* with a spoon. Doug must be shaking in his knee-high boots for fear you'll steal all his box-office take."

Roscoe chuckled. "Doug's pictures are a different kettle of fish than mine, Marty. You know that." Roscoe had a point. Although Fairbanks's old signature had been short, sometimes quirky comedies, now that *Robin Hood* had started the trend and *The Three Musketeers* had apparently sealed the deal, no doubt Doug wouldn't appear in anything without a sword to brandish for years.

On the other hand, Roscoe's stock in trade was broad comedy, trading on his girth, his moon face, and his unexpected physical agility.

"You don't do too badly, though."

"Once again, can't complain. Say, Marty, a bunch of us are heading up to San Francisco for the long weekend. Putting up at the St. Francis for a little party. Want to come with?"

Martin startled and stared at the telephone as though he could somehow see through it. He and Roscoe were friends, but he'd never been invited on a road trip before. *Ah.* "I take it Buster won't be going?" Buster Keaton was Roscoe's closest friend, although his recent marriage to one of the Talmadge sisters would probably curtail their carousing.

"Nah. He's still all honeymoonish. He's taking Natalie to Catalina." Martin heard a smack through the line. "Shoot. I didn't—I mean, I always *meant* to ask you too."

Martin chuckled. In some ways Roscoe was still as ingenuous as Robbie. "I'm not insulted. I know Buster's your best mate."

"Please, Marty?" Roscoe's voice held a childlike desperation. "It'll be way more fun if I've got a real friend there."

Martin tipped his head back and stared at the ceiling. To get away from Hollywood, even for a few days. *Why not?* He could put *The Three Musketeers* debacle behind him. While the news story had focused on Wesley, Martin didn't want to be in town when someone looked more closely at that blasted photograph and asked why Martin hadn't been inside the theater with all the other Hollywood notables.

He probably *could* swing it if he wanted to—shooting on *The Imaginary Husband*, the picture he was *almost* in with Evelyn if you didn't blink too quickly, wasn't scheduled to resume until the day after Labor Day. He could take the train back from San Francisco on Monday and be in decent enough shape to face the camera Tuesday morning.

Or maybe I could have Robbie drive me up.

But if Roscoe wasn't thrilled about the company, Martin would be even less so, and Robbie would probably be scandalized. The picture of Robbie's shock, disillusionment, and possible outrage when faced with the standard lack of decorum at one of Roscoe's parties sent Martin's belly into a tailspin.

When did Robbie's opinion start to matter more than my own amusement?

It hardly mattered when or how, only that it did, and Martin refused to give it up for a single moment before Robbie inevitably realized that Martin's feet were made of the most common of clays.

"I don't think it would be wise, Roscoe. Evelyn and I are still shooting until the middle of the month, and I'm under strict orders from Sid to keep my nose clean. I'm not sure my reputation would survive one of your parties."

Roscoe guffawed. "Aw, c'mon, Marty. That's what the studio fixers are for. Besides, you'll be with me. What could happen?"

Martin tapped the newspaper with one finger. Roscoe had a point. He was a huge star. If the studio could cover up Wesley's very public breakdown this quickly, any minor infractions of the Volstead Act committed in Fatty Arbuckle's presence would disappear almost before they occurred. Besides, it wasn't illegal to buy or to consume alcohol—only to manufacture, sell, or transport it. No doubt Roscoe had that angle covered, although the fewer details Martin knew, the better.

But there's Robbie. Even if Robbie weren't at the party, Martin would feel his gaze on his back anyway. Not judging—Robbie didn't judge. But Martin discovered suddenly that he didn't want to give Robbie a *reason* to judge. *Shite, he's turning me into a better man, even when he's not here.*

"I'm sorry, Roscoe. But it really wouldn't be prudent of me. Jacob is being… well, Jacob."

"Looking for any excuse to boot you out on your rump, is he? Okay, Marty. I get it. No hard feelings."

"I hope not. But we'll get together when you're back in town. How's that?"

"That'd be swell."

"Have a good time, my friend."

"Oh, you know me. Always the life of the party." But from the forlorn note in Roscoe's voice as he signed off, he wasn't expecting much from the weekend.

Martin nearly relented and telephoned Roscoe back, but then he glanced at the clock on the mantelpiece. *Robbie is waiting.* The thrill of anticipation flushed all thought of Roscoe's uneasiness from Martin's mind.

He settled his boater at the perfect angle, locked the door behind him, and strolled toward the street. Robbie was leaning against the hood of the Flyer, his gaze trained on the sidewalk. As soon as he saw Martin, he straightened up, and *there*—the smile that warmed Martin from his toes to his hat brim.

"Good morning, Mr. Brent—I mean, Martin." His smile faded as his eyebrows bunched together. "Is that all right? Am I still supposed to call you by your given name?"

Martin allowed himself the indulgence of patting Robbie's arm. "Indeed you are. I wouldn't rescind that kind of invitation."

Robbie's shoulders sagged. "Good. I wouldn't want to offend you."

"I doubt there's anything you could do that would offend me, Robbie. I'm rather difficult to shock."

Robbie ducked his head as a hectic flush stained his cheeks. He parted his lips as though to say something, but instead he nodded jerkily and opened the car door.

Martin didn't get in. Instead he unfolded the newspaper and thwacked it with one finger. "Our crisis of last evening has been averted."

Robbie peered at the article with its accompanying photograph of the two of them manhandling Wesley down the sidewalk, several gaping onlookers in the background. "Wow. Do I really look like that much of a hick?"

"Nonsense. You look quite capable and determined. And very handsome. Anyone would be forgiven for thinking *you* were the film star."

"I know I shouldn't contradict my boss, Martin, but that's the bunk." Robbie's flush had deepened. "They'd never make a mistake like that. You look just as perfect as you always do."

"I'm flattered." He folded the paper with the photograph topmost. "And what about Wesley?"

Robbie tilted his head and squinted a bit, which only made his eyes bluer. "He doesn't look so good."

"No. But Leo made certain to give the public an explanation they could swallow."

Robbie looked closer. "His grandfather died? Does Wesley have a grandfather?"

"He does now. Or rather he doesn't." Martin studied the photograph more closely. "You know, Robbie, I wasn't wrong before. You and Wesley share a certain resemblance—build, hair color, face shape—but if I were pressed to tell someone which of you belonged on the screen based on this photograph? It wouldn't be him."

Robbie gripped the top of the open door. "You know that's not what I want. I didn't come to Hollywood to be in pictures."

"No." Martin tapped his chin thoughtfully. "Why *did* you come to Hollywood, Rob?"

Robbie's gaze darted to the left. "Because this is where my last lift dropped me. If you don't get in the car, you'll be late on the set. You don't want to keep Miss Trent or Mr. Brody waiting."

Martin chuckled but didn't pursue Robbie's obvious dodge. "Of the two, it's Evelyn who strikes the most terror in my heart." He climbed into the automobile, but as he watched Robbie circle in front of the hood, he wondered—not for the first time—what had really cast Robinson Crusoe Goodman adrift and caused him to wash up on the highly improbable shores of Hollywood.

Robbie was silent until they were halfway to the studio. "Martin?"

"Yes, my dear?" Martin winced the instant the words left his mouth, but Robbie didn't seem to notice the inadvertent endearment.

"That story in the paper. It's a lie."

"Yes it is. Does that trouble you?"

"Well, the thing is…. Papers are how most regular folks find out about things, things that are happening farther away from them than their own town. If the papers print lies sometimes and truth other times, how are regular folks supposed to tell the difference?"

"That, Robbie, is a very good question, and one that studio publicity departments hope your 'regular folks' never think to ask. If the truth were known about the stars they revere so, they'd rise up en masse and slaughter the lot of us."

Robbie chuckled as he turned onto Melrose. "They wouldn't do that. They all love you too much. Why, Dottie told me you get at least a dozen proposals of marriage every week."

Was that a note of jealousy in Robbie's voice? Martin could only hope.

"At one point, that may have been true. But my popularity with the country's unmarried ladies—and even the married ones—has fallen off sadly since Mr. Valentino danced his famous tango."

"Dottie told me about that too. But I don't think that's the whole story. Folks have room in their hearts for more than one favorite. That's what *I* think anyway."

"Do you? I hope that's true." *For my sake as well as yours.*

They pulled into the studio drive and waved to Pops when he ambled out to open the gates for them.

When Robbie parked the car next to the stage, he didn't jump out the way he usually did. Instead he sat with his hands gripping the steering wheel and stared at the stucco wall in front of him.

"Robbie? Is something the matter?"

"Last night, Mr. Thornhill said the studio expected him to work even though he was hurt."

"That's right. Some contracts do include nonperformance provisos." Roscoe had one. Martin's current contract didn't, but Sid suspected that the next one would, provided it was offered.

"But that's wrong. It's like they're using people up and throwing them away. On the farm we'd never throw something away because it was broken. We'd fix it. And if it couldn't do what it was intended to do, we'd find another place for it. We didn't waste things. We couldn't. But here? It's like Hollywood's wasting people."

Martin sighed. "You're not wrong, Robbie. And sadly, they can afford to, because no matter how many they throw away—no matter how big the name or how bright the star—ten more will be waiting in the wings, ready to step in and take their place." What was even sadder was how unlikely the public was to notice the difference.

CHAPTER EIGHT

Robbie walked Martin to the set the way he always did, so he could find out when the director expected to be done. Afterward he wandered through the building. On one set a couple of guys in baggy pants and suspenders were whacking each other with giant sausages. On the next a fellow in a toga reclined on an uncomfortable-looking marble bench while a pair of listless ladies fed him grapes. On the next—Robbie stopped and squinted at the throne room set. He could swear that the same woman in the same hooped dress was sobbing over the same bewigged guy that he'd seen on his first day on the lot. The only difference was the musician in the corner was playing "Hearts and Flowers" on a piano instead of a violin.

He shook his head. *Couldn't be.* He'd been around long enough to know that most pictures were shot incredibly fast, to feed the public's appetite for new entertainment. He was tempted to watch for a while, just to be sure, but this morning, he wasn't in the mood.

So he headed for the cutting room, where he was always assured of a welcome.

But for once, Dottie didn't greet him with a smile. She wasn't even at her cutting table. Instead she was sitting in a chair, jabbing a pencil into a pad of paper, over and over, until the point snapped.

Robbie eased the door closed behind him. "Dottie? Is something wrong?"

She stared irritably at her pencil and then flung it onto the floor, where it skittered into the corner. "I have to keep script for Aurelia Arthur's next picture."

Robbie picked up the pencil and scooted the other chair—a wooden slat-backed number they'd liberated from the Italian restaurant set—so it faced her. He pulled out his pocket knife and sharpened the pencil. "I thought you liked keeping script because it makes it easier for you to cut the picture later if you can make notes during filming."

She wrinkled her nose. "I do like it. Mostly. But *not* Aurelia Arthur's pictures. She's so... so... *insipid.* Jacob hired her because he needed an ingenue with golden ringlets, his own Mary Pickford or Mary Miles Minter. But she doesn't have Pickford's intelligence or the edge of crazy Minter can never quite hide."

"So, you're mad because you don't like Aurelia?"

"Yes. No." She slid down in her chair until her chin was on her chest and laced her fingers across her stomach. She was wearing pleated, high-waisted trousers today, and although Robbie had been startled by her wardrobe choices at first, now he rather admired her for them. "Do you know how old Anita Loos was when she sold her first scenario to Griffith? Twelve. Twelve! And Pickford starred in it."

Robbie dropped the sharpened pencil in the can that held a dozen others, a few pens, and even a chopstick or two—Dottie had introduced him to the wonders of Chinese food, and he'd be forever grateful. "So you're mad at this Anita too?"

"Of course not. But I'm twenty-two, Robbie. How can I ever match her?"

"Who says you have to?"

"That's what I want, though. I don't want to just *keep* the script. I want to write it. Maybe even direct."

"Do they… um… let women direct?"

Dottie kicked the leg of Robbie's chair. "They pretend they don't, but Pickford all but directs herself."

"Then why not get started? I see ads in the fan magazines all the time about writing schools. You could—"

Dottie scoffed and pushed herself upright, the better to glare at him. "Those? Nobody ever learned diddly from those phonies. I know more about how to put a scenario together than any ten of them."

"So do it."

"Do what?"

"Write a scenario. Do you have an idea for one?"

She scrubbed her hands through her frizzy bob. "Are you kidding? I've got *dozens* of ideas. *Hundreds.*"

"Then write one and give it to Mr. Ira. Couldn't hurt, right? All he can do is say no." Not like they'd put her in jail for doing what could make her happy. *Not like me. Not like Frank.* "So you wouldn't be the first or the youngest. So what? You don't have to be. You just have to be the best. Think you can do that?"

Her eyes kindled as she took the bait—as Robbie knew she would. Dottie was the most determined and competitive person he'd ever met.

"You think I can't?"

He shook his head. "Nope. I know you *can*. If it's good enough, maybe Mr. Ira'll assign somebody else to keep script on Aurelia's picture."

She jumped up and grabbed his arm to pull him to his feet. "I could kiss you, Rob, except neither one of us want that. Come to the commissary with me. I feel like celebrating."

He let her pull him out of the room. "Celebrating with what?"

"I don't know. Pancakes. A ham sandwich. *Something.* I want to mark this day as the beginning of my new career."

They weaved their way through the rabbit warren of sets where directors shouted instructions and assistants darted about. One of the assistants, a spindly fellow in tweeds, with a large Adam's apple and spectacles thicker than Dottie's, caught sight of them and beckoned them over.

He thrust a folded paper at Dottie. "Can you run this over to the costume department? Antoine is waiting for it."

Dottie took the note. "Sure. Do you need us to wait for an answer?"

"Nah." He glanced over his shoulder at the throne-room scene. The woman in the hoop skirt was giving the fellow in the wig a piece of her mind in a voice that didn't need a megaphone to be heard. "It's more in the nature of a warning, if you get my drift."

She grinned. "Gotcha. See you later, Alfie." She waited until he'd returned to his spot next to the cameraman and then turned to Robbie. "You know, Rob, you could do his job."

"What? Hand people notes, you mean?"

She gave him a look that clearly said *don't be a dope*. "No. Assistant director. Pops told me the other day that for some hick who'd never so much as visited a nickelodeon two months ago, you know more about making pictures than half the ADs on the lot." She blew on her fingernails and polished them on her shirt. "Of course, a lot of that's thanks to me."

Robbie laughed and held the door for her. "I can't deny that, at least the part about you teaching me the nuts and bolts of the place. But I don't think I know enough to actually help *make* a picture."

"You know plenty." She strolled across the pavement to the three-story brick building that housed the commissary as well as the costume department. "Between me and Pops, not to mention the time you spend watching them shoot Martin's pictures, you've got a better idea about how this place works than half the people at Citadel, *including* some of the directors."

A chill skated down Robbie's spine, even though his uniform was far too heavy for the warm weather. *She's seen me watching Martin. Does she suspect anything?* "I'm happy where I am."

"As a driver? You could be so much more, Rob." She didn't wait for him to open the door for her. Once inside, she turned around to face him and walked backward down the corridor. "Don't you have any ambition?"

"I have ambition." *Keep my head down. Don't tell anyone about that night. Stay as close to Martin as I'm allowed.* "I have a lot of ambition. It just doesn't have anything to do with pictures."

"Uh-huh." Dottie opened a door with *Costumes* lettered in gold on its frosted glass panel. She pointed to the end of the long room. "There's Antoine." She strode between two vast tables littered with peach satin fabric scraps and stopped next to a slight man in a pale gray suit and lavender tie.

Antoine's blond hair was slicked back, and his hands, pale and long-fingered, punctuated his words as he explained something to a harried-looking girl with a tape measure around her neck and a mouthful of pins. She was draping wide swaths of peach satin around a bored-looking actress, who was virtually naked from the waist up.

Robbie quickly turned sideways, heat rushing up his throat, but nobody else seemed to think the woman's lack of covering was remarkable at all.

"Hey, Antoine. I've got a note here for you from Alfie."

"Don't tell me," Antoine said. "That Wentworth harridan is complaining about her dress again. Perhaps somebody should tell her that she's acting—allegedly, I might add—in a period drama." His gaze caught Robbie's. "*Hel*-lo. Who have we here?"

"This is Robbie Goodman, Martin Brentwood's driver. Robbie, Antoine."

"Charmed." Antoine gave him a once-over and an appreciative smile that made Robbie want to duck out the door to catch his breath. *Could men* do *that here? Be so blatant? Didn't they know it wasn't* safe?

"I'm s-sorry. I didn't catch your other name."

"Antoine will do. Surnames are so bourgeois, don't you think?"

Robbie swallowed. "Um, sure."

Dottie poked Antoine's arm. "Behave."

"Never." Antoine flicked a glance at Robbie from under his lashes. "But do come back any time."

Dottie shook her head, grabbed Robbie by the elbow, and towed him, unresisting, out of the room. She didn't say anything to him until they were settled at a table in the corner of the commissary.

Dottie unwrapped her ham sandwich. "What did you get?"

Robbie looked down at the table in front of him. "I—I'm not sure." He lifted one corner of the wax paper. "I think it's a pickle." He peered into his cup. "And tomato soup?"

She set her sandwich down. "Rob, did Antoine knock you that far off your pins?"

"I just—What—How did he—" He gave up and took a bite of his pickle, and as the sourness hit the glands at the back of his tongue, he remembered that he hated pickles. He dropped it onto its wax paper.

She sighed. "I think we need to talk about a few things."

He nodded and then took a sip of his soup. *And I hate tomato soup too.* "I think that's probably a good idea."

Propping her elbows on the table, she leaned toward him. "The thing is, Rob, some men like men."

"Of course they do. Everyone has friends."

"I don't mean *that* kind of like. Not as in friendship. As in love. As in sex."

Robbie gaped at her for what might be forever. Dottie waited patiently until he'd gotten his head around the fact she was *speaking* about that. *Nobody* spoke about it. Even Frank had whispered things in bits and pieces, never giving Robbie the whole picture—never *naming* it—until they were hunkered down in that basement hallway, waiting for their turn *in there.*

But Dottie acted like she was talking about whether to order lemonade or iced tea with her sandwich.

"I—I know that."

"You do? Then that makes this easier. In Hollywood, there's regular work—" She held out one hand, palm up. "—and there's queer work." She held up the other hand.

"Queer. Is that what they call them? Men who… who like men? Do they make them all stay together? Where the queer work is?"

Dottie chuckled. "They don't *make* them, but there are definitely certain places where producers think it's okay for queers to work. The costume shop is one place. Set design and decoration is another."

"Not acting?"

Her expression darkened. "Not *openly*, but that doesn't mean there aren't queer actors. See, for all the power the studio heads have, they're working stiffs under the skin. The artistic types, the *sophisticates* they call 'em, have class. So the producers depend on fellows like Antoine or George Hopkins, over at Famous Players-Lasky."

Robbie nodded jerkily. "I've met George."

"Honey, *everyone's* met George. He's been here since he was seventeen and started designing for Theda Bara. But George and Antoine…. Well, the producers defer to them because they make the studio's pictures look good." She shrugged. "And if the pictures look good, audiences pay to see 'em. Which makes the producers happy."

"Okay. That makes sense, I guess."

"But the thing is, those same producers—and all the 'regular' folks—don't want queers to show up anywhere else. Directors? Stuntmen?" She pointed to a table nearby where the sausage-slinging actors were eating hot dogs. "Actors? Nope. They've got to be he-men. Because what they do isn't 'queer work.'" She jerked her thumb over her shoulder toward the corridor leading to the costume shop. "In there, it's safe for Antoine to be who he is, because he's where he belongs. But to be queer on the set? Behind the camera?" She shrugged. "You've got to have thick skin, a convincing cover story, and the courage of a whole pride of lions. You also need someone to stand by you, or you'll get kidded by every bull-necked yahoo on the lot." She took a huge bite of her sandwich.

"Does that happen? The… the kidding?"

She swallowed, then took a swig of her lemonade. "It can. If a director thinks an actor isn't he-man enough for him, he'll let a scene go on a little too long before calling 'cut'—not long enough for any real injury, but long enough for discomfort and fear. That happened to Jack Kerrigan all the time."

"Somebody should have stood up for him." Robbie's throat was tight. *I didn't stand up for Frank.*

"Rob. God, your face." She reached across the table and grabbed his hands. "It doesn't happen all the time. Look at George. He and Bill Taylor are pretty much untouchable because they work together, so they've always got each other as backup. Although when Bill was in London last year, George could have had a little trouble if it weren't for the fact that his mother has almost as such influence as he does."

Robbie's stomach dropped. "Bill Taylor? As in Mr. Taylor, the director?"

"Yep. William Desmond Taylor."

Robbie tried to speak but could only manage a croak. He took a gulp of his cold soup. "You mean they're… they're…."

"Together. Yes. *Like that.*" She let go of him, although she still watched him as if she were afraid he was about to burst into flames. *She's not wrong.* "Not that they make a production out of it in public. What Hollywood tolerates here in town, in our own circles, is different from what the ladies in the temperance unions or the preachers in the revival tents can handle."

Robbie clutched his knees, his head whirling. If someone like Mr. Taylor could do that, *be* that, and have his… his lover by his side….

"But Mr. Taylor is such a gentleman. He makes all those speeches to the ladies' temperance clubs and all. Even the censorship groups listen to him."

Dottie gave him a pitying look. "Rob, just because a man likes men more than girls, it doesn't make him a monster."

Did that mean...? Robbie took a breath that filled his lungs for what felt like the first time since he'd left Boise. But then he remembered Pa's fury and disgust, the preacher thundering about the wages of sin, the police that night, beating a man as he whimpered, *"I'm sorry, I'm sorry,"* until Frank grabbed their arms and they turned on him instead.

"But the law... the raids.... There was one a week or so ago." He'd seen the headlines in the paper, and he'd huddled under his blankets, trembling all night long. He'd been a wreck the next morning, haggard enough that Martin noticed and asked if he thought he was coming down with a cold.

"Don't worry," Dottie said around another bite of sandwich. "Even if anyone in the business gets picked up, the studios take care of it."

Robbie licked his dry lips. "What do you mean? If someone breaks the law, they'll go to jail."

Dottie snorted. "You really are naive, Robinson, my boy. Not everyone who's guilty gets punished, and not everyone who's innocent goes free. And in Hollywood, the studio has connections to make sure their assets are protected."

Another one of Robbie's beliefs crumbled into dust. "But if the laws don't hold for everyone equally, then—"

"Then you're living in America. Really, Rob, things've never been fair. Why would Hollywood be any different?"

"Darling, if we weren't such very great friends and if we weren't so well acquainted, I might be tempted to be insulted."

Martin tore his gaze from the window and looked at Evelyn across the expanse of white linen, china, and crystal. With shooting on *The Imaginary Husband* complete, she'd suggested a celebratory dinner, and of course Martin had agreed. And then proceeded to ignore her, apparently.

The restaurant's low lighting and candlelight made her appear even more beautiful than usual as it cast a glow on the lovely skin that was too often hidden under thick film makeup.

"I beg your pardon, Evie. I didn't catch what you said."

"No, you didn't. You haven't all evening. I ordered for you, by the way."

He blinked at her. "You did?"

"I had to, darling. The poor waiter was growing roots waiting for you to choose. You're having the sirloin."

"Thank you." He took a gulp of water, and his gaze drifted away from her again.

"Ever since we sat down, you've spent more time staring out the window than you have looking at me. Is it just absence of mind, or—" She glanced out the window and chuckled. "Ah. I understand now."

Martin's hand clenched around his water glass. "Understand?"

"It isn't that you find *me* tedious, it's that you find *someone else* mesmerizing."

Martin stared at his lap. "I'm not *mesmerized*, for the love of God."

"Of course not, darling." The ice tinkled as she took a delicate sip of her mineral water. "That's why your attention has been riveted on your chauffeur for the last half hour, even though he's doing nothing but sitting behind the wheel, reading a newspaper." She leaned back and tilted her head as she gazed out the window with the heavy-lidded, midnight-dark eyes that had made her a star. "Although whatever article he's reading can't be very interesting. He spends more time staring at this window than he does at the page."

"He does?" Martin winced at the eagerness in his tone. "I mean, he didn't need to stay while we dine. I told him to pick us up in two hours' time. He could have—"

"Could have what? Returned to the studio only to turn around and drive back? Most of the stores have closed for the evening, so it's not as though he could do a spot of shopping while he waits. What did you expect?"

Damn the Volstead Act. Martin could really use a whiskey—a double. "I should have taken a taxi."

"Nonsense. He'd have probably been crushed. That lovely young man is paid for driving you about and being at your disposal—" She smiled up at the waiter as he delivered their meals. "Thank you." Once he'd left, she leaned forward, smiled slyly, and lowered her voice to a murmur. "Is that the problem? You want him to be at your disposal for more than an automobile ride or two?"

Martin grabbed his knife and cut viciously into his steak, even though its aroma—perfectly cooked, or he missed his guess—didn't tempt him in the least. *Why the hell did I think going out for dinner would be a good idea? I'm not remotely hungry.* "Robbie is not *disposable*."

She reached across the table and laid her hand on his. "Of course not. But darling, if you're that fond of him, why not do something about it?"

Martin stared down at her hand—long-fingered, perfectly manicured, soft—and felt not the least hint of attraction or arousal, although several men at nearby tables cast him envious looks. What man wouldn't be flattered by Evelyn Trent's attention and obvious affection?

The fool who's more moved by the brush of his driver's sleeve, that's who.

"He's an innocent, Evie. He doesn't know anything about the life or what it means. He's undoubtedly a virgin. He may never even have kissed a girl in his life."

"Ah." She tapped his hand with one finger and sat back. "But has he kissed a boy?"

Martin glanced around wildly. "Evelyn. Don't."

"Darling, this is Hollywood. Nobody cares." She winked at him. "Have you seen the way most of the men here have been eyeing our waiter's ass?"

Martin glanced at the waiter. The arse in question was worth eyeing, but it didn't hold a candle to Robbie's. Martin swallowed, his mouth dry when he remembered yesterday. He'd walked out of the shooting stage to find Robbie, his jacket discarded, bending over the Flyer's open hood. He'd had to make a brisk turnaround and hurry to the men's room to splash cold water on his face. Although splashing cold water on his cock would have been more effective.

"Before he came to Hollywood, he'd never been to a city bigger than Boise."

"He seems to have found his feet rather quickly. Whenever you've escorted me, he's never made a wrong turn or showed the least hesitation."

"Learning the streets is one thing. Learning a culture we never talk about is another. Most of America doesn't even have a word for being in the life."

"Neither do we, apparently, since we're still calling it 'in the life.'" She cut a tiny sliver from her filet. "You should put it to the test, Martin, if only so you'll stop mooning about. This inattention is so bad for my reputation." Her smile took the sting out of the words, but Martin squirmed with guilt, nonetheless.

"You're right. I've been a complete boor lately. I apologize." He took her hand gently and brushed his lips against her fingers. "I'll do better."

"What would be better is if you made a move."

Martin released Evelyn's hand and gazed out the window again. Robbie wasn't looking their way, despite Evelyn's claims.

Instead, he was peering out the windshield at a newsboy hawking papers on the corner.

"I'm too much of a coward, Evie. What if he says no? Or worse, what if he denounces me like Vernon threatened to do?"

"Vernon? Oh, your previous chauffeur. How could I forget?"

"I wish I could. You know, Bill Taylor's driver threatened him as well." He tried to smile, but it felt more like a grimace. "What is it about chauffeurs that makes them prone to blackmail?"

"Well, they do have information about your comings and goings, who you spend time with, your state when you leave any clandestine drinking establishment. I suppose for some, the temptation is too great to resist." She ate another morsel of filet. "From what I've heard, though, Robbie isn't the type to succumb to that sort of temptation. He seems devoted to you."

"But is it the devotion of an employee, or is it something more?"

"As I said, darling, you'll never know until you ask. Think of Nazimova. The word is she groped Erich von Stroheim's daughter in the Ambassador Hotel ladies' room, but it didn't affect her popularity, nor her brash self-confidence, in the least."

Martin lifted an eyebrow. "Perhaps not, but it might have affected the daughter." He paused while cutting another bite of steak. "Does von Stroheim even *have* a daughter?"

"Well, whoever it was knocked La Nazimova on her well-known behind for her pains." Evelyn's expression softened. "Darling, you really do like him if you're so worried about hurting him that you'll never give him the chance to tell you no." She laid her knife across her plate and dabbed her lips with her napkin. "You know how to be discreet. You know how to be subtle. You needn't throw him up against the wall and grab his crotch like that beast Gilbert Flint would do."

Martin clutched his silverware. *I'll kill him.* "Gilbert's sniffing around Robbie?"

"I'm speaking in the general sense, not the specific. As far as I know, Gilbert has no more idea of who Robbie is than the Emperor of China."

"I don't think China has an emperor anymore," Martin murmured as he toyed with his green beans.

"The emperor of Japan, then. I have it on good authority from both sexes that Gilbert is a grab-and-throw man." She sniffed delicately. "Not that I care if someone's tastes are eclectic, but one needn't be so ham-handed and vulgar about it."

Martin gave up even pretending to eat. "I don't know, Evie. What if he's disgusted?"

"Then at least you'll know. You can ask for another driver if it makes you uncomfortable."

"Wonderful. Then he'll think I had him fired."

She shrugged one shoulder in a ripple of satin. "Simply make it clear to him that his livelihood doesn't depend on saying yes. That shouldn't be hard."

"Oh really? I suppose you have personal experience?"

Her expression turned cagey, and her glance slid off Martin's face. "I might. Or perhaps I'm simply working out my own scenario. For heaven's sake, Martin, it's our *business* to tell stories."

"Yes, but we do it without words."

"Then don't use words. Or at least only use the ones that matter." She chuckled. "Perhaps you should ask someone to prepare a few pertinent title cards for you. You can hold them up whenever you can't think of the right thing to say. Or hire a violinist to play 'Hearts and Flowers' outside the window as you declare yourself."

Martin couldn't help but laugh at the notion. "Even if I wanted musical accompaniment, I wouldn't choose 'Hearts and Flowers.' That's traditional only for death and despair. I'd hope for a more cheerful outcome."

"Hmmm. You may have a point. Don't go *completely* in the other direction, though. Stay away from seltzer bottles and cream pies. Only Roscoe Arbuckle can get away with that."

Martin's gaze strayed to the window again in time to catch Robbie getting out of the car to approach the newsboy. "Robbie must have finished his paper if he needs to get another one. Have we lingered too long?"

"One can never linger too long over a fine meal with a good friend. However, if I haven't convinced you to declare yourself to your chauffeur, I may have to order dessert."

"I'll… consider it."

"Martin." Evelyn's voice was laced with steel. "You need to do more than consider it. All joking aside, I hate to see you so unhappy. Please, if not for yourself, consider him. If he really is as fond of you as he seems, you might be hurting him more by not declaring yourself than by waiting for some sign from God that the time is right."

Was she right? Do I owe it to both of us to say something? To put it to the test?

He watched Robbie wander back to the car, the paper held close to his face in the yellow light from the street lamps. His brows were drawn together, possibly because it was difficult to read in the wan light. But then he glanced at the window, and the expression on his face made Martin's belly plummet.

He gestured to the waiter and threw his napkin on the table. "Something's wrong. We've got to go."

Evelyn, to her credit, didn't balk, although she did glance outside, where a group of excited people were clustered around the newsboy. When the waiter brought their bill, she smiled up at him. "Pardon me, but do you know what all the fuss is about?" She indicated the gathering crowd with a wave of her hand. "Has something happened?"

The waiter glanced toward the maître d' and then leaned closer. "It just came in over the wireless. That film star? Fatty Arbuckle? He's been arrested for murder."

CHAPTER NINE

Every day for almost two weeks, Robbie had reported to the studio faithfully, ready to sign out the Dixie Flyer and head to Martin's house. But every day the story was the same—Martin wasn't scheduled on set, and he hadn't arranged to go anywhere else. Or at least he hadn't arranged to have Robbie take him anywhere else.

Since Mr. Arbuckle's arrest, the studio seemed subdued. It still buzzed but more like a beehive at night, with all the workers inside for safety. Some pictures were still shooting, but some had been put on hold. As usual when he didn't understand something, Robbie talked to Pops about it.

"Citadel doesn't have anything to do with Mr. Arbuckle's pictures. Are the Mr. Schlossbergs cutting back out of respect? Like a funeral?"

Pops snorted. "It's got nothin' to do with respect. For one thing, Jacob's always resented Fatty, same as he resents Buster and Charlie and Harold Lloyd. Citadel hasn't ever found a comedian who could match 'em."

"So why's he doing it?" *Why isn't Martin here, where he ought to be?* But Robbie couldn't ask that question. It would give too much away. Because the question he really wanted the answer to was *Why isn't Martin with me?* Robbie missed Martin with an ache he hadn't felt since he realized Frank didn't want *him*—he'd just somehow recognized Robbie was a kindred spirit. *Wish I knew for sure if Martin was the same.*

"Why? Money, a' course. For Jacob, no matter what the question, the answer's always money. The temperance groups, the morality watchdogs—they're out for blood. The blood of the film industry. They're using Fatty's arrest as proof that pictures are as degenerate as they've always claimed." Pops's jaw worked like one of Pa's cows chewing a cud. "Feh. Bunch of hypocrites. If they can tell sin the first time they see it, why'd most of 'em sit through six showings of *The Four Horsemen of the Apocalypse* and *The Soul of Youth* before they got around to denouncing 'em?"

"So people aren't going to see pictures anymore?"

"They're not going to *Fatty's* pictures. And where one sheep goes—or doesn't go—the others'll follow. The Schlossbergs, Zukor, Schenck, Mayer, Laemmle—they're afraid this'll kill pictures. Put 'em all out of business." He stared at the empty gates, his face bleak. "They need somebody to take the blame." He turned back to Robbie, jabbing a finger in the air. "You mark my words, young feller. No matter what the jury says when Fatty goes to trial, the public has already found him guilty, and the producers'll sacrifice him if it means they save themselves."

Pops subsided into silence, and after a while, Robbie wandered over to the shooting stage. The big barracks of a building seemed to echo with emptiness today. Sure, Robbie could hear one or two competing violins or pianos, but without the lights and bustle and noise of a normal day, the flimsy sets and tawdry finery seemed somehow woebegone, like a doll whose little-girl owner had graduated to lipstick and rouge.

Robbie hoped that the destiny of this building, these sets, the people who worked to bring make-believe to life, would be better than the fate of that discarded doll.

When he got to the cutting room, he found Dottie hunched over a newspaper, much as she'd been every day since the news broke about Mr. Arbuckle's arrest.

"Dottie? What's the matter?"

She thrust the paper at him. "Read this."

Robbie scanned the front page, with its usual screaming headlines about Mr. Arbuckle's upcoming trial. "The whole thing?"

She scowled at him and jabbed her finger at a column near the bottom of the page. "Right here."

In the dim light of the cutting room, Robbie peered at the article and his stomach dropped. "Universal's putting a morality clause in all their contracts?"

"Only for the actors so far, but who knows when that will change? Read that last paragraph out loud." She slumped in her chair, arms crossed over her chest. "For maximum effect."

Robbie cleared his throat. "The actor agrees to conduct himself with due regard to public conventions—"

"Public conventions. Which public? Which conventions?"

Robbie didn't think Dottie wanted an answer—which he couldn't give in any case, so he continued. "—public conventions and morals and agrees that he will not do or commit anything tending to degrade him in society or bring him into public hatred—"

"Hatred and degradation. Jesus H. Christ, how can we help that when Hearst and his reporters are practically dancing on Roscoe's grave before he's even gone to trial? And Universal isn't even Roscoe's studio!"

Robbie didn't know the answer to that either, but with every word, the pit in his belly grew. "—public hatred, contempt, scorn, or ridicule, or tending to shock, insult, or offend the community or outrage public morals or decency, or tending to the prejudice of the Universal Film Manufacturing Company or the motion picture industry."

"Covering all their bases, aren't they? Not just Universal, but anything anywhere in the whole film industry. But you haven't gotten to the best part." She made a get-on-with-it gesture.

"In the event that the actor violates any term or provision of this paragraph, then the Universal Film Manufacturing Company has the right to cancel and annul this contract by giving five days' notice to the actor of its intention to do so." Robbie let the newspaper drop from nerveless fingers. "They can fire anyone who violates the clause within five days?"

"Think about it, Rob. This means they can fire anybody, anytime. Because who decides what it means to lose respect? Who decides what's decent? Who decides whether *outrage* is justified? Pictures are subjective, like poetry or painting. *Everybody* is offended by something. Who gets the last say?"

"I'm guessing," Robbie said slowly as he retrieved the paper and handed it back to Dottie, "that whoever's got the power."

"But that's the thing. Does the power rest with the distributors who refuse to show the pictures, like Sid Grauman, yanking *Gasoline Gus* after Roscoe was arrested? Or with those picture-hatted harridans in the temperance unions who won't set their dainty toes inside a theater unless the film has been gutted of everything that might force them to *think*?" She ripped the page out of the paper, balled it up, and flung it across the room. "Rob, this could destroy pictures. It could destroy Hollywood."

"Know what I think?" Robbie said slowly as he stared at the crumpled paper. "I think your picture-hatted harridans are just an excuse. What this clause does is give the men who do the hiring and firing even more power than they've already got. I mean, they've always had it, but now they'll have more."

Almost complete power, in fact, since the studios owned the police and the press. All they had to do was feed the papers a story that would cause public hatred, contempt, scorn, or ridicule for an actor they wanted to get rid of.

Or not stop a story for one they'd decided not to protect.

"I need to talk to Martin."

"Good luck with that. He's not on the lot."

"I know. I'm going over to his house."

Dottie shot him a sharp glance. "Without him asking for you? Don't let Pops know about that."

"This doesn't have anything to do with the studio. I'm checking in on a… a friend."

"A friend." Dottie's tone was neutral. "Sure."

"I mean it, Dottie." Robbie pointed at the newspaper crumpled on the floor. "Martin is going to take that badly."

"I can't argue with that. *I'm* taking it badly." She smiled crookedly. "Do what you can, Rob."

"I will."

Since he wasn't on official studio business, he didn't feel right taking the car. So he changed out of his chauffeur's uniform and into the spare clothes he kept in a locker in the studio garage and then hopped the streetcar.

By the time he got off on Alvarado in front of the bungalow court, he was having second thoughts. Sure, Martin had invited him in that one time, but there had been extenuating circumstances. Robbie didn't expect to be asked inside, but would Martin be offended that Robbie had the presumption to knock on his door? He'd told Dottie he was checking on a friend, but he wasn't entirely sure Martin saw him that way.

He squared his shoulders and marched up the sidewalk, the September sun nearly as hot on his shoulders as it had been in July.

When he got to the door, he could hear music from inside— probably a Victrola or maybe the wireless. *At least he's home.* He raised his fist but hesitated for an instant until he worked up the gumption to knock on the door. Then he had a moment of panic. *What if he's not alone? What if he's with someone? What if—*

The door opened, and there stood Martin. His usually smooth dark hair was rumpled, a shock falling forward over his forehead. Instead of his usual suit, he wore a red silk dressing gown open over trousers and an undershirt. He peered at Robbie out of bloodshot eyes.

"Oh. It's you."

Okay, that's not very promising. "Are you all right?"

"What do you think?" The scent of gin was evident on Martin's breath. "One of my friends has been accused of rape and murder. The press is having a field day excoriating him along with the entire motion picture industry. And now Universal has decided to judge its actors by the threadbare moral yardstick of middle America."

"I don't think yardsticks have threads, Martin."

"You know what I mean." He held the door wider. "You might as well come in."

As an invitation, it wasn't the most elegant or welcoming, but Robbie didn't care. He'd take it because right then, all he wanted was to comfort Martin—and maybe comfort himself in the bargain.

God, Robbie was the last person Martin wanted to see in the state he was in. *There won't be much admiration in his eyes today, will there?* So Martin didn't look at his face. He just walked back to the sideboard and picked up the gin bottle.

"You want some?" Martin held up the bottle, but Robbie shook his head. "You sure? Bound to be outstanding. Barstow's claw-foot porcelain products are far superior to that swill from Pasadena."

"Won't that—I mean, I've heard alcohol can blind you."

"That's the idea." Not for the first time since Sid had given him the news about Universal's diabolical maneuver, Martin poured a good three inches of the stuff into his tumbler.

But before he could raise it to his lips, Robbie gently grasped Martin's wrist and eased the glass from his fingers. "Martin, it's only ten o'clock in the morning."

"Is it?" He peered at the light trying its best to sneak in through his blinds. "I suppose. However, I'm positive that when you haven't yet been to bed, the morning after counts absolutely as part of the night before."

"Let me make you some coffee."

The note in Robbie's voice—was that actually pity? It had been so long since someone had pitied Martin that he wasn't sure. Perhaps it was simple kindness. Or charity. *God, I'm a charity case.* "That's not in your job description." The shame curdling his belly—or maybe it was the gin—made his voice come out rougher than perhaps was called for. He winced and turned away but didn't protest when Robbie collected the gin bottle too.

"I'm not here as your chauffeur, Martin." Ah, he recognized *that* tone. Hurt. Betrayal. *That's what Hollywood has become. One giant pit of remorse and betrayal.* "I'm here as your friend."

"My friend," Martin murmured. "I suppose I could use one of those."

"You have lots of those."

"Roscoe thought he had friends too, and look where that got him."

The clink of glassware on wood was followed by Robbie's hand, warm on Martin's elbow. "Come on, Martin. Sit down. I'll be back in a minute with the coffee."

"How? You don't know where anything is."

"I was here the other night, remember? I made coffee for Wesley before I drove him home."

"Of course." The other night. *The Three Musketeers.* Proof that Martin meant rather less to Citadel than Roscoe meant to Paramount. Of course, Martin wasn't worth a million dollars a year. *And now Roscoe isn't worth that either.* And Universal was leading the way for the studios to escape expensive deals if they —or the public—should change their minds. *For any reason whatsoever.*

Because that's what the morality clause meant. It meant the studios could dictate the lives of their performers. Cage them. Trot them out on demand, dressed in their tawdry finery. "Just as if we're bloody trained monkeys," he muttered.

"Here. Take this."

Martin gazed blearily at the glass in Robbie's hand. "That's not coffee."

"No. It's water. You should try it sometime."

Martin faked a shudder. "Too dangerous. That's a good way to catch some dreadful disease."

The glass wobbled a bit and water sloshed onto Martin's trousers. "Shoot. I'm sorry. I'll get a towel—"

"No." Martin wrapped both of his hands around the glass—and by extension, Robbie's hand. "I'm the one who's sorry. Did I do something to hurt you?" He glanced at the gin bottle. "Something else to hurt you."

"You didn't."

"I did." God, Martin wished he didn't stink like a bootlegger's truck bed. "What is it, Robbie? What is it about water that's made you sad?"

Robbie smiled crookedly down at him. "Not water. Disease. My brother... my older brother died of Spanish Influenza."

Martin's stomach rolled. "Oh, God, Robbie. I'm so sorry."

Robbie didn't answer. He just eased his hand out from under Martin's and returned to the kitchen. Martin got up and followed. He stood in the doorway so his stench wouldn't overpower poor Robbie, who was fussing with the percolator and unerringly opening the cabinet with the heavy ceramic mugs Martin preferred for coffee. For the first time, Martin realized Robbie wasn't wearing his chauffeur's uniform. *It's the first time I've seen him in other clothes.* Instead, he was in workman's dungarees and a shirt with no collar, and his shoulders looked somehow broader under the lightweight cotton.

Robbie's spine was ramrod straight as he fumbled with the cutlery drawer. "You like cream and one sugar, right?"

"Rob." Martin kept his voice gentle. "What happened to your brother?"

"He died."

"I understand. Was the epidemic very bad in Idaho?"

"He didn't die in Idaho. He died in New York." Robbie dropped a spoon on the floor with a clatter and a soft curse.

"So far away from you."

"He'd been farther." Robbie stopped pretending to be busy and gripped the counter with both hands. "He was coming back from the war. He'd been in France. Survived all that... that *awfulness*." He choked on something that could have been a laugh or a sob or maybe something in between. "He wrote to Ma about it, you know? Making a joke out of the conditions—the food, the rats in the trenches. He didn't want her to worry."

Martin took a few steps closer. "But she did."

He nodded. "She knew. We both did. We could read between the lines. Not Pa. The letters made him mad. He thought Eddie should... I don't know. Brag more? Be more stoic? Be a *man* about it. After all, he was a soldier."

"I'd think that soldiers, of all people, would need something to lighten their load. I know I did."

Robbie looked up at that. "You served in the war?"

Martin shrugged. "I'm not sure my service was that useful. I never got out of Camp Wadsworth in South Carolina."

"I wish Eddie had never enlisted," Robbie said fiercely. "I don't care what people would've said about cowardice or duty. It would have been better for him to be alive. Better for him not to have died that stupid, senseless death when bullets and gas couldn't kill him. All it took was a tiny bug that nobody can even see."

More than anything, Martin wanted to put his arm around Robbie. Hug him. Offer him some kind of comfort for an unimaginable loss. *Irony. God, I hate that shite.* But he stank of gin and sweat and despair. So instead, he squeezed Robbie's shoulder.

"I'm so very sorry, Robbie."

Robbie hitched one shoulder. "It's all right."

"No. It's not all right. I'm being incredibly self-indulgent, and I have no reason for it. I really have very little to complain about." *For now. The future may be another question.* "If you'll excuse me for a moment, I'll go and make myself a bit more presentable. And less odiferous."

Robbie chuckled. "You're not so bad. Remember, I've lived on a farm. We raised pigs."

Martin lifted his wrist to his forehead in a pretended swoon. "I smell better than pigs. You have no idea how that lifts my spirits." He tugged on the satin lapels of his dressing gown. "Nevertheless, I would prefer to remind you more of the flowerbed than the pigsty."

In a flare of red silk, Martin executed a dramatic pivot and stalked out of the kitchen. But once outside of Robbie's sight, he dropped the sham display and hurried upstairs.

A bath, a shave, and clean underdrawers made a world of difference in both his smell and his mood. *Perhaps that was my problem. I smelled too much of the tenement, the sweatshop, and those lonely days without hope.*

He wasn't ready to brave leaving his house yet, so he didn't bother to don a suit. Trousers, a clean shirt—he hesitated, but decided to forgo the collar. He stared down at his bare feet. *Perhaps a bit* too *casual for our current relationship.* Although Robbie had come to him today as a friend, not an employee. Perhaps there was hope for Martin after all.

After he put on shoes and socks, he descended the stairs in a more or less dignified manner, even though his instinct was to gallop down and steal every possible moment in Robbie's company.

Robbie was sitting in the wingback chair next to the window, holding a white ceramic mug in both hands. Another cup sat on the table next to the davenport. Martin caught it up and took a sip. *Ah.* He sank onto the sofa. "That's perfect. Exactly as it should be." Robbie smiled, and Martin noticed that his own coffee was black. "I take it you don't agree."

Robbie shrugged. "I got used to it. Not a lot of options when you're on the road."

"No. I suppose not." Martin studied Robbie's face. Even though his cheekbones were still sharp, the hollows underneath them that Martin had noticed at their first meeting were gone. *He's eating regularly now. Before, he was starving.*

The cup trembled in Martin's hand. *Robbie starving.* If Martin hadn't already been sitting down, he'd have fallen on the floor, a howl of outrage and despair ripped from his throat. *But it didn't happen. He's here now. He's well.* And if Martin had anything to say about it, he would *stay* well.

Since Robbie had opened up about his brother, Martin was tempted to see if the confidences would continue, and if he could encourage Robbie to reveal why he'd left Idaho with such obviously slim resources. But that would be selfish. *He's offered me something, but I haven't given him anything in return. I have nothing to give.* So much of Martin's *self* was locked up in lies. Besides, how did you open the conversation that would lead to *by the way, I sleep with men—do you*?

Robbie took the decision away from him, thank God. "I guess you saw the notice about the morality clause."

Martin cocked an eyebrow. Now that he was clean and safely behind the armor of his clothing, his persona settled around him again. "I suspect every actor in Hollywood has seen it by now. And possibly reacted to it in the same way that I did." He nodded at the gin bottle. "Poorly."

"Is anything else the matter? I mean, I know you and Mr. Arbuckle are friends."

"Yes." Martin sighed, the guilt that had dogged him since news of the arrest souring his stomach. He set the coffee down. "He asked me to go with him, you know."

Robbie blinked. "No. I didn't."

"I made an excuse about still shooting *The Imaginary Husband*. But I could have gone. I could have been there over the weekend and returned on the train on Monday." *But I didn't want to leave you, and you probably don't even see me the way I see you.* "If I had been there—"

"Don't." Robbie scooted forward and set his own cup down with a clatter. "You mustn't blame yourself."

"Mustn't I? What are friends for if not to help each other, keep each other out of trouble, be a trusted presence in a room where others may not have your best interests at heart?"

"But you can't know you'd have made a difference." Robbie's voice was strained, as though he were forcing the words out of a throat screamed raw. "Maybe you'd have been caught too—accused, imprisoned, *worse*. All those newspaper articles, saying all those awful things about Mr. Arbuckle. They could be saying them about you too."

"Suppose I deserved them?"

Robbie shook his head, his expression earnest. "You don't. You're a gentleman. As fine a gentleman as... as Mr. Taylor." Robbie swallowed. "Th-the temperance clubs and morality groups love him."

Martin laughed mirthlessly. "Bill Taylor. You realize that's not his name, don't you?"

"It's not? But—"

"He's one of those fathers I told you about. The ones who disappear. He abandoned his wife and daughter in New York to head west. They only found him again when they spotted him on-screen in a picture."

"But... but *you* wouldn't do something like that, would you?" Was the tone of Robbie's voice a little desperate? "You're not married."

"No, my dear." Martin heaved another sigh. *But neither am I the son of an impoverished British baronet.* "It was inevitable, you know."

"What was? That Mr. Taylor's family would find him?"

"No." He laughed mirthlessly. "Although how foolish would you have to be to appear in a picture seen by thousands, perhaps millions, when you were trying to hide from your past? No, it was Roscoe's fall that was inevitable. The fall of a man people used to worship in the dark of the theater, with their dimes and their attention and their laughter." Martin toasted Robbie with his coffee cup. "No matter how much people love their heroes, Robbie, they love it even more when the heroes fall."

CHAPTER TEN

"Was it Mr. Brentwood who called?" Robbie heaved the heavy, wet sheets out of the washer and started to feed them through the wringer for his landlady. He hadn't heard from Martin for five days, not since the morality clause announcement, and he was getting desperate for something, *anything*.

Mrs. McGuire pushed a limp lock of hair off her forehead. "I'm sure I don't know. That new girl don't know how to take a message."

Mrs. McGuire was never in the best mood on laundry day, but today she was especially irritable. Her last maid had left with no notice when she got picked to be an extra in Mr. Von Stroheim's picture, and the new one wasn't working out. Robbie had been pitching in with the heavy work, since he wasn't doing any driving lately and Pops usually sent him home by noon—once he made sure Robbie had gotten his lunch.

Today someone finally telephoned for Robbie from the studio, but the new maid hadn't asked the identity of the caller or gotten many details. All Robbie had was a time—six thirty— and a place—shooting stage two on the Citadel lot. Did that mean Martin was filming another picture? If so, why wouldn't he ask Robbie to pick him up at the Alvarado bungalow? It wasn't unusual for actors to be called in to film at odd hours. Sometimes they started at six and worked until two or three in the morning. They'd done that once or twice on *The Imaginary Husband*. But nobody had mentioned anything to Robbie about a new picture or a late schedule.

Maybe the call had nothing to do with Martin. Maybe the Mr. Schlossbergs had gotten tired of paying Robbie for sitting around on his backside and decided to assign him to somebody else.

Despite the damp heat in the laundry room, a chill chased across Robbie's skin. Not to see Martin every day. Not to have those precious minutes when the two of them were alone in the automobile together. Not to catch the smile that dawned on Martin's handsome face the moment he caught sight of Robbie waiting for him, the door of the Flyer open and ready.

And those other times—the *best* times—when Martin's fingers would brush Robbie's as he got in the automobile.

Maybe I should have said something the other night, put it to the test like Dottie said I ought to. But what if Martin didn't want that? Not seeing him at all would be worse than seeing but not touching.

Wouldn't it?

Robbie hauled the sheets out to the clothesline. Mrs. McGuire trailed after him to hand him clothespins while she continued to complain about the new maid. Then he excused himself from her offer of tea and ran upstairs. Most of the other residents bathed in the morning or late evening, so not only was the bathroom free, but there was a little hot water left. After his bath and shave—he really needed a haircut again—Robbie dressed in his uniform and took the streetcar to the studio.

Pops wasn't at the gate, and the guard who let him in just shrugged when Robbie asked if Martin was on the lot. He trotted to the stage door and slipped inside.

Production still hadn't picked up again after Mr. Arbuckle's arrest, and Robbie had never seen the place so echoingly empty before. There had always been something going on—a picture with a late filming schedule, fellows from the set department knocking together the scenery for a new picture, janitors cleaning up for the next round of shooting.

But tonight? Nothing. Not even the squeak of wheels from one of those rolling mop buckets. Robbie made his way through the dim, silent building—a graveyard of stories in the midst of being told. The cutting room was dark—no Dottie inside, peering at the tiny negatives.

Had the maid gotten the message completely wrong? Was he supposed to report at six thirty tomorrow morning? *Shoot, I'll bet that's it.*

A little nugget of excitement mixed with dread had burned in his chest since the call. But it shriveled and died, leaving him cold and empty. He sighed and trudged back across the floor, past a jungle where fake banana leaves and palm fronds rustled in his wake, past a drawing room where the ghost of cigarette smoke hung in the air, and past a schoolroom with the same old-fashioned double desks that had stood in Robbie's long-ago schoolhouse. But Robbie doubted if the curse word scrawled across the chalkboard in foot-high letters was an official part of the production.

"Goodman! What are you doing here?"

Robbie startled at the voice with its New Jersey accent, one he'd learned to recognize since his first day at the studio. Sure enough, Gilbert Flint was striding toward him, dressed in full evening gear. *He doesn't look nearly as good in a tuxedo as Martin does.* "Good evening, Mr. Flint. I'm sorry to disturb you. I got a message I was to report here, but I think the girl who took the call got the time wrong." He touched the brim of his cap. "You have a good evening."

Mr. Flint chuckled, for once not sounding like he was laughing at Robbie's expense. "She got more than one thing wrong. Brentwood's expecting you to pick him up at Pershing Square to take him to the *Camille* screening."

Robbie's heart stuttered, then leaped. "He is? Why there?"

Mr. Flint shrugged. "A meeting with a reporter. A producer. Somebody. I'm not his social secretary. But I heard him say he'd arranged for you to watch the picture from the balcony."

A glow spread through Robbie's chest. After the disastrous attempt to get into *The Three Musketeers* showing, he'd been afraid Martin either regretted his offer to get Robbie a ticket or had forgotten. *He didn't. He remembered.* "I'll head right over."

"Hold on." Mr. Flint gestured to Robbie's uniform. "They'll never let you in wearing chauffeur's duds."

Robbie glanced down at his ridiculous jodhpurs, shiny boots, and double row of black buttons, and his heart sank. "I don't have anything else to wear. All my other clothes are at home, and they're not fancy enough for a premiere."

Mr. Flint waved one hand in dismissal. "Nobody'll expect you to look swank up in the balcony. Come on." He tilted his head and looked Robbie up and down. "There's a suit over in wardrobe that ought to fit you well enough."

Robbie trotted along at Mr. Flint's side as he strode toward the door. "But I thought the studio only made the actresses' clothes. Aren't the men supposed to supply their own?"

"I didn't say there were a lot of suits. But there's one that ought to fit you close enough. Come on."

Martin loitered in the lobby of the Million Dollar Theater, mostly ignored by the press who were all outside awaiting the arrival of Nazimova and Valentino. If Martin knew anything about Nazimova's ego—and he did—the two would not be arriving together.

At least this time the studio hadn't neglected to get him a seat, although Martin suspected Sid had more to do with it than either of the Schlossbergs. Valentino was Martin's chief rival these days in the smoldering-leading-man department. Sid wanted him to pay attention—and find a way to make himself distinctive. *Valentino plus athleticism. Fairbanks plus sex.*

He sighed and pasted a smile on his face to greet Joe Schenck and Norma Talmadge. Although, like most actors, he distrusted the studio owners' motives, Schenck at least had stood behind Roscoe, unlike Paramount. Maybe that was Norma's influence —she was an actress, after all, and her sister was married to Buster Keaton, Roscoe's closest friend.

He stopped to kiss Marion Davies on the cheek and chat for a few moments. If only Marion could exert a little influence on Hearst, who continued to drown Roscoe in a vast sea of yellow journalism. But as lovely and kind as Marion was, she always deferred to W.R., more's the pity. She was such a brilliant light comedienne, but Hearst wanted her to do those ridiculous overblown costume pieces. He didn't want anyone laughing at her, and since he held the purse strings on all her productions, he always got his way.

A cheer arose from outside, which meant either Nazimova or Valentino had arrived. But Martin didn't have a chance to find out, because Gilbert Flint sauntered over to him, a self-satisfied smirk on his face.

"Marty, old bean." Gilbert always tried to mock Martin's assumed accent with one not nearly as successful—New Jersey always bled through. "I almost don't recognize you without your faithful dog in attendance."

"I haven't the faintest notion what you're referring to, nor do I wish to find out." Martin turned away and scanned the throng for somebody he could use as an excuse to escape Gilbert.

"Who else? Your golden boy of a driver, that's who. He's done nothing for weeks but sit on his can while you mope around at home. But does Pops let him earn his keep honestly when other people could use an errand boy? No."

"They're paying him to be my driver. If I don't need him one minute, it doesn't mean I won't need him the next." He spotted George Hopkins across the lobby. *Thank God. I can always count on George.*

Gilbert grinned like a toothy shark—although Martin supposed that was redundant. "Hope you won't need him in the next few minutes, because I've got a feeling he'll be tied up for a while."

Martin froze in the act of raising his hand to greet George. "What do you mean?"

"Nothing much. But I hear a couple of ships docked in San Pedro tonight. The sailors'll all be heading into town, and if they happen to spot a punk in a purple tie when they hit Pershing Square, they'll know what to do with him."

"Robbie doesn't own a purple tie."

"But you do. Too bad you're so careless with it."

Martin's hands turned ice-cold. "What have you done, you bastard?"

Gilbert's eyes blazed. "What do you care, Marty? If you got a soft spot for the hayseed, I'm doing you a favor. After tonight, he won't be so stupid no more."

Martin shoved Gilbert's shoulder and half ran out of the lobby and into the crush of fans outside just as Valentino stepped out of his limousine. Martin alternated between cursing and apologizing as he shouldered his way through. God, it took him forever to burst onto a clear part of the sidewalk. Cars and limousines still lined the street in front of the theater, but none of them were free—they were all waiting to disgorge their rich or famous passengers—and Martin could hardly commandeer one.

So he sprinted for the streetcar, cursing Gilbert from dawn to Hades. Why had the bastard targeted poor naive Robbie? *Strike that. I know why. Because Gilbert knows how to get under my skin, and he's a worse bully than the entire set construction crew put together.*

But Robbie didn't deserve to pay the price of Gilbert's feud with Martin. Chances were Robbie hadn't had so much as a kiss from a high school sweetheart, let alone any clue about Martin's hidden world. People—the so-called decent people who'd voted for the Eighteenth Amendment, who packed the film censorship boards, who sat piously in their pews of a Sunday—barely acknowledged that his sort existed. If they did, it was to deride them as perverted, deviant, unnatural.

Who's to say they weren't right?

Martin had had glimmerings of hope that Robbie might be inclined that way, but a trial by fire like this—or rather a trial by sailor—wasn't the way to introduce him to the life. *It's my duty. My privilege.* And if Robbie was disgusted, then Martin would let the matter drop, along with the burgeoning friendship that had become so important to him.

But one way or another, Martin would rescue Robbie from Gilbert's spite. Because nobody deserved to have their innocence ripped away like that.

Nobody deserved to be raped.

Dang, but Pershing Square was a busy place. Robbie battled the crowded streets, trying to catch sight of Martin from behind the Flyer's windshield. Mr. Flint hadn't known exactly where the meeting—whatever it was—was taking place, and Robbie could hardly drive through the streets forever, hoping for a sight of Martin's profile.

So he searched for a parking spot, finally located one six blocks away, and then ran all the way back. What if Martin was looking for him and couldn't find him? Would he think Robbie was falling down on the job? Taking advantage of the secrets Martin had shared with him?

That first day, Martin had accused Robbie of using his job as a stepping stone to stardom, and Dottie had told him stories about other chauffeurs who had betrayed their employers. That driver of Mr. Taylor's? He was an out-and-out villain, and no mistake.

Once he got back to the square, Robbie skirted the park and took a moment to catch his breath. He smoothed the lapels of his borrowed suit. It was so much nicer than anything he'd ever worn—the wool fine and closely woven, the lining real silk. He couldn't believe someone would just leave it behind in the wardrobe department. Although, when Robbie dropped a couple of coins into the pants pocket, they'd fallen straight down his leg and rolled across the floor. The other pocket had a big hole in it too, so maybe whoever owned it before hadn't wanted to bother with mending.

That would never have happened on the farm. Folks who depended on the land for their living learned how to make do. His pa would have been outraged at the waste—although he'd probably sneer at the suit as too fancy for a man to wear. But then, Pa would be outraged at almost everything about Robbie's life now, including the reason he'd wound up in Hollywood in the first place.

Good thing he can't see me now. But Martin will see me. Soon, I hope. With Robbie in a nice suit, even if it was a little too big, would Martin finally think of him as somebody other than the driver? Robbie straightened the swell tie Mr. Flint had pulled out of a box for him. It wasn't a color Robbie would have chosen —purple was a little flashy for him, even though he'd passed a couple of other men wearing similar ones tonight.

A packed streetcar pulled up across from the park and disgorged a mob of men, some in sailor's uniforms, some in suits, some in the rough clothing of laborers. Robbie pushed aside a sagging banana frond, a real one this time—this park was lousy with banana plants. He craned his neck and scanned the crowd, but he didn't spot Martin's sleek dark hair or aristocratic profile.

A burly man in laborer's clothes peeled off the laughing group in front of the nickelodeon across the street and stared at Robbie with a grin splitting his broad face.

The man shoved his hands in his pockets and sauntered across the street with the kind of swaggering confidence of Mr. Flint. Behind him the clump of men began to disperse, but

Robbie couldn't spot Martin on the sidewalk there nor anywhere else along the boulevard.

Could Mr. Flint have been mistaken? He'd seemed so sure. Might Martin already be at the theater or waiting at Alvarado Court for Robbie to pick him up?

He turned, ready to bolt back to the Flyer, but the man from the streetcar blocked his way.

"What's your hurry?"

Robbie ducked his head. "Sorry. I'm looking for someone."

"You're in luck. You found him." He tapped the side of Robbie's face with one blunt finger. "Pretty." He hitched up his pants. "You got a room?"

"Um…." Could this fellow be a policeman? Pops had warned him that first day that the cops were tough on vagrants. "Yes. I do. I've got a job and everything."

"Well now, ain't you just the cat's pajamas. Got a bottle in your room?"

Robbie's eyes widened. A trap. It must be a trap. But it wasn't illegal to drink liquor you already owned, only to sell it or buy it or transport it. Not that he had any anyway. "N-n-no."

The man moved closer. "Too bad. But you're pretty enough I'll let that pass. Let's go."

"Go?"

His mouth lifted in a sneer, and he shook his head. "Why're the pretty ones always stupid?" he muttered. "Yeah. To your room. Unless you want me to fuck you in the bushes yonder."

"What?" Robbie backed up, panic rising from his belly to choke him. He barely knew his secret desire himself. How had he given himself away?

The man laughed through his teeth, hissing like a snake ready to strike, and advanced, herding Robbie toward the shrubbery in the center of the park. "The bushes it is. You at least got some slick? If not, this ain't gonna be easy. I been without for too long."

"Get away from him." At the lash of Martin's voice, Robbie's knees threatened to buckle.

The man turned with a glare. "Who're you to tell me what to do?"

Martin strode over to them, his shoulders back, the steely glint in his eyes visible even in the yellow light from the street lamps. "I'm his employer."

"So I need to pay you for a go at him?"

"What you need," Martin said, his voice like a saw blade, "is to move along before you're arrested for solicitation. I'll wager your commanding officer won't be pleased when you end up in jail, particularly for that reason. Unless of course you *want* a dishonorable discharge."

"How'd you know I'm a sailor? I ain't in uniform."

Martin smiled, thin-lipped. "You walk like the deck's still under your feet."

"Fuck this." The man spat on the sidewalk, inches from Martin's shoes. "There's other fish who don't raise this kind of stink." He turned and strode off, hitching his pants a bit higher.

Martin turned to Robbie. "Let's go."

Robbie's lips were so numb he could barely speak. "The car's parked a ways away. I don't know if we'll get to the theater in time."

"We're not going to the theater."

Robbie cringed at the anger in Martin's tone. "But *Camille.* Aren't you—"

"Screw *Camille.* I'm not in the mood to watch Nazimova and Valentino slink about on the screen. Let's just go home."

The walk to the car seemed to take forever, and at every step, Martin longed to take Robbie in his arms and comfort him. From the way he stumbled along at Martin's side, his arms crossed in front of him like a shield, he was obviously still in shock from the encounter with that bloody sailor. But that kind of public display could get both of them arrested for the same crime he'd threatened the sailor with.

God damn Gilbert Flint.

Martin didn't trust himself to speak, so he stayed silent until they got to the car. He wanted to get in the front seat, sit next to Robbie, perhaps put a soothing hand on his thigh, but there were far too many people on the sidewalk tonight, and based on the murmurs and occasional pointed fingers, some of them recognized Martin.

So he let Robbie open the door for him but hesitated a moment before he climbed inside. He let his fingers brush Robbie's on the door handle, only to have Robbie flinch away from the touch.

God damn *Gilbert Flint.*

Martin kept a close eye on Robbie from the back seat as they drove back to Hollywood, but although his jaw was set and he drove perhaps a bit slower, he didn't seem otherwise distracted. When they pulled up to Alvarado, though, and Robbie would have parked at the curb, Martin surrendered.

"Pull around to the garage, Rob. Please. I think we need to talk."

Robbie didn't release the steering wheel. "You're not—Are you mad at me?"

"God, no! But you've had a shock. I'd like to take care of you for a bit, if you'll let me."

Robbie's shoulders slumped, and Martin held his breath. *Please, oh please don't go yet. If you do, you might never come back.* But Robbie nodded and put the car in gear. When they reached the garage and Robbie would have gotten out to open the door, Martin put a hand on his shoulder.

"I'll get it."

"But—"

"I'm capable of opening a door or two, Rob. Let me do this for you."

"All right." Robbie's voice was small. *God damn Gilbert Flint to hell.* "Thank you."

Somehow Martin managed to get Robbie into the bungalow without wrapping him in a hug, but it was a near thing. Once inside, he pointed to the davenport. "Sit, please. I'll be back in a moment."

Robbie shuffled across the room and plopped gracelessly onto the leather cushions. *God damn Gilbert Flint to the* lowest circle *of hell.* Martin stalked to the sideboard, flung open its door, and retrieved his precious bottle of brandy from behind the bootleg gin. He sloshed two fingers of amber liquid into a snifter and swirled it gently to warm it.

"Take this, please."

Robbie barely glanced at it. "I don't drink gin."

"It's not gin. It's brandy. Real brandy. I bought it before Prohibition, since I'm not stupid."

"But—"

"Take it, Rob. You need it tonight."

Robbie jerked a nod and took the snifter in his shaking hand. He lifted it to his lips and took a gulp. His eyes popped wide and he inhaled on a gasp. Then he coughed, eyes watering.

Martin took the glass and sat down next to him, rubbing his back. "It's not water, my dear. You're supposed to sip, not guzzle."

"Sip," Robbie wheezed. "Got it."

Martin stood and walked into the kitchen to procure a glass of water. When he got back, Robbie seemed to have recovered his breath and was taking a cautious sip of brandy. His cheeks, which had been deathly pale when they'd walked inside, sported a bit more color.

"I didn't know…." He cupped both hands around the brandy. "Do people… do men *do* that?"

"Some do. If you want to make it in this town, you'll see worse on the set five days out of seven. Bill Taylor and George Hopkins had a scene in *The Furnace* where all the extras were buck naked, and only doctored the prints to add flames covering the important bits later."

Robbie glared at him from under his bunched eyebrows. "Jehoshaphat, Martin. I'm not talking about copulation. I know all about that. I was raised on a farm. I mean forcing someone. Someone who says no. Like that sailor tonight. Like they say Mr. Arbuckle did."

Martin resumed his place next to Robbie but didn't presume to touch him again. "It happens more often than I like to think about. Sometimes even when someone says yes, it's only because they don't think they have a choice. It's not about sex, or even one-sided gratification. Not really. It's about power. And when the person with the power dangles something in front of you that means the difference between starvation and survival? Between subsistence and comfort? Or even just something that you deeply desire? In those cases, even if your heart is screaming no, yes can seem like the only option."

Robbie swallowed and his Adam's apple slid under the smooth skin of his throat above the stiff Arrow collar. "That sailor tonight, he didn't give me a chance to say yes or no. He didn't even ask the question. Why would he think I'd say yes?"

Martin gestured to Robbie's chest. "The purple tie. It's a code —a sign. A way for men who are in the life to recognize one another."

"In the life?"

Shite, this is not how I wanted to have this conversation. But it looked as though the choice had been taken from both of them. Martin forced himself to gaze calmly into Robbie's eyes. "Men who prefer the company of other men. Who prefer sex with men rather than women."

Robbie exhaled slowly, but it seemed like a release rather than an unraveling. "So it has a name. I never knew."

CHAPTER ELEVEN

Robbie swallowed hard, and the tight collar added to the constriction in his throat. "Are you—Do you—I mean, have you ever...."

The strong line of Martin's jaw tightened, and he averted his eyes. *No. Please no. Not* that *look.* Not the one he put on with the Mr. Schlossbergs or Mr. Flint. "You've had a shock tonight, Robbie. You should go. I'll—"

Robbie grabbed the sleeve of Martin's jacket, hardly believing he had the guts to do it. "Because if you do... if you did, I wouldn't think any less of you."

"No? What if I told you that suit used to belong to me? What if I told you the slit pockets were deliberate?" Martin's eyes couldn't have looked darker or more intense if he'd had his full makeup on. "What if I showed you what those slits were for?"

"I...." Holy God, Robbie's mouth was so dry he could barely get the words out. His hands trembled so badly that he had to curl them into fists lest Martin mistake this thrill, this anticipation, this *need*, for fear. "I would say... please."

"Please what? Please stop? Please go away? Please never come near me again?"

"Please. Show me."

Martin shut his eyes, and the expression that flashed over his face didn't match the *want* coiling in Robbie's middle. "I will not be like that sailor."

"You're not. You could never be." His belly swooping like a barn swallow, Robbie shed his coat and folded it reverently. Now that he knew it had belonged to Martin, it was doubly precious. He laid it carefully over the back of the armchair and stood, his arms at his sides. "Martin. Would you please, please show me wh-what the slit pockets are for?"

Martin's shoulders rose in a sigh, but he stood up and faced Robbie, their chests no more than a handspan apart, and suddenly Robbie's breath was stoppered under his throat. "Turn around, Rob," Martin murmured, his voice headier than the brandy.

Robbie couldn't do anything but obey—not because he felt he *must*, but because he craved knowing what came next. *This is it. The thing I never knew how to ask for. The thing I didn't have a name for. The thing Frank would have shown me if they hadn't taken him away.*

After Robbie was facing the curtained windows, Martin stepped closer, and then—*Holy God*. Martin's chest was warm behind him, his legs tight against Robbie's, and in between... in between....

Robbie gasped, his pecker so hard in his pants that he was afraid he'd disgrace himself right there in Martin's lovely home, in Martin's lovely suit. But then Martin's lovely *hands* were on Robbie's hips.

"Do you want me to show you, Rob?" Martin murmured, his breath stirring the hair over Robbie's ear. "We don't have to go any further. I can stop. Just tell me no."

"Jehoshaphat, Martin," Robbie choked out. "Why the devil would I want to say *no*?"

Martin's chuckle caught on a sharp inhale. *Guess he's not as calm as he seems.* "Very well."

Then Martin's hands slid down and forward, into Robbie's pants pockets, and then down and down and down until Robbie jerked when Martin's fingers nearly scalded his inner thighs through the thin cotton of his underdrawers. And then.... And *then*....

"One usually doesn't wear anything under these trousers, you know." Martin cupped Robbie's balls with one hand and gripped his pecker through the cotton with the other, and Robbie's knees turned to jelly as his pecker turned to steel.

"God. *Martin!*"

"Oh, my darling boy. You feel so wonderful."

Robbie leaned his head back onto Martin's shoulder. "I—I don't know what to do."

"Exactly what you're doing now. So lovely. So hot and hard and eager in my hands." Martin pressed his lips to Robbie's throat. "How would you feel in my mouth?"

"*Martin!*" Robbie grabbed Martin's forearms, but it was too late. Fire shot down his spine and into his balls and then he was spending in Martin's house, in Martin's suit, in Martin's *hand*. *Oh God, what have I done?* But he couldn't speak, could barely hold himself upright as he waited for Martin's reprimand.

But it didn't come.

Instead, Martin stroked him through his release and then slowly withdrew his hands from Robbie's pockets. He kissed Robbie's throat again and gripped Robbie's shoulders, regardless of the mess Robbie'd obviously made on his hands. *Maybe my drawers caught most of it.*

"You," Martin murmured, turning Robbie until they were face to face, "are a bloody miracle."

And then Martin's lips were on his, soft and warm and so delicious that Robbie opened his mouth, the better to taste, and was rewarded with the flick of Martin's tongue.

This is what I've waited for. What I've wanted.

Robbie wrapped his arms around Martin's neck and gave himself up to the kiss, to Martin's chest, firm against his own, to

Martin's hands roving down Robbie's back to his behind. When Martin tucked Robbie closer, Martin's erection nearly seared Robbie's belly despite the cooling mess of semen in his underdrawers.

"Will you come upstairs with me, Rob? I'd like to see you. All of you."

Robbie bit his lip, his heart pounding so loudly he could barely hear. "Can I see you too?"

Martin chuckled. "Of course. I'd like nothing better than to show you what we can accomplish when we're both naked."

"Then yes. Let's go. Because I really want to touch you."

"Then you shall."

And he did—with his hands, his lips, his tongue, and possibly every inch of his skin.

Afterward, as Robbie lay gasping in Martin's bed, with Martin's hand warm on his chest, he turned his head on the pillow.

"Martin?"

"Yes, my darling?"

"Is that really your suit?"

Martin laughed, the corners of his eyes crinkling. "It is."

"Will you promise me something?"

"If I'm able."

"Never wear that suit for anybody but me."

Martin's slow smile lit his face. Jesus God, if that look ever got captured on film, there'd be riots in the theaters, both men and women. "You have my solemn word."

Martin traced Robbie's cheekbone with one finger. "It's too bad you don't want to go into pictures. This face was made for the screen."

Robbie turned on his side so he could rest his hand on Martin's bare hip. And the realization that he had permission to do that nearly stopped his breath again. "It's just a face. A pretty ordinary one. Not like yours."

"Mine? Mine is a dime a dozen, or so Jacob Schlossberg keeps telling me."

"He's wrong." Robbie caught Martin's hand against his cheek. "There's nobody like you."

Martin's smile was wry. "The American public may not agree. But as long as *you* believe it? I'm perfectly content."

Robbie watched the light play across Martin's face for a moment, the scent of orange and almond wafting from the soft linen sheets, the breeze from the window ruffling the curtains and drying the sweat on both of their bodies.

"Martin?"

"Hmmm?"

"What happens now?"

Martin propped himself on an elbow to peer down at Robbie in the dim light. "I suppose we could bathe. Perhaps eat something."

"I don't mean right this minute, although all those things sound good. I mean tomorrow and the next day and the one after that. Will we—" Robbie swallowed around a lump in his throat. "Will we do this again?"

Martin threaded his fingers through Robbie's hair. "We will do this many times, my darling. At least if I have my way, we will, but you have a say in this as well." His brows drew together, although his lips were still curved in a smile. "Do *you* want to do it again?"

Robbie nodded. "It's more than I ever—That is, I never knew what—Jehoshaphat, Martin, you must know this is *everything.*"

His smile quirked up a notch. "I don't. Not unless you tell me. And in any case, it isn't *everything.* It can't be. We both have jobs to do and people looking to us to do them."

"I know we're not on a deserted island, like stupid Robinson Crusoe. It would almost be easier if we were. Dottie says.... Dottie says that men who... who like men can get away with it in Hollywood, despite the law, because things are different here. That it's all right to have a lover who's the same sex as you."

Martin stroked Robbie's hair. "That's true and not true. It's safer here for people who have a studio's power behind them. But for the ordinary man in the street? I'm not sure it's any better here than in Springfield or Schenectady."

"Does that mean we have to keep things quiet?"

"Not entirely quiet. I think—I *want* to be able to be with you when it's safe, which might not be all the time. Also, you're my driver. If Jacob or Ira suspected there was something else between us, they might take it poorly, to say the least." He scowled. "Despite the fact directors and producers bed would-be actresses every day."

"Is that what you meant about power?"

"Yes. Partly. Technically, I'm in a position of power over you because you're in service to me, even though the studio is your employer."

Robbie grinned up at him. "If you're asking if I feel exploited...."

Martin chuckled and tugged one of Robbie's curls. "No, you cheeky brat. But I'd never want you to feel that way, or for anyone else to be able to accuse you—"

"Or you."

He inclined his head. "Or me, of impropriety. Not that Hollywood knows what impropriety is. But I think we can chart a course through the rocky shoals around our desert island while keeping the island all to ourselves. Are you willing to try?"

Robbie didn't reply, not with words. But he drew Martin down and let the kiss be his answer.

CHAPTER TWELVE

Robbie's skin was just as glorious as Martin had imagined—pale, smooth where a man's skin ought to be smooth, rough where a man ought to be rough. The palms of his hands, for instance, where his calluses caught Martin's skin as Robbie stroked his face, his arm, his hip.

"I can't believe I'm here," Robbie murmured, wonder tinging his voice. "That *you're* here."

Martin nudged Robbie's chin up so he could drop a kiss on that lovely mouth. "Will I shock you if I tell you I've been imagining you here, *wishing* you here, since the day we met?"

Robbie's blushes indeed went all the way down. "I've been, um, imagining you too, but I never imagined *this*." His flush deepened as he glanced down at their groins. "Or *that*."

"Did you like this?" Martin kissed Robbie again, this time openmouthed, and was rewarded with Robbie's groan. "And that?" He trailed a finger down Robbie's chest and over his cock to cup his balls.

"Jehoshaphat, Martin," Robbie gasped. "What do you think?"

Martin stopped teasing and wrapped his arms around Robbie. He held them flush together from chest to hip. "I think I'm the luckiest man in Hollywood." He rolled his hips. "We've covered this and that. Would you like me to show you the other thing?"

Robbie's eyes widened. "There's another thing?"

"Oh, so many more things. You've only to say the word."

"Then I—Jehoshaphat, is that the time?"

Martin followed the direction of Robbie's gaze to the top of the dresser. *Damn clock.* "I fear it is. Are you tired? Would you prefer to sleep a while before trying the *other thing*?"

But Robbie pushed away and sat up with an apologetic smile. "I can't. I've got to return the Flyer to the studio."

"Why? They don't mind if you keep it overnight, especially if you have an early pickup in the morning."

"But I don't, because *you* don't, and everyone knows it." Robbie picked up his underdrawers, but then he screwed up his face and balled them in his fist. Of course. He spent in them last night.

"Second drawer of the bureau, Rob. Help yourself."

Robbie shot him a grateful glance. "You're sure you want to loan me your underdrawers?"

"Not loan. Consider them a gift. Trust me," Martin said, gazing at the play of light and shadow on the curve of Robbie's arse. "I'm being well compensated." *And there's the blush again.* "Although I'm getting a few *very* interesting ideas. Are you sure you can't stay?"

Robbie shook his head and crossed to the bureau. "I wish I could. But my landlady isn't expecting me to be out all night, and—Jehoshaphat, Martin, are you *sure* you want to give these to me? They're fancier than anything I've got."

"They're only underdrawers, Rob, not the full soup-and-fish."

Robbie froze with the garment in his hands. "The what?"

Martin laughed and propped himself on his elbow. "It's slang, Rob. It means evening dress—a tuxedo."

Robbie shook his head. "I've got a lot to learn."

"Remind me to show you my thirteen-and-the-odd sometime."

"Now you're just kidding me." He pulled on the underdrawers, adjusted them for his narrower waist, and then picked up his trousers.

My trousers. My underdrawers. Martin wanted to crow, to announce to the world that this man was *his*, but that could never happen. His elation paled for an instant, and he levered himself up to sit on the edge of the mattress. "No, I assure you. White tie and tail coat. Ask Sid if you don't believe me." *Good God, the flex of his back muscles. It's a crime to cover those with a shirt.* "Are you sure you can't stay?"

He shrugged into his shirt. "Mrs. McGuire leaves the door on the latch for me, and I lock up when I get home. I can't let her down."

"Very well." Martin sighed theatrically. "I suppose I must suffer." He got up and retrieved his dressing gown. Then he followed Robbie down the stairs. Robbie reached for the suit jacket, but Martin stayed his hand. "Allow me."

He held up the jacket for Robbie to slip his arms into the sleeves, just as he'd done for clients when he'd been a tailor's apprentice—although he'd never dropped a kiss on a client's neck, as he did now. "I'll miss you."

Robbie turned and wrapped his arms around Martin's waist. "I'll miss you too. Will we get back to a regular schedule soon?"

"I don't know. It depends on how long Jacob and Ira overreact. But I'll think of some way we can meet without any tongues wagging." He grinned. "Except our own, of course."

So Martin was able to send Robbie on his way with a kiss and a chuckle before returning to his bed, where he spent the rest of the night staring at his bedroom ceiling, alternating between dizzy elation and sheer terror.

He'd revealed more to Robbie than anyone in Hollywood knew about him, even Sid. Not that Martin would have wanted to share any details with someone who wasn't in the life—or really with anyone who *was*. Although there were some in their unofficial fraternity who indulged in more... *extravagant* behavior, Martin had never been one of their number. He socialized with Bill Taylor and George Hopkins and met with others who were similarly discreet for what Sid mocked as "steak and pinochle parties" up at Mount Lowe Lodge.

They weren't overt, but among themselves they didn't have to pretend either. Martin wondered when he'd have a chance to take Robbie to one and introduce him to his friends with the tacit understanding that Robbie was his lover, even though the words would never be spoken.

They didn't have to be. Robbie's presence at that sort of gathering would speak for itself.

Having Robbie continue as his driver was both a blessing and a problem. At least they still had a reason to see each other every day—or they would once Citadel's production ramped up again. *I can only hope I'll still be employed.*

A chill skated across his skin, and he pulled the sheets over his chest. What would he do if Citadel instituted its own morality clause? For that matter, what would Citadel do with that kind of contract verbiage? Would they stop protecting men like Martin, whose tastes might legitimately draw "hatred, contempt, scorn, or ridicule" should the public discover them? Would they turn Martin into a sacrificial lamb for the studio, much as Roscoe was being sacrificed for the whole motion picture industry?

If they did, Martin's career would be over, and although he wasn't the spendthrift that Valentino was, he hadn't saved as much of his generous salary as he should have. How could he protect Robbie if he lost his job?

On the other hand, Robbie wasn't in the public eye. So far, the morality clause only applied to actors, because they were the only ones the fan magazines—and by extension, the fans—cared about. However unfair that was, at least it meant that Robbie would still have a job. *Maybe I'll end up being kept by my chauffeur instead of the other way around.*

The chill prickled Martin's scalp. Would Robbie's reputation be tarnished by association with Martin? Would he be sacrificed too, should their relationship become known?

Martin set his jaw, the sheets bunched in his fists. Somehow, he needed to find a way to protect Robbie yet keep him by his side. Because now that he knew Robbie shared his own desires, now that he'd tasted Robbie's innocent enthusiasm, Martin knew one thing for certain.

I'm never giving him up.

Because Robbie, warm and open and giving in Martin's arms, was a true miracle at the end of a night that could have turned disastrous on so many levels.

As dawn crept through the blinds, Martin finally gave up any attempt at sleep. He threw on his dressing gown, unwilling to wash the traces of Robbie from his skin quite yet, and shuffled downstairs and into the kitchen.

He brewed himself some coffee and retired to the living room to brood. He still had no idea what direction his career was going. If he—

The telephone shrilled, making him slosh coffee onto his robe. "Shite!" He set the cup down and held the steaming fabric away from his skin as he crossed to the telephone. "Hello?"

"Marty, I've got great news!" Sid didn't need to say the words —the glee in his voice was obvious.

"Hearst sold all his papers and is retiring to a monastery?"

"Better! *Camille* is a total stinker, and Valentino stinks the most. This is the chance we were hoping for."

"I'd never hope for a picture to fail. That's not good for any of us."

"Nuts to that. Listen, I've got a meeting with Ira Schlossberg later today. The rushes from *The Imaginary Husband* have looked so good that even Jacob can't fault them."

He wouldn't anyway. Not as long as Evie keeps him salivating at arm's length. "That's gratifying, of course, but it's Evelyn's picture. I'm just there to light her cigarette, as you've pointed out before."

"Ah, come on, Marty, don't be sore."

Martin sank down in the chair next to the telephone table. "I'm sorry, Sid. I've simply got a lot on my mind. Gilbert Flint pulled a very nasty trick on Robbie last night, and—"

"Robbie? Your driver?"

"Yes."

"You're not getting in over your head there, are you, Marty?"

"I'm not sure what you mean by 'over my head,' but nobody deserves the mean-spirited and possibly physically hurtful stunt Gilbert pulled last night." And when Martin considered the high incidence of syphilis in the transient population.... He shivered. It wasn't only Robbie's innocence that had been threatened last night. It was his life.

"You know what I mean. Keep your nose clean, Marty, at least till the dust-up with Arbuckle blows over."

"He's accused of rape and murder, Sid. It's hardly a 'dust-up.'"

"They can't make it stick. It's all a stunt by that DA shyster, Brady, because he wants to run for office. Arbuckle'll be acquitted, and we'll be back to business as usual."

Martin leaned his head against the wall. "Give it to me straight. Do you think Citadel will tack a morality clause onto their contracts?"

"They'll forget about it once Arbuckle is clear. It'll be too much trouble to put in place, and you know how Jacob hates trouble." *Yes, but he hates queers more.* "Listen, I want you to be on the lot this afternoon. If my powwow with Ira goes the way I think it will, I'll need you on the spot. Can you do that?"

"I'll try to fit it into my oh-so-busy schedule."

"Don't be an ass, Marty."

Martin sighed. "What time, Sid?"

"Make it three. No, two. I may have some talking to do before we're ready for you, but I don't want to give Ira a chance to waffle if he has to wait. I'll get him primed, but you'll need to be there to close the deal."

"Do we have a plan? Any lines you want me to say?"

"Nah. Just agree with whatever I say."

"Business as usual indeed. Very well. I'll see you this afternoon."

Martin replaced the telephone earpiece. He had hours to go before he needed to be presentable, but since he'd be seeing Robbie, presentable wasn't sufficient. He needed to be perfect— a man who wouldn't shame someone like Robbie, even if nobody could ever know they were together.

Of course, when he was shaving, he couldn't keep his mind from drifting back to the night before, to Robbie in his bed and the wonder in his eyes as Martin showed him what two men could do together. And there was so much more—places Martin had never gone, things he'd never done with his other partners because he'd lacked that one thing with them that he had with Robbie.

Trust.

Robbie Goodman's name wasn't merely a collection of letters. It defined him. He was truly a *good* man, a rarity in Hollywood. Martin's hand trembled so severely that he had to set his razor down. *What if Hollywood changes him, corrupts him?* It had done as much to so many others. Even the best man might ignore his conscience in the quest for fame and money and power.

Not Robbie. Never Robbie.

The kiss Robbie gave him when he left this morning had been shy and as full of wonder as the first, as though he couldn't believe his luck.

I'm the lucky one. How many people found that one person who completed them, soul of their soul? George had found that person with Bill Taylor. Doug and Mary had been so enamored that they'd flouted public outcry to divorce their spouses and marry each other—and the public treated them like royalty now.

Of course, it was doubtful the public would have done the same if Doug had declared his undying love for, say, Charlie Chaplin instead of Mary Pickford. Martin snorted. Charlie wasn't in the life any more than Doug was, although Charlie was skating on thin sexual ice in other areas.

Still, even Charlie's penchant for very young women could be forgiven more readily than a loving relationship between two men of legal age.

Someday, maybe that would change. Pictures could do that. Pictures could reach as many as—or more than—a fire-and-brimstone preacher at a revival meeting. Bill Taylor was starting to ease some of those ideas into his own work, all while presenting the gentlemanly front that the conservative groups adored.

One day—maybe not soon, maybe not for another ten years or so—the public wouldn't blink at two men holding hands, two men kissing, two men together as though they were married. Once people saw it in pictures, it would start to seem like it had always been there. And once they saw it portrayed as beautifully as someone like Bill could do it, it wouldn't seem shocking or immoral at all.

Robbie wasn't entirely sure his feet were touching the ground this morning. He smiled at everybody on the streetcar, so widely that a mother snatched her pinafored little girl out of his way. Robbie didn't care. He bowed and offered them both his seat and then jumped off the trolley. Today he didn't need the ride.

He was pretty sure he could fly.

He stopped at the diner to buy half a dozen doughnuts for Pops and Dottie and left an extra quarter for a tip, to the wide-eyed amazement of Earlene, the waitress who'd seen him at his threadbare worst. He couldn't really afford it—that quarter would cover at least two dinners if he was careful. But today Robbie wanted to make other people as happy as he was, even if it was just with an extra couple of nickels.

Besides, he wasn't hungry. His belly still fluttered when he remembered Martin's lips on his, Martin's skin against his, Martin's—

"Hey! Watch where you're going!" A scowling man in a gray fedora shoved irritably at Robbie's shoulder.

Robbie ducked his head. "I'm sorry." He touched the brim of his cap. "Here. Have a doughnut." He held out the paper-wrapped treat and the man took it, his scowl fading into a bemused half smile. Robbie nodded and walked on, whistling. But then his steps faltered as he realized what song was on his lips.

"Wildwood Flower." Frank's favorite.

A little of Robbie's joy faded. How could he be happy with Martin when Frank was stuck in Idaho, possibly in prison, possibly worse.

But Frank never wanted to do that *with* me. *Only with some man he'd never met before.*

Robbie had never stopped trying to find a mention of Frank in the Boise newspaper, but he'd never seen a single word. Would the paper judge it worth the ink? Even if they did, would they have printed the whole truth, or only what would sell the most papers?

He'd learned a lot since he'd come to Hollywood, and some of it was wonderful—his belly swooped again at the memory of Martin's kiss—but other things? He used to trust the newspapers. He used to trust the police. But not anymore.

Now the only people he trusted were the ones he knew for a fact wouldn't lie or cheat or betray him. Pops. Dottie. *Martin.*

And when it came down to brass tacks? That was enough.

At the studio gates, he waved to Pops and brandished the paper bag of doughnuts. Pops ambled over, shaking his head as he chuckled.

"If I'd known you'd spend all your dough at that diner, I'd never have taken you there." He opened the smaller door set into Citadel's massive wrought iron gates.

Robbie slipped inside. "You don't fool me. You're just a big softy." He followed Pops to the booth and unloaded a couple of wrapped doughnuts onto the shelf inside. "I had Earlene wrap 'em all separate, so you can have one later on if you want."

"You're a good boy, Robbie." Pops patted his shoulder. "Best thing I ever did, picking you up off the street that day."

"Hey! I wasn't on the street." Robbie grinned. "Okay, I was on the street, but I wasn't *on* the street. I'd have found my feet eventually. But Pops?" Robbie gripped the older man's shoulder. "I'm powerfully glad you did. Thank you from the bottom of my heart."

"Bah." Pops waved his hand as though shooing a fly, but Robbie caught the brightness of tears in his eyes. "Didn't do it for thanks. I did it because I needed a good worker. And a little bird told me you've been making yourself useful on the lot, besides being a driver, so looks like I made the right decision." He handed Robbie a slip of paper. "Here. Looks like Mr. Brentwood's coming back on the lot today. You're to pick him up at one thirty."

Robbie's belly didn't only swoop, it did a full barrel roll. Martin had promised they'd find a way to see each other, but Robbie hadn't dared hope it would be so soon. He'd missed those moments alone in the car, the drive so familiar now that he didn't have to pay such close attention to the road and could chat and laugh with Martin instead. If Martin was starting a new picture, then those days were here again. *And maybe I'll be able to watch him work, as long as I stay well back and don't distract anyone.*

Robbie cringed when he remembered his first foray onto the shooting stage. Thank goodness Mr. Brody never found out who spoiled that shot. *Maybe I should have brought cake for Dottie as well as doughnuts.* She'd saved his bacon and no mistake. While Robbie owed Pops plenty for getting him in the door at Citadel, he owed Dottie that he wasn't tossed out on his ear that first day… or any day since.

He had plenty of time before he picked up Martin, so he made his way to the cutting room and knocked on the half-open door. "Dottie? I brought you some—*whoa!*"

Knocked off-balance when Dottie yanked hard on his arm, Robbie stumbled into the room. Then he nearly landed on his behind when she leaped on him and hugged him tightly around the neck.

"He bought it," she sang, crushing the doughnut bag between them. "He bought it, he bought it."

"Dottie," Robbie gasped. "Air. Neck. Breathe."

She dropped the stranglehold, stepped back, and clasped her hands under her chin. Her eyes behind her steel-rimmed spectacles sparkled, and her hair stood out as though she'd been pulled through a bramble bush backward in a windstorm. "Sorry, sorry, sorry. But, Rob, he—"

"Bought it. You said. But who bought what?"

"Ira. He bought my scenario. He said it's exactly what the studio needs right now."

This time Robbie was ready for the leap and caught her around the waist before she could throttle him again. He squeezed her in return. "That's stupendous, girl. Congratulations." He set her back on her feet and then held up the mangled bag. "These used to be doughnuts before you turned them into pancakes, but will they do for a celebration?"

She grinned up at him. "They'll do for a start." She grabbed the bag and danced around the crowded room, expertly avoiding stacks of film cans. "I can't believe it. I'm a real scenarist now."

"You can finally get out of the cutting room, see the light of day, right?"

She smacked him on the shoulder with a balled fist. "Are you crazy? I'm not letting any ham-handed yahoo touch my story. I'm cutting it. I'm keeping script too. They won't let me direct, not yet, but my fingers are gonna be in every piece of that pie. You watch. It'll be so good, so amazing, make the studio so much money, they'll have no choice but to give me my shot." She smirked at him like Ma's cat when she got into the cream pitcher. "I've already got the director I want—Boyd Brody."

Robbie froze with a flattened doughnut halfway to his mouth. "Mr. Brody? But—"

"Don't worry. He still doesn't know about you."

"But he's Citadel's top director now. Nothing against you, Dottie. You know I think you're aces. But how'd a first-time scenarist land that big a fish?"

She grinned. "Easy. I just happened to leave the scenario on the set where I was keeping script for him. When I rushed back, all frantic, he asked why. So I pretended like it was a big secret, something the Schlossbergs didn't want anybody to know about. Naturally he was wild to read it, so I oh-so-reluctantly handed it over."

"And he liked it?"

"He stormed into Ira's office and demanded to direct it." She did another jig, her doughnut overhead, raining bits of chocolate icing into her hair. "I'm getting the cast of my dreams too."

"Stand still for a minute. You've got chocolate dandruff." Robbie steadied her with a hand on her shoulder while he brushed the crumbs out of her hair. "How will you get around Mr. Brody, though? Won't he have the final say? And actors can refuse a role, can't they?"

"Not if they're under contract here rather than on loan from another studio." She grabbed his hand, although he hadn't cleared all the icing from her hair, and towed him over to their usual seats in the corner. "Normally the director has the say over the big parts, the name actors. The assistant director handles everything else. The AD for *The California Trail*—"

"Is that the name of your picture?"

She nodded, eyes shining. "Mmhmmm," she mumbled around a mouthful of doughnut. "It's about the first successful wagon train to cross the Sierras. The Stephens-Townsend-Murphy party."

"Oh sure. That's a good story."

She blinked. "You know about it? Most people only know about the Donner party, the one that wasn't so successful." She wrinkled her nose. "People do love other folks' misery."

"I know about it because—"

"We'll be filming on location in Nevada and later in the Sierras. Months, Rob, months. And I'll be on the spot the whole time."

"Months?" His days at the studio would be awfully empty without Dottie. But maybe he could spend the time watching Martin's picture. Make himself useful so the director wouldn't send him packing.

She grasped his hands, hers still sticky with chocolate. "Rob, you've got to help me. The AD is a friend of mine, so I can steer him toward the actors I want for some of the smaller parts. But I really really *really* want Martin Brentwood for Dennis Martin."

Robbie shifted uneasily on the hard wooden chair. "I don't think he and Mr. Brody get on so well."

"They hate each other. But Boyd directed *The Imaginary Husband*, and even he says that Martin's good in it. But *you* have to convince Martin to take the part."

"I thought you said he'd have to take anything they offer him."

"He does. But they won't think of him for this part. He's been stuck playing the suave leading man for too long. You have to convince him to *ask* to be in the picture."

Robbie reared back in his chair. "Me? What makes you think he'll do what I ask?"

She peered at him over her spectacles, grabbed the last doughnut out of the bag, and let the silence stretch out between them. Robbie tried to keep a straight face, he really did, but with terror climbing his rib cage, he probably looked like a shop window dummy. *If I open my mouth, the truth will spill out.*

Finally she sighed. "Are you picking him up today?"

"Yes. At one thirty."

"That's for a meeting with Ira."

He gaped at her. "How do you find out these things?"

"Never mind that. I already dropped a few hints that Evelyn Trent would be perfect for the part of Elizabeth Townsend. Ira will do anything for Evelyn. And Evelyn will do anything for Martin. Mention that she'll be in the picture, and I'll bet he'll say yes."

Does that mean Martin will do anything for Evelyn? Robbie finished off his doughnut, but it was like sawdust in his mouth. "I'll try. But I can't make any promises."

She leaped up and hugged him around the neck again, knocking his hat off. "Thanks, Rob. You're the best. It'll work out. You'll see."

Months and months? Robbie smiled weakly, unwilling to dim her joy. But without Martin, Hollywood was bound to seem as grim and joyless as the farm in the Bitterroots.

CHAPTER THIRTEEN

Martin was waiting on the sidewalk when Robbie drew up to the curb in the Flyer. He smoothed the front of his best suit, unable to contain his grin. But when Robbie climbed out, he didn't meet Martin's gaze. Instead, he kept his head down as he circled the car and opened the rear door.

Ice formed in Martin's belly. Did Robbie regret what they'd done? Had Martin misread the situation? God, had he forced Robbie to do something he didn't want to do?

But then Martin remembered the guileless joy on Robbie's face the first time he'd trailed trembling fingers over Martin's bare chest. *No. I won't believe it. I* can't *believe it.*

Martin raised his hand, about to take Robbie's arm, when Edna Purviance, a fellow actor and one of his neighbors, stepped out of the court onto the sidewalk.

"Good morning, Martin. Lovely day."

He touched the brim of his fedora. "Indeed." She didn't move on, seeming perfectly happy to stand on the sidewalk and fuss with her parasol. A *parasol*, for the love of God. Martin surrendered and got into the car because he couldn't have any kind of conversation with Robbie while someone else was watching.

Robbie trotted around to slide behind the wheel, but he didn't cast a smiling glance over his shoulder as he'd begun to do since that dreadful evening with Wesley. Martin studied the set of Robbie's jaw as he pulled out into traffic, and the ice in his middle reached up to his throat until he wasn't sure he could speak.

Say something. If he's hurting, if I've ruined everything, he needs to know I never meant any harm.

But they were almost to the studio before he finally forced himself to say, "Robbie?"

Robbie jerked, his hands gripping the wheel. "Yes, Martin?"

At least he'd said *Martin* and not *Mr. Brentwood*. They hadn't backslid that far.

"Is anything wrong?"

Robbie's shoulders hitched up another inch. "No. N-nothing."

Martin pinched the bridge of his nose. "Robbie, *nothing*, when said in that tone of voice and with that little conviction, always means *something*. And not just something, but something big. Do you—Do you regret what happened last night? Because if you do—"

"No." He cast a brief, panic-stricken glance over his shoulder before the blare of a horn jerked his attention back to the road. "I wouldn't—That is, last night was the best night of my life."

"Have you changed your mind about a repeat performance?"

Please say no. Please say no.

"No. Never."

Thank God. Martin took a deep breath and finally relaxed against the squabs. "Then could you please tell me what's deprived me of your smile this morning?" Robbie didn't move, so Martin, greatly daring, reached forward and squeezed his shoulder. "Please, Rob?"

Robbie shuddered under Martin's hand, so Martin loosened his grip, but then Robbie clapped his hand over Martin's and held it in place for an instant before he had to let go to turn in at the studio gates. "You can touch me. I'd like that. It makes this a little easier." He choked on a laugh. "Or else harder. I'm not even sure anymore."

"Then why not come out and say it, whatever it is?" Martin's heart was attempting to climb into his throat. "Because you're starting to scare me."

Robbie didn't say anything as he maneuvered the automobile through the lot and parked in his usual spot. Then his hand crept up to cover Martin's again. "You know I'm grateful for everything you've done for me."

Martin drew his brows together. "You don't owe me anything." *It's not your gratitude I want.*

Robbie swallowed, his chin nearly on his chest. "The very first day we met, you thought I was... you know... using this job as a way to get ahead in Hollywood. Do you remember?"

Martin swore at himself silently. "Yes, and I'm sorry for it. If I never apologized then, please accept my profound regrets now."

"No. It was fine. You didn't know me. But—But I don't *ever* want you to think that's all you are to me. That last night was a way to... to *bargain* with you." Robbie's voice had sunk to a near whisper, but he spat out those last words like a curse.

"I know you by now, Rob. You're not that kind of man. I trust you."

"You might not anymore when I tell you.... When I ask you...." Robbie heaved a sigh and released Martin's hand. "The thing is, Martin, you know Dottie's a friend of mine?"

"Yes." Martin drew out the word, uncertain where this conversation was heading. Was Robbie interested in a relationship with Dottie as well?

"She wants me to ask you if... if...."

If she wants to share him, I'm not sure I can handle it. "If what?"

"If you'll take a part in the picture she wrote, even though Boyd Brody is directing and they'll be off on location for months."

After the words tumbled out of Robbie's mouth, he clenched his eyes shut as though he were expecting a blow. But the relief that bubbled up inside Martin made him want to laugh.

"Robbie." He kept his tone gentle and managed to keep the amusement out of his tone. "It's not usually taking advantage of someone if you're giving *them* work instead of asking for it for yourself."

Robbie opened his eyes and peered over his shoulder. "It's not? You're not mad?"

Martin gave Robbie's shoulder another squeeze and then released him. "Not in the least. And you may have given me a vital clue about this meeting. Will you walk up with me and tell me more?"

"Um, sure." Robbie swiped a hand under his eyes. Then he clambered out of the car and raced around to open Martin's door. *Oh, you lovely man. You don't know the meaning of selfishness or guile.*

As they entered the main door, Martin's shoulders were straighter, his chin higher, his smile wider than it had been in months, precisely because of the man at his side. *It doesn't matter if nobody knows what he means to me. I know it.* He nodded at the receptionist as Robbie snatched off his chauffeur's cap and tucked it under his arm.

"Good afternoon, Jenny." Martin removed his own fedora. "I believe someone is expecting me?"

"Yes, Mr. Brentwood. Upstairs. The meeting room next to Mr. Jacob's office." She turned back to her typewriter.

Jacob was involved in this too? Maybe the meeting wasn't about Dottie's scenario after all. "Thank you." Martin led Robbie to the stairs but didn't rush. "Tell me about this scenario," he said as they began to climb. "What's the story?"

"It's a pioneer picture. About the first wagon train to cross the Sierras."

Martin frowned. "This isn't about those poor people who were trapped up by Truckee? The ones who may or may not have—"

"No. The Donners came later. This party actually made it through. All of them. In fact, they ended up with two more than they started with because a couple of the women had babies along the way."

Martin continued to mount the stairs, steadily but slowly. "A pioneer picture. I haven't sat a horse since my first days in Hollywood. I'm not sure I remember how."

Robbie grinned at him, sunny nature reasserting itself as they entered the antechamber of Jacob's office. "You know what they say. You gotta get back on the horse."

Martin shouted with laughter, startling Mrs. Hodge, Jacob's secretary. She glanced between him and Robbie. "You can go right in, Mr. Brentwood. Everyone else is already here."

Martin studied the massive oak door that led to the meeting room, and his mouth dried. This could mean a new direction in his career, or it could mean its end. He needed to remain calm, project the same urbanity that he did in all those drawing-room pictures. Somehow that was easier to do with Robbie next to him.

"Rob, would you please fetch me a glass of mineral water?"

"Of course, Mar—Mr. Brentwood."

Martin smiled at Mrs. Hodge. "You'll let him in when he returns, won't you?"

"Certainly. But they're waiting. If you could…?" Mrs. Hodge made her stately way over to the door and held it open.

Martin gave her his most gracious noblesse-oblige nod and strode over to the door as though he weren't quaking in his shoes.

If he'd known what awaited him inside, he might not have found the courage to enter. The room held not only Jacob, Ira, and Sid, but also Boyd, Evelyn, Dottie, Leo, and Gilbert bloody

Flint. Martin forced himself to smile at everyone. "I'm so sorry to keep you waiting. I was told two o'clock."

Jacob waved his cigar. "Siddown, siddown. We're about to get started."

Martin sat at the end of the table next to Sid and across from Evelyn, a couple of empty chairs on the other side of him. Evelyn smiled serenely and then turned her attention back to Jacob.

"What did I miss?" Martin murmured to Sid.

"Nothing. Just listen and nod."

"I live to serve." His voice was barely audible, but Jacob glared at him anyway.

"Listen, we've gotta put Citadel's best foot forward. A big picture. Something that'll wow the audiences and have 'em lining up twice, three times, four. This Arbuckle shit pile could either bury the whole motion picture industry, or it could be our chance to rise to the top of the heap. Ira?"

Ira cleared his throat. Martin wondered, as he did every time, how the two men could be brothers. Jacob, the bluff, barrel-chested blowhard, and Ira, the brainy, reed-slender aesthete. They had two things in common, though. First, they were both razor-sharp negotiators, although their styles couldn't be more different. Jacob browbeat you into agreeing to his terms. Ira maneuvered so you believed his ideas were your own.

And second? They were both determined to marry Evelyn Trent.

"Miss Dashwood—" Ira nodded at Dottie. "—has given us the best scenario I've seen in years. It has scope, adventure, pathos, action, suspense—and it's based on a true story. This could be the biggest thing since *Way Down East*."

"That's right," Jacob said, his teeth clenched on his cigar. "We'll spare no expense." He glared at Ira. "Within reason."

Robbie slipped in the door, a crystal glass in his hand, his hat still tucked under his other arm. Everybody looked at him, and he blushed and ducked his head. Jacob plowed ahead as Robbie made his way around the table to Martin.

"We'll have the set department make authentic Conestogas."

"If we make them, they won't exactly be authentic, will they?" Martin asked mildly. Sid jabbed Martin with his elbow.

Ira rolled his eyes, and Jacob scowled behind a blue cloud of cigar smoke.

"Listen." Jacob punctuated his words with jabs of the cigar, scattering ash across the gleaming black-lacquer conference table. "If we're dropping half a million bucks on this opus, we're doing the damn thing up right."

Robbie set Martin's water on a marble coaster. "But Conestogas aren't authentic. Not for a trip like this. They were too big and heavy."

The subtle shifting and rustling of papers stopped. Even Jacob's cigar froze like a broken film splice. "And how," Jacob's growl set the room stirring again, "do you know about Conestogas?"

Robbie's eyes widened and he glanced at the faces around the table, all focused on him. He gulped. Martin suppressed the urge to take his hand and patted him on the shoulder instead.

"Tell us about it, Rob."

"Well…." Robbie perched on the edge of the leather chair next to Martin and clutched his hat in his lap. "My ma's people came out on a wagon train. Settled in Oregon. In fact, they were in that same train that Stephens and his group traveled with from Iowa to Idaho."

The reaction of the men at the table was comical, synchronized double-takes that rivaled the Keystone Kops at their best. "You know about this story?" Jacob demanded.

Robbie shrugged. "Not the California part of it. The Oregon pioneers never heard from the Stephens group again, far as I know. But I do know they had to use lighter wagons to get over the mountains. We still use that wagon base on our farm."

Martin coughed into his hand to hide his laugh at the uproar Robbie's casual comment produced.

"You can't be serious," Ira said faintly.

Robbie shrugged diffidently. "Homesteaders, farmers—we have to make do. Repair broken equipment, not replace it. I bet you could advertise and get most of the wagons you need for the picture from people who are still using them."

Jacob turned to Leo. "You heard the man. Do it." He clamped the cigar between his teeth and rubbed the palms of his hands together. "What do you bet we can get the wagons and half our extras for five bucks a day plus meals? That's one chunk off this overblown budget. You." He pointed a stubby finger at Robbie. "You're now the official technical advisor on this picture."

"I am?" Robbie cut a glance at Martin, and his knuckles shone white on his crumpled hat, which might never be the same. "Um, what does that mean, exactly?"

"Means you're on set all the time. You do what Boyd tells you, but you tell him what you know too. And in the meantime...." He nudged his empty mug across the table. "Get me some coffee."

Leaving everyone else in the meeting room to discuss contract details, Robbie tried to keep up with Dottie as she rushed headlong down the stairs.

"Dottie, hold up, will you?"

She tossed a grin over her shoulder. "I've got things to do. We start shooting as soon as those contracts are signed."

"But—"

"You've got things to do too, Mr. Advisor."

"Just wait a second. Please?" He grabbed her elbow and eased her to a stop in the middle of that vast marble staircase. He blew out a breath, feeling like one of the butterflies in Ma's collection, pinned on a white mat with no way to escape. "What exactly *am* I supposed to do? I don't know anything about making a picture."

She smiled at him slyly. "You know more than you did a month ago. And by the time we're on location, you'll know even more. I'll make sure of it. So come on." She tugged at his sleeve, and rather than get knocked down the stairs and break his fool neck, he let himself be towed along as she plunged downward again.

"I can't *believe* you didn't tell me your mother was actually on that journey."

"It wasn't her. It was her people. My great-grandparents. Besides, I told you I knew the story."

"But you didn't tell me *why*. The first-hand experiences...." She threw up her hands. "The mind absolutely boggles."

"But I don't have first-hand experiences."

"You knew about the wagons."

"Sure, but everybody knows that."

She eyed him and raised one brow. "Jacob didn't. Ira didn't. *I* didn't, and I'd read the travelers' journals."

Robbie shrugged. "Guess they thought everybody knew too. You don't mention stuff that's obvious."

"Then it's going to be your job on this picture to tell us the obvious stuff." She clasped her hands behind her back as they walked across the lot. "In fact.... What's life like up on that farm of yours?"

Robbie snorted as he tried to reshape his hat. *What the heck did I do to this thing?* "It's not my farm. It's Pa's. It was supposed to be Eddie's. But now that he's gone, guess Pa'll just have to figure out how to hold on to it after he's dead."

She glanced at him curiously, her hand on the stage door handle. "Why wouldn't he leave it to you?"

"There's the little matter of me not being there."

"A point, I admit. Would he have given it to you if you'd stayed?"

Robbie thought about it as he followed Dottie inside. "Pa has his notions of what it means to be a farmer, what a farm should be like. Crops in straight rows. Animals in their pens." *Sons doing as they're told.* "No time or effort wasted on anything except what increases the yield."

"Is that bad?" She unlocked the cutting room door. "I mean, I'd expect you'd want lots of crops and fatter animals and all that."

"Yes, but all that plainness.... My ma was a schoolteacher before she married Pa. Her family lived in a place that wasn't as hardscrabble as Pa's place. She loved flowers. Used to paint beautiful pictures of them before she moved to the farm. But Pa didn't hold with painting because it didn't serve a purpose. Flowers too. He didn't believe in planting anything you couldn't later eat."

She plopped down in her chair. "Not exactly a barrel of laughs, was he?"

"You have no idea." As awful as that night in Boise had been, at least Robbie was no longer trapped under Pa's thumb on the farm. He stared down at his mangled hat. *I'm not going back. Not ever.* He tossed the hat on the floor, settled across from her, and leaned forward with his elbows propped on his knees. "I planted some morning glories and sweet peas for her once, for a birthday present. They were on the side of the house where the clothesline was, someplace Pa never went."

"Did she like them?"

He nodded, his throat closing up. "She said it was the best present anyone'd ever given her. When Pa—When he found out, he pulled up all the plants and fed them to the pigs."

She reared back, her jaw sagging. "He did *what*?"

Robbie's backside had been sore for a week after that beating. *But he can never do anything to me again. He'd have to find me first.* And Pa would never think of looking in Hollywood, of all unlikely places. "Said at least then they'd be worth something."

"You're kidding?" She held up her hands. "Never mind. I know you don't kid about things like that. But you're here now, right? And you're going to be working on my picture." She bounced a little in her chair. "You'll be right there with me on location, behind the camera with me when—"

"Hold on." Robbie's hands shook a little, so he grabbed his knees. "I'll be going on location? With you? With Mar—With everybody?"

She blinked at him. "Well, sure. Didn't you hear Jacob?"

"I know, but I thought that just meant when we were here." *I'm going with them. I'm going with Martin. We won't be separated.* But would they have any time alone? "What's it like? On location?"

"Depends on the location." She snagged an overstuffed loose-leaf binder from a stack on the table and opened it in her lap. "I've made notes on all the locations we'll need. We'll be filming the big prairie-crossing scenes in Nevada. The scenes of Moses Schallenberger's solitary months near Truckee, close to the site of his actual cabin. We can use Inceville for the Sutter's Fort scenes, since we'll need the Hollywood posse for most of the horseback stunts."

"Hollywood posse?"

She grinned. "All the cowboys who used to work in the Wild West shows or on actual ranches. They show up in any picture where we need a bunch of fellows riding hell-for-leather."

"*Real* cowboys?" Robbie's eyes widened. "Wow."

"You bet. Some of 'em will be coming with us to Nevada to take care of the oxen and horses, so you'll get to know them. But that's for later." She popped up again. "Come on. They're building some interiors for the Iowa leave-taking scenes. Let's go see."

She zipped out the door, catching Robbie by surprise. He retrieved his hat, although it was too misshapen to sit flat on his head anymore, and lurched after her. He nodded apologetic greetings to a couple of carpenters as he ducked under the planks they were carrying between them, and caught up with her at the opposite corner of the stage. The place was a hive of activity—hammering, sawing, shouting—and Robbie wanted to cheer. *We're finally getting back to normal. Everything will be all right now.*

Dottie rocked on her heels, her hands in the pockets of her trousers as she surveyed the work with a proprietary smile. "Jacob and Ira didn't want to waste any time, so the designers and decorators started right away. This place—" She pointed to the tallest of three sets. "—is Stephen Townsend's family home. He was a doctor, so he was well-to-do." She strolled to the next in line. "Elisha Stephens was a mountain man and trapper. A blacksmith too. He always carried his knife on his hip." She glanced up at him. "Gilbert Flint's playing him."

Robbie nodded curtly. He expected Mr. Flint would be involved somehow, since he'd been in the meeting. While he didn't like it much, the flare of panic he'd felt at that first sight had faded, leaving behind a barely simmering anger. *I can ignore him. I know what he is now. He can't hurt me.*

Or could he? If Mr. Flint had known what the purple tie meant, what the slit pockets meant, and that the suit had belonged to Martin, did that mean he could expose them both? The panic started to crest again. If he—

"Rob?"

He glanced down to see Dottie peering up at him, her forehead wrinkled in concern. He forced the panic down. "I'm sorry. You were saying?"

She squinted at him for a moment but then shook her head and turned back to the sets. "Stephens was single, but Dr. Townsend was married, and his wife's younger brother lived with them too. All three of them, plus at least one servant for Mrs. Townsend, went on the trail."

"Well, sure." Robbie was proud that his voice didn't wobble. "If you took a trip like that, you were going for good. You'd want your family with you."

She threw up her hands. "You see? That's another thing that's important. I need to make a note. Maybe we can have a couple of scenes of family left behind." She turned and sped back toward the cutting room.

Chuckling ruefully, Robbie trotted after her. "Slow down, Dottie. You're bouncing around like water on a hot skillet today."

"I can't help it." She clasped her hands under her chin the way she always did when she was trying to hold in her excitement. "It's my scenario. We're making *my* picture, with Boyd and Evelyn and Martin and Evelyn—"

"You said Evelyn twice."

Her cheeks flushed a blotchy red. "I meant… well, never mind what I meant. It's still my dream come true." She wrinkled her nose. "Except for Gilbert Flint and Aurelia Arthur."

Robbie's middle tried to turn over. *Just when I'd managed to calm down.* "Did you ask for Mr. Flint?"

"No." Her tone was laced with disgust. "But I have to admit, he's perfect for Elisha. And we're stuck with Aurelia because she's Citadel's answer to the Marys."

"Marys?"

"Pickford and Miles Minter. The golden-haired sweethearts. But anything less sweet than Aurelia, I have yet to see. And don't get me started on her mother." She rolled her eyes. "You need to keep an eye on them. Elisha Stephens might wear his knife in his belt for everyone to see, but those two'll stab you in the back before you ever see the blade."

"I'll keep it in mind." Robbie peered ruefully at his hat. He'd need another one before he picked up Martin. Luckily he'd brought his spare uniform to the lot after—

He nearly choked on his own spit. *Uniform. Driving. Martin.*

"Holy cow. What about my *real* job? If I'm supposed to stick to Mr. Brody like a cocklebur, how will I drive Martin where he needs to go?"

She chuckled. "Well, I expect Martin will be where you are most of the time anyway. He's got a big part. Dennis Martin was the one who returned to the lake to rescue Moses Schallenberger."

Robbie slapped his cap on his head, only to have it slide over one ear. "I need to talk to Pops."

She saluted him. "Go ahead. But don't be surprised if you get called into a meeting on your own account."

Robbie hurried through the stage. *Jehoshaphat. Meetings?* He'd never been called to a "meeting" in his life. Not on purpose, anyway. He didn't count when Pa ordered him into the barn to tell Robbie exactly how he'd failed and the reasons the coming beating was all Robbie's fault. He wouldn't know how to behave in a meeting that didn't involve a belt against his backside.

He practically sprinted to the booth and skidded to a stop as Pops closed the gate behind a departing automobile.

Pops raised his bushy eyebrows. "What's your hurry, young feller?"

"Pops." Robbie's breath sawed in his lungs from his rush. "There's this thing that's happened."

"Is that right? You found your true love?" Pops cackled as if he'd made a joke, but heat rushed up Robbie's throat. He ducked into the shade of the booth's overhang.

"Mr. Jacob told me I have to be the technical advisor on Dottie's picture."

"Oho. So you're moving up in the world? Don't forget your friends when you're sitting pretty up there."

Robbie snatched off his cockeyed cap. "You know that's not my idea of a good time. I'd be just as happy driving Mar—Mr. Brentwood. But that's the problem. I have to stick by Mr. Brody all the time. Mr. Jacob made it sound like that's my job now." Robbie ran one hand through his sweat-damp hair. "*Is* it my job? I mean, do I have to talk to somebody about it? Sign some more papers? Hand in my—my uniforms?"

"Easy there, son." Pops took his elbow and herded Robbie inside the booth. "Sit yourself down and take a minute to settle."

Robbie nodded. He hunched forward with his hat between his hands and tried to slow his breathing.

"Now," Pops said, "if Mr. Jacob said you've got this job, then you've got this job. Mrs. Hodge might be snooty, but she knows how to get things done. I expect you'll be paid more as a technical advisor than as a driver."

"I don't need more money. What I'm making now is fine."

"Ah, but what you're making now is for a job that gives you a lot of time to sit around on your backside and wait. If you're workin' for Boyd Brody, won't be much sittin' involved. So whatever they pay you, you'll be earning it. Don't you forget that."

Robbie nodded, swallowing convulsively. "I won't, Pops. But what about Mr. Brentwood? He still needs a driver. If I'm not there—"

Pops patted his shoulder. "You just take it easy. I'll find out what the shooting schedule's likely to be. Chances are if Mr. Brentwood is in the picture too, he'll be right there along with you. If not, I'll find somebody else."

But I don't want you to find somebody else. If somebody else was driving Martin, taking him home, picking him up, what chance would they have to be together? Especially if Robbie's time would be taken up with his new job as... as what? Boyd Brody's toady?

"I'll give you a piece of advice, though." Pops's expression turned somber. "A driver's no threat to anybody, so nobody's got it in for them. But as an assistant director?"

"I don't think I'm that. From what Dottie says, they've got way more important jobs."

Pops held up one hand, palm out. "You're on the first rung up that ladder, son. And once you're on the ladder, if there's nobody behind you, raring to knock you off, there'll be someone above you, ready to kick you in the face."

CHAPTER FOURTEEN

Barely a week into shooting on *The California Trail*, Martin knew Wesley Thornhill was in trouble. Wesley was supposed to be playing an eighteen-year-old, but with shadows under his eyes that even heavy film makeup couldn't hide and the way his hands shook, he seemed more like an old man.

The two of them had several scenes together, since Martin's character, the Canadian Dennis Martin, was supposed to be friends with Wesley's Moses Schallenberger. Since Dennis was the one who returned to rescue Moses in the picture's climax, Dottie had crafted some very clever ways to seed the depth of their relationship, and the nature of both men—Dennis's loyalty, Moses's perseverance—but Wesley couldn't get through the scenes without at least one mistake.

It's a damn good thing this isn't a stage play. If he had to remember his lines, he'd have been fired for sure.

"Cut!" Boyd hollered for the umpteenth time. He tossed aside his megaphone and stormed onto the set. "Thornhill, what the devil is the matter with you? You're supposed to be a kid who could survive three months in a snowbound cabin by himself, but you act like someone who couldn't survive the next week in a featherbed."

Wesley raised a shaking hand to his face but stopped short of touching himself lest he smear his heavy makeup. "I'm sorry, Boyd. I'll do better, I promise. Can we go again?"

Boyd scowled and snatched off his flat cap to scrub at his thinning hair. "No, we can't. It's fucking one AM, and we're due at the station tomorrow at eight for the train to Dodge Flats. Go home. Pack. We'll do retakes when we get back after the location shoots. Goodman!"

Robbie rose from his spot behind Boyd's chair. "Yessir?"

He pointed a beefy finger at Robbie. "Make sure the costume department gets the clothes loaded."

"Already done, Mr. Brody. They're in the truck, ready to head to the station."

Boyd grunted. "You got everybody's tickets?"

"Yessir. And the car assignments."

"Right, then. Help Howard load the camera and film and the supplies for developing, and—"

"Boyd?" Martin said mildly. "Shouldn't Robbie have a chance to pack too?"

"What? Oh." He looked Robbie up and down. "Don't look like he's got much to pack. He wears pretty much the same thing every day. For that matter, he's the same size as Wesley. He can borrow a shirt if he must. I need him here."

"It won't take me long to grab my gear, Mr. Brody," Robbie said. "I've got it ready to go. I'll just take Mr. Thornhill and Mr. Brentwood home and be back in a jiffy."

Boyd's jaw worked as though he were chewing over Robbie's words. "Fine. But no more than an hour, you hear?" He strode off, leaving Howard, his long-suffering cameraman, grumbling in his wake.

Martin walked over to Robbie. "Are you all right, Rob? Boyd's been working you like a navvy all week. I'm not sure this is what Jacob had in mind by 'technical advisor.'" In truth, the instant Boyd had found out Robbie was competent, the poor man's fate had been sealed.

And so had Martin's, for that matter. They hadn't had the opportunity for another evening together since shooting started.

"I don't mind." Robbie leaned in to whisper, "Do you *know* how much they're paying me? Two hundred and fifty dollars a *week*."

Martin smiled at him, the urge to stroke Robbie's cheek nearly irresistible. "Don't ask me how much the actors are making, then, nor Boyd himself, or you'll be appalled at how little we do to earn it."

"You earn every penny, Martin, all of you, no matter how much it is. You're putting yourself up there for everyone to see. For everyone to judge. That's a lot. I couldn't do it."

"Robbie, my dear, I don't think there's anything you couldn't do if you put your mind to it."

"Hey, Robbie?" Wesley staggered over, his makeup smeared where he'd tried unsuccessfully to remove it. The traces of cold cream still glistened on his forehead and throat. "Could you take me home now? I need…." He licked his lips and wiped his palms on his trousers, leaving a set of greasy handprints behind. "I've got stuff to do before we leave tomorrow."

"Of course, Mr. Thornhill." Despite having been run off his feet all day, Robbie still sounded as cheerful as he had that morning when he'd picked Martin up after having already been at the studio for two hours. "Are you ready, Mr. Brentwood?"

"By all means."

"If both of you will meet me by the door, I'll bring the car around." Robbie trotted off.

Good God, this job is going to kill him. Martin made a mental note to make sure Robbie was eating and getting at least a bit of sleep. With luck, he'd be able to nap on the train—Boyd was notorious for holing up in the club car and playing nonstop high-stakes poker on train journeys, so Robbie might be able to get a bit of a break.

Of course, they still wouldn't have any time alone together. Martin ground his molars as he practically dragged Wesley across the stage.

"Cut it out, Martin. You're gonna leave a bruise."

Martin stopped and backed Wesley into the corner of a throne room set. "How much are you taking, Wes? How often?"

Wesley's gaze darted to the side as he plucked at the edge of his jacket. "Don't know what you mean."

"You do. Are you still taking something for that injury?"

He pressed his lips together, and Martin could see the denial about to come, but then he nodded. "I can't help it, Marty. The pain—"

"That stuff makes you sleepy, though, and you look like you haven't slept for a month, and you're twitching like a spastic marionette." Martin grabbed both of his arms. "You're still taking the coke too, aren't you? For the love of God, Wes, are you insane?"

"I don't have a choice, remember?" Wesley jerked out of Martin's grip and hugged himself, although it didn't stop his tremors. "That fucking nonperformance clause. Roscoe has one too. Did you know Paramount fired him while he was in jail? If they can do that to one of the biggest names in Hollywood, you think they'll waste a second doing the same to me? I need the stuff to make it through this picture."

"I've got news for you. You could get fired for nonperformance anyway." Martin jabbed his finger back the way they'd come. "Because you've been staggering around on set like a damned somnambulist."

Wesley hunched his shoulders, and his mouth took on a sullen downward curve. "The studio doc says it's okay. He's the one who gave me the prescription."

"I don't care if Hippocrates himself gave it to you. It's not doing you any good. You need to get clear or—"

"Or what, Marty? You gonna turn me in?" Wesley sneered, settling his jacket on his shoulders. "At least my… *medicines* are studio-approved. Think they'd approve of your little... treatments?"

Martin jerked back, Wesley's words like a blow to his chest. He moistened his lips. *He can't know. There's barely anything* to *know.* "If you mean that I'm trying to talk you out of an early drug-addled grave—"

"You know what I mean." He flipped up his jacket collar. "Now I have to go *pack,* and I'm sure you have *things* to do as well. Like maybe after you drop me off?" He gave Martin a cruel, knowing smile and headed toward the exit, his swagger marred by his inability to walk in a straight line.

"Judas priest," Martin muttered as he followed him outside to where Robbie was waiting next to the Flyer, smiling as though nothing could make him happier than holding the door for them.

As Wesley climbed in, Martin stalked around to the other side and waited for Robbie to close Wesley's door and circle the car. When Robbie grabbed the door handle, Martin murmured, "Drop me off first, Rob. I know it's out of your way, but...." He shrugged. "Wesley's being difficult."

Was that hurt that flickered across Robbie's face? Martin couldn't tell in the uncertain light, but Robbie nodded. "Of course. I'll be by to pick you up at seven tomorrow."

"Rob." Martin sighed. "Try to get some rest, all right? I don't want you to collapse from exhaustion."

Robbie grinned, although it didn't seem as bright as usual. "This isn't nearly as bad as harvest time back at the farm. At least I don't have to haul bags of potatoes around."

Martin cocked an eyebrow and nodded toward Wesley. "By the time you drop him off, he might be doing a fair imitation of one, so don't count your chickens just yet."

Robbie chuckled. "We never bothered to count 'em. It was a thankless task." He opened the door for Martin to climb in. "Don't worry. I'll be fine."

But when Robbie showed up, hatless, on Martin's doorstep at six thirty the next morning, he was nowhere close to fine.

"Martin. I—" Robbie's breath had gotten lost somewhere on the wild drive from Wesley's apartment. He was afraid his heart would jump out of his chest right there on Martin's front stoop while he gasped like a landed trout.

"Rob?" Martin stood in the open door, fully dressed, his suitcases lined up in the vestibule behind him. "What's wrong?"

Robbie just shook his head, the nightmare of the last hour stopping his voice somewhere south of his throat. He wanted nothing more than for Martin to *hold* him.

Luckily, Martin seemed to realize that. He took Robbie's arm and drew him inside.

That gentle *tick* of the closing door sparked the explosion, and a sob tore out of him. Martin immediately embraced him and drew Robbie's head against his shoulder. "My dear, what is it? What's happened?"

For a moment Robbie allowed the bottled-up awfulness to escape, but then he realized that he'd get tears and snot all over Martin's nice suit if he kept it up. Pa's words echoed in his mind. *Men don't cry. Toughen up and get over it.* So he took a shuddering breath, ready to step away, but Martin held him closer.

"Let me hold you, Rob. Please. If not for yourself, then for me."

Robbie nodded, his cheek rubbing against the smooth wool of Martin's coat. He probably should fight harder, but he *needed* this. "Thank you."

"Don't thank me. You're doing *me* the favor. Do you know how much I've longed to have you in my arms again?" A chuckle rumbled through Martin's chest. "Although I admit I was imagining rather different circumstances." He kissed the top of Robbie's head. "Not that I'm complaining—I rather like easy access to your lovely hair—but where's your hat?"

Robbie's hand twitched toward his head, but he grasped Martin's lapel instead. "I have no idea."

"Can you tell me what's wrong? I don't want to rush you, but we do have a train to catch."

"Wesley…."

Martin stiffened, his arms tightening around Robbie's ribs. "Did he threaten you? By God, I'll kill him."

"No, no. Nothing like that. But when I got to his place, there was an ambulance. Reporters. Mr. McCorkle. Mr. Jacob."

"The damned fool," Martin muttered. "Was it the drugs?"

"Mr. McCorkle told the reporters it was pneumonia, brought on by worry over his grandfather's health."

Martin shut his eyes and pinched the bridge of his nose. "The same grandfather who died the night of *The Three Musketeers* premiere?"

Robbie drew back and blinked up at Martin. "Oh. I'd forgotten. Maybe the other grandfather?"

"My dear, Wesley may have half a dozen grandfathers—"

Robbie's chuckle caught on a hiccup. "That'd be kind of hard."

"Not if Leo has anything to do with it. In any case, I doubt any one of those legions of grandfathers, should they exist, is ill. Wesley has apparently learned nothing since we rescued him outside the theater that night. He's certainly ignored all *my* warnings about indulging in those highly suspect medications. I suspect they'll take him to one of the discreet sanitariums up in Santa Barbara to recover."

"But—but what about *The California Trail*? He has one of the main parts. The location shooting schedule is so tight because we have to beat the first Nevada snows. Does this mean the picture will get shut down?"

Martin swiped his thumbs under Robbie's eyes, wiping away the tears. "I don't know. That will be up to Ira and Boyd. But let's at least act as if we believe Leo's banana oil, shall we?" He smiled wryly. "If production is canceled, I'm certain Boyd will assign all of the grunt work to you."

Robbie sighed. "You're probably right."

"I know I'm right. The man could get on better without his right leg than he could without you. I think you've literally changed his life." Martin kissed his forehead. "As you've changed mine, but in an entirely different and more pleasurable way."

Taking another deep breath, this one not so shaky, Robbie stepped back. "Then we'd better—"

"One moment." Martin cupped Robbie's face in both hands. "If we're about to head into the wilds of Utah—"

"Nevada, actually. Dodge Flats." Robbie's voice had gone faint and scratchy at the feel of Martin's fingers against his skin.

"It hardly matters. Anything between New York and Los Angeles is the wilds, as far as I'm concerned. And I have to fortify myself in case we're so surrounded by the cast and crew that we never get a moment alone. Or in case Boyd keeps you running at his beck and call twenty-four hours a day."

Martin dipped his head, and his lips met Robbie's in the softest, sweetest kiss. Robbie turned boneless, moaning at the touch, and the kiss turned insistent, from his side as well as Martin's. *Jehoshaphat, this is worth anything.* Lack of sleep. Mr. Brody's incessant demands. Petulant tantrums from Wesley and the other actors. As long as he got moments like this with Martin, he'd pay any price.

At the same time, he was filled with such a huge nameless *want* that he was terrified that these moments would never be enough. He craved *every* moment, even the ones where they weren't actually touching. The conversations in the car about ridiculous things like how annoyed Martin was that he had to let his hair grow for this part. How fastidious he was about his wardrobe, giving his tailor such precise instructions that the man rolled his eyes when he turned away. Not where Martin could see, of course, but Robbie had been there, and Robbie had seen, and then shared a secret smile with Martin because Martin had *known*, even though he hadn't said anything.

But Robbie treasured that shared smile like a gold nugget.

Martin drew back with one final kiss to Robbie's forehead. "Now. Let's get to the station and find out what our fate is to be, shall we?" Robbie nodded and picked up Martin's case. Martin grasped his wrist. "I can carry my own luggage, Rob."

As sweet as that was, Robbie knew it wasn't an option. "I'm still your driver. Folks would think it odd if I'm empty-handed and you're not."

"Nobody can see us here."

"You never know. Someone could be looking out of their window as we leave. Half the other bungalows are occupied by picture people."

Martin sighed and settled his gray fedora on his head. "Sadly, you're right. Am I allowed to carry my Gladstone? I'd like to keep it with me since it holds items I'll need on the train." Robbie nodded. "When did you get so wise, my dear?"

Robbie snorted. He held the door open with one foot while he reached for Martin's other bag. "It's not wisdom. But you can't spend more than ten minutes in this town without figuring out that what's *real* isn't as important as what *looks* real. That's what pictures are all about, aren't they?"

Martin frowned as he passed Robbie and walked down the front steps. *He looks worried.* Well, of course he was worried. So many things were wrong—Wesley's collapse, the morality clause, Mr. Arbuckle's ordeal. His trial was set to start in a couple of weeks, and Robbie knew Martin was sorry he couldn't be there to support his friend.

So when Martin was quiet on the drive to the station, Robbie tried not to take it personally.

"Do you know what track our train is on?" Martin finally said as they drew up to the station.

"Two. If we're still taking it."

"Let's be optimistic, shall we? We'll assume we're taking it until they throw us off."

But when Robbie got out, one of the studio runners rushed over, pushing a luggage trolley. "Good morning, Mr. Goodman, Mr. Brentwood. I'm Julius." Robbie blinked. *Mr. Goodman? Nobody calls me Mr. Goodman.* "Mr. Brody is waiting inside. I'll take the car back to the studio for you. Do you need any help with your bags?"

"N-no. I've got it. Thanks." But Julius helped pile Martin's matching suitcases onto the trolley, as well as Robbie's second-hand carpetbag. Then he climbed into the Flyer and pulled away.

Martin watched him disappear into the morning traffic. "I trust we're proceeding on schedule, otherwise we've just allowed someone to abscond with a studio vehicle."

Robbie chuckled as he pushed the trolley toward the station door. But a uniformed porter approached, touched his hat brim respectfully, and took over. "Which track, sir?"

Robbie gaped at the man, who waited patiently. First being addressed as *Mr.* and now having someone offer to wheel a cart he was perfectly capable of doing himself.... He wasn't entirely sure the world hadn't shifted under his feet.

Martin stepped in and passed the porter a coin. "Two, please. Isn't that right, Rob?"

"Uh...."

But the porter nodded and wheeled the cart away. Martin touched Robbie's elbow. "You needn't look so astounded, Rob. It's his job to take care of passengers' needs, including stowing their bags on the train."

"But how will he know which car to put them in? I'd better go—"

"We won't need most of them." Martin brandished his Gladstone. "Everything I need for one night is in here."

"Jehoshaphat!" Robbie darted after the porter and rescued his carpetbag from the top of the stack. Then he trotted back to

Martin's side. "Pretty much everything I have is in here, for tonight or the rest of the stay."

Martin frowned at the bag. "Rob, we're going to be out in the middle of nowhere for weeks. Surely you'll need more changes of clothes than will fit in there."

Robbie glanced away, hoping Martin couldn't see the heat painting his cheeks in the wan early light. "These are all I've got."

Martin stopped in the station portico as another porter held the door for them. "Why? You're making enough now that—"

"Martin." Robbie glanced at the porter, who was studying them in patient inquiry. "Not here, please?"

Martin shook himself like Pa's retriever after a dip in the pond. "Of course. Sorry. Shall we?"

In truth, Robbie *could* have bought some clothes, and he probably should have. But when he was still a driver, his uniforms had been provided by the studio. As Mr. Brody's assistant, the cheap but durable workman's clothes he'd bought at the five-and-dime were fine—better than fine, since he didn't mind if they got dirty or stained and they stood up to the long hours he'd been putting in.

But the other reason, the *real* reason, was because he didn't want to spend the money. It might disappear at any time. In fact, if production on *The California Trail* got canceled or postponed, it might disappear *today*. And if Robbie had learned one thing on the farm, it was that saving for a rainy day wasn't just prudent, it was *essential*.

Because sure as anything, rainy days were bound to come. Probably sooner rather than later.

As Martin strode toward the cluster of studio folks in the center of the station—both Mr. Schlossbergs, Mr. Brody, Dottie, and Mr. McCorkle—Robbie dropped a step or two behind him. It wouldn't do to seem like he believed he was Martin's equal in the eyes of the most important people on the picture.

"Jacob, Ira," Martin said with a nod at both men, "Dottie, a pleasure." Martin didn't single out Mr. Brody or Leo, but since neither of them were paying attention, they didn't notice. "I trust we're proceeding on schedule despite Wesley's—"

"Visit to his grandfather," Leo said.

"But didn't his grandfather die?" Robbie blurted.

"Of course. His grand*mother*." Leo turned to Mr. Ira. "The press junket'll arrive in two weeks. Can we get Thornhill back on his—back from his *grandmother* by then?"

Mr. Jacob chewed on an unlit cigar. "We'd better. Or he'll be looking for a new—"

"Jacob," Mr. Ira said with a glance at the curious passengers streaming by on the way to the train. "I'm sure things will work out."

Mr. Brody stopped pacing and glared at Mr. Ira. "How am I supposed to shoot without one of the leads? We don't *have* two weeks. If he—"

"Robbie can stand in."

Everybody, Robbie included, turned to stare at Dottie, who looked more than ever like a schoolboy in her round cap and pea coat.

"What?" Mr. Brody barked.

Dottie remained unperturbed. "He's the same height and build as Wesley. Same blond hair, and since all the men have grown their hair out for the picture, they look even more alike. If Robbie were to slick his hair back now, you'd never be able to tell them apart from the back."

"Me?" Robbie squeaked. "B-but—"

"Hmmm." The way Mr. Brody squinted at Robbie, eyeing him up and down, made Robbie want to hide behind the nearest high-backed bench. "He's a little broader through the shoulders than Thornhill, but you're right. Unless they were standing side by side in the same shot, they could be twins. Or brothers at least." He turned to Mr. Jacob. "Get Thornhill out to our location by a week from Saturday or I can't guarantee we'll meet this crazy schedule you've dreamed up."

"We're releasing this picture in April, Boyd." Mr. Jacob chomped on his cigar as though it were breakfast. "Do what you need to do, but don't let the schedule slip. Come on, Ira."

Mr. Ira glanced irritably at his brother's retreating back. "I'd like to say don't worry about it, but Jacob's right. We're banking a lot on this picture, so whatever you need, Boyd? Say the word and it's yours."

"How about a cast that doesn't show up for work high as a kite?" Mr. Brody muttered. He gestured peremptorily at Robbie and Dottie. "You two. With me. We've got a lot to discuss before we get to Dodge Flats."

"Boyd, don't you think you could let Robbie get settled in his berth first?" Martin said.

"What's he need a berth for? We're not gonna be sleeping. We've got too much to do." Mr. Brody strode off toward the tracks.

Dottie shrugged. "He's probably right. Sorry, Rob." But she grinned at him, her spectacles glinting in the overhead lights. "But don't worry. Everything'll work out. In fact—" She hugged the massive script that she hadn't let out of her sight since before shooting started. "—it'll be *brilliant*."

Robbie glanced helplessly between Martin and Dottie. "But I'm not an actor. I don't know the first thing about it."

Martin patted Robbie's shoulder. "It'll only be long shots, Rob. And you'll have business to do."

"Business?"

"Stage business. Boyd may be an annoying SOB, but he's a decent director, and he'll give you things to do in the scene. You'll be so busy you'll forget that the camera's rolling."

"Martin's right. All you have to do is pay attention to what's happening in the scene. If you're supposed to be talking to someone, look at them the way you look at me or Martin. That's all acting is really. Just paying attention."

Alarm shot up Robbie's spine. "Talking? I'm not going to talk to anybody. Nothing but long shots, right?"

Dottie's gaze turned steely. "D.W. Griffith may not care about matching his close-ups to his long shots, but this is *my* picture. We're shooting the close-ups too, even if we have to redo them with Wesley later, because it'll be easier to cut the picture."

"'If' we redo them? Dottie—"

"Don't worry, Rob. You'll be fine."

From down the platform, a conductor shouted, "All aboard!"

"Let's go." Dottie tugged on Robbie's arm. "We don't want to miss the train."

Robbie gazed helplessly over his shoulder at Martin as Dottie towed him down the platform to the car where Mr. Brody was leaning out the door, irritably beckoning to them.

Martin lifted his hand in farewell and strolled toward the club car. "I'll see you in Nevada, Rob. Try to convince Boyd to let you sleep for at least a few hours."

"Sleep," Dottie muttered. "Who needs it?"

With a sinking feeling in his belly, Robbie jogged to keep up with her. Sleep was the least of his worries. He'd be up on the screen, twenty feet tall, for anybody in America to see. If Martin was right—and he always seemed to be right—appearing in a picture had given away Mr. Taylor's whereabouts to the family he abandoned. *What if somebody recognizes me? What if Pa finds me?*

He comforted himself—a little—with the notion that only his back would be on display. Nobody—except maybe Frank—would be able to recognize him from the rear, not even Pa, despite Robbie's backside's familiarity with Pa's belt.

He held on to that thought as he climbed aboard the train in Dottie's wake. Because otherwise he might never sleep again.

CHAPTER FIFTEEN

"What the devil is *that*?" Martin stood, arms akimbo, the bitter wind whipping his coattails as he stared at the monstrosity in front of him.

"That," Evelyn said, holding her hat on with one hand, "is our princely accommodation for the next month or so."

"It's a circus train, Evie." The faded paint on the box car featured a lion snarling at an elephant. "A goddamned *circus* train."

"Yes, darling, but I have it on good authority that we won't have to share our rooms with the animals."

"Is it even heated? It's bloody freezing out here." And it was barely November. What would it be like at the beginning of December, when they finally returned to Hollywood?

"At this point, all I care about is getting out of this wind. So shall we? I believe my car used to belong to the bearded lady. So perhaps it will at least have a decent mirror."

"A circus train," Martin muttered as he followed her toward where Robbie stood, attempting to keep the papers on his clipboard from being ripped away by the wind. "I had no expectations of an actual hotel, but I cherished hopes for at least a hut or two."

Robbie handed Evelyn into a car where other members of the cast were visible through the grimy windows. Then he turned to Martin. "Hello. I hope your trip was pleasant."

Martin snorted. "Pleasant enough. But is the studio mad? A *circus* train?"

Robbie's tentative smile faded. "I know it's a little, um, rough, but it's not so bad really. It's got room for the entire company, and it's mobile, so we can move it from one location to the next without making everybody pack up."

"Yes, but a *circus* train." Martin glared at the lion's faded snarl. "Let me guess. This is one of Jacob's cost-saving measures."

"Well, it was definitely cheaper than building a hotel out here in the middle of nowhere."

Martin started at Robbie's uncharacteristically tart tone. When he put aside his own travel weariness and really *looked* at Robbie, the signs of fatigue were hard to miss. "Rob. I'm sorry. I know this isn't your fault."

Robbie ran a hand over his face. "No. I'm sorry. I shouldn't have snapped. But I've been getting the same song, different verse from everybody. In fact, Mrs. Arthur is demanding that she and Aurelia be driven to the nearest town and put up at a hotel immediately, then picked up again each day for shooting."

Although those demands didn't sound totally unreasonable, Martin objected to anyone ordering Robbie about. "How far is the nearest town?"

"One with a hotel? About thirty miles. But that'll change as we move on to the prairie-crossing scenes."

"So in other words, it would waste everybody's time."

"Well...." He shrugged. "Mine mostly."

"Rob. You don't have the time to waste. You're not a driver anymore. You're not even a director's assistant. You're an actor."

Robbie groaned. "Don't remind me." But his smile flickered to life again. Martin chose to believe it was for his benefit alone.

"The rest of the company's inside. Mr. Brody wants to address everyone first. Then I'll show you to your car."

Martin grasped the handle next to the door. "Very well." He paused, one foot on the step, and looked down at Robbie. "Promise me Gilbert's been assigned the gorilla's car?"

Robbie cracked a laugh. "Nobody's living in the animal cars. We're using those for costume and prop storage."

"Wonderful. We'll all end up with fleas." But he climbed aboard with a reasonable facsimile of his usual aplomb, Robbie's presence behind him reconciling him to the sight of Gilbert, lounging in a threadbare armchair, his legs stretched halfway across the car. And Mrs. Arthur, her back poker-stiff as she sat next to her blue-eyed, blonde-ringleted daughter, both of them swaddled in furs. *Now* those *will collect fleas.*

The thought cheered him considerably.

Boyd rose from his seat at the head of the car, megaphone in hand. "Martin. Nice of you to join us."

Martin didn't rise to the bait. "My pleasure." Evelyn cast him a sly, sideways smile as he joined her on a love seat that had seen better days.

Boyd lifted his megaphone halfway before annoyance flickered across his face. He must have realized he didn't need it here, despite how the wind rattled the ill-fitting windows and whistled around the car like a teakettle. Boyd thrust the useless thing out, and Robbie hurried forward to take it.

"Okay, people. Here's the scoop. You'll have the rest of today to get settled into your quarters while Howard and I scout the area for the best angles." He pointed through the window at a distant cluster of buildings. "We're using that little burg over there for the Iowa leave-taking scenes."

Mrs. Arthur rapped the end of her umbrella on the floor. "If there's a town that close, I fail to understand why we can't simply remove to a hotel there."

Boyd's grimace *almost* passed for a smile. "Because the town hasn't got a hotel. It's barely got a street. The sets our crew threw up last week only have three walls and they're swankier than those houses. Trust me, this train is a step up."

"Nevertheless—"

"Mother." Aurelia's soft voice held a steely edge. "I'm sure we'll be fine." She favored the group with a sweet, wistful smile, one she probably practiced in the mirror for several hours a day, and lingered an extra moment on Martin.

"Uh-oh," Evelyn murmured. "Watch out, darling. That one has claws."

"I'm aware." He tucked her hand in his elbow, which dimmed Aurelia's smile a bit. "I'm sure this train will provide admirable accommodations." He kept his voice bland. "After all, if it's good enough for—" Martin nodded at a faded poster featuring a lion that he fervently hoped was not to scale. "—Leo the Magnificent, Scourge of the Savannah, then it's good enough for us."

Dottie choked on a laugh, but Boyd's trademark glower never wavered. "Tomorrow we're shooting the leave-taking scenes, one family at a time, while we set up the wagons for the group scenes. Rob has the schedule." He scowled out the window. "If this damn wind doesn't die down, we may have to change things, but that's the plan for now. So everybody, get settled. Dinner's in the dining car, but it's small, so you'll eat in shifts, by department. Rob has that schedule too."

Gilbert waved a hand. "You got a schedule for when we take a shit too, Rob?"

"Well, I never," Mrs. Arthur said.

"Simmer down, Flint," Boyd said. "Everybody break. Rob, Howard, you're with me."

"You'll have to do without Robbie, Boyd." Nettie Warren, their costumer, stood, a steely glint in her eye. "I need him right now if you expect me to alter all of Wesley's costumes for him."

Boyd scowled at her. "Haven't you done that yet?"

"When? You kept him holed up with you in the club car the whole trip out to this godforsaken place, although I suppose I should be thankful you bothered to tell me about recasting the role."

Robbie glanced from Nettie to Boyd. "I'm just the stand-in until Wesley's back with us."

"We still have to match the costumes in all the shots. Right, Dottie?"

Dottie nodded decisively. "Absolutely. It'll be impossible to cut otherwise." She stood up, her script book in her arms. "I'll go with you, Boyd. I'll need to make notes about the shots anyway."

Boyd scowled but finally nodded and strode out of the car, Howard and Dottie at his heels.

Nettie cornered Robbie at the other end of the car. "Let's go. We've got a lot to do."

Robbie brandished a clipboard. "But I need to hand out the car assignments. The dining schedule."

Martin stood up. "I can do that, Rob. You go with Nettie. After all, it wouldn't be appropriate for Moses Schallenberger to be naked, even in a long shot."

Robbie dropped his gaze as a blush suffused his cheeks. Good God, but Martin ached to touch him. He settled for taking the clipboard and a box of carefully labeled keys and then retreating to his seat next to Evelyn as Nettie towed Robbie out of the car.

Martin glanced down at the list. "Well, Evie, my dear, it looks as if you'll be sharing your car with Wilma Dean."

Evelyn shuddered and glanced at where Wilma was flirting with Gilbert. "I don't think so. Let me see that list." She held out an imperious hand, and rather than fight her on it, Martin handed it over. "Hmmm. A little judicious rearrangement is called for. Do you have a pencil?"

"Do I look like someone who would have a pencil?"

"Then give me your fountain pen. I know you've got one of those. In fact, you've got three."

"I left two of them at home," Martin grumbled, but he retrieved the pen from his inside pocket.

She bent over the list and slashed lines across names right and left, making changes with her elegant penmanship. "Wilma can share with Nettie. I'll room with Dottie."

"Are you sure? Dottie's bound to be up until all hours. Hardly a way to get your rest, my dear."

Evelyn cast him a sidelong glance. "I'll make sure she takes a break or two."

Martin's grin dawned. "Oho. Like that, is it?"

"If I play my cards right. And I always do." She tapped one perfectly shaped nail on the paper. "There. You can thank me later."

Martin peered at the list. Whereas he'd originally been slated to share with Cyril Mathison, who was playing Stephen Townsend, Evelyn had put him with Robbie instead. "Evie...."

"Martin." She mocked his inflection. "Although a great many people in Hollywood are fools, I'm not one of them. But take care. Even a fool can occasionally be clever if their ambition or malice is strong enough to overcome their cowardice." She stood up and shook out her skirts. "It's far easier for people to accept rooming arrangements like this after they've happened once. Suddenly, it will seem normal to them. It's called precedent, darling. Lawyers are very fond of it."

"And you're very fond of lawyers?"

"On the contrary. I avoid them whenever possible. But it's always wise to know your enemy."

Robbie tugged at the neckerchief that Nettie had tied way too tight. "I don't know what I'm supposed to do, Dottie. I can't act."

"Then don't. Sheesh, the last thing we need is somebody else emoting all over the place." She glared at Aurelia, who was busy having a very unbecoming tantrum because she considered her costume to be too plain. "That's not what this picture is about."

"What *is* it about?" Ever since his unexpected and unwanted rise from crew to cast, Robbie hadn't had an instant to read the scenario. On the train from Hollywood, Mr. Brody had monopolized every minute with details about the shoot and lists of things—every one of them top priority—that Robbie was expected to do once they reached Dodge Flats. And since the meeting yesterday, he'd had to delegate everything to Alfie, the assistant director, because Nettie hauled him off to the makeshift costume shop and storage, formerly the home of Lydia the Incomparable and her Deadly Vipers, who looked a lot like boa constrictors in the poster.

He'd stood there, wasting time for what seemed like hours while Nettie pinned things around him, muttering about his shoulders being too wide or his waist too narrow, and barked at him to stop fidgeting.

"It's about a real journey, Rob," Dottie said, eyes sparkling. "Real people. Real triumph. The audience should feel like they're making the trip with folks who could be their neighbors, their friends, their family. It should feel…." She made a circular motion with her hand.

"Real?" Robbie suggested.

"Exactly. Like when the audience in *The Great Train Robbery* all dove out of their seats when the train barreled down the track toward the camera."

"So what should I do?" Robbie wished he could talk to Martin, ask his advice, but even though they were sharing the car that belonged to Boris the Mighty, the circus strongman, they hadn't both been in it at the same time yet. Besides, it wasn't as though they'd have any privacy anyway. Otis Browning, who was playing Mr. Murphy, was bunking with them because his assigned car had a hole in the floor the size of an automobile tire.

Dottie pointed to the scene in front of them. The camera was set up to face the set's false front, rather than the rear with its open-sided interior. A couple of the cowboys were hitching a team of oxen to a wagon that could be a double for the one back on the farm, the one that had carried Ma's dowry and hope chest to Idaho from Oregon after she married Pa. "You're supposed to be helping your brother-in-law load the wagon. You know how to load a wagon, right?"

"Sure." In fact, he'd had to give some of the other actors pointers on how to do it. *Jehoshaphat, you'd think none of them had ever seen a wagon before.* But Robbie tried to be charitable. They were all from Hollywood. Chances were they never *had* seen one outside a film set.

"Then load the wagon, just as if it was *you* about to take that trip across the prairie to a place that seems almost imaginary. You're leaving everything you've known, but your sister and brother-in-law are heading west. They're all the family you've got, so you're willing to take the leap. You're eighteen, so the adventure is probably exciting to you, but you're a responsible kid, so you'll do your chores with a good heart."

Robbie nodded. *I wonder if Ma thought moving to Idaho would be an adventure.* He'd never been sure why she agreed to marry Pa in the first place. "I can do that."

"Then Martin, as Dennis, will come around the corner of the house and talk to you. You're friends, so you should be glad to see him."

That won't take any acting. "What do I say to him?"

"It doesn't matter, as long as you don't recite the 'Song of Hiawatha.' Nobody can hear what you say, but it'll be obvious if you talk more than the title cards."

"What will the title card say?"

"We're establishing the relationships of everyone in the party, so it'll say something like 'Dennis Martin, Moses's Canadian friend.' Boyd'll probably shoot that a couple of times from the top of that hill. Then we'll move in and shoot from across the road. We'll finish up with some close-ups."

Robbie shifted uneasily and tugged on the neckerchief again. "I don't know why you need to do close-ups of me. Wesley will be back soon."

"I told you. I need the footage here, where the light and the background are the same, so I can cut the picture." Her jaw tightened. "The splices are going to match *perfectly*. I've got my standards."

"But—"

"You'll be fine, Rob. Now I've got to head up the hill. Just do what Boyd told you."

Despite the chilly wind that had dropped but not dissipated, sweat prickled on Robbie's forehead. "Um, what was that again?"

"Don't worry. You'll be doing the same thing so many times that you'll be able to do it in your sleep." She grinned. "Assuming you ever get any."

She strode off, leaving Robbie to wander the set where everyone but him seemed to know what they were doing, even the locals who'd been hired on as extras to fill out the crowd.

A cluster of the cowboys—the real ones who'd come with them from Hollywood to handle the horses and livestock and to play the men in the party who didn't have named parts in the scenario—stood laughing at the corner of the blacksmith shop set. Robbie envied them their ease. *They look like they could be part of the town, part of a real wagon train.*

Robbie still felt like an impostor.

Then one of the cowboys turned, and it wasn't a cowboy at all—it was Martin, in his costume as Dennis. Martin's pioneer getup wasn't that different from the clothes folks wore back home, barring a more old-fashioned coat and heavy, square-toed boots. Robbie's breath caught in his throat because Martin was so beautiful.

He slapped one of the cowboys on the back and said something that made them all laugh, and then walked toward Robbie, his stride different from the way he moved in Hollywood—looser, freer, yet determined. *Like a man about to head out on a wagon train.*

Martin grinned, his hair waving over his forehead under his flat-brimmed hat. "Rob. You look just like a pioneer."

Robbie tugged on his neckerchief again. "I don't feel like one." He glanced around. "Pretty soon everyone'll figure out I'm not real."

"Real?" Martin threw back his head and laughed, and even that was different from how he behaved in Hollywood. "Look around, Rob. That blacksmith shop has an anvil made of gypsum plaster. The Stephens house only has three walls. The flour sacks are full of sand. The only real things around here are the horses and oxen." He touched his hat brim. "And the wagons, of course."

"The cowboys are real."

Martin's smile turned crooked. "They were once. Not anymore. Pictures make it possible for them to pretend their way of life isn't gone, but it is. The world is changing, Rob."

"But is it changing for the better?"

Martin's brows drew together, and his gaze returned to the group of cowboys. Then it drifted to the scatter of *real* townspeople who were staring openmouthed at the film crew. "I like to think it is." He met Robbie's eyes, and his smile was intimate. "For both our sakes."

Robbie swallowed around a lump in his throat. "I hope so too."

"Good." He slapped Robbie's back, but let his hand rest on Robbie's shoulder blade a few seconds longer than he had with the cowboy. "Remember what we'll be doing?"

Robbie could swear the dang neckerchief was about to strangle him. "Jehoshaphat, Martin, I can't remember which end of me I should put my hat on, let alone what to do when Mr. Brody yells action."

"You're nervous?"

"What do you think?"

"The best thing to combat nerves is to have something to do to take your mind off it." Martin glanced around until his gaze lit on the wagon that "belonged" to the Stephens family. "Come on." He strode over to it, and Robbie hurried to catch up. "What are you supposed to do in this take?"

Robbie pointed to a couple of burlap sacks. "Load those into the wagon and then stand here until you come over. But I don't know what to do with my hands."

"Hmmm." Martin glanced around until he spotted Ned Philpott, their properties master. "Hey, Ned. Got a minute?"

Ned ambled over. He never seemed to move at more than half speed. "What's up, Marty?"

"Seems like the Stephens family should have more than a couple of bags of whatever this is supposed to be when they uproot themselves and move across the country." Martin glanced at Robbie. "What did your mother's family bring with them, Rob?"

"Well, food supplies, of course. Things they wouldn't be able to hunt. Stuff to repair the wagon if it broke. Trunks with their personal belongings. Dottie says Dr. Stephens brought along a lot of books."

"Can you get us a small keg or two, Ned? A couple more of those fake flour sacks? Maybe a nice trunk that looks like it could hold beloved objects?"

"Sure, Marty. I've got just the thing." He strolled off.

Martin shook his head. "I'm never entirely sure how he gets anything done. He must move faster when nobody's looking." He turned back to Robbie. "Now here's what we're going to do. You'll heave those two bags into the wagon. That's not a problem, right?"

Robbie snorted. "Hardly. They may say *potatoes*, but they're full of hay."

"Well, you should at least pretend that they're heavier than they are. We can load them with rocks if you think that would help."

"No, thanks."

Martin grinned. "That's what I thought. Then after you do that, try to lift the trunk—but imagine it's full of books. Lift one end and let it drop like it's heavy. Can you do that?"

"Sure."

"Good. Then I'll come around the end of the wagon and ask if you need some help."

"Won't that be a problem?"

"For whom? Pictures don't have sound. We can say whatever helps us with the scene, and it might as well be something that makes sense. So I'll ask if you need help. You nod and say yes. Then we'll lift the trunk into the wagon together. Afterward, you jump up into the wagon bed, and I'll hand you the other things."

"What other things?"

"Whatever Ned finds us. You know how to load a wagon, so you can tell me what you want, and I'll hand it to you."

Robbie blinked. "Is that all there is to it?"

Martin laughed. "That's all, at least for this scene. Simple, right? By the time Dottie's finished with it, most of it will probably be on the cutting room floor, but as long as we do the same thing every time the camera's pointing at us, whether it's on that rise—" Martin pointed to the hill. "—or right next to us, we'll be doing our job. So how about it? Ready to load a wagon with me?"

Robbie smiled and ducked his head. "I'd do anything with you," he murmured. *Preferably when nobody else is watching.*

CHAPTER SIXTEEN

Otis's snoring woke Martin at dawn. He groaned and pulled his scratchy blanket over his head. He'd never get back to sleep with that racket, but if he got up, it meant braving the frigid air. *Whose idea was it to film in Nevada at the asscrack of winter?* Living in Hollywood gave people an unrealistic idea of real weather.

He heard a soft click, and then the aroma of coffee wafted under his blanket tent. He drew the covers back and met Robbie's apologetic gaze.

"I'm sorry," he murmured. "I didn't mean to wake you."

"You didn't. Otis took care of that quite nicely. Is that coffee for me?"

"Yes, if you want it."

"Don't ask silly questions." Martin sat up, wrapping the blanket around himself. He was sleeping in two shirts plus a heavy sweater and two pairs of pajama pants, but these damn circus cars weren't heated or insulated. He took the mug from Robbie and wrapped his hands around the almost-too-hot ceramic. "You are an angel." He patted the bed next to him—if you could call the berth a bed. Boris the Mighty must have had the hide of an elephant and a back of steel. "Sit. If you've got a minute."

Robbie cut a glance at Otis, who muttered in his sleep, smacked his lips a couple of times, and then recommenced his stentorian snoring. "Won't it be... you know?"

"Nothing this side of Armageddon will wake Otis before his call time. I've worked with him before." Robbie perched on the edge of the berth, obviously poised to leap up again at the least hint of danger, but he didn't flinch when Martin patted his knee. "How are you doing, Rob? Boyd isn't running you too ragged, is he?"

Robbie shrugged. "It's not so bad. Dottie's taking up a lot of the slack, and he's starting to depend on her for answers to all his questions, which suits her just fine."

"He has little choice when you're in the scene and not available to bow to his merest whim."

Robbie smiled wryly. "I'm not sure that wouldn't be easier."

"Here now." Martin set his cup on the floor and swiveled to take Robbie's hands. "You're doing a wonderful job."

"I'm not doing anything but what Mr. Brody tells me."

Martin chuckled. "In pictures, my dear, that counts as doing a wonderful job. Directors may *say* they want to work with those high-profile, temperamental stars, but give them an actor who will do their best to actually *take* direction? They'll do everything in their power to make that actor look good."

"It's easier when I'm doing scenes with you. Then, it's you and me talking. Normal-like. With Miss Trent too." He chuckled low. "It's as though she's really my sister. She scolds me if I'm not wearing a scarf. Orders me to eat extra potatoes at dinner. Reminds me to get to bed on time. Eddie used to do the same thing. So when we're in front of the camera, it's... comfortable. Familiar."

"You work well with the others too. The actual townsfolk we've corralled into being ersatz townsfolk for the benefit of the picture hang on your every word when you explain what Boyd wants them to do."

"That's because I really *am* one of them. They don't understand picture people. They think you're all some kind of mythical creatures. One of them asked me whether you all had to use the outhouse just like *real* people."

Martin snorted. "I hope a trip past the latrines answered that question for them."

Robbie grabbed Martin's wrist. "You aren't drinking from that creek behind the tracks, are you? You're only taking boiled water from the dining car, right?"

"Don't worry, my dear. I have no more desire for dysentery than any other halfway intelligent man."

Robbie slumped in relief. "Thank goodness. The fellow who runs the town general store said that they lost three children and two adults last summer."

Martin scrubbed his hands over his face, over the beginnings of the beard that would keep getting bushier over the next months, since Boyd had forbidden them from shaving. "Good God. We forget sometimes that while we're playing at hardship and suffering, others are actually living it."

Robbie shrugged. "People like this—farmers, homesteaders, pioneers—they're a pragmatic bunch. Sometimes their lives are bleak, but I'm starting to think that's why they *need* pictures, just like Ma always said people need books. Stories to remind them that there are other ways to think and do and be. Otherwise they'll get so buried in their ideas that you couldn't chisel 'em loose with a pickax. My pa was like that. But he must not have always been that way, or why would Ma have married him?"

"Maybe she was trying to escape from something that was worse? A life that made what he was offering—drawbacks and all—better than what she already had."

"Maybe." He sighed. "I hope she was happy once. Everyone deserves that, don't they?"

"In my opinion everyone deserves more than a single shot at happiness." Martin retrieved his mug from the floor. "Well, everyone except Flint. He deserves to be consigned to the lowest circle of hell and as soon as possible."

Robbie's smile held a hint of slyness. "Oh, I don't know. I'll always be grateful to him for loaning me that suit."

The cup wobbled in Martin's grip. "Good God, Robbie. Don't say things like that when I'm holding coffee hot enough to scald my bollocks off."

His brows pinched together. "Sorry. I—"

"Shhh." Martin set the cup back on the floor with exaggerated care. "Observe me removing the immediate danger." He glanced at Otis, but the older actor was still impersonating a buzz saw. Then he cupped Robbie's jaw and leaned in for the briefest—and sweetest—of kisses.

Robbie jerked but didn't pull away. Instead he placed his hand, so warm and real, on Martin's chest.

Martin didn't let the kiss go on—for one thing, they weren't alone, and he wouldn't risk Robbie that way. For another, he didn't want to torture either one of them when they couldn't hope for more, not for at least another two weeks, when the company was scheduled to return to Hollywood before the next location shoot. But he indulged himself by resting his forehead against Robbie's for one precious moment, breathing in his familiar, seductive scent overlaid by campfire smoke.

What would it be like if they had more than these moments? If their lives consisted of nothing *but* these moments?

"I know we can't be together in public," Martin murmured. "Not yet. But when we get home, I want to talk to you about—"

A clatter of heavy footsteps outside made Robbie leap up an instant before the door burst open and crashed against the wall. Martin clutched the blanket around himself, heart hammering, as Robbie retreated to the corner.

Otis muttered under his breath and turned over.

Wesley stepped into the car and struck a pose like he was waiting for a photographer's flash, arms spread and hat at a rakish angle. "I'm here!"

"Good God, Wesley, it's practically midnight." Martin could barely hear with his heart pounding in his ears.

"Nonsense. The sun's been up for... well, for minutes. Rise and shine." He turned to Robbie. "My luggage is outside." Then he surveyed the car with its faded paint, messy berths stacked against the walls, and ill-fitting windows that were only clean because Robbie had washed them. "Christ. They can't really expect me to stay *here*, can they?" He glanced at Robbie. "Well?"

Robbie blinked and then started for the door, but Martin stood up and blocked his path. "You're not a driver anymore, Rob. Remember?" He stared Wesley down with as much dignity as he could summon, considering he probably looked like he'd spent the night in a flophouse. "Why are you here, Wes?"

Wesley's gaze darted to the side, and Martin noticed his hands twitching before he shoved them into his overcoat pockets. "I'm the star of this picture. Where else would I be?"

Why the hell did they release him? He's obviously still doped to the gills. "This is an ensemble piece, Wes. There are no stars."

Wesley edged farther into the car, his gaze never landing anywhere for more than a second or two. "I'm the biggest name in the cast." A tic danced in his cheek. "No offense, Marty."

Martin sighed. "Wes, I'll ask again. Why are you here? You clearly should still be in the sanitar—"

"Visiting my *grandmother*, you mean?" Wesley sneered. "Funny thing, that. She got better."

"From your grandfather's death?"

Wesley blinked. "Oh. Er, yes. Recovered from her grief and all that. I took the first train out here. Can't hold up production, after all. The fan mags are already full of stories about this picture. A wholesome tale of pioneer survival and perseverance, they say. A story to remind us of Hollywood greatness and the indomitable human spirit." He snorted. "Had to prove I'm just as indomitable as the rest, eh?" He spun and scowled at Robbie. "Now *will* you bring in my luggage, for God's sake?" He strolled over and levered himself up onto Robbie's neatly made upper berth. "It's so hard to find competent help these days."

Despite Martin's tart reminder to Wesley that Robbie wasn't a driver anymore, Robbie didn't see any point in rocking a clearly sinking boat. So he brought in Wesley's bags—all five of them—and quietly removed his own from the corner.

Then he went back to the cowboys' campfire to bum another cup of coffee. The cowboys refused to eat in the dining car. The grizzled old fellow they called Lefty did all their cooking for them, and Robbie had to admit that the man's biscuits were lighter than any he'd ever tasted outside his Ma's kitchen.

Luckily for Robbie, the cowboys had taken a shine to him when he showed that he knew how to care for animals, because now that he'd been displaced in the already overcrowded train and unless he wanted to bunk down in a boxcar, he'd have to beg a place in one of their tents.

Mug in hand, he trudged down the length of the train until he got to the boxcar that Dottie and Howard had fitted up for developing the exposed film. Robbie had spent most of one day helping them tack tarpaper over the walls and make the place light-proof. Apparently they weren't processing any film yet this morning, because the big sliding door was ajar, and Dottie was sitting on the edge of the car, swinging her feet like a kid. From the circles under her eyes, he suspected she'd been up all night, but she grinned at him as though she were having the time of her life.

He held up the cup. "Need some courage?"

She held out her hands in their fingerless gloves. "Gimme!" He passed it over, and she wrapped her hands around it, inhaling the steam that curled around her face. "Mmmm. You didn't get this from the dining car. This is Lefty's coffee."

"How'd you guess?"

She peered up at him through the steam. "The posse always brings him along. He was a trail cook before his old boss passed away and his daughter sold the ranch. Now?" She shrugged. "The way he sees it, he's still cooking for the cowhands. The trail's just a little different."

Robbie nodded, shading his eyes against the sunrise with one hand so he could see the cowboys' camp, neat tents pitched upwind and a safe distance from the latrines. "I wonder if they miss the days when the only thing they had to worry about was a stampede."

She snorted. "Of course they miss it. But this life isn't half-bad for them. They still work with the horses they love. There are enough Westerns still being shot that need their skills, and even the Biblicals hire 'em because a lot of 'em have translated their team-driving skills to handling chariots." She slurped her coffee. "Everyone likes to be needed."

"Yeah. I guess that's true."

She glanced up at him sharply. "What's the matter, Rob?"

"Matter?" He returned his gaze to the sunrise so he could squint and blame any stupid stray tears on the light. "Nothing."

"Don't give me that bull. Something's put you off." She set her mug down and jumped to the ground. "You're as easy to read as a book. That's why you're such a dream on camera."

It was Robbie's turn to snort. "I was only a stand-in. But that's over now."

Behind her spectacles, her gray eyes widened. "Holy simoleon. Wesley showed up?"

"Yes. A few minutes ago. He—" Robbie stared at Dottie's getup. "What the heck are you wearing?"

She glanced down at herself. "Soldier's uniform pants. They're wool and warm, even if they're not exactly stylish. I cut armholes under the waistband." She grinned up at him. "Don't tell Nettie. She'll have a fit."

"There are soldiers in this picture?"

She waved a hand at the plains spread out in front of them and the mountains rising in the distance. "Not in these scenes. But when we get to the ones with Sutter and how he coerced the men into joining the Micheltorena War before they went back to resupply the women and children, we need an easy way to differentiate the pioneers from the soldiers. I don't know if Sutter's troops wore uniforms, but I doubt anybody else does either." She jabbed him in the chest. "But you're avoiding the question."

"Er, what was that again?"

"How do you feel about Wesley barging in to steal your part?"

Robbie sighed and set his carpetbag down at his feet. "It's his part, Dottie. It always was."

She narrowed her eyes. "No. It wasn't. From the first minute he stepped in front of the camera, I knew he wasn't right for this role. He might have been, a couple of years ago, before he started to get so... so *Hollywood*. But he doesn't belong in this picture. He belongs in one about the dangers of drugs and alcohol."

"*Dottie.*" Robbie glanced around wildly. "You can't say things like that. What if somebody heard you?"

"They don't have to hear me. All they have to do is look at the rushes. Wesley's all wrong for Moses Schallenberger. But you?" She jabbed him again, and he pushed her finger away before she could tell how fast his heart was beating. "You're perfect."

"Stop it. I never wanted to be an actor. I still don't."

"Then why the long face?" She glanced down at the bag at his feet. "Oh. He moved into your car, didn't he?"

Robbie nodded. "Now I have to find another place to bunk. The only car with any room is Mr. Flint's, and I'm not—" He swallowed. "That's not an option."

She scowled. "You're darn right it's not."

"If the cowboys don't have a spare tent, I might try to bunk in with one of the townspeople in exchange for chopping wood for them or something."

"Rob." Dottie shoved him backward until he hit the edge of the car. "You are not expendable here. No matter what you think, *I've* seen the rushes. I've seen your work. And I'm telling you, you've got more right to be here than Wesley does."

Robbie managed a weak smile. It was nice of Dottie to say things like that, but even if they were true—and Robbie knew for a fact he hadn't been acting—he was still just the hick from Idaho who did whatever the people in power told him to do. And no matter what Dottie thought, no matter how much she was able to steer this particular picture, Robbie had no illusions that her influence would extend beyond it. Since Dottie knew a lot more about the inner workings of Hollywood than he did, she probably had no illusions either.

Any hopes she had for a different career after *The California Trail* depended on how well it did at the box office, and since Dottie was his friend, he owed it to her to make sure the picture was as successful as possible. *Which means making sure the* real *actors can do their jobs.*

It also meant rousing Mr. Brody and getting instructions for the day, so he'd better get to it.

"I gotta get going. Is it okay if I leave my bag here with you?"

"Sure. But Rob—"

"Great." He chucked the carpetbag inside the boxcar, making sure it landed out of the way. Then he saluted her. "See you on the trail."

He hurried down the train to the fancier cars, where Boyd was billeted. Today they'd be filming some of the prairie-crossing scenes, which meant the teams had to be hitched to the wagons. The cowboys who had team-driving experience were handling that, but they needed to be costumed and in place.

The actors with named parts, like Martin, Gilbert, and—Robbie swallowed against something awfully like grief—*Wesley* would be on horseback. The women would all be riding next to the drivers, or inside the wagons. He ran through the shot list in his head. *Long shots from the hill first. Medium shots of the wagon train heading toward the camera. Shots from the perspective of the village, with the wagons retreating, with Aurelia peering out the back of one and waving.*

Then, while that was happening, the circus train had to move on another two miles to where they'd film the river crossing. Robbie needed to check with the engineer and make sure he was ready. *After Mr. Brody, I can....*

He slowed down as he saw the cluster of men outside Boyd's car. *Jehoshaphat, both Mr. Schlossbergs? And Mr. McCorkle? What's going on?* Mr. Brody was gesturing wildly, and Robbie could tell he was shouting although he couldn't make out the words. He started to back away, but Mr. Brody spotted him and gestured peremptorily, so Robbie trotted over as everyone's head swiveled to look at him.

Robbie touched his hat brim and nodded to the group. "Yes, Mr. Brody?"

"Rob, I need you to get Dottie up."

"She's already up, sir." He pointed back the way he'd come. "She's in the dark car."

Mr. Brody grunted. "Good. Jacob, Ira, Leo, you come with me and I'll *prove* it."

Mr. Jacob chewed on his unlit cigar. "Don't matter what you prove. The contracts—"

Mr. Brody jabbed a finger at Mr. Jacob's face. "You're the one who writes the fucking contracts, Jacob. You can damn well write another one."

Mr. Ira held up his hands in a placating gesture. "Now, Boyd. You know it doesn't work like that."

Mr. Brody transferred his scowl to Mr. Ira. "You're the one with the artistic eye. You come with me and *then* tell me it's impossible." He stormed off toward the dark car, with the Schlossbergs and Leo trailing behind.

Robbie stared after them for a moment, scratching his head. *What the heck is up with them?* He hoped Dottie wasn't in trouble. If she got pulled off this picture, it would kill her. For an instant he considered following in case she needed support. *But why would any of them listen to me?* He'd help her more by making sure the day's shoot proceeded as planned.

He shaded his eyes as he scanned the cowboy encampment. The men were already striking their tents, the ones who were extras on horseback today loading them behind their saddles. Others, probably the ones who'd be driving teams, were stowing their gear in the boxcar set aside for them. Robbie waved at them and got nods and grins in return. No need to worry about the cowboys. They knew their jobs and didn't need to be herded like the actors did.

With one last glance at where Mr. Jacob was heaving himself into the dark car, Robbie headed toward the locomotive.

He grabbed the handle and mounted the step that led to the platform between the engine and the firebox and waved to the engineer. "All set for the move today, Floyd?"

"Sure thing, Rob. Want to come aboard?"

Robbie grinned up at the apple-cheeked engineer who looked like the illustration of Saint Nicholas in one of Ma's books. "Not today, thanks. Got some other things to check up on."

"If you want to ride with us this time, let me know. You'd be welcome."

"I'd like that, but it depends on what else Mr. Brody has for me to do today."

Floyd's grizzled eyebrows rose. "Do? Ain't you acting in this picture?"

Robbie shrugged. "I was just a stand-in. The real actor arrived this morning, so I'll go back to my regular job. Which includes getting the cast and crew up and off the train so you can get moving."

"Suits me. Let us know when we're clear."

"Will do." As Robbie was about to jump down, he caught a glimpse of windblown blond hair above a dark coat. *Someone's on the other side of the train*. Robbie frowned. The only thing over there were some abandoned latrines and the stream that flowed down the hill to a scum-covered pond. Nobody should be over there. He'd made sure everyone in the company knew of the danger. He ran to the front of the locomotive and crossed the tracks in front of the cowcatcher.

Wesley.

The actor was on his knees next to the stream, hunched over in apparent pain. As Robbie started toward him to see if he needed help, Wesley cupped both hands in the creek and raised them, dripping, to his face.

"Stop!" Robbie raced toward him. "Don't drink the water!"

Wesley stared at Robbie with overbright eyes. "Don't tell me what to do." But the water dribbled away between his fingers.

Thank goodness. "I'm sorry, but this water is tainted. Go to the dining car. They've got safe water there. Coffee. Breakfast."

Wesley dropped his gaze to the stream, so innocent and clear in the morning light. "It looks fine to me." He cast Robbie a scornful look. "What do you know anyway? You're nothing but a driver."

"Wesley—"

"That's Mr. Thornhill to you."

"Mr. Thornhill, then." Robbie reached for Wesley's sleeve but dropped his hand at the flare of anger in Wesley's eyes. "Please. You didn't drink the water, did you?"

Wesley stood up and wiped his hands off on his waistcoat. "I believe I'll have that breakfast now." He sauntered away with only a slight wobble.

Robbie glanced back at the stream. Maybe he'd caught Wesley before any damage was done. *I hope*. Because Wesley—Mr. Thornhill—didn't look strong enough to withstand a sideways shove, let alone a bout of dysentery.

CHAPTER SEVENTEEN

When Martin emerged, shrugging into his costume coat, most of the company was already buzzing. Mrs. Arthur was complaining loudly about having to vacate her car so the train could move.

"Mother," Aurelia said with something less than sweet patience, "you don't have to dog my every step. Just stay on the train while they move it. I'll be inside a *wagon* all day with a bunch of *children*. Nobody's going to *debauch* me."

"Really, Aurelia," Mrs. Arthur huffed. "Your language."

Aurelia turned melting blue eyes on Martin and took his arm. "Tell her, Mr. Brentwood. Tell her I don't need a chaperone."

Martin smiled down at her and disengaged. "It's not my place, Miss Arthur. If you'll excuse me."

For an instant, anger flickered across her face and her Cupid's bow lips tightened into a petulant pout. But then she smiled sunnily and gazed up at him through her lashes. "Of course, Mr. Brentwood."

As he tipped his hat to Mrs. Arthur, he detected a decidedly calculating look on her face. Although, considering the dancing shadows cast by the massive plumes on her prairie-inappropriate hat, he couldn't be sure. Besides, she was a stage mother. They all looked like that 90 percent of the time.

He shoved his hands into his jacket pockets and ambled down the train, trying not to be too obvious about looking for Robbie. But as he passed the dark car, Ira Schlossberg stuck his head out the door. Martin did a double-take worthy of Roscoe. "Ira? What are you doing here?"

"Martin. A moment if you please." Ira beckoned for Martin to step into the car.

"Of course." He climbed aboard and blinked at the people gathered there. The car wasn't spacious at the best of times, considering all the paraphernalia that Howard and Dottie had lining the walls, but Jacob Schlossberg with his bulk and Boyd Brody with his attitude could fill a space three times as big. Add in Ira, Leo, Dottie, and Martin himself, and the place was reminiscent of one of the Marx Brothers' vaudeville routines. Martin half expected the *blatt* of Harpo's horn to hail his entrance.

"Brentwood," Jacob barked, "what's this about your driver acting in this picture?"

Alarm chased down Martin's spine. *Is Robbie in trouble?* He schooled his face into his usual bland smile. "I believe you changed his job title, Jacob. Isn't he Boyd's technical advisor?"

"Yes, yes. That's not the point. Is he *acting*?"

"He's been standing in for Wesley, since he was instructed to obey Boyd's every whim, and that's what Boyd ordered him to do. That seems inside his purview."

Jacob's face took on an alarming red hue. "Brentwood—"

"Martin," Dottie said, her expression nothing short of smug, "I think what Mr. Schlossberg is asking is if Robbie is giving a good *performance*."

"Oh. Well, that's easy. Yes."

Jacob jabbed his unlit cigar toward Martin's face. "Why didn't you tell me he was an actor?"

"It, er, never came up. Robbie didn't come to Hollywood to pursue a career in pictures."

"Nonsense," Jacob snapped. "Everybody comes to Hollywood to pursue a career in pictures. Why else move here?"

"Why indeed?" Martin murmured.

"The point," Ira said, rather more gently, "is that Dottie has shown us the rushes of the scenes between you and Robbie."

Martin's hands started to shake, so he shoved them into his pockets. "She did? And?"

"The kid's a genius," Jacob muttered. "I mean, who *is* this guy, and why isn't he under contract with us?"

"I believe he *is* under contract. As a director's assistant."

"Well, change the fucking contract, then, before he gets away." Jacob stuck his cigar in the corner of his mouth. "Ira. Take care of it. Leo, I want a big splash about it. Citadel discovers new talent. Get the kid listed in that New Stars column in *Picture Play*." Jacob paced the very small space, making it even smaller. "We need a story for him. A good one. And get him a girlfriend." He snapped his sausage-like fingers. "What's-her-name, the blondie on this picture. She'll do."

Over my dead body. "I'm not sure Aurelia's mother will agree to that. She's quite strict about who her daughter is allowed to see."

Jacob snorted. "Bunch of hogwash. She'll do what she's told." He pointed at Leo. "So tell her."

"I see one small problem with this," Martin said mildly.

Jacob scowled at him, chewing on his cigar. "What?"

"Wesley Thornhill has the part. And he arrived this morning to film it."

"Thornhill?" Jacob's eyebrows descended farther. "What the fuck is he doing out of that sanitarium?"

"Back from his grandmother's," Leo murmured.

Jacob bared his teeth. "He's not back on set until *I* say so, and I don't. Furthermore, since he's missed more than five days of work, I can fire him from this picture."

"Jacob," Ira murmured.

"What? You've seen the rushes, both the ones from this week and that dreck from the studio. Which would you rather use? Do I have to remind you that this picture is supposed to put Citadel at the top of the studio heap, not bury us under a pile of stinking garbage?"

"Yes, but—"

"We've got a nonperformance clause for a reason, Ira. Execute it on Thornhill's ass and get him back to that sanitorium—"

"His grandmother's house," Leo corrected, earning a glare from Jacob.

"He's a liability, and I'm done carrying him. Do it. And you —" Jacob pointed at Martin. "—keep turning in performances like this last week and Fairbanks and Valentino can kiss my ass."

Fairbanks plus sex. Valentino plus athleticism. Sid was right. Although the sex in this case was something the audience would read as friendship. *I hope.*

"Mr. Schlossberg," Dottie piped up. "I can write some extra scenes to develop the friendship between Moses and Dennis so it's reasonable that Dennis would return alone to rescue Moses from the cabin."

"That's what I'm talking about." Jacob rubbed his hands together. "Do it. All of it. And meanwhile, get that kid under contract." He stared at them all. "What are you all standing around for? Get moving!"

"Who's going to tell Wesley that his, er, services are no longer required?" Martin asked.

Jacob squinted at him. "You volunteering?"

"God, no. That seems like something that should come from studio management, don't you think?"

Jacob *harrumphed*. "Fine. Ira. Take care of it."

Ira shot Jacob a disgusted glance. "Should I wipe your ass while I'm at it?"

Jacob chuckled. "No need to get snitty, Ira. Your reputation is riding on this picture too, so make the ride a smooth one, right to the top."

Jacob hove across the car and got down—not without some cursing—followed by Ira and Leo. Boyd stopped in front of Martin, and Martin could swear his expression was almost sheepish.

"Look, Marty. I know we haven't always seen eye-to-eye, but the Schlossbergs are right. Your performance—yours and Robbie's, the relationship between Moses and Dennis—is what's going to put this picture over the top. The men and boys'll like the adventure, but the women are gonna come for the sentiment. So keep delivering it, and we're square." He clapped Martin on the shoulder and jumped down from the car.

"What just happened?" Martin shared a bemused glance with Dottie. "Did Boyd actually *forgive* me for the fact that he's spent years treating me like shite?"

She hugged herself, and Martin noticed she was wearing cavalry uniform pants as a kind of overall. "We made Robbie a star, that's what."

Martin thought back to Robbie's comments about Hollywood and his own hopes about building a discreet life together despite the klieg-light glare of the motion picture business. When Martin's career had been modest to dwindling, that seemed like an achievable dream. But if Robbie became a star— with a studio-appointed girlfriend, for the love of God—what chance did they have?

"Martin?"

Martin looked up at the tentative note in Dottie's voice. "Yes?"

"Aren't you happy for him?"

"Of course." *Am I? Happy for him, perhaps, but not for me, not for us.* And how selfish was that? "It's a wonderful opportunity for him."

Her eyes narrowed behind her steel-rimmed spectacles. "I'm not stupid, you know. I hear what you're *not* saying perfectly well."

He laughed mirthlessly as he took off his hat and dragged a hand through his overlong hair. *Good God, I look worse than Chaplin.* "Then perhaps you could tell me what it is, because at the moment, I'm not entirely sure myself."

"You're afraid everything'll change," she said, her voice matter-of-fact. "That you won't have a reason to spend time with him anymore. That people will start *paying attention*, and when that happens, sometimes they notice things you don't want them to see."

"I don't know what you're—"

"Like the way you look at him. The way he looks at you."

Panic turned Martin's insides to jelly. "We don't—There isn't anything—I can't—"

She grabbed his sleeve and shook his arm. "Take it easy, Martin. Most folks won't recognize it because it's so far outside their imagination. But I've seen the rushes. It's right there on the screen. How you both feel when you look at each another. *I* know what it is, because, well, I know what it is." Her cheeks pinked, and while that might have been due to the cold snaking in through the open boxcar door, suddenly Martin wasn't so sure. Men weren't the only ones who sought out their own kind for companionship, and Evelyn had made those not-so-subtle comments....

"I see."

"But Mr. and Mrs. America, sitting in the dark in picture palaces from Philadelphia to Pasadena? They won't know. And the people in the business—Jacob and Ira and Leo—the ones who *do* have the words? Well, they know what side their pocketbooks are buttered on."

Martin couldn't help a chuckle. "Interesting image."

"You know what I mean." She bunched his sleeve in her fist. "This is my picture, Martin. I want it to be the best. But Robbie's my friend. So are you." She shook his arm. "Don't you see what I've done?"

"Other than thrust him into the limelight, which, by the way, I'm not sure he wants?"

She grinned up at him, and Martin could suddenly see why Evelyn might be willing to risk her tightrope act between the Schlossbergs. "I've given him armor."

"Armor?"

"He's an *asset*. He has dollar value to the Schlossbergs. They'll move heaven and hell—heck, they'll move the police and the press, which is more useful—to protect him. And if he's protected, *you're* protected." She patted his arm. "Don't worry, Martin. You're safe."

He opened his mouth but couldn't find the words. Was his disguise so pathetic that *anyone* could see through it? He peered down into Dottie's thin, clever face, with those spectacles that seemed to allow her to penetrate his very soul. "I—"

"And if you're worried about Robbie turning into Wesley, or worse, Gilbert? Don't. He won't change."

"How do you know?" Martin's voice had somehow turned desperate, needy.

"Because we're not giving him anything that he wants. Well, nothing other than you." She stepped back and shoved her hands into the pockets of her oversized jacket. "Now are you gonna give him the bad news, or shall I?"

"I can't." Robbie glanced wildly from Dottie's face to Martin's. "I'm not an actor."

"That's why you're so good, Rob." Dottie hugged her scenario binder to her chest. "You don't *pretend*. You just *are*."

"She's right." Was Martin's smile a bit strained? It was so hard to tell in the dim light of the boxcar. "The worst thing for this kind of picture is for someone to *act*. You *look* at the other people in the scene. You listen to them. You *do* what you're supposed to be doing instead of faking it. That comes across on film."

"How do you know?"

Martin's smile cranked tighter. "Dottie showed me the rushes. And you're good, Rob. Really good."

"But that was only me. It wasn't hard because I knew Wesley would be doing the *real* job later."

Dottie bounced on her toes. "But that's the thing. *You* already did the real job. The job the picture needs. Anyone who looks at that footage won't see some Hollywood type trying to show off. They'll see Moses Schallenberger, a pioneer who knows how to ride a horse and pack a wagon and talk to his friend. That's what I want, Robbie. That's what I *need*. What the picture needs. Please?"

"But… but what about Wesley?" Robbie wanted so badly to touch Martin for a little bit of reassurance, nothing more. But he couldn't. They couldn't. And it didn't seem like Martin was in an especially reassuring mood. "Won't that mean—"

"Wesley's off the picture anyway." Dottie pushed her spectacles up her nose. "Jacob's ordered him back to that sanitarium—"

"Grandmother's house," Martin murmured, and this time his lips twitched in what might actually be amusement.

Dottie glared at him. "*You* know and *I* know and *Robbie* knows—heck, everyone in *Hollywood* probably knows that Wesley's got a problem and it isn't his grandmother. You're not doing him out of a job, Robbie. He managed that all on his own."

Not entirely on his own. Not really. Robbie swallowed, his mouth drier than the wind sweeping across the prairie. *It was the studio. The injury. The contract.* How could anyone *want* this kind of life—want it so badly they'd nearly kill themselves to get it?

And how angry would Wesley or any of those other desperate actors be that Robbie got it only because he knew that a Conestoga was the wrong kind of wagon for *The California Trail*? Jehoshaphat, he was barely even a chauffeur, and he'd only gotten *that* job because Pops felt sorry for him.

"What if I keep standing in for him? Just until he's back on his feet?" Robbie glanced at Martin. "I mean back from his grandmother's?"

Dottie grimaced. "He's never coming back, Rob. He's sick."

"Oh, God." Robbie's knees wobbled. "Is it dysentery? I tried to stop him, to warn him about the water, but he wouldn't listen."

"Dysentery? No. It's the drugs." She rolled her eyes. "He fell off his damn horse when he was trying to prove to Jacob he was fit for the job. Even if his health improves—and it won't if he doesn't cut out the dope—the Schlossbergs are done with him. If you don't take the role, the picture will fold, and we'll have wasted all this money and time."

She didn't have to add that it would kill her dreams because Robbie knew—heck, *everyone* knew—that if *The California Trail* didn't live up to the Schlossbergs' box-office expectations, they'd never give her another chance.

Martin moved closer and brushed the back of his hand against Robbie's. "I know this isn't what you want, my dear, but look at it this way." He tangled their fingers together, and alarm skittered across Robbie's skin. *But it's only Dottie. She knows.* "You don't have to do any more pictures if you don't want to."

"I don't?"

"I'll contact Sid. Have him take a look at the contract for you. He'll make sure you've got options. The timing is perfect, because right now you've got all the power on your side. Everyone wants you in this picture—Dottie, Boyd, Ira, even Jacob." He smiled again, and this time it reached his eyes. "And me, of course."

"You do? Really?"

Martin's smile widened into a grin. "I'm looking forward to our next location shoot. Just you, me, and a cabin in the Sierras."

He chuckled. "Well, you, me, Dottie, Boyd, Howard, the crew, and a cabin in the Sierras. But I've loved having you on set, where I can look up and see you any time I want, rather than waiting until the end of the day. When we can sit down together in the dining car and share a meal. Where I can look into your eyes and not at the back of your head."

Out of the corner of his eye, Robbie saw Dottie slip out of the door and slide it shut behind her with a *whuff* and a *thump*, enclosing him in the half darkness with Martin.

Martin cupped the back of Robbie's neck. "Don't you see, Rob? This is one way we can be together that nobody will question. Out in plain sight."

"But—but won't they know? Won't they see?"

Martin carded his fingers through Robbie's hair. "What they'll see is two men who are friends, who aren't denying or hiding that friendship. People only get suspicious if you behave as if you're doing something wrong. Do you think we're doing anything wrong?"

Robbie sucked in a shaky breath. "It doesn't *feel* wrong. But the law says.... And the Bible...."

Martin chuckled, his dark eyes glinting. "My dear, in Hollywood, the Bible is only useful as material for DeMille or Griffith to make their next overblown costume picture. Unless...." Martin's brows drew together, and worry flickered across his face. "Do *you* think the Bible—"

"No! No, I never did. If it was so perfect, how come folks spend so much time arguing about what it means?"

"Exactly. At the end of the day, what we do in private is nobody's business, because we won't *make* it anyone's business."

Something fluttered at the base of Robbie's throat, and he allowed himself to rest his palms on Martin's chest. "Will that.... Can that really work?" His voice wavered. "Really?"

Martin's grip tightened on the back of Robbie's neck, and he pulled him closer. "It will work because we'll make it work."

Martin kissed Robbie's forehead. "I've been waiting my whole life for someone like you. I'm so proud of you, proud that you want me—"

"You are?" Robbie searched Martin's face for any sign of a lie. "But I'm nothing but a hick from Idaho. I'm nobody."

Martin laid his finger across Robbie's lips. "I won't let you denigrate a man who's infinitely precious to me."

The fluttering in Robbie's throat threatened to steal his breath. "P-precious?"

"Yes." He smiled—not the wide, practiced smile he aimed at the cameras, but something softer, more intimate. Something just for Robbie. "Robbie Goodman, I've never met anyone with a more appropriate name. You're a good man, my dear. Loyal, brave, true."

"I'm not. Not really." If Martin knew the truth, he'd run away from Robbie as fast as Robbie had run from Boise.

"There you go again, casting aspersions that I simply cannot allow."

"Martin—"

"Hush. I said I'm proud of you, and I meant it. You've been there for me in some difficult times, and I want to be there for you, for us to be there for each other. The danger of being in the life isn't as great for us now." He chuckled. "The studio would never allow us to be taken up on an indecency charge."

Robbie's stomach tried to hide behind his spine. *Frank.* "You mean they'd lie for us."

"I mean they'd take care of us."

"How is that fair? Other people don't have that. They have to face the consequences. Face their family. Go to prison or worse. Why should we get different treatment just because... because...."

"Because thousands of people will pay to see our faces on the screen?"

Robbie nodded unhappily and clutched Martin's heavy frontiersman's coat. "It doesn't seem right."

"What's not right is the law. What's not right is the attitude that says what we feel for each other is wrong. What's not right is the *rest* of the country. Not here." Martin lifted his eyebrows and cast a pointed glance at the surrounding boxcar. "Or rather, not Hollywood. In fact, as far as I'm concerned, it's our *duty* to take advantage of our good fortune, to live our best lives, as our best selves, to prove we're not the monsters they paint us to be."

Robbie laughed weakly. "Not sure anybody who's in danger of losing his balls for deviant behavior would agree with that."

"Rob. Look at me." Martin tugged at a lock of Robbie's hair until Robbie raised his chin. "We can't be responsible for anybody but ourselves. Our choices. Our actions. Our lives. But the point is, they are *ours*. So let's own them and make them the best they can be."

Could it be possible? Could Pa have been wrong all these years, with his constant harping on how Robbie owed him for not being the son he wanted, for not working hard enough, for being alive when Eddie wasn't? "Isn't that selfish? Don't we owe it to other folks not to put ourselves first?"

"The way I see it, if we don't put ourselves first, who will? Are those people putting us first? I mean, who's at the front of the line? Who are we sacrificing for? And will whoever it is ever thank us for the sacrifice?"

Robbie thought of Pa's face, contorted in anger, plowing over the kitchen garden, ordering Robbie to plant everything in straight rows instead of the pretty groupings Robbie had arranged for Ma. Pa was at the front of the line at the farm, for sure. He wasn't about to put anybody else first, even Ma. Maybe Martin was right. Maybe trying to please everybody else at the expense of his own happiness was a losing battle. "Probably not."

"Then let's take this opportunity for what it is—a gift, something very few men like us will ever receive. If anyone should ever question our… relationship, we have only to point to our time making this picture. Other men might make friends on the playing field or on campus. But this is Hollywood. Here, we make friends on set. Our time on *The California Trail* let us forge our friendship." Martin dipped his head and kissed Robbie softly on the lips.

Yes. This. If I can have this, I'll take it. Robbie wrapped his arms around Martin's waist and leaned into the kiss. He was rewarded by Martin's groan and the feel of Martin hard against Robbie's hip.

Someone pounded on the boxcar door and they broke apart. Robbie turned toward the corner and wiped his mouth. His heart tripped in his chest as the door slid open.

Dottie stuck her head inside. "Sorry to bother you fellows. But word's come in about Roscoe's trial."

Martin braced his hand on the wall as though he were having trouble standing upright. "God, Dottie. Tell me they didn't convict him."

She shook her head. "No. But they didn't acquit him either. The jury couldn't agree, so the judge declared a mistrial. He's got to go through it all again."

Martin glanced at Robbie, his expression bleak. *Guess Mr. Arbuckle isn't at the front of anybody's line either.*

Or else there were some things that could never be fixed.

CHAPTER EIGHTEEN

Martin set his Gladstone down inside the cabin door. "Well. This is slightly less than palatial. Although I suppose it's a step up from a circus train."

Robbie nudged him out of the way and brought his carpetbag inside, along with a string bag full of oranges. "You didn't have to come along so soon. Dottie says we won't be ready to shoot the scenes with Dennis until next week." He peered out the grimy window. "Assuming we can get any filming done at all. For all the snow on the ground up here, we might as well have stayed in Inceville."

"Boyd wanted real snow or at least the *chance* of real snow, which we can hardly get in Santa Monica. But he's already put this off as long as he could. This is the last sequence—Moses in the mountains." Martin checked the path that led up to their cabin. *Empty.* He closed the door to be safe, before he took Robbie in his arms. "Besides, you know why I came up now."

Robbie grinned and clasped his hands at the small of Martin's back. "You didn't want to inconvenience the crew by making someone drive all the way back to the Sacramento train station to pick you up?"

"Yes. That must be it. Crew inconvenience." Martin nuzzled Robbie's neck, just under his ear, his overlong hair tickling Martin's nose. "I do so hate inconveniencing the crew."

"Martin." Robbie's voice caught on a laugh. "I have more luggage and supplies to bring up. I can't do it with a tent in my trousers."

But Robbie didn't pull away, so Martin took the opportunity to steal a kiss, something he'd been starving for since they boarded the train in Los Angeles yesterday evening. He rested his forehead against Robbie's. "Do you realize the absolute torture I endured? You were merely in the next Pullman, yet I couldn't go to you. Or worse, the agony of sitting next to you in the automobile all the way up here? Not to take your hand? Not to stroke your hair? Not to kiss you right here—" He dropped a kiss on Robbie's perfect cheekbone. "—or here—" *Eyebrow.* "—or here?" *Lips, oh God, Robbie's lips.* "Excruciating."

Robbie ran his hands up Martin's back. "Yes, Martin. I'm aware of exactly that torture and agony. I was *there*, remember?"

"How could I forget?" Martin looked around at the rough plank walls of the cabin. "And now we're here. In rustic splendor."

Robbie kissed him once more, tenderly for all it was too quick to suit Martin. "If you had waited until next week, you could have stayed in the main lodge with Dottie and Boyd and everyone else. By that time, some of Mr. Vidor's *Sky Pilot* crew should have packed up and headed back to Hollywood." He eased out of Martin's embrace and picked up both of their bags. "For that matter, you could probably have asked to swap into one of the crew's bunks. You're a star, after all."

Martin followed Robbie across the room. God, was the ground actually visible between the floorboards? "But that would have *inconvenienced* somebody—probably me. Have you ever heard Howard snore? He's worse than Otis."

"Martin—"

"*Robbie.*" He took the bags from Robbie's hands and set them on the floor next to an old-fashioned washstand equipped with a hand pump. "I came here to be with you. Why in the world would I choose to stay with somebody else when we have a perfect studio-sanctioned opportunity to be together?"

A smile quivered on Robbie's mouth. "It's a studio-sanctioned opportunity to be together with no indoor plumbing."

"What?" Martin glanced around the big single room—a couple of wide cots, the washstand, a pot-bellied stove in the corner, a table with two chairs... but a notable absence of bathtubs or toilets. Martin closed his eyes and shuddered. "Please tell me there's at least a chamber pot."

Robbie chuckled. "Are you sure you don't want to swap with someone up at the lodge? They've got all the modern conveniences."

Martin opened his eyes, and just like always, Robbie's beauty rendered him weak at the knees. "They might have toilets and bathtubs—"

"And a kitchen."

Martin inclined his head. "And a kitchen. But they don't have you. As far as I'm concerned, I've got the better bargain."

Robbie blushed adorably. "Jehoshaphat, Martin. When you say things like that, I want to—"

Somebody pounded on the door. "Rob?" Dottie called. "Martin? Are you in there?"

Martin lifted an eyebrow. "At least she knocked. I don't suppose the door boasts a lock."

"Sure it does." Robbie nodded at a two-by-four leaning against the wall next to the stove. He grinned when Martin rolled his eyes. Then he strode over to let Dottie in. "Hey, girl. What's up?"

She peered over his shoulder, her eyes widening as she took in the interior of the cabin. "Golly. I thought the circus train was roughing it."

Robbie gestured for her to enter. "Compared to Moses Schallenberger, we've got it good."

She laughed and socked him in the arm as she walked by. "Darn right. Maybe we should arrange for you two to sleep in a tent instead."

"Thank you, but this is quite primitive enough." Martin caught her hand in its fingerless woolen glove and brought it to his lips. "I trust your accommodations are satisfactory?"

"Are you kidding? It's lush." She wrinkled her nose. "Well, lush by location standards. The food's great too. That's why I'm here. Because the place is so packed, what with us and Vidor's *Sky Pilot* bunch, the innkeepers are running two meal shifts. They're about to serve lunch for our crew, so you fellows should get up there before it's all gone."

Martin tugged on the collar of his coat. "We can't have that. Tell me, are these jolly innkeepers of yours charging as much for this cabin as they do for rooms in the main building?"

She grinned. "More, I think. It's their 'pioneer experience' lodging."

Martin pretended to be shocked. "You mean people choose to live like this *on purpose*?"

Robbie laughed and tugged a knitted cap over his curls. "I hate to tell you, Martin, but this isn't all that different from some of the places up in the Bitterroots. Not everyone's got a snug little bungalow in Hollywood."

Martin followed Robbie and Dottie onto the narrow porch. "Are you telling me you chose this room deliberately, Robinson?"

Robbie cut a glance at Martin. "I volunteered. I figured I'm more used to roughing it than anyone else in the crew. Besides —" He gestured to a pile of logs next to the cabin. "—if I've got to chop wood as Moses, I might as well get to use it in the stove."

Martin's mouth dried at the notion of watching Robbie chop wood. Of course, in this weather, he wouldn't be shirtless, particularly if he was being filmed in his pioneer garb. But the concentration and power behind every physical thing Robbie did—and Martin was privileged to be on the receiving end of some *very* physical things—always left him breathless.

The California Trail audience was going to eat him up with a spoon.

He let Robbie and Dottie precede him up the trail that wound through the trees for half a mile before it opened out in front of the lodge. Martin could recognize Boyd and some of the other crew through the windows of what was apparently a dining room up on the second level. He scanned the blank wall in front of them.

"Where's the door?"

Dottie jerked her thumb to where Howard was standing on a wide deck, holding a steaming mug. "Up there."

"Why not put the door down here, where the people are?"

Robbie chuckled. "Because down here is where the snow is, Martin. They put the door up there so they can get in during the winter."

"Of course. How foolish of me." *The things you forget in Hollywood.*

They climbed the stairs to the deck, but once they stepped inside the snug lobby, Robbie said, "You two go on in and have a seat. I've got a couple of things to take care of first."

Dottie propped her fists on her nonexistent hips. "Rob. You're one of the stars of this picture. You're not the runner anymore or even the AD. If you want something done, you can *ask*."

He grinned at her. "Then I'm *asking* you to go have lunch. Don't worry, Dottie. Nobody's oppressing me." With a brief smile in Martin's direction, he strode over to the reception desk.

"Well," Dottie said. "There's no point in arguing." She tugged Martin's elbow and led him through a white-painted archway into the dining room. "Once Rob sets his mind on something, nothing's gonna stand in his way."

"I've noticed," Martin murmured as he settled at a white-clothed table by the window.

"Yep." Dottie sat across from him and shook out her napkin. "He gets the job done, whatever it is." She glanced over her shoulder at Boyd, who was scowling at his plate and shoveling in mashed potatoes. "That's why Boyd's so discombobulated. On the one hand, he's over the moon about Robbie's performance. On the other, he misses having somebody that reliable to fetch and carry for him."

"I'm surprised he doesn't expect Rob to do both."

She chuckled as a server in a red-checked apron set plates of meatloaf, mashed potatoes, and green beans in front of them. "He forgets sometimes, and I have to remind him." She met Martin's gaze, her fork poised over her meatloaf. "You know, Martin, Hollywood doesn't have many people like Robbie. He's special."

Was that a warning note in her voice? "Yes. I'm well aware of that fact."

She studied him for a moment out of narrowed eyes. "Good. Long as you don't forget it."

"That's hardly likely." Martin gestured at the other diners at the room's dozen tables. "I have daily reminders of what Hollywood people are like." He took a bite of meatloaf, and the caramelized onions and tomato nearly melted on his tongue. "My God, you weren't kidding about the food. Not fancy, but —"

"Delicious. I know."

She dug into her meal with obvious relish. By the time they'd polished off some excellent apple pie and the rest of their crew had finished their meals and departed, Robbie still hadn't returned. Since King Vidor and Colleen Moore were visible beyond the archway, the staff probably wanted to set up for the *Sky Pilot* lunch service.

"I suppose we'd best clear out." Martin folded his napkin and laid it on the table. "I hope Robbie didn't get corralled into assisting Boyd, and miss lunch entirely. Maybe King will let him eat with them."

Dottie rose, peering at where King was smiling down at the diminutive Colleen, the girl who was the definition of the term *flapper*. "I have a feeling King and Colleen wouldn't appreciate a third at their table, if you know what I mean."

Martin blinked. "King and Colleen? But he's married. And she's—"

"Catholic?"

"*Seventeen*, for the love of God." But as he and Dottie threaded their way through the tables, Martin caught a glance between the director and the actress, and his heart stuttered in his chest. *Good God, are Robbie and I as transparent as that?*

He nodded at King, who'd always been decent to him, and smiled at Colleen as he passed, vowing to himself to be more careful in public, for Robbie's sake if not his own.

"I've got a meeting with Boyd, so I'll see you around." Dottie lifted a hand in farewell and trotted down the stairs ahead of him to where Boyd was glowering at the snow-free ground.

Martin made his way down the trail to the cabin, and as he cleared the trees, he saw a plume of smoke drifting out of the chimney pipe. *Robbie.* He hurried up the steps and across the porch, and when he opened the door, he almost turned around, thinking he was in the wrong place.

The floors were bare no longer. They were covered by several layers of overlapping rugs, worn but not threadbare. Brightly patterned blankets hung over the now-sparkling windows, providing insulation as well as privacy. A blue-checked cloth covered the table, and a shelf against the back wall, which had previously been empty, now held a cast iron skillet, a battered coffeepot, and a short stack of plates and bowls.

But I can't be in the wrong place. There's only one cabin on the property.

Then a clank from the corner caught his attention, and he turned to see Robbie rising from a crouch in front of the stove, a fire now burning merrily in its belly.

"Rob." Martin croaked and had to clear his suddenly thick throat. "Where did you get all this?"

Robbie shrugged, smiling shyly. "The lodge owners. They lived out here when they were building the place, so they had some stuff from back then, plus things that were a little too beat-up for their nice rooms."

Martin closed the door behind him and leaned against it, and if the way he looked at Robbie revealed the depth of his feelings the way Vidor's had, so what? They were alone here, away from prying, judgmental eyes. "I can't believe this. It's like a different place."

Robbie's gaze was as full of love and longing as Colleen's had been. "I might be used to roughing it, but you deserve better."

"As long as I deserve you"—*and, God, I don't, but I wish I did*—"everything else can go hang." Martin took two steps across the room and wrapped Robbie in an embrace.

His arms loaded down with split logs, Robbie pushed the cabin door open with one hip. The wind caught it and sent it banging against the wall, so cold air *whoosh*ed into the room. He winced, glancing at where Martin was still huddled under the blankets, and let the firewood tumble out of his arms next to the woodstove.

"What's next?" Martin grumbled. "A brass band?"

Robbie grinned as he shut the door and dropped the bar into its brackets. "Sorry. Stay under the covers for a while until I get the fire built back up."

He knelt in front of the stove. Dang it, Pa would have walloped him for letting the fire nearly die overnight. *But I was… distracted.* Robbie shivered with the memory of how exactly Martin had distracted him. He fed in kindling and then laid a couple of small branches on top. Once they'd caught, he added a bigger log. When he clanged the stove closed and stood, Martin was sitting up in bed, grinning at him, his hair tousled. *So gorgeous.*

Robbie wiped his hands on his trousers. "What?"

Martin shook his head. "Just admiring my mountain man, that's all." He lifted the blankets, revealing his long, lean body, which was unfortunately covered by a red woolen union suit. "Come back to bed."

"I can't." Although it was so tempting. The last week here with Martin had been magical. They'd had complete privacy, protected by everyone's horror over the cabin's lack of modern conveniences. Once shooting wrapped for the day and the company had eaten dinner, Robbie and Martin had retreated to their hideaway-in-plain-sight.

Sure, they had to keep it clean until bedtime in case Boyd demanded that Robbie come back up to the lodge for a meeting or in case Dottie got fed up with the rest of the crew and came down to join them, bringing cookies and hot chocolate and the ideas for her next scenario.

But once they turned out the oil lanterns, they were alone in the dark for the night.

Robbie had never realized how much you could discover in the dark.

But with the dawn, the rest of the world had claims on them, and this morning more than most. "Sorry it's a little chilly in here. I let the fire burn down." He tapped a fingernail against the pot on top of the stove. "But the water's still warm, if you want a wash. I'll have the coffee ready in a jiffy."

"Rob. You don't have to take care of me quite so assiduously." Martin tossed the blankets back, stood up, and stretched his arms overhead. "I may complain about the primitive nature of the accommodations, but I'm fully capable of enduring them, even relishing them at certain times." He smiled slyly. "After all, two under a blanket can keep warm far more effectively than one." He grabbed the pot off the stove and headed toward the wash stand.

"Martin? The, uh, barn door's open."

Martin glanced over his shoulder and then down, where the back flap of his union suit was hanging open, revealing the smooth pale globes of his behind. "Really, Robinson, you should learn to close up after yourself." He grinned and dumped the water into the basin—but didn't button up.

Robbie licked his lips. *Oh, the things you can discover in the dark.*

Martin pumped some water into the basin and then dabbled his fingers in it to test the temperature. "Drat. Did you want me to leave some warm water for you?"

"Nope. I took a bath up at the lodge. Nobody in the crew was up yet, so the bathroom was free."

Martin glanced over his shoulder again. "How early did you get up?"

"Early. But I don't mind."

Martin's smile tilted crookedly. "No. You never do, do you?" He leaned over the basin and splashed water on his face.

Jehoshaphat, when Martin leans over like that….

Robbie cleared his throat and forced himself to look away. *The fire. Yes, I need to tend the fire.* He knelt in front of the stove again. "Dottie's back from Truckee. She says the rushes from the scenes with Dewey and Conrad look good." Dewey and Conrad were the actors playing Joseph Foster and Allen Montgomery, the two men who stayed behind with Moses Schallenberger when the rest of the group pressed on to the survival camp on the Yuba River.

Robbie had spent the last week filming scenes of building the cabin with them and of the attempted escape over the snow when Moses had to give up and turn back. Unfortunately, they'd had to move farther up the mountain from their original scouted location just to find enough snow to escape over.

"That should make Dewey and Conrad happy. I trust they're returning to Hollywood as fast as they can shake the alleged snow off their boots?"

Robbie chuckled. "Not until after breakfast. They're not stupid. But Dottie got a call from Mr. Ira while she was down in Truckee. He and Mr. Jacob love the footage of the Sutter's Fort battle scenes—"

"They would." Martin's voice was muffled behind a towel.

"—and they wanted Dottie to add more of them."

"Are they mad? This isn't a picture about the squabble over California's prestatehood governorship. It's a picture about the triumph of the pioneer spirit, about survival, about loyalty and friendship."

Robbie propped his arm on his knee and grinned up at Martin. "You sound like Dottie."

He slung the towel around his shoulders. "After listening to her every day for three months, across more locations than I care to count, not to mention the studio scenes, I've seen the light at last. I trust she refused their gentle request?"

"In a red-hot minute. Boyd backed her up too, but I guess Mr. Jacob isn't taking it lying down. He's coming up here next week."

Martin's eyebrows shot up. "Jacob? Here? He's hardly the mountaineering sort."

"Well, not *here*. But to Truckee. So Boyd wants to speed up filming so we can prove the story works without more bloodshed. He wants to wrap by February first."

"That gives us all of three days! Judas priest, we've got the Moses/Dennis scenes, plus all the Moses-alone shots. How are we going to—"

"By starting now. Get ready, Dennis." Robbie picked up Martin's flannel shirt and tossed it to him—mostly so he wouldn't be tempted to take Martin's union suit *off*. "You're on set in an hour."

Robbie knelt in the snow, the stiff carcass of a fox next to him as he fumbled to reset the snare. His fingers were so cold in their battered gloves that he couldn't get it right. The rope was stiff and uncooperative. *I can do this. I've done it before, more times than I can count. If I can't do it again, I'll—*

"Moses!"

Robbie jerked his head up, and there, on top of the snow-covered ridge, stood Martin. *No, not Martin. Dennis.* He let the trap drop from his fingers and scrambled to his feet. Then he was staggering through the snow, his feet breaking through the crust of ice and making it impossible for him to run. But Martin —*Dennis*—*shush*ed toward him, snowshoes on his feet, and then he was there, dropping to his knees in front of Robbie.

Robbie lifted a shaking hand to touch Martin's face. "Are you really here?"

Martin smiled, but a sob caught at his voice. "Yes. I'm here. I've come to take you home."

Then Martin enveloped him in a hug while Robbie let his arms drop and leaned his head against Martin's shoulder. He closed his eyes and murmured, "Thank God."

"Aaaand cut!" Boyd called through his megaphone. "That's a wrap, folks."

Martin patted Robbie once and drew back, grinning down at him. "Good job, sweetheart," he whispered.

Robbie blinked up at Martin, his head still reeling a bit from exertion and lack of sleep, not to mention the emotional roller coaster of pretending to be Moses Schallenberger. The past few days, Boyd had interspersed Robbie's solo scenes with scenes of Moses and Dennis trudging through the snow, and they had been draining to say the least. They'd filmed from before dawn until late into the night for the interior cabin scenes, working relentlessly to finish before Mr. Jacob descended on them to force them to make *his* kind of picture instead of *theirs*. And yes,

Robbie had tipped over into a feeling of ownership of this picture, for all he'd never wanted to be in it.

But now, after the last scene was shot, as the prop man collected the stuffed fox that had played the part of every one of Moses's trapping victims, Robbie was so weary he could barely move. Was it nuts that Robbie felt sorry for the fox? That he ached for Moses's ordeal? That his gratitude toward Martin-as-Dennis was so great he wanted to weep?

In fact he *was* weeping, his tears nearly freezing on his cheeks in the wind.

It didn't matter that Robbie knew the end of this story, that they'd filmed the joyous reunion of Moses and his family weeks ago back in Inceville. Being out here on the set, farther up the mountain from the lodge, in the rough cabin that Robbie had partially built in earlier scenes.... Other than Boyd shouting directions through his bullhorn, Howard cranking away from a half a dozen different angles, Dottie watching intently from her folding chair next to the cameraman. Other than that? He'd felt nearly as isolated and desperate as Moses must have felt, feelings that were all too familiar.

Since his flight from Idaho, Robbie had experienced isolation, hunger, and desperation first-hand. And although Moses's story had ended well, Robbie still wasn't sure how his own would turn out.

Mine. Or Frank's.

Lately, they'd both been so tired after filming that Robbie and Martin hadn't done much overnight except fall asleep in each other's arms. But even that felt like a benediction Robbie didn't deserve. Every time Martin heaped praise on him for doing something any decent man would do, the guilt burrowed deeper.

I need to tell him. He needs to know the truth about me.

"Rob?" Martin gripped Robbie's shoulders and peered down into his face. "Are you all right?"

"I... I don't know."

"Shite, you're exhausted. Boyd!" Martin shouted over his shoulder. "I'm taking Robbie back to the cabin before he falls over."

Boyd barely glanced their way as the wind kicked up snow from around his feet. "Yeah. Fine." He huddled into his coat and resumed an intense conversation with Howard.

As Martin led him away from the bustling crew, Dottie slogged over to them. "I'm heading down to Truckee with Howard as soon as he's got the film ready to go. You fellows want to come with us? The drivers don't want to come back after dark in case the roads are icy."

Robbie just blinked at her, unable to put anything into words.

Martin chuckled. "Don't worry about us. Take Boyd or one of the crew. Rob needs to rest and recover for a bit, so we'll wait for the morning run."

She smirked at them, but her expression morphed into one of concern. "Yeah. You may be right. See you tomorrow, then." She trudged through the snow to join Boyd and Howard.

"Come on, sweetheart," Martin murmured. "Let's get you home."

CHAPTER NINETEEN

"Are you sure you two don't want to leave tonight?" Dottie marched along the path next to Martin, carrying a cardboard box with the spoils of a raid on the lodge larder—a raid with full lodge staff cooperation. "There's not much room in the automobiles with all the camera equipment, not to mention that Boyd refuses to let anyone ride with him, but one of the drivers could come back up."

"Out of the question." Martin adjusted his grip on a tin washtub loaded with soap, towels, and even more food. "The minute we get down to Truckee, Jacob will be there. Leo too, and if I know Leo, he'll have at least one reporter along. Robbie's not ready for that. Not yet."

She stumped up the porch steps next to him. "You could both move up to the lodge, though. There'll be room now, with our gang leaving, even though Vidor's crew is still there." She nodded at the tin tub. "You could at least have real baths."

Martin sighed as he set the tub down and took the box from Dottie's hands. "You've worked in pictures for a while, Dottie, but you've never been an actor. It takes a toll, especially in this kind of story and with the performance Robbie's been turning in. He needs time—time to recuperate, time to come back to himself, time where nobody is asking anything of him."

She eyed the contents of the box. "Not even what he wants for dinner, I guess."

"Not even that." He peered at the sky. Above the treetops, daylight was fading fast. "You better get back to the lodge before you miss your ride."

She smirked up at him. "I'm not worried about that. I've got the keys to all their hotel rooms in Truckee."

He laughed as the wind whipped around the corner of the cabin, tossing the ends of Dottie's scarf and making Martin clap a hand over his hat. "You'll go far in this business, girl."

"Don't I know it." She threw a saucy smile over her shoulder as she descended the rickety stairs. "I'll send a driver up for you tomorrow."

"Not too early, if you don't mind."

She turned around, walking backward, her eyes wide and innocent behind her glasses. "You know how absentminded I can be, Martin. I might forget you're even up here until I miss you at lunch." She waved and then turned and trotted up the path to disappear into the trees.

Martin eased the door open in case Robbie was asleep, but he was sitting on the edge of the bed, his hands dangling between his knees, staring at nothing. Martin brought the supplies inside and shut the door.

"Hey, are you hungry? I brought dinner."

Robbie shook his head but didn't say anything.

"Actually, I think I've got half the larder here. When I told the cook it was for you, she gave me free rein to take anything I wanted, plus she packed up some fried chicken from tonight's menu." He unpacked the box and the tub—a loaf of bread, a giant wedge of cheddar, a bottle of milk, enough fried chicken for six people, a half dozen apples, some potatoes—raw potatoes? What the hell were they supposed to do with those? He took the milk and cheese to the little wooden box built against the wall next to the door and lifted its hinged lid. "This is really clever, don't you think? The double-sided box? I know it's intended to let you grab the milk delivery without going out onto the porch, but in this weather, it's as good as an icebox."

Still no response from Robbie. Martin eyed the stack of wood next to the stove. They'd need more before morning. He stepped onto the porch, only to have the wind nearly tear his hat off again. He tossed it inside so he could grab a double armful of split logs without the damn thing flying off into the forest.

Back inside, he let the wood clatter down next to the stove. "I think you stacked enough wood on the porch to get us through until spring." He turned to bar the door again.

"A month, maybe."

Martin's heart leaped to his throat at the barely audible words. "A month? I don't know. That's an awfully big stack." He turned, not making any sudden moves. Robbie was still sitting on the bed, his hands loose on his wrists, but at least he was looking at Martin now. "Why so much?"

Robbie shrugged. "It's the wood I split for the picture. While I was Moses. It seemed stupid to let it go to waste."

"No wonder the innkeepers adore you." Martin shed his coat and muffler. Then he sat next to Robbie and put his arm around his shoulders. "But not nearly as much as I do."

Robbie turned in Martin's embrace. "Martin, I don't—Why do I feel this way? Like I'm empty? Like my head doesn't have anything inside but blowing snow?"

Martin kissed Robbie's forehead and stroked his cheek with the back of his fingers. "It's because you're finding your way back to *you*, back to Robbie from Moses."

"But I've been doing the job for months. It's never felt like this before."

"That's because before, you always had the next scene, the next shoot, the next day ahead. You didn't have time to stop. And in the last week, Boyd's been working you into the ground in one emotional scene after another. It's a reaction, Rob. It's natural. You need time to adjust."

Robbie's eyes were huge, their blue faded to gray in the dim light. "Does it happen to you?"

"Every time." Martin smoothed Robbie's tangled hair back from his forehead. "Some pictures cut deeper than others. But I've been doing this long enough that I know what to expect. I'm used to it. This is your first time. Next time, it'll be better. Trust me."

Robbie shivered and clenched his eyes shut. "I'm not sure I want there to be a next time."

Martin gathered Robbie against his shoulder and stroked his hair, his neck, his back. "That's your choice, Rob. Sid took care of that when he drew up your contract. But you're so good. It would be a shame to rob audiences of the chance to see your light."

"I wonder…."

Martin waited, but Robbie didn't continue. "Wonder what, sweetheart?"

He felt Robbie swallow, his throat moving under Martin's palm. "I wonder if this is what it's like for Ma. Why she still sits at the window, waiting for Eddie to come home, even though we know he never will. I wonder if she can't see through the snow."

Martin's heart squeezed. "Ah, Rob. I'm so sorry." Robbie's shoulders started to shake, and a moment later, he was sobbing against Martin's chest. Martin lay down and brought Robbie with him to nestle at his side. "It's all right. You'll be all right." He continued to croon the same meaningless platitudes while the room darkened, the fire crackled, and the wind seemed to cry in sympathy.

But eventually Robbie took a deep, shuddering breath. "Thank you," he murmured.

"For what?"

He lifted his head and gazed into Martin's eyes, and although Martin could only see half his face clearly in the orange light from the stove, the tenderness there cut right through Martin's chest. "For understanding. For helping me understand. For being here." His lips quirked up on one side. "For not making me sit with everybody else at dinner."

"My pleasure." Martin kissed Robbie's almost-smiling mouth. Soft. Lingering. *A promise, not a demand.* "Would you like something to eat now? I understand that fried chicken is the specialty of the house. And there's biscuits."

"Why didn't you say so?" But Robbie didn't move away. Instead, he levered himself up on one elbow to look down at Martin, but with the firelight behind him, Martin couldn't read his expression. He laid his palm against Martin's cheek. "I don't know what I did to be so lucky. I don't deserve it."

Martin caught Robbie's hand and pressed it against his face even though the beard he'd grown for the picture had to prickle Robbie's palm. "You deserve every bit of happiness you get, Robinson Crusoe Goodman. And I'm pretty sure *I'm* the lucky one."

"You think so? Why's that?"

Martin grinned and kissed Robbie's palm. "Because I didn't have to chop all that wood."

Robbie laughed, as Martin hoped he would. "Then let's make good use of it. I'll build up the fire. You set out this famous fried chicken, and we'll have our own private feast."

"Private feasts are my favorite kind." Martin waggled his eyebrows. "Because the dessert can go on for hours."

"Hours?" Robbie's voice squeaked a bit, and if the light were better, Martin had no doubt he'd be able to see Robbie's delectable blush.

"Hours. But we've got all night, and you still have some recovery to do. Besides, dessert is always better for the anticipation." He kissed Robbie again, slowly and sweetly, and was rewarded with Robbie's subtle whimper. "And I'm not talking about the pie."

Robbie looked down at the washtub as Martin emptied the last pot of warm water into it. "I'm not sure about this."

Martin nudged the tub with his toe. It didn't budge. "It seemed much more spacious when I was lugging it the half mile from the lodge." He glanced up, his expression apologetic. "It's not too late for us to go up there. You could have a bath in a real tub, have your own room, and get a hot dinner served by somebody who knows what they're doing."

Robbie dropped his towel on the floor and wrapped his arms around Martin's waist. "I don't want my own room. The dinner we've got is perfectly fine." He kissed Martin's mouth, and Martin's fuller beard tickled his lips. "And I've bathed in a tin washtub before. But it's not pretty. I'll look like some kind of pale, spindly insect that's been folded in half and shoved in a knothole. Are you sure you're ready for that?"

Martin grinned at him. "I never realized until now, but I've been craving just such a sight my entire life."

"Anyway, from the sound of that wind, we might get blown off the mountain before we got halfway to the lodge." He kissed Martin again. "I'm happy here. With you."

"I was hoping you'd say that. Now into the tub with you. You stink."

Robbie widened his eyes, pretending insult. "*I* stink? I thought that smell was you."

"It is. That's why I'm about to heat more water so I can clean up next." Martin brandished a pot and headed to the wash stand, the creak of the pump handle and the splash of water oddly complementary to the tune he was humming under his breath.

So Robbie undressed, removing the clothes he'd worn as Moses for the last week. The costumer had three identical copies of the whole outfit, but Boyd had insisted Robbie stay in the same one the whole time and hadn't allowed anything to be washed. Verisimilitude, he called it. Unnecessary, Robbie called it. After all, the audience couldn't *smell* pictures.

He lowered himself into the tub and hissed when his bare behind hit the water. It was a little warmer than he expected, which banished the gooseflesh on his skin. The cabin was warm enough—he'd gone a bit overboard building up the fire—but drafts still sneaked in where the walls weren't sealed properly and the wind had really picked up.

Using an enamel pitcher, Robbie scooped up water and poured it over his chest. The sound of the pump ceased, as did Martin's humming. Robbie glanced over his shoulder, and Jehoshaphat, the look on Martin's face... "Martin?"

"You are"—Martin's voice was rough and thrilling—"beyond a doubt the most beautiful thing I have ever seen in my life."

Heat rushed outward from Robbie's chest—up his throat to his face and down to his groin, where his pecker tried to rear itself above the water. "You've seen me before. In situations a lot less awkward."

"Every sight is like the first, my dear." He abandoned the pot at the washbasin and moved toward Robbie like a stalking cat. "And I can't imagine ever growing tired of it." He hunkered down next to the tub, wrapped his hand behind Robbie's neck, and drew him in for a kiss that was hotter and wetter than the bath. Then he leaned his forehead against Robbie's temple. "I am, without a doubt, the luckiest son of a bitch on the planet."

"Martin...."

"But you still stink." He grinned and slapped Robbie's wet shoulder. "Wash up. I've got plans for you once we're both clean."

"P-plans? What sort of plans?"

Martin stood and sauntered back to the pump to collect his abandoned pot of water. "Why, getting dirty again, of course. In the best possible way and as many times as we can manage before dawn."

Robbie blinked. "Those are good plans."

"Then get moving, Robinson. We've got things to do."

While Martin took his bath, Robbie, dressed in fresh clothing, eyed the stack of wood next to the stove. At the rate they were going, they'd need to bring more in from the porch, but he didn't want to open the door and let in the cold while Martin was naked in the tub.

Martin is naked in the tub.

Robbie tripped over the edge of a rug on the way to the table but managed to keep on his feet. *Not that I'd've banged my head. My pecker would have stopped my fall.*

He sorted through the supplies on the table. Dinner. They were going to eat dinner. Fried chicken. Biscuits.

Martin is naked in the tub.

Robbie dropped a potato, and it rolled across the rug to bang against the side of the washtub.

Martin stopped humming. "Rob? Is everything all right?"

"Y-yes. Fine. Everything's fine."

"You're sure?"

Robbie nodded and fumbled with the loaf of bread. *We don't need the bread. Biscuits. We're having biscuits.*

"All right. If you're sure." The sound of splashing resumed, as did Martin's humming.

"What—What's that song?"

"Hmmm? Oh." He chuckled. "It's called 'Old-Fashioned Garden.' It's from a show called—if you can believe it—*Hitchy-Koo*."

"Did you sing it? In the show?"

"Me? No. That was after I'd gotten my start in pictures, but I wouldn't have rated a solo anyway. Sid and I never made it out of the back row of the chorus."

"Sid?" Robbie set the bread down. "Your manager Sid? The one who fixed up my contract? He used to be an actor?"

Martin stood up and water sluiced off his haunches in a very distracting way. "Only in the very loosest sense. Like I said, we never made it out of the chorus. If it weren't for pictures, we'd probably both still be there."

"So Sid decided he didn't want to be an actor?"

Martin stopped toweling himself dry. An odd expression flickered across his face—or maybe it was the shadows cast by the lantern. "He did. We both did. But I'm the one who got tapped."

"Because you're handsome, and Sid... well...."

"Sid isn't. Yes. It's not fair, because to be frank, he was a better chorus boy than I was. He at least had taken dance classes, even if they were social dances, not ballet or tap. But audiences have expectations about the faces they'll pay to see projected twenty feet high, and Sid's didn't make the cut."

Martin resumed humming as he stepped out of the tub and finished drying off.

"There's that song again."

Martin chuckled. "So it is. The lyrics talk about a 'dear little shack.' I suppose I'm feeling sentimental about our cabin." He tossed his towel aside, advanced on Robbie, and trapped him against the table. "Although I wasn't in it, I saw the show on Broadway. The song was written by Cole Porter. He's... one of us."

Robbie's brain was having difficulty focusing on anything other than Martin's skin, because it was all *right there*. "Us?"

"He's in the life."

Robbie swallowed convulsively. "You mean—"

"Yes, my dear. I do. He likes to have sex with men, for all he's married and extremely devoted to his wife."

Robbie's eyes widened. "Does she *know*?"

Martin smiled gently. "Of course she does. And she's equally devoted to him regardless. Marriage is hedged around with expectations and laws and religious pomposity, but really it's a contract between two people, not so different from the contracts we have with the studio. What Cole and Linda do—or don't do

—in their bedroom is nobody's business but theirs, provided it makes them both happy and contented."

"Does that happen a lot? Those kinds of marriages?"

"More often than you might think, particularly in Hollywood, where we're granted a great deal of personal license and conversely are under far greater scrutiny than the average shopkeeper in Omaha. A lavender marriage can grant both partners security and a certain legitimacy that keeps the morality bloodhounds at bay. For instance—" Martin's gaze slid away from Robbie's face. "—you could marry your friend Dottie."

"Marry Dottie? Why would I want to do that? I don't want to sleep with her."

"And unless I miss my guess, she doesn't want to sleep with you either."

Robbie blinked. "She doesn't? Who does—" He shook his head. "Never mind. It's none of my business."

Martin caressed Robbie's cheek. "Evelyn, of course. Dottie is absolutely smitten with Evelyn. Why do you think she wanted her for Elizabeth Townsend?"

"Because she's a good actress?"

"She is, but there are other good actresses. No, she wanted the chance to spend time with her, just as I wanted the opportunity to spend time with you."

"But I thought—That is, you and Miss Trent seem so close."

"We are. We're very dear friends. But we are not, nor have we ever wished to be, bed partners." He trailed a finger along Robbie's throat. "And despite how much easier it could make both of our lives—assuming one or both Schlossbergs wouldn't try to murder me before the wedding night—we've never considered marrying each another either. Neither one of us wanted to live with that kind of deception."

"Oh."

"Dottie and Evelyn are luckier than we are in certain ways. The public is willing to accept a close friendship—one that involves sharing interests, a home, a life—between two women with relative equanimity. But God forbid anyone suggest the same is possible between two men. On the other hand...." Martin gestured to the room around them. "Our two very dear friends aren't fortunate enough to be ensconced, as we are, in a dear little shack where the weather and primitive conditions keep everyone else at bay. But if I know Evelyn—and I do— she'll find a way to arrange something equally romantic."

"You think she likes Dottie too? In that way, I mean?"

"Besotted, my dear. Absolutely besotted. Evelyn could never resist the little feisty ones, especially when they've got such obvious talent. But do you know what?" Martin stepped closer, still completely naked, his erection seeming to reach for Robbie's—which was reaching right back. "Now that I'm clean, I don't want to talk about them anymore."

"Y-you want to have dinner, then? F-f-fried chicken? B-biscuits?"

"Dinner," Martin said as he threaded his fingers in Robbie's hair and pressed his mouth against Robbie's neck, "can wait."

CHAPTER TWENTY

Afterward, with Robbie lying against Martin's chest and the fire and wind singing a subtle duet, Martin allowed himself to drift, to pretend that they could have this feeling, this closeness, forever.

And why couldn't we?

He had an extra room in his bungalow. Robbie could move in, ostensibly to occupy it. That kind of thing happened all the time. Sid's warning about Jack Kerrigan and his "secretary" wiggled its way into Martin's head, but he banished it. He wasn't Jack. Robbie wasn't... whatever the fellow's name was. And thanks to Leo, the fan magazines had already been primed with stories about Martin's friendship with Robbie and the fairy-tale beginnings of Robbie's career.

The fans did love a good fairy tale. Martin wondered if any of them realized that every word printed in those magazines was just as preposterous as anything by the Brothers Grimm.

But with that groundwork already laid, having Robbie move in wouldn't be shocking. Although the bungalow *was* a bit small and the neighbors rather too close—the shared walls between his half of the building and Mr. Pendergast's introduced a bit of risk, given Robbie's rather, er, *vocal* enthusiasm for their lovemaking. *A house. I've been wanting to buy a house.* Maybe up in Pasadena. No, that was too far from the studios. Where would Robbie like to live? In the hills? By the ocean? They could start looking as soon as they got back to town.

"Martin?"

"Yes, my dear?"

"You said Sid had taken social dance classes. But didn't you? I mean, aren't aristocrats expected to be able to dance at parties?"

Suddenly Martin was wide-awake, the sweet post-lovemaking lethargy banished. *He doesn't know the truth. How can I ask anything from him when he doesn't even know who I am?*

"Ordinarily, yes."

Robbie rose up on one elbow, his blond eyebrows bunched in obvious concern, probably because he detected the wariness in Martin's tone. "I don't mean to pry, but I don't know anything about aristocrats." He uttered an awkward half chuckle. "I didn't even know they were... you know... bare." His eyes flicked to Martin's waist. "Down there."

"Circumcised, you mean?"

Robbie winced. "Sorry?"

Martin sighed and took his courage in both hands. "I'm circumcised because I'm a Jew, Rob."

"You are?" Robbie's eyes widened. "Really? I didn't think they let Jews be aristocrats. I mean...." He covered his face with one hand. "Jehoshaphat, Martin, I'm such a hick. I don't mean to insult you."

An unexpected smile ambushed Martin's mouth. *Good God, he's so marvelous.* He gently drew Robbie's hand down and kissed his mouth. "You needn't be so mortified, my dear, because you're perfectly correct. They don't really allow Jews to be aristocrats."

"But—"

"I'm not an aristocrat."

"I know. Your father disowned you after you got kicked out of that last school, and you came to America, to that farm in

Kansas where they sent wayward nobility. The same one Mr. Taylor was at. You had to—"

"Hush." Martin placed his fingers across Robbie's lips. "Yes, that's Martin Brentwood's story. But I'm not Martin Brentwood." Martin swallowed and deliberately let his accent slip back to the way he'd spoken before Sid had taught him better. "I'm Marvin Gottschalk. A tailor's apprentice from Flushing, Queens." He laughed mirthlessly and let his hand fall to his chest. "And the name of the borough is as close as I've ever been to royalty."

Robbie blinked. "Does Sid know?" His whisper was nearly inaudible above the wind whistling around the cabin, rattling the windows behind the heavy blanket curtains.

This time, Martin's laugh was bitter. "Darling, *Sid* is the disgraced aristocrat. We've been friends since he ditched that Kansas reform farm and ran away to make it in show business. We traded life stories back when we tried to break into pictures. I got the jobs because of how I looked—which was exactly why Sid didn't. So he cut his losses and became my manager instead."

"So Sid isn't Jewish either?"

"Hardly. But my persona was perfect for him as a manager." Martin flicked his fingers. "The Schlossbergs. Mayer. Zukor. Schenck. They're all working-class Jews. My life, my backstory, put him on equal footing with them, made them less defensive, less suspicious." He shrugged. "It's worked out for both of us."

"Wow," Robbie breathed. "I'd never have guessed. You sound so... so *English*."

Martin chuckled. "I was always good with accents. Sid had more trouble learning to speak poorly than I had learning to speak well. It helped that I had a fairly decent early education, although that was purely by accident. Now?" He shrugged. "It's second nature. I even *think* in British idioms."

Robbie hadn't settled back against him again. *Oh God. I've ruined it. I've finally told somebody the truth, and he's the one person who could completely destroy me. What in blazes was I* thinking?

Martin flung an arm across his eyes and blessed the dimness in the cabin that would keep him from seeing the disgust on Robbie's face. *Maybe I should have told him this when it was possible for us to leave gracefully.* Because they were stuck here. Yes, he supposed one or the other of them could trudge his way up to the lodge, but with the way the wind was keening, it would be a miserable half-mile hike in the dark, with no way into town until the morning.

In fairness, I suppose I should be the one to offer. I was the one who lied, after all.

"If you want me to go, I'll understand."

"Go? It's nighttime, and it sounds like the wind's about to take the roof off anyway. Why would I want you to go?"

"You just found out that you're in bed with a Jew. Isn't that reason enough?"

Robbie chuckled. "I think the fact I'm in bed with a *man* is a little more shocking than that I'm in bed with a Jew. It doesn't matter, Martin. None of it matters as long as we've got this."

"Don't you understand? I'm a completely imaginary person, Robbie. There's nothing real about me. Not my name, not my voice, not my life story. It's all a sham."

"That's not so."

Martin lifted his arm and glared. "I've just *told* you—"

"Yes, I know. The stuff you put on for Hollywood. I get it. But it's not *you*, Martin. It's like another part you're playing for the pictures. It's nothing but window dressing. The real Martin is a man who'll give an ignorant, bewildered country boy *directions*, even though that idiot is suppose be his chauffeur, for crying out loud, then tips him five dollars to boot. The real Martin runs to the rescue when that same ignorant, bewildered country boy nearly gets raped in a public park. The real Martin grounds the... the...."

"Ignorant, bewildered country boy?" Martin murmured, his heart lodged somewhere in his throat.

"Yes, him. The real Martin was there, grounding him when he was tossed in front of a motion picture camera where he had no business. Then held him when it all got to be too much." Robbie gazed down at Martin in the flickering light, his expression tender, and stroked Martin's hair and then his cheek. "The real Martin is right here. The rest of it, all the stuff that you put on for Hollywood, that's not the real Martin. That's for the benefit of the studio. The producers. The audience. And if that's all they want? They don't *deserve* the real Martin."

"Then it's a good thing I don't want them to have him." Martin drew Robbie down against his chest and wrapped his arms around him. "Now that I consider it, the only person who deserves the real Martin is Robinson Crusoe Goodman. And I intend to let Robinson Crusoe Goodman have every. Last. Inch. of Martin Brentwood. Now."

Last night had been…. Robbie didn't even know how to describe it. Martin had been tender one moment, masterful and demanding the next, and Robbie realized that, despite how wonderful their lovemaking had been in the past—the few times they'd had during the busy shooting schedule—Martin had always been holding something of himself back.

The real Martin.

He'd still been acting, at least a little bit, never fully naked even when neither one of them was wearing a stitch of clothing.

But last night, after he'd told Robbie the truth about his past, about how much of his life was just another kind of performance, his lovemaking had changed too.

If Robbie hadn't experienced *before*—the mannered, careful Martin, who took Robbie apart at the seams, and, while he obviously enjoyed their encounters, never lost that last bit of suave self-control—then *now* wouldn't have been such a revelation.

Because last night Martin had been different, free to show Robbie what he really wanted. Free to want, to ask, to *beg* for Robbie's every touch. Everywhere.

When he'd risen on his hands and knees, and in a shattered voice that held no trace of the sophisticated Martin Brentwood accent, begged Robbie to take him, to enter him, to… to *fuck* him? That was something Robbie would never forget, not as long as he lived.

And when Robbie did as Martin asked, slick with oil and so hard he *hurt*, the heat, the tightness, the *rightness* of it all…. If Robbie hadn't already been kneeling behind Martin, he'd have genuflected right there.

But this morning, lying next to Martin, the wind howling outside couldn't drown out the clamor of his own thoughts.

He told me the truth. He bared himself to me in so many ways. But he doesn't know me.

The idea of telling Martin the truth about his own cowardice, his betrayal, his flight, made Robbie's pecker forget that Martin was stretched out next to him, warm and naked under the blankets, keeping the cold of the cabin at bay.

If I tell him, will he look at me differently? If I tell him, will we ever have another night like this again?

Coward that he was, he didn't want the answers to those questions, because he was afraid of what the answers would be. But if he didn't tell the truth, Robbie might never be able to meet Martin's eyes in the daylight again. *And he'd probably notice that.*

To put off the decision as long as he could, he eased out of bed and scrambled into his clothes. The air was chilly, but not frigid, so if he built up the fire and put water on to heat, they ought to be comfortable bathing in the washtub this morning before they braved the wind to walk up to the lodge to catch their ride into Truckee. Although maybe Martin would prefer to go up earlier and bathe in a real tub.

Call him selfish, but Robbie pushed that idea away. If Martin suggested it, he'd go along of course, but he sure wasn't going to bring it up on his own. Because once they left the cabin, they'd be back in the world where Martin had to pretend again.

So. More wood.

He filled a bucket at the pump and set it a foot or so away from the door—far enough away to let him slide through but close enough to keep it from blowing open. Then he lifted the bar, slipped outside, and latched the door behind him.

"Jeee-*hosaphat*."

The world was white. Snow was blowing straight sideways, and drifts had built up against the cabin and spilled onto half the porch. The trees, which Robbie knew were only twenty yards away, were invisible. Heck, he couldn't see two feet beyond the porch rail, and even that was nothing but white.

Luckily, the wood pile was on the side of the porch not buried in snow. Robbie gathered an armful and bundled it inside, then went back three more times before barring the door against the storm.

"Robbie?" Martin sat up, his chest bare in the light sneaking in from behind the blankets. "We'll be leaving this morning. Do we really need that much wood?"

"We're not going anywhere." Robbie stripped off his coat, hat, and gloves, and knelt in front of the stove.

"But the driver will be picking us up in—" Martin fished his pocket watch out from under the bed. "God, an hour. I didn't realize it was so late." He grinned. "I must have been worn out."

"The car won't be here." Robbie shoved logs into the stove with shaking hands. Then he stopped and took a deep breath before he smothered the embers completely. "There's a storm, Martin. A blizzard. We can't go anywhere until it lets up, and even then, if the snow gets too high, we might be stuck for a while."

"Shite," Martin muttered. "I should have taken you up to the lodge last night. Then at least you'd be comfortable. Oh, well. We can head up there now to wait it out."

"Martin, it's a *blizzard*. I know they don't have them in Hollywood, but they must have them in New York."

"Probably. But I don't recall—"

"A fellow a couple of farms over from ours got lost in a white-out blizzard like this, walking from his house to his barn, a trip he'd taken every day for his entire *life*. They found him three days later, frozen to death in a field two miles in the other direction."

"So what you're saying is…." Martin's grin grew. "We'll have to stay here. Alone. Together. Until the storm clears up?"

"Yes. That's exactly what I'm saying."

"What a hardship." He lay back down. "Come back to bed."

Robbie didn't move. "As long as it doesn't last more than a couple of days, we'll be all right. We've got water. Food. We can bake those stupid potatoes in the stove. It won't be fancy, but we won't starve."

Martin frowned and rose up on one elbow. "Robinson, if I didn't know better, I'd think you were avoiding me. Which is patently impossible in a one-room cabin with a storm raging outside. What's wrong?" Something flickered across Martin's face, something very like… fear. "You don't regret—"

"No! Jehoshaphat, Martin, I'll *never* regret that. Not ever. But…." Robbie rubbed his hands on his trousers. "I can't…. You don't know…."

"Rob. Tell me what's wrong. Please." He patted the bed. "You can tell me anything."

Anything? Robbie wasn't sure about that, but it wasn't fair *not* to tell now. Despite wanting nothing more than to feel Martin's touch, his reassurance, Robbie stayed where he was, the stove heating his backside until sweat prickled his skin. *Or maybe that's fear.* "I told you last night that pictures don't deserve the real Martin."

Martin smiled, a light in those incredible dark eyes. "You did, and I'm uncertain whether I properly expressed my appreciation." He patted the bed next to him. "Come here."

"The thing is, Martin, I don't think I deserve you either."

Martin's smile turned tender. *I definitely don't deserve* that. "You're the best man I know, Rob. The best I've *ever* known. If there's a question of *deserving* here, I'm pretty sure I'm the one who'd be found wanting."

"You don't know the whole truth. About why I came to Hollywood."

Martin's brows drew together—not in a frown, but in concern. "You don't owe me anything, Rob. We've agreed, haven't we, that the past will remain firmly in the past, that we'll only look forward from now on?"

"Yes." Robbie nodded jerkily. *Now. It's now or never.* "But first I want to tell you. About my best friend. About Frank."

Martin's expression didn't clear. "All right. Go ahead, but only if you want to."

Robbie crept forward and sat on the edge of the bed, far enough away that he couldn't feel Martin's heat next to him. "Frank Westin was my best friend. Had been since we were boys. His pa's farm and mine were right next to each other, and when Ma was still running the school, Frank and me were always in the same lessons." Robbie couldn't help a smile then. "Always in the same trouble too. Frank could pretty much talk me into anything, but he never let me take the blame. He was an adventurous fellow, but a stand-up one. He'd never make anyone take a risk that he hadn't taken first. He—" Robbie's breath hitched in his chest.

"It's all right, Rob." Martin rested his hand in the small of Robbie's back. "Go on. I'm here."

I shouldn't let him touch me. He won't want to touch me when he knows. And since this might be the last time Martin would want to touch him, Robbie decided to be selfish a second time. He didn't move away.

"Frank was smart. Way smarter than me. He went to college down in Boise while I stayed back to work on the farm. Eddie was already gone by then, so things weren't too great. Pa was angry. Ma was... lost. So when Frank came home at Christmastime, he didn't have to work very hard to convince me to run down to Boise with him. There was a thing he wanted to show me, he said. A thing he thought I'd like." Robbie's voice disappeared on the last word.

"Rob, he didn't force you, did he?" Martin's tone was fierce, dangerous.

"What? No. Never." Robbie took a deep breath. "But the thing is, Frank knew before I did that I'd never want to marry a girl. That I wanted something—*somebody* else."

"You wanted Frank."

"No. Or not really. More the *idea* of Frank. Of what it meant that if I had to pick somebody to kiss and had to choose between all the girls I'd ever met and him, that I'd have picked him. Same as he'd have picked me."

"Ah." Martin began to rub small circles on Robbie's back. "I see."

"Anyway, he and I took off for the city. I didn't tell Pa I was going. I told Ma, but she didn't hear. She never does anymore."

"Rob." Martin's voice was choked nearly as much as Robbie's.

"No, it's okay. I'm used to that by now." He tangled his fingers together between his knees. "There was this place you could go in this building, he told me. You could stand on one side of a wall. Take your pecker out and... and...."

"I know what you're talking about. You don't need to say more."

"But I do!" Robbie turned and gripped Martin's wrist so his hand wasn't touching Robbie's back anymore. "I do." He let go and turned away again. He couldn't look in Martin's face when he said this, when he confessed. "Frank had told me in the truck on the way down that he'd found some other fellows at college like him. Like us. That what we liked, what we wanted, wasn't shameful as long as we weren't hurting anybody else. That he knew I wasn't sure, but there was a way to find out."

"So he took you to a glory hole for your first experience? Good God."

"No, see, one of these other fellows he'd met, he'd taken Frank there first. So Frank knew. He wanted me to have the same chance. So we went there. To the place. We weren't the only ones. Some other fellows were ahead of us, but just as one came out, buttoning up his trousers, the police came."

"Shite. A raid?"

Robbie nodded. "We tried to get out. Suddenly there seemed to be way more men there than I'd realized. Frank and me and the fellow who'd just come out, we made it down a hall and out the back door. Frank pushed me in one direction and told me to run. He went the other, but the other fellow, he ran the same way I did. The police—they'd come around the other side of the building and caught another man. They—they *beat* him, Martin, and he was *apologizing*, but they kept hitting—"

Martin wrapped his arms around him, and this time Robbie didn't pull away. "Shhh. You mustn't blame yourself for not interfering."

Robbie's stomach felt as though it were filled with red-hot stones. "No? Because Frank saw what they were doing, and he *went back*. He tried to stop them, and when they turned on him instead, started beating him? I didn't help. My best friend in the world and I didn't help. Instead, I turned my back on him and ran. And kept on running. For *weeks*."

"Until you fetched up on the shores of Hollywood, exactly like Robinson Crusoe."

Robbie punched his thigh. "If Crusoe was a damned *coward*."

"Robbie—"

"I ran away, Martin. I got away clean and left him there, being beaten by three policemen. Even if he s-s-survived, do you know what they do to men who're convicted of… of *that* up in Idaho?"

"No," Martin murmured. "But I can imagine."

"*Anything they damn well please,* that's what. And the worst part is, I don't even know what they *did* do to him."

"Do you *want* to know?" Martin said, his voice way kinder than Robbie deserved.

"I've tried to find out. I get a Boise newspaper delivered to my boarding house. There's never been a word about him, but whatever it was could have happened while I was on the road. I had no way of finding out anything then."

"Rob, you do realize we work for a studio with a positive *spiderweb* of connections in the newspaper industry, don't you? You've also got a manager."

"Wh-what do you mean?"

"I mean, we can ask Sid or Leo or both of them to investigate. To find out what happened."

"But what if we find out that he… that he…."

"This uncertainty is eating you alive, sweetheart." Martin twined his fingers with Robbie's. "Wouldn't you rather know for sure? And who can tell? There might be something you could do about it to make amends."

Could there really be a way? "Sid, then. I don't want Leo to know."

"You're probably right." Martin kissed him. "Now get undressed and get under the blankets. There's a blizzard raging outside, and I need you to keep me warm."

CHAPTER TWENTY-ONE

"Martin. Wake up." Robbie's voice pulled Martin out of a deep sleep. "I want you to see something."

"Mmmphm." Martin burrowed farther under the blankets, because damn it was *cold* in the cabin this morning. "If it's not your naked skin, I'm not interested." He patted the cot, but he wasn't foolish enough to do so on top of the blankets. "Come back to bed."

Robbie's chuckle was a lovely low burr. "No, really. You need to get up. You can bring the blanket with you."

Martin peered over the edge of the covers. Robbie was fully dressed—including coat, hat, gloves—and was smiling at him from inside the doorway. Snow was scattered on the mat around his boots. "Is the storm over?"

Robbie nodded. "Come and see."

Martin wrestled himself out of the bed, but as Robbie had suggested, he wrapped the blanket around himself and shuffled across the room. "Here I am."

Robbie grinned and unlatched the door.

"Robinson, what are you doing? You'll let the cold—oh!" Martin's jaw dropped, and he shuffled the last few feet to step out onto the porch, cold be damned, because the world was *magical*. There was no other word. Not a breath of wind stirred the trees, and the sun just clearing the treetops set the snow—which came all the way to the top of the porch railing—sparkling like a field of diamond shards. Somewhere a fox barked, but otherwise there wasn't a sound. "It's beautiful."

"Yes." Robbie closed the distance between them. "The morning after a storm can be like this." He chuckled again. "And we're lucky. We don't have to stay here and shovel it all away."

Martin turned, and the blanket parted to let a *very* unwelcome chill skate over his skin. "We don't? Surely the studio cars can't make it up here with *this* on the roads. Do they even plow this far?"

"No, but the innkeeper came out while I was getting more wood." Robbie pointed to a double line of disturbed snow leading from the tree line. "He said King Vidor's crew is planning to walk down to Truckee this morning. We should join them."

"It's eight bloody miles," Martin grumbled. "I haven't walked eight miles at one time in my entire life. And have you seen the snow out there? It's as high as my waist."

Robbie grinned and pointed to a jumble of bent wood and leather at the edge of the porch. "The innkeeper brought snowshoes as well as information."

Martin choked on a laugh. "Not the ones we wore for the picture, I hope."

Robbie joined his laughter, and the sound seemed to spiral up to the sky. "Of course not. Modern ones. But they're not really so different. And at least you've had practice."

"Too much of it. Why it waited until now to present us with perfect *California Trail* snow instead of forcing us to cart it down from higher up the mountain, I'll never know."

"The studio may control the press and the police, but they can't control the weather."

Martin huffed and wrapped the blanket tighter around his shoulders. "Give Mayer and Zukor and the Schlossbergs time and they'll figure out how to do it."

"In any case, I don't think the blizzard was personal."

"You'll never convince me of that."

Robbie's face turned serious, and he cupped Martin's jaw with his gloved hand. "We've both got responsibilities back in Hollywood. If nothing else, we need to be there to support Dottie in her fight to save *The California Trail* from becoming *The California Cavalry Brigade*. I'd feel better if we weren't making the trek alone."

He nudged Martin back through the door and closed it behind them. "And think of the publicity, the headlines Leo can spin. *Actors Relive Their Characters' Real-Life Trek*, or something like that."

Martin couldn't resist Robbie's grin, nor could he argue that Robbie made an excellent point. Recreating Moses and Dennis's journey—or at least a part of it—would feed the studio publicity machine like nobody's business. "You know, you may need to reconsider your skepticism about the studio controlling the weather. Because now that you've mentioned it, this is exactly the kind of thing Jacob would have ordered." He sighed and then dropped a kiss on Robbie's mouth. "I suppose a snowshoe trek is in our future, then. But if you love me, could we have coffee first?"

Robbie's cheeks, already pink with cold, reddened further. "I —"

Martin realized what he'd said. "Oh God, Rob. I didn't mean to imply that—"

"No. It's all right. I've never said it, have I?" Robbie's clear blue eyes met Martin's, steady and unflinching. "I love you, Martin. Of course I do."

Heat bloomed in Martin's chest. *To hell with the blanket*. He dropped it and snaked his arms under Robbie's coat. "Good. Because I love you. So much." He kissed Robbie, but not so deeply as to start something, because despite the fire and the warmth from the avowal, not to mention from Robbie himself, Martin had just been outside in nothing but a blanket, and his bollocks were still attempting to crawl inside his body. "Does that mean you'll make coffee?"

Robbie chuckled. "Yes, Martin. I'll make coffee. But before you drink more than one cup, you might want to think about whether you really want to pull your pecker out halfway down the mountain to pee against a pine tree."

"Hmmm. Good point." He glanced around the room, at the narrow beds they'd pushed together to make one larger one, at the clothes scattered about, at the remains of the meals they'd shared—really, how brilliant was Martin to choose a lover who could make biscuits in a skillet on top of a woodstove? "I suppose we should clean up a bit."

"A little. I'll toss the leftovers into the trees as we're leaving. We should, um, move the beds."

Martin smiled at Robbie's flush. "Yes, I imagine that would be wise."

"But the innkeeper said they'll pack everything else up for us and send our luggage into town on a sledge later. We only need to bring ourselves."

"And you, my darling, are a surfeit of riches."

So that's what they did. As they trekked down the hill, the only sounds the *shush*ing of their own footsteps and the faint shouts and laughter from King Vidor's group up ahead, Martin was able to simply enjoy the beauty of the woods and the sharp, clear morning. The exercise was keeping him warm, there was no wind to cut through their coats, and his lover was next to him.

Could anything be more perfect than this?

He cut a glance at Robbie, who was gazing up at an eagle soaring above the treetops, the sun burnishing its feathers from brown to gold. *I can't lose this. I can't lose* him. *There must be some way we can continue to live together, sleep together, wake up together.* Bill Taylor and George Hopkins managed to keep their personal relationship a secret, hidden in plain sight behind their professional collaboration. Could he and Robbie do the same?

After this picture, Robbie was bound to be a star, probably a brighter one than Martin had ever been or could hope to be. Martin turned that idea over in his head. Did he care? If he wasn't a Star With A Capital S, he wouldn't have the same pressure on him to present a pristine image to the press and public. Joseph Henabery had made a respectable career out of playing character parts once he wowed Griffith with his portrayal of Lincoln in *Birth of a Nation*. Edward Everett Horton had never aspired to stardom, but as a dependable supporting actor of a particular type, he was never out of work.

Martin wouldn't mind that kind of career. Sid could probably arrange it, although he might complain. But if he had Robbie's career to guide, maybe he wouldn't complain *quite* as much.

If only I knew how to do something besides acting. He huffed a laugh at that notion. He had no other skills outside of pictures. His tailoring abilities had never risen above the adequate, and nobody in pictures needed Martin's ability to coax round tones and appropriate accents out of less than stellar voices, as he'd done back in his vaudeville days for stage performers who were trying to jump from chorus to featured players.

"Martin?"

Martin turned his head to find Robbie gazing at him with a smile that melted his bones. "Hmmm?"

"What's so funny?"

"Funny? Nothing."

"But a moment ago, you laughed."

"I did?" Martin retraced his thoughts. *I don't need to share my lack of marketable skills with him.* "I suppose I did." He checked the snow-covered road ahead, but Vidor's group was out of sight around a curve. Although he couldn't wrap an arm around Robbie or move in for a kiss for fear their snowshoes would get tangled and they'd go down in a heap, never to be found until spring, he laced their gloved fingers together. "Maybe it's because I'm happy."

Robbie ducked his head and peered at Martin from under his hat brim. "You are?"

"I am. *You* make me happy."

He blinked, and his cheeks pinked above his blond beard. "I do?"

"Never doubt it."

"You—" Robbie swallowed, his gaze dropping to his feet. "You make me happy too, Martin. More than I ever thought I could be."

If he's happy and I'm happy, who has any right to say we can't be happy together?

Martin cleared his throat. "So I've been thinking. Are you still renting that room?"

Robbie glanced up, obviously confused by Martin's non sequitur. "Yes. Three dollars a week."

Sid's voice murmured in Martin's memory, warning him about the flimsy tale of Jack Kerrigan's "secretary" holed up with him in his "Kumfy Kerrigan Kottage." *Shut up, Sid.* "My bungalow has a second bedroom. What would you think about moving in there?"

Robbie's eyebrows shot up. "Move into your house? With you?"

"It's not unheard of. Bill Taylor had a live-in assistant." Martin winced. "Although perhaps that's a bad example, since the bastard robbed Bill and wrecked his car. But other people who work in pictures share accommodations. It's convenient, especially when we're going to the same place for work every day."

"So… you want me to live in your spare bedroom?"

Martin squeezed Robbie's hand. "No, my dear. I want you to live in *my* bedroom. But nobody else in the world needs to know that. With the publicity Leo's already spreading about our friendship on *The California Trail*, it might even play well to the press."

"We'd be pretending?" Robbie's voice held an odd tone, but Martin couldn't tell whether it was reluctance or simply consideration.

"Yes. Exactly. Although...." He mentally reviewed the other inhabitants of the bungalow court. Far too many of them were involved in the industry. While the average American had no notion about what it meant for two men to be in the life, Martin had no illusions about anyone in motion pictures. "I've been thinking it might be time for me to buy a house. We could find one that's too big for one man, but perfect for two."

"A house?" Robbie's smile glimmered into being. "With a garden?"

"Do you want a garden?"

"More than anything. I laid out Ma's kitchen garden once, because I didn't see any reason it couldn't be pretty, same as a flower bed. Pa made me plow it under and do it properly."

"If you want a garden, then a garden you shall have, to plant whatever way you want. What do you say?"

Robbie's smile was brighter than the sun on the snow. "I'd love that."

Martin glanced down the road again. The roofs of Truckee were visible, but the road was deserted. Vidor's gang must already have reached town. He pulled Robbie to a stop and leaned in for a kiss, the mist of their breath surrounding them, Robbie's mouth fiery compared to the frigid air. "Then that's what we'll do. As soon as we get back to Hollywood, we'll start looking."

"All right."

Both of them were still grinning like loons when they walked into the bar attached to the hotel where Citadel had installed their staff. The room was strangely subdued, but as soon as he and Robbie cleared the door, Dottie rushed over to them, her mouth pressed in a straight line and a hint of fear in her eyes.

Good God, I forgot. The trial. The jury deliberations. He grabbed her hands. "They convicted him? Roscoe?"

"No."

Martin clenched his eyes shut. "Thank God."

"But they didn't acquit him either. It's another mistrial. But —"

"What? How many times are they going to put him through this? That damn DA—"

"Martin." The rawness in Dottie's normally cheerful voice cut Martin's tirade off at the knees. "There's something else. Something worse."

"Worse?" Martin glanced around at the other people in the bar and noticed for the first time that there was a somber cluster of Hollywood folks in the corner, where King Vidor was huddled with an older man. *His father.* "What could be worse?"

"It's Bill Taylor."

Ice washed through Martin's belly. He released Dottie's hands. "The press," he croaked. "Did they find out about George? About the Mount Lowe evenings? Surely the Famous Players-Lasky publicity department can fix it. They can fix anything."

"Not this." Dottie put a gentle hand on Martin's arm. "He's been murdered, Martin. William Desmond Taylor is dead."

At the table in the club car, blocked in by Jacob Schlossberg's bulk on one side and Leo McCorkle on the other, Robbie didn't hear more than one in ten words that the two men kept flinging at him. Not that it mattered. If he tried to speak, they talked over him anyway.

Mr. Jacob's cigar smoke curled around Robbie's head, making his eyes water and the back of his throat burn. *That's what I'll tell them, if anyone asks.* Because the real reason for his leaking eyes and burning throat was his distance from Martin—and not only physical distance.

"—interview with *Photoplay*—"

"—next picture with Boyd—"

"—appointment with a photographer—"

"—find the right co-star—"

"—escort to Zukor's party—"

Robbie nodded occasionally and let them interrupt each other, his attention fixed on Martin, who was sitting on the other side of the car, staring out the window, his hands white-knuckled on his knees. They'd barely spoken since Dottie gave them bad news and *worse* news. Robbie hoped that was because Mr. Jacob and Leo had descended and hadn't left them alone or stopped talking since—not in the smoky room at the hotel in Truckee, not in the limousines to Sacramento, and not after they'd all boarded the train back to Hollywood.

Robbie *ached* to hold Martin, to touch him, to talk to him. Because the look on Martin's face when he'd heard that Mr. Taylor was dead.... *Jehoshaphat.*

Not that Robbie wasn't pretty cut up too. He'd met Mr. Taylor several times, heard him speak, respected his gentlemanly ways. But Martin had been his *friend*. They'd worked together on several pictures and still saw each other socially. What must he be feeling now?

And George Hopkins, Mr. Taylor's... friend. Before Robbie took over Moses for real, Boyd had sent him over to Famous Players-Lasky to consult with George on some set decoration details for *The California Trail*. George was funny and helpful and kind—at least he was to Robbie.

If it was me, if I'd lost Martin that way, I don't know what I'd do.

Mr. Jacob slapped the table, causing Robbie to flinch. "So that's settled."

Robbie tore his gaze from Martin. "I'm sorry. I didn't catch that."

Mr. Jacob narrowed his eyes, but Leo brayed a laugh and clapped Robbie on the shoulder. "That's perfect. That whole corn-fed aw-shucks innocence. Keep that up. The fans'll eat it up and beg for more."

"What?" Robbie's head was throbbing, and the clanging of the signal outside as the train pulled into the station didn't help. "I don't understand."

Mr. Jacob hove to his feet. "You don't have to understand. Just do what you're told. Leo." He turned and waddled off as the train pulled to a stop.

Leo jumped up, and for some reason, Robbie was reminded of a hen back on the farm who'd taken to following one of the hogs around. "I'll be in touch." He darted after Mr. Jacob, and Robbie drew the first full breath since he and Martin had walked into that hotel.

He turned toward the window where Martin had been sitting, but he wasn't there anymore. Robbie caught a glimpse of his hat and the billow of his overcoat as he swung off the train and onto the platform.

Dang it. Robbie grabbed his coat and his carpetbag, but before he could hurry after Martin, Dottie appeared at his elbow.

Everything about her seemed to droop—her shoulders, her mouth, even her usual unmanageable hair seemed flatter. *Just like today. Just like everything since we heard the news.*

How could everything be so wonderful one minute and so horrible the next? Shouldn't there be a moment in between? A chance for everyone to catch their breath? A title card, like in the pictures, warning them that life was about to go to hell?

Robbie cast one more glance at Martin's retreating back and sighed. He let his bag fall to the floor and gripped Dottie's shoulders. "You doing all right?"

She shrugged, and he could swear he felt her bones move under his hands. "I'm managing. I didn't know Bill Taylor that well, but he was a nice man. And Roscoe.... He's facing *another* trial now." She hugged her ever-present script to her chest. "Mabel must be devastated."

"Mabel?"

"Mabel Normand. She's a friend of mine. She did a lot of pictures with Roscoe and was really close to Bill. I'm going to telephone her as soon as I—" She wrinkled her nose. "Rats. I can't. Ira wants me in the cutting room right away. He wants to screen the dailies from our last shoots tonight."

"Tonight? Dottie, you've been traveling for almost twenty-four hours. And it's Sunday. Surely they can give you time to rest."

She looked at him over her spectacles and then pulled away to walk down the aisle, where a conductor holding a pocket watch was glaring at them. "This is Hollywood, Rob, and the studio is owned by two Jewish men. Sunday doesn't mean a lot to them." She ignored the conductor's hand and climbed down the steps without his help. "Besides, the way I see it, we owe it to Bill to make the best pictures we can. To keep our whole industry from dying."

He hopped down after her. "You think it could? Die? But there are hundreds, maybe thousands of nickelodeons and picture palaces all over the country, and audiences flock to them every day."

"There were thousands of taverns too, but that didn't stop Prohibition. And all those temperance societies need *something* to do with their time now that they've gotten their way over liquor. They've been squawking about the *immorality* of pictures practically since the beginning. You've seen what Hearst and the other papers have done to Roscoe." Her mouth flattened. "Bill had his own secrets to hide. If all of it should get out...."

"Jehoshaphat," Robbie murmured. *Martin.* "Excuse me a minute, would you, Dottie?"

Martin had already disappeared into the station, so Robbie sprinted down the platform and then charged through the doors, narrowly missing a porter pushing an overloaded baggage cart. He caught sight of Martin's fedora rising above a garden of flowered picture hats. The ladies in those hats blocked Robbie's path, and he lost precious moments pardoning his way through the crowd.

But finally he reached the exit and burst outside. Martin was a dozen yards down the sidewalk, standing next to an automobile—a Dixie Flyer. *Their* Dixie Flyer. But the uniformed man holding the door for him was a stranger.

"Martin!" Another baggage cart trundled past in front of Robbie, and by the time he'd ducked around it, Martin had already climbed into the back seat. "Martin!"

Martin didn't even glance Robbie's way. He said something to the strange chauffeur, who nodded curtly and closed the door.

By the time Robbie was close enough to reach the automobile, the engine had already started. He lunged for the handle, but his fingers only grazed the fender as the driver slid into traffic, and Robbie nearly took a header into the street before he could regain his balance.

Someone behind him tittered, but Robbie couldn't bring himself to care. *Before*, Martin had told Robbie he wanted them to live together, to find a house together, to *be* together. Yet Martin hadn't spoken a word to him in over a day, even though they'd never been more than a dozen yards apart.

Until now. Jehoshaphat, Martin had *left him at the curb*.

Robbie's ribs were suddenly too small. He couldn't breathe. He couldn't breathe. He couldn't *breathe*.

Is this what Frank felt like when the police closed in with their truncheons? When the cell door clanged behind him? When the judge stared him down, contempt in his eyes, and pronounced his pitiless sentence? I'll never know. Because I fucking ran away.

Like Martin had done just now.

"Rob." Dottie was suddenly there, taking his elbow and drawing him into the shelter of the station's portico while

Robbie tried not to drown in exhaust from the line of automobiles and his own panic.

"He left me." Robbie's wheeze was barely audible over the putter of engines and the blare of horns. "He *left* me, Dottie."

She patted his arm. "I know. But how could he do anything else? He could hardly kiss you in the middle of the train station."

"K-kiss? I—"

She added a bit more force to one pat until it could almost have been a punch. "I'm not stupid. You *know* I'm not. The thing about folks like you and me and Martin? The way we stay safe and free is to keep our private business *private*. All these people here? Most of 'em have no idea about what we want and how we live. *And that's how we want to keep it.* Because anything else —"

"Could kill us."

She smiled wryly. "Well, maybe not *kill* us. But—"

"No, Dottie. It could kill us. What if it killed Mr. Taylor?" *What if it killed Frank?*

She blinked, her gray eyes wide behind her lenses. "Don't think that. Please, Rob. Don't. But don't be careless either."

He stared down at her, his breath still trapped somewhere inside the vise of his rib cage. "I need to talk to him."

"Then do it. But do it privately. Not in the middle of a crowd." She stopped patting and gripped his forearm. "And remember—he's probably trying to protect you too." She let go of him and tapped her script. "You've both got a lot more to lose now."

"You think I care about a *picture*? About a bunch of people pretending to be something they're not?"

She stared at him stonily. "You ought to care. For one thing, it pays your salary—which is about to get one heck of a lot bigger, if I read Jacob right. And for another? It's damn good practice for what you'll have to do if you expect any kind of a life with Martin."

"Practice," Robbie scoffed.

"Yes. Practice. Practice until you don't even have to think about it anymore, like you did in those last days of shooting." Her shoulders rose and fell with a huge sigh. "It doesn't mean it can't be real, Rob. It doesn't mean it can't be good. It only means it can't be *public*." She gave him a little push. "Now go on. I need to get home and change before I head over to the cutting room. And you need to go—"

"Practice?"

"*Talk*." She grinned, but it was a shaky grin. "But a little practice wouldn't hurt."

CHAPTER TWENTY-TWO

Martin slumped on the davenport, legs stretched out in front of him and a half-full glass of gin cradled on his belly. He peered blearily at the glass in the dim light. *Maybe I should open the drapes. Or turn on a light.* Because it looked like the glass was empty. That couldn't be. Could it? What the hell. He grabbed the gin bottle off the table at his elbow—although he had to try twice, because for some reason it wouldn't stay still—and sloshed more into the glass.

"There. *Now* it's half-full."

A knock sounded at the door. *Go away. There's nobody here.* Had Bill heard a knock at the door? Had he answered it and let his murderer inside? There had been no sign of a struggle. Sid, who could winkle information out of a razor clam, had given him the whole scoop, and it was even worse than Martin had feared.

Famous Players-Lasky knew. And if one studio knew about the clandestine activities of its employees, regardless of how high their profile, surely all the others had similar knowledge.

If Martin never answered his door again, maybe he could pretend that he was safe.

The knock came again. "Martin?"

Robbie. God, Martin didn't want to see him. Not when he was half-drunk—or more than half. Not after he'd avoided Robbie since Dottie gave them the news. *Not after I admitted I loved him. Not after I asked him to move in.*

Because what if Robbie took him up on it? Neither one of them would ever be safe again. Somebody could knock on the door, and all Robbie's light and grace and goodness would be snuffed out, just as Bill's had been.

"Martin, I know you're in there. Please open the door."

Martin sighed hugely and nearly toppled his gin. *That would be a tragedy.* No, the tragedy would be Robbie seeing exactly how pathetic Martin Brentwood-nee-Marvin Gottschalk really was.

"Martin, please. I don't think you should be alone. I—I don't want to be alone."

Damn it. Martin could have resisted if he only had himself to torture. But torturing Robbie too? Unacceptable. He heaved himself to his feet and shuffled to the door, not daring a glance in the mirror for fear of what he'd see. *The truth. The real Martin Brentwood. How he crumbles at the first sign of adversity.*

He opened the door, and there was Robbie, standing on the doorstep with his hat in his hand and hurt all over his beautiful face. Martin choked on a laugh. "Are you *sure* you want to come in? I mean, look at me." He held out his arms, his dressing gown hanging open over his undershirt and wrinkled trousers. "You deserve so much better."

"Yes. I'm sure. May I?"

Martin executed a mocking bow and gestured grandly for Robbie to enter. "Mi casa es su casa."

Robbie frowned slightly as he passed into the living room. "I don't know what that means."

Probably just as well, since it will never be true. "Never mind." He brandished his glass. "Want some gin?"

"What? No." Robbie's nose twitched. "And I don't think you should have any more either."

"On the contrary," Martin said as he advanced on the sideboard where his liquor was stashed. "I think I should have a *lot* more." He blinked down at the bare spot where the gin bottle usually lived. "Except somebody stole my gin."

"Uh, Martin? If you're looking for the bottle, it's over here."

Martin swung around, and damn if Robbie wasn't right. The bottle was right there next to the davenport. But it was empty. Huh. *I need to call my bootlegger.*

Robbie sat on the davenport and patted the cushion next to him. "Sit down before you fall down."

Hmmm. That might not be a bad idea, considering that the floor seemed to be heaving in a very uncharacteristic way. He sat, but not too close. *Don't want to be tempted.* So he resumed his slump and let his head fall back. *This damn cushion is as hard as a rock. Why did I buy such an uncomfortable piece of shite?*

"You know what? I'm going to make some coffee."

"Coffee? I don't need that. I've got gin." Martin reached for the bottle, but Robbie snatched it out of reach. "Hey!"

"No more, Martin. Not now. It's not helping you, and you'll be sorry later." Robbie strode into the kitchen, taking the bottle with him.

"I'm sorry *now*," Martin called. *But I'll be sorrier yet if this whole situation causes Citadel to clean house.* He closed his eyes, only for a minute, to keep the room from spinning. But when he opened them again, the lamps on the desk and in the corner were lit, Robbie was sitting in the wingback chair with a book, and Martin's mouth tasted like crap. He squinted at the lights. "What time is it? Did I fall asleep?"

Robbie set his book aside. "About eight. And yes, but I think it was a good idea. How do you feel?"

"Like Doug Fairbanks tossed me off a castle onto my head."

A smile glimmered on Robbie's mouth for an instant and then disappeared. "Here. This should help." He handed Martin two aspirin and a glass of water, and Martin sighed but downed them. He got up and staggered to the bathroom to piss. While he was there, he brushed his teeth and washed his face, although nothing could help his bloodshot eyes.

When he returned to the living room, Robbie was setting a steaming cup on a coaster on the end table. "Would you like something to eat?"

Martin shuddered, his belly threatening to revolt, and dropped onto the davenport. "God, no." He took an injudiciously large gulp of coffee and burned his tongue and throat, but so what?

"Martin. I'd like to talk to you. About what happened. About Mr. Taylor and Mr. Arbuckle." Robbie's tone was bleak. "I want to understand why you ran away from me."

And there's the hurt. I knew it was coming.

How could it not? Martin had done everything short of bludgeoning Robbie with a hammer to put it there. Yet Robbie sat next to him anyway.

Martin stared into his cup, the coffee as black as his mood. "Do you know what they did? Famous Players-Lasky? Eyton, their general manager, sent George to Bill's house. While he was lying there, dead on the floor."

Robbie's hand was warm on Martin's back, and Martin didn't have the courage to pull away. "Maybe Mr. Eyton didn't know what Mr. Taylor was to George."

"Oh, he knew." Martin considered fighting Robbie for the gin bottle but settled for another scalding gulp of coffee. "Trust me. He knew."

"Then maybe... maybe his motives were purer than you think. Maybe he wanted to give George a chance to say goodbye."

Only Robbie could be that naive and good-hearted. "With the police and who knows who else swarming the place? Not likely."

"What other reason could there be?"

Martin tightened his hold on the cup until he was surprised it didn't shatter in his grip. "Because Eyton knew there might be evidence."

"Evidence of what?"

"That Bill was in the life. That he and George were… what they were to each other. And he knew George would know what to look for."

"But—"

"George took a box full of stuff from the house that morning, while they still thought Bill died of natural causes. And boxes can take things in as well as take things out. But they were covering up the *wrong fucking crime*. They'll never figure out who murdered Bill because the studio staged the whole scene to tell a different story, one that would cover their own sorry asses, and *screw* how George or Mabel or anybody might feel about it. Hell, I wouldn't be surprised if they tried to pin it on Mabel. She's the last one who saw him alive."

Robbie's eyes widened, their pupils large and dark in the dim room. "Surely they wouldn't. Miss Normand is a big star."

"Roscoe was a big star too, and that didn't make any difference. Hell, at this rate, Roscoe could be on trial for the rest of his *life*." Martin stared into his cup. *Just like we would be.*

"Surely that won't happen."

"No? And if he isn't, they could convict him. He could end up as dead as Bill." Martin stood, wobbling a little as the room swayed around him. "And you know what's worse? All those Christian ladies in their white lacy dresses and picture hats. All those preachers looking down from the bulwark of their pulpits. All the fine, upstanding moral leaders of the country. All of them, Robbie. All of them will say that he deserves it. That he deserves to die because of something he didn't even do!"

"Martin—"

"There's this Pinkerton man." Martin pounded his forehead with his fist. *What was his name?* "Hammett. That's his name. Roscoe's lawyers hired him to investigate on Roscoe's behalf.

And he says the whole thing was a frame-up, arranged by some of the corrupt local newsboys. Roscoe was good copy, so they set him up for a fall. Them and Brady, the fucking DA who imagines himself riding into the governor's mansion by trampling over Roscoe's life."

"But Martin, a woman *did* die. Surely she didn't deserve that either."

Martin's shoulders slumped. "No. She didn't. But she's not here to tell anyone what happened. Other people—people who weren't even *there*—are lying about it. *I* should have been there." Martin slammed the mug onto the sideboard. It came to pieces in his hand. He stared at the blood welling across his palm. "I should have been there."

"Martin!" Robbie grabbed Martin's wrist. "Jehoshaphat, you're bleeding like a stuck pig." He dragged Martin into the kitchen. "Here. Hold your hand under the water."

Martin let Robbie tend to him, hoarding the touches against a bleak future. The pain in his hand was a dull ache, far less acute than the pain in his chest. *Barstow gin makes a poor martini, but as an anesthetic, it's not bad.* "He asked me, you know. To go with him to that party. But I said no."

"You can't blame yourself. My ma always said the what-ifs could kill you faster than a shot in the heart." He cradled Martin's hand and peered at the cut. "I don't think you'll need stitches. It's not as bad as I thought. Do you have any bandages? Some gauze?"

"There's a first aid kit under the sink." Martin let Robbie lead him to the kitchen table and press him into a chair before he hustled over to collect the supplies. "Do you think she's right? Your ma?"

Robbie paused, his knuckles whitening as he gripped the cabinet door. "She sits at the window, waiting for my brother to walk down the lane, even though there's no question he's dead. I think what-ifs are killing her slowly, as sure as the influenza killed Eddie." Robbie stood up, the metal box in his hand. "At least Eddie went quick."

He knelt in front of Martin and, head bent, began wrapping Martin's hand in gauze. Martin longed to stroke those bright curls, drop a kiss on the skin peeping out above Robbie's collar. *Just to hold him and be held. To pretend for one minute or ten or a hundred that we have only ourselves to please. To comfort. To love.*

But the world was too cruel—people were too cruel—to allow them that peace.

It's time they both faced the truth.

Martin didn't say a word the whole time Robbie was bandaging his hand. *That can't be a good thing.* He hadn't voluntarily touched Robbie since Robbie walked in the door. *And that's* definitely *not a good thing.* It was almost worse than the trip down from Truckee. At least there was a reason for the distance then—not only the double dose of bad news, but because they were in public.

It's not fair. We should have as much right as anybody to take care of each other, whether we're in public or in private. Because Robbie had no doubt that Martin needed taking care of. Look at what he'd done today—drunk himself into a stupor on lousy gin and then cut his hand open.

Maybe if Mr. Taylor hadn't been alone, if he and George had been allowed to live together openly, he wouldn't have died alone. Heck, he might not have died at all if there'd been someone there to look after him.

There I go with the what-ifs. But if he didn't want the what-ifs to torture them both for the rest of their lives, Robbie needed to do something about it.

He taped the bandage gently but didn't let go of Martin's hand. He looked up and caught an expression on Martin's face that scared the bejesus out of him. *That's a what-if face for sure.* Regret and pain and determination were etched in the lines around his mouth, the pinch of his eyebrows, the set of his jaw. Robbie's first instinct was to back away, leave before Martin could say the words, the final words that would shatter their world into even tinier pieces, but he forced himself to stay put. *I ran once. I won't do it again.*

"Martin, I've been thinking about what you said. About me taking the room upstairs. I don't have much back at the boarding house. I could move in tonight." *So I wouldn't be alone. So you wouldn't be alone.*

Martin sighed and withdrew his hand from Robbie's grasp. "You know that's not possible anymore, Rob."

"Why?" Robbie's voice came out on a breathy squeak. "All the reasons you wanted—*we* wanted to do it are still there."

"Yes, but the reasons it would work have all been shattered. Don't you see? The press is already sniffing around for scandal. The trail might be so polluted now by false assumptions and inept investigation and studio interference that the truth about Bill's death will never come out. But that won't stop the press from looking at his *life*. And when they look, they'll find. And if they don't find, they'll invent."

"But what does that have to do with us? We weren't even in town when it happened. Reporters aren't going to be interested in us."

Martin stared down at his lap, where he'd rested his bandaged hand. "The more they dig into Bill's history, into his movements, into his world, the more likely they are to find out about us." He held up his hand when Robbie would have protested. "Not us per se, but men like us. People like us."

"People in the life, you mean."

"Yes. Most of the country doesn't even have a *name* for what we are. We can't risk giving them that name. Because once you name something, then you can start to hate it. And once you start to hate it, then...." Martin ran his uninjured hand through his hair. "Well, then you want to destroy it."

"But—"

"No buts, Rob. We had our time up in that cabin. For a moment—" A heartbreaking smile curved Martin's lips. "—a very precious, but very finite moment, we were able to shut out the truth. But that moment is over. It's time to face facts." Martin stood up. "And those facts are that we cannot live together. We can't even *be* together, not alone. From now on—" Martin's voice broke, but he cleared his throat and squared his shoulders. "From now on, we're nothing more than colleagues. We co-starred in one picture, but it's unlikely we'll ever work together again. After all…." His smile turned brittle. "Your star is rising, whereas mine is most definitely on the wane."

Robbie stood. "Don't say that. It's not so."

"I may be an expert at pretending to be this person called Martin Brentwood, but even I can't deny this particular truth. You'll be a star, Rob. And I couldn't be happier for you."

Robbie clutched Martin's arms like a shipwreck survivor clinging to a floating spar, and for the same reason. *Don't let me drown. Don't let me drift. Don't leave me castaway in this bewildering place.* "I don't want to be a star. I never did. I told you so on the day we met. It's not important to me. *You're* important."

Martin gently detached Robbie's hands. "Ah, but that won't last. Stardom has a seductive power that's hard to resist."

"*You're* the only thing I can't resist. Martin, please. Don't make me leave. Or if we can't live together, at least say we'll *be* together."

"How would we justify it? You're not my chauffeur anymore. We're not in the same picture. There's no reason for us to spend time together."

"The reason is because we… we *love* each other," Robbie cried.

Martin's eyes hardened. "But *that's* the reason nobody can ever know. Now please, Robbie. For my sake if not for your own, you need to leave."

"But—"

"Please, Rob." Martin clenched his eyes shut. "Don't make this harder than it is."

Robbie's chest was as hollow as a gourd. *I don't see how it could be any harder.* But he nodded and returned to the living room to retrieve his hat and coat. He paused, his hand on the doorknob, Martin an ocean away in the kitchen doorway. "Just promise me one thing."

"If I can."

"Don't drink anymore, Martin. Don't drink and don't take any of those drugs. I couldn't bear it if you ended up like Wesley."

Martin gazed at him, expressionless, for a moment, and then nodded. "I promise."

"Good."

"And, Rob?"

For an instant, hope fluttered in Robbie's chest. "Yes?"

"Please don't come back."

Robbie nodded, stumbled out the door, and sucked in a lungful of crisp night air that turned into a sob somewhere under his heart. There were still people milling about down by Mr. Taylor's bungalow, so Robbie turned in the opposite direction and made his way to the streetcar. A trolley was just arriving at the Third Street stop, so he climbed aboard, sat down heavily, and stared straight ahead, the headlights from passing cars flashing in his blurry vision.

Somebody tugged on his sleeve. "Mister?"

He glanced down at a boy, probably nine or ten, in short pants and a flat cap. "Yes?"

"Are you okay?"

No. "Of course. Why do you ask?"

"'Cause you're crying."

So I am. Robbie wiped the tears off his face with the back of his hand. "It's nothing. I appreciate you wanting to make sure, though. That means you're a good person."

"Th-thanks. I guess." The boy chewed his lip. "I thought being a good person was learning your Bible verses and doing what your pa and ma tell you with no back sass."

Robbie gave a watery chuckle. "You can be a good person without doing any of those things—although I'd be careful about the back sass if your pa has a heavy hand. All you need to do is be kind to others. Make things better for them. Offer to help them when they need it. Just like you did with me."

"That's all?"

"That's all." Robbie stood up as the trolley reached the stop near his boarding house. He swung down to the pavement and looked up at the boy. "Keep up the good work."

As the streetcar rattled away, the boy raised his hand in farewell. Robbie returned the wave and then shoved his hands in his pockets. He slouched across the street, shaking his head at his own presumption.

Who am I to tell somebody else how to be a good person? If I were a good person, I wouldn't have left Frank. If I were a good person, I'd know how to make things better for Martin.

Robbie slowed to a stop halfway up the boarding house steps. *Make things better?* Could he do that? Could he head the what-ifs off at the pass by *doing* something about them?

He took the remaining steps two at a time but eased into the house quietly so he wouldn't disturb any of the other residents. He crept down the hallway to the niche where Mrs. McGuire kept the telephone. He'd never made a call from here, only taken a couple, but he knew the rules. He inserted a dime in the metal box next to the telephone, lifted the earpiece, and clicked its hook several times.

"Hello, operator? Please connect me to Melrose 6847." A moment later, a voice with a heavy New York accent came on the line.

"Sid Howard. Who's this?"

Of course, Robbie now knew that accent was completely fake. *If Martin's the one who taught Sid how to talk like that, he'd make a fortune as a vocal coach.* "Sid, it's Robbie Goodman. Sorry to bother you so late, but—"

"No problem with that. I've been trying to reach you. Jacob Schlossberg's been after me about a new contract for you."

"Yes, I want to talk to you about that. But there's a couple of other things I want to discuss first. Can I come by your office tomorrow?"

"Sure, sure. You name the time."

"Seven?"

"In the morning?" Sid spluttered. "I thought only roosters were awake then, and thank God there aren't a lot of those in Hollywood."

"All right, eight. But I want to get going on these things as soon as possible."

Sid chuckled. "I'm just kidding with you. Seven's fine. Jacob would probably push for six. Five, maybe. He really wants to get your contract locked down."

Robbie leaned against the wall, staring at the sampler hanging opposite. Whoever'd stitched it had left out the letter Q —or rather they'd put P in twice. *Maybe they never needed Q. Maybe two Ps make sense in their world.* "How good are you at negotiation, Sid?"

"Nobody better. That's why all the producers hate me."

"Good. Because I've got my own ideas about the contract. But there's two other things that don't have anything to do with the studio that I need your help with."

"I'm your manager, Robbie. You can ask me anything."

Robbie took a deep breath. *Here goes.* "I'd like you to take a trip to Idaho."

Sid was silent for a moment. "Idaho? Isn't that where potatoes are born?"

"Some of them. Sometimes."

"I assume you have a good reason."

"The best."

"All right. We'll talk about it tomorrow. You said two things. What's the other?"

Robbie smiled at the sampler. *No Q. Two Ps.* "I want to buy a house."

CHAPTER TWENTY-THREE

Bill Taylor's funeral was a circus—one where none of the clowns were funny, the ringmaster only pretended to be in control, and where the aerialists could topple off the high wire at any moment. As one of the aerialists in question, Martin teetered on the edge of falling throughout the service because Robbie was there.

Martin hadn't gotten near enough to greet him—easy enough to blame the crowd for that. But still raw over Bill's death, still ashamed of how he'd behaved to Robbie afterward, Martin was afraid his precarious equilibrium would slip if he got too close.

When he returned home afterward—alone—he was still empty and off-balance, as though he were missing a leg. *Or a heart.*

In the week that followed, Martin half hoped Robbie wouldn't keep his promise. That he'd show up at Martin's door as sunny, capable, and genuine as he'd been from the first day they met. But Robinson Crusoe Goodman didn't break promises, so he didn't come.

To fill the Robbie-shaped hole in his life, Martin did something he'd never done before—he bought fan magazines. Since he couldn't trust himself to see Robbie in the flesh, he stalked him via the press. He'd slink out to the newsstand in one of his cheap vaudeville suits, a cap pulled low across his face, and snap up every issue of *Picture Play* that had a hint of a mention.

For the first time in his life, Martin could sympathize with the fans desperate to get close to their idols but having no way to do it except through magazines.

So he knew exactly when Robbie started filming a new picture about Billy the Kid up in Inceville, directed by Boyd and with a scenario by Dottie. He also knew he needed to get out of town or he'd weaken and show up on the set.

He was packing when someone knocked at the door. His first thought was *Robbie*, so he hurried downstairs and checked himself in the mirror by the door. *God, I need a shave.* But when he opened the door, it was Sid standing on the doorstep.

"Oh. It's you."

Sid pushed past Martin to set his briefcase on the floor next to the first of Martin's suitcases. "Nice to see you too."

Martin closed the door, leaned against it, and waited for his stupid heart to resume its normal rhythm. "Sorry, Sid. You know you're always welcome."

"Am I?" He nudged the suitcase with his toe. "Then why haven't you mentioned that you're leaving town?"

"I was going to." Martin stalked past Sid into the living room. *But not until I was already gone.* "I'm heading up to San Francisco. I've been asked to take a part in—if you can believe it—*Hitchy-Koo*."

Sid snorted. "Back to your chorus days?"

"No indeed." Martin put his hand on his chest and lifted his chin. "I am a *headliner*." He dropped his pose. "At least until they hear me sing. It's only for a month." *Maybe by the time I get home, I'll be used to living without him.*

Sid *harrumph*ed and retrieved his briefcase. "Have you been dodging me because I told you I'd have the new Citadel contract for you?"

"No. Why would I?" Oddly, it was true. Martin hadn't thought about his own contract since they'd returned from the Sierras. "Do I need to deal with that now?"

"Given your triumphant return to the stage?" Sid said dryly. "I can put the Schlossbergs off for a while, but not forever."

Martin toyed with the glasses on the sideboard. "Does the new contract include a morality clause?"

Sid huffed a sigh. "You know it does."

"Did… did *his*?"

"You're gonna have to say his name *sometime*, Marty. Reporters are already asking about the friendship between the two of you that mirrors Dennis and Moses."

Martin let go of a tumbler and it clattered against its neighbor. "God. You have to head them off, Sid. We can't run with that story now. Not after Zukor made that asinine comment that he knew for a fact Bill wasn't intimate with *any* woman." Martin crossed the room and dropped onto the davenport. "Did he really think that would head off Hearst's bloodhounds? All it does is beg the question of who Bill *was* intimate with." He froze, gazing up at Sid. "George. They're not sniffing around George, are they?"

"As far as the newsboys are concerned, the only people involved in pictures are actors, directors, and producers." Sid sat in his usual spot in the wingback chair. "They could care less about art directors. They probably don't know what an art director *is*."

"If they dig deep enough, they'll find him. Then—"

"For cripes' sake, Marty, calm down. George is too valuable to the studio for them to let the press take potshots at him. Besides…." Sid's gaze slid away from Martin's.

"Besides, he does *queer work*. He's where the studio bosses think he belongs."

"Marty…." Sid's voice gentled, and a little of his real accent crept in. "George is where he wants to be. You don't need to worry about him. Between him and his mother, they've got enough clout to keep Zukor in line."

But Robbie doesn't have that kind of clout. Robbie, Dottie, Evie—all of them were at risk. As long as the producers controlled their lives, they always would be. *Somebody needs to take a stand.*

And who better than someone who had nothing left to lose? "I'm not signing."

Sid's jaw sagged. "Are you nuts? If you don't sign, you don't work."

Martin shrugged. "Then I don't work." He leaned forward, elbows on his knees. "It's probably a futile gesture, one the Schlossbergs won't even notice, but somebody has to be the first one. I can't do anything for Roscoe or Bill. But I can do this. For the rest of us."

"It'll kill your career, Marty."

"Then maybe it doesn't deserve to live."

Sid squinted at the ceiling and drummed his fingers on his knee. "I won't tell the Schlossbergs yet."

"Sid—"

Sid held up his hands. "Hear me out. You've had a hell of a one-two punch, what with Roscoe's second mistrial and Bill's murder. I'm not saying you're not thinking clearly, but, well, you're not thinking clearly. I'll use that ridiculous play as a reason for the delay. You'll be back for *The California Trail* premiere, right?"

"It's a contractual obligation, isn't it?"

"Yeah, but like I said—"

"I'm not thinking clearly?"

"Exactly." Sid shifted in the chair and once more avoided Martin's gaze. "I'm, uh, going out of town myself actually."

Martin grinned for possibly the first time in weeks. "You, Sid? You never venture farther afield than Pasadena. Where to?"

"Nowhere I want to discuss with you. If you…." Sid frowned, then tilted his head at an awkward angle, his eyes sharp. "I thought you never bought the fan mags?"

Martin followed the direction of Sid's gaze. *God.* His *Picture Play* stash was spilling out from under the coffee table. Martin pushed off the davenport and knelt on the rug, shuffling the stack upright. "It's, um, research."

"Uh-huh." Sid stood up. "You're gonna have to face him sometime, Marty. Don't you think it would be better to get it over with before the premiere?"

Martin stayed on the floor, his fists bunched on his thighs. "No."

"Suit yourself." Sid grabbed his briefcase and clapped on his fedora. "But to answer your question—no."

"No?"

"No, Robbie's contract doesn't have a morality clause." Sid walked to the door, leaving Martin gaping on his knees. "He refused to sign on until they struck it, and they wanted him bad enough that they caved." He opened the door. "I'm not sure they'll do the same for you."

Robbie had just finished rubbing down Bandit, the strawberry roan he was riding in this picture, when Alfie, the same AD who had worked on *The California Trail*, poked his head into the stables.

"Hey, Rob. You've got a visitor." Alfie jerked his thumb over his shoulder. "Over at the production office."

Robbie fumbled the currycomb, his heart lurching sideways as it had done countless times since the day he'd walked out of Martin's house, promising not to return. *Is it him? Has he changed his mind?* It had only been about a month—*five weeks, three days, seventeen hours*—but it felt like forever.

"Thanks, Alfie. I'll be right there." He shut Bandit's stall door. *Do I have time to clean up?* After a full day of filming, most of it on horseback, Robbie looked like he'd really been on the trail. But with his hands trembling in anticipation, he didn't want to take the time. If it *was* Martin, he'd be forgiven. *I hope.*

He hustled out of the stables and through the dusty streets. It looked like a town in the Old West, but its buildings housed prosaic things like prop storage, administrative offices, the cutting room. He rounded the last corner, his heart lodged in his throat, but instead of Martin, Sid was standing on the porch of the production office. In his natty suit and fedora, he was out of place among the men in cowboy duds—both actors and actual cowboys—and the production crew in their dusty work clothes.

"Sid." Robbie wiped his damp palms on his worn dungarees, trying to be sneaky about scanning the street for another out-of-place suit.

He must not have been successful, because Sid grimaced. "Sorry, Robbie. Martin's not here."

With his heart somewhere by his knees, Robbie couldn't manage a smile. "Is he…. That is, how is he doing?"

"I couldn't say. I haven't seen him for a couple of weeks."

"No? Don't you see him on the regular? You're still his manager, right?"

Sid raised one heavy eyebrow. "That's the rumor. However, I've been out of town." He paused. "Oregon."

Robbie scratched the back of his head under his cowboy hat. "Oregon? But—"

"And Idaho."

Robbie grabbed the porch railing to keep himself from dropping onto his behind. "You found him? Frank?" he croaked. "Is he alive? Did they arrest him? Is he all right?"

Sid stood aside and gestured to the door. "Why don't you let him tell you himself."

Robbie goggled at Sid, who was as poker-faced as though rescuing people from hell was something he did every day and twice on Sunday. "He's here? You brought him—" Robbie lunged for Sid and wrapped him in a very dusty, sweaty hug. "Thank you. Thank you so much."

"Yes, yes." Sid patted Robbie's back. "That'll do. You reek of horse."

"That's because I've been on one since seven this morning." Robbie stepped back and swiped his hand under his eyes. "He's really here?"

"Yes, he really is." Sid mopped his face with a linen handkerchief. "I understand the commissary serves a decent lemonade. I'll wait there while you speak with him. Which, by the way, will never happen unless you actually go inside."

Sid strolled off down the street, ignoring the looks cast him by the cowboys. Robbie stared at the door. When he asked Sid to look for Frank, he'd expected *news*, not the man in the flesh. *How can I face him after what I did?* He swallowed convulsively and then took off his hat and tucked it under his arm. He owed it to Frank to take whatever was coming, so he might as well get it over with.

He crossed the porch, his boots *clunk*ing hollowly on the warped boards, and slipped inside. A man was standing at the window across the room, staring out at the street. He was dressed in rough workman's clothes—and leaning on a cane.

Robbie swallowed and licked his dry lips. "F-Frank?"

Frank turned, aided by his cane, and Robbie had to steady himself on the door frame, because Frank's left eye was covered by a black patch. For an instant, they simply gazed at each other. Without saying a word, Frank walked toward Robbie, his awkward gait aided by the cane.

If he wants to deck me, I'll take it. I deserve it, after all.

Robbie squared his shoulders. "Frank, I'm so sor—oof!" His apology was cut off when Frank wrapped him in his arms and hugged the stuffing out of him, his cane bumping against the back of Robbie's legs.

"You got away. Thank God, Robbie. You got away."

Robbie buried his face in Frank's shoulder and returned the embrace. "I was so afraid of what they'd do to you in prison."

"Prison? They didn't even bother to arrest me. Either of us, me or Len. They just left us there."

Robbie drew back. "What? After that beating?"

289

Frank nodded. He released Robbie and shifted his weight onto his cane. "I guess they figured they'd handled justice fine without getting any lawyers involved."

"I can't believe they left you there. Didn't they at least send for a doctor?"

Frank lifted an eyebrow—the one above his eyepatch. "For a couple of queers? They didn't think we deserved it. I managed to flag down a passerby, but it was a while before we got any medical help. I got off easy." He rubbed his nose, which was crookeder than Robbie remembered. "Broken nose. The leg of course. My eye was a loss, but I've still got one that works fine. Len, though. I'm not sure he'll ever be right again."

"Right how?"

Frank sighed. "They broke his ribs. His arm. Those have gotten better. But they hit him in the head too, Robbie. Cracked his poor skull." Frank's hazel eye glistened with unshed tears. "Don't get me wrong. He's a good worker. Kind. Cheerful for the most part. Doesn't talk much. But he was studying to be a doctor before. I... I brought him along with me. I didn't want to leave him behind."

Robbie's belly knotted like a snarled lariat. "I'm so sorry. I shouldn't have run. I should have—"

"Hey." Frank let his cane clatter to the floor and gripped Robbie's shoulders. "The one thing that kept me going these last months was the hope that you got away. I don't blame you. Hell, I *told* you to run."

"Yes, but if I'd stayed—"

"They'd have beaten you too. They were armed, Rob. Armed, angry, and backed by the full authority of the law. We didn't stand a chance." Robbie jerked his chin down, not able to meet Frank's steady one-eyed gaze. *His eye. If I hadn't run....* "I'm serious. This isn't your fault. I'm the one who dragged you to that spot, if you recall." Frank smiled crookedly. "I've prayed to God every day that you didn't pay a price for being my friend."

He glanced around. "Do you mind if we sit? My leg's got a ways to go yet."

"Jehoshaphat. I should have thought of that." Robbie retrieved Frank's cane and kept pace with him in his shuffle to the chairs in the corner. "Will you...."

"Recover?" Leaning heavily on his cane, Frank sank into the chair with a grunt. "The leg should mend, although I'll probably never lose the limp. They broke it in two places."

"Frank...." Robbie plopped onto his own chair and buried his face in his hands.

"Hey. What did I tell you?" Frank grasped Robbie's arm and gave it a little shake. "Not your fault. I'm real glad you found a place for yourself. Some friends who'll look after you better than I did." He jerked his chin at the door. "Like that fellow out there. Your friend Sid."

"He's my manager."

"I think he's more than that. Do you know what he did?"

"Besides bring you here?"

"Yep. Besides that."

"He didn't say anything." Robbie drew his eyebrows together. "Wait. He mentioned going to Oregon. Is that where you were?"

"No. Me and Len were still in Idaho." Frank poked Robbie in the arm. "He took your ma back to her sisters."

Robbie's jaw dropped. "Wh-what?"

"Remember Lula Mae down at the feed store?" Robbie nodded. "She told my sister who told me that Sid showed up at your pa's farm, read him the riot act, and packed your ma out that very day. He hired Lula Mae to bear your ma company on the trip and take care of her." Frank chuckled. "He probably didn't have to ask Lula Mae twice. She's been dying to get out of Pierce since she was ten years old."

The lump in Robbie's throat threatened to choke him. "And... and Pa?"

Frank grimaced. "Your pa is still your pa, I'm afraid. Once he found out where you were and what you were doing, he washed his hands of you."

Robbie slumped in his chair. "Thank goodness. I was half afraid he'd show up at the studio one day and drag me home by my ear." He took a shuddering breath and straightened up. "What have you been doing... since? Did you go back home?"

Frank snorted. "Are you kidding? My pa's as bad as yours." He stacked his hands on the head of his cane. "Once I could walk again, I started picking up work here and there. Gardening and field work mostly. Len was a big help with that."

"Field work? But you wanted to be a landscaper."

Frank tapped his eyepatch. "Hard to design with no depth perception."

"Frank," Robbie moaned.

"Stop it. I'm serious. Besides, you always had a better"— Frank winked—"*eye* than I did."

Robbie scowled at him. "Now *you* stop it."

"Come on, Robbie. If I can't laugh, I might as well turn up my toes. My life still has plenty of good things in it." He patted Robbie's shoulder. "And now it has even more."

Robbie managed to smile. If Frank could be cheerful about his prospects, Robbie had *nothing* to complain about. "What are you and.... Len, was it?" Frank nodded. "What are you and Len going to do now?"

Frank's gaze drifted to the window, where a swath of hillside was greening with the onset of spring. "Probably more of the same. I suppose people in Hollywood have gardens too."

Robbie blinked. Only last week, he'd been forced to escort Aurelia Arthur and her mother to the premiere of *Beauty's Worth*. Escorting the Arthurs was painful, but he'd met the picture's star, Miss Marion Davies, who'd been so kind and gracious, chatting with him about the garden she hoped to plant behind her bungalow if she could ever find the time with her busy filming schedule. She'd asked him to call on her. *What if I call on her with an answer to her gardening woes?*

Robbie hadn't stopped to consider what he'd do after his contract with Citadel concluded. He just knew it wouldn't involve acting—or *anything* to do with pictures, if he had his way. But the thing about picture people was that they mostly had more money than time, and often more time than taste.

"Frank, I've got an idea."

CHAPTER TWENTY-FOUR

"I invited Roscoe to the premiere." Martin focused on adjusting his white tie, although Sid's silence from the other side of the room nearly deafened him.

"It's only been five days since the verdict. You really think he wants to expose himself to the press again so soon?"

"Why not? It only took the jury six minutes to acquit him, with an abject apology thrown in. Everyone knows he's innocent now."

"No." Sid leaned forward in the wingback chair, his elbows on his knees, completely uncaring of how it creased his tuxedo jacket. *Giving up the aristocratic backstory has some advantages.* "They know he wasn't *convicted*. But after seven months of the press painting him as some kind of depraved maniac, you think everyone's opinion will have changed? Depravity sells more newspapers than apologetic jurors. Half the country probably still thinks he's in jail."

"That's exactly why he should get out. Act normal. Remind people of who he is and how much they loved his pictures until...."

"Yes. Until." Sid sighed and leaned back in the chair. "It's a nice sentiment, Marty, but it won't work. Years from now, you think anyone'll remember Roscoe as the man who performed at a prison because some guy sent him a letter and asked him to? The man who picked up the tab for every stinking party he ever attended? The man who gave so much to charity, to the war effort? No. Now and forever, he'll be the man who killed a girl with sex."

Martin removed a speck of lint from his sleeve. "He said no anyway."

"He's smarter than I took him for, then." Sid pulled out his watch. "The limousine should be here in ten. Evelyn's expecting us in twenty. You want to fortify yourself with some of your rotgut gin first?"

God, do I ever. But.... "I got rid of it all."

Sid's eyebrows rose toward his hairline as he tucked his watch away. "You did? *You?*"

Martin dropped his gaze and picked more nonexistent lint from his jacket. "I promised Robbie I wouldn't drink anymore."

"Shite," Sid muttered, and since he'd slipped back into his real voice, he must be powerfully moved. "It's been two months."

"More, actually." Nine weeks and six days since he'd last seen Robbie at Bill Taylor's funeral.

"I thought you'd moved on."

Martin steeled himself to ask the question, although he knew at least part of the answer. He'd read it in interview after interview in his vast collection of fan magazines. "Like he has?"

"Jesus, Marty. You of all people should know better than to believe all the banana oil Leo feeds to the press. Robbie's no more dating Aurelia Arthur than you're dating Evelyn." He jabbed his forefinger at Martin, a gesture he'd learned from Jacob Schlossberg. "If you hadn't hared off to San Francisco for that play the week after Bill's funeral, you'd know."

"I needed the distance, Sid. I'm—" Martin swallowed against a lump in his throat. "I'm not strong. Not where Robbie's concerned. I don't think I ever will be."

Sid muttered something under his breath. "Don't get me wrong. I like the kid. He's gonna make me a mint, thanks to the contract I got him with Citadel." Sid chuckled. "You should have seen Jacob's face when I laid out the deal."

"Frankly, I'd be happy never to see Jacob's face again, but I expect I won't be able to avoid it tonight."

"They've been after me, you know. Jacob and Ira." Sid shrugged one shoulder. "Well, mostly Ira. He thinks *The California Trail* is going to be a hit, and he wants you back under contract."

Martin walked over to the coat tree. "Yes, but I don't want to *be* under contract. Not another long-term one anyway, and definitely not one with a morality clause." He draped a silk scarf around his neck. It wasn't cold—April had been almost balmy so far—but this was a premiere. A certain manner of dress was expected. "I've been chatting with Edward Horton." Martin stared irritably at the scarf and then yanked it off and hung it back on the coat tree. *Damn expectations anyway.* "He doesn't believe in long-term contracts."

"He probably couldn't get one if he did. He's not hero material. He'll always be the best friend, the rejected lover, the timid clerk. If you go down that path, you never get the girl."

"That's fine with me." *I don't want the girl. I want a man I can't have.* Martin held the door and gestured for Sid to precede him. "Besides, when you're not in the spotlight, it's easier to be invisible."

Sid grunted a response as he stepped outside.

Martin locked the door behind him. "You know who else was in that show in San Francisco? Florence Salomon."

"From vaudeville days?"

"Mmhmmm. I'd forgotten how good she was at tricking mediocre singers into delivering a performance. At bullying patsies from Hoboken into sounding like they'd never gone anywhere south of Forty-Second Street." Martin glanced sidelong at Sid. "Turns out I'm not so bad at it either."

Sid snorted. "So what? Pictures are silent. It's not like anybody here needs elocution lessons."

"Maybe not. But there's always theater, Sid. Musicals." Martin pressed a hand to his chest and the opposite wrist against his forehead and strode down the sidewalk like Aurelia Arthur at her most melodramatic. "I have such a deep and abiding love for the theater. Surely you can relate, Sidney, old fellow, old chap." Martin dropped the pose when they reached the curb, since the chauffeur, standing ramrod straight next to the open limousine door, looked a bit white around the eyes. *This is Hollywood, pal. Get used to it.*

But getting used to it didn't make it any easier to take. Or to survive. *Just ask Wesley Thornhill.* The poor sod never made it out of that sanitarium the second time.

Martin climbed into the limousine and slid across the seat to leave room for Sid so the chauffeur didn't have to run around and open the other door. Once they pulled into traffic, Martin took his courage in both hands. He'd resisted pressing Sid for details about Robbie since the day they'd gotten back from Truckee. *Screw resistance. I want to know.*

"How long is Robbie tied up with Citadel? Five years? Seven?" That's another reason Martin didn't want another contract with the Schlossbergs. Seeing Robbie on the lot but being unable to touch him would be torture.

"Neither. Two pictures."

Martin goggled at him. "Two pictures? Jacob would *never* agree to that."

"It was two pictures or nothing. Robbie was ready to walk away." Sid's dark eyes were kind in the flare of passing headlights. "He doesn't want to be a star, you know. He never did."

"I know." Robbie had told him so, more than once. Deep down Martin had never believed that anyone would *want* to give up the glamour, the fame, the money. *Yet I'm about to do it myself.*

"He wanted enough money to get himself set up. Buy a house. Send something to his mother. Spring a friend from— Never mind."

Martin grabbed Sid's elbow. "Don't try that shite with me. *What* friend? Spring a friend from what?"

Sid sighed and pried Martin's fingers off his arm. "Just a pal of his who'd had a little run in with the law."

Martin sucked in a breath. *Frank.* It had to be. *His first love.* Or was he? Martin rubbed his temples and tried to remember exactly what Robbie had said back in that cabin. But while Martin could remember every touch, every kiss, every inch of Robbie's skin, he couldn't remember all their words. *Because words hadn't been as important as how I felt.*

"Did you find him? This friend?"

Sid nodded. "He was working on some farm out in the middle of nowhere. He'd obviously had a hard time. Busted nose. Walks with a limp. Lost an eye too."

Martin closed his eyes. *Poor Robbie. Although I probably should think "poor Frank."* But while Martin couldn't remember what exactly Frank had been to Robbie, he remembered Robbie's guilt and shame perfectly well. Robbie would blame himself, possibly forever.

"Does Robbie know?"

"Of course he knows. He paid for the fellow to move down to Hollywood. Found him work doing landscaping for Marion Davies, of all people."

Martin nodded. "That's good. Marion is lovely. She'll make sure he's treated right."

Sid gazed out the window, a show of nonchalance that Martin didn't buy for a moment. "I could cut you a deal just as good, you know. After tonight… well, I thought you were a fool to refuse to sign the Schlossbergs' first offer, but it made 'em hungry, more likely to concede to our demands. And since I let slip I've fielded a couple of calls from Thalberg over at Universal—"

"That's not why I did it, Sid. You know that."

Sid sighed hugely. "I know. But it turns out it was the right decision." He pounded his knee with a fist. "I never thought I'd say this, but keeping away from Robbie isn't the right decision. Not anymore. It's changed you, Marty. Being away from him."

Martin offered Sid a smile. "Maybe I needed to change."

"Not this much. You're my friend, my oldest friend in this country. Hell, probably my oldest friend in the world, since everybody I ever knew across the pond prefers to pretend I don't exist. I hate to see you unhappy."

"Maybe not everyone deserves happiness. Ever think of that?"

"Bollocks. The only people who don't deserve to be happy are producers after I've buggered them over the contract table."

Martin chuckled. "Watch out, Sid. Your vocabulary is slipping."

"I mean it. You know what's another bad idea? Seeing Robbie again for the first time at the premiere tonight. Between the klieg lights and the photographers' flash powder, you won't have anywhere to hide."

Martin leaned his head against the window. "You're probably right, but it's too late now." He rolled his head so he could watch Sid's profile. "Tell me about him, Sid. Is he all right? What's *really* happening?"

"He's making that Billy the Kid picture that Dottie wrote. You know that, right?"

"Yes. Evelyn told me." *And I read about it in* Picture Play. "Is he having any trouble with the Hollywood posse? They can be hard on a tenderfoot."

Sid chuckled. "Nah. They love him because he knows how to ride and treats his horse so well. They've tried to talk Dottie into changing the end of the picture so that Billy lives."

Martin snorted. "That sounds like them." Of course they'd love Robbie. The real cowboys who played cowboys and soldiers and Roman legions on the screen had no patience for the fake and phony. They'd have spotted how genuine Robbie was in a heartbeat. "But Will Hays would never stand for that. According to His Highness, the Czar of All the Rushes—"

"Don't call Hays that, not where anyone else can hear it, anyway."

"—wickedness must be punished. Or at least not rewarded." Martin ran a finger down the crease of his trousers. "So he's all right, then? Robbie?"

"What do you think? He's lonely."

"He can't be. He's got you, Dottie, the posse." *Frank.* "He's too busy to be lonely."

"You can be lonely in a crowd. He misses you. That's obvious by how careful he is to never ask me about you."

"He probably doesn't ask about me because I burned that bridge to cinders."

"I think you're wrong. And I think you need to talk to him."

Martin sighed. "I will. But not tonight." Tonight, he had to endure his first sight of Robbie in nearly ten weeks, all while preserving his star persona, smiling at the crowd, and answering reporters' prying questions.

I might as well be naked.

The giant searchlights sweeping the sky weren't anything Robbie hadn't seen before, nor were the red carpet, the crowds jostling one another behind velvet ropes, and the near-constant pop and flare of flash powder. He'd only seen a hint of it the night of *The Three Musketeers* premiere, when he'd still been Martin's chauffeur, but he'd seen it in all its overblown glory in the last couple of months, every time Leo insisted that Robbie escort Aurelia Arthur and her mother to some opening or other.

While he hadn't minded *Beauty's Worth* and getting to meet Miss Davies, who was being just as kind to Frank and Len as she had been to Robbie that evening, other outings hadn't been so enjoyable. During *The Heart Specialist*, for instance, Aurelia kept making rude comments under her breath through the whole thing. Its star was Mary Miles Minter, who looked an awful lot like Aurelia—and both of them looked an awful lot like Miss Pickford. Robbie had squirmed in his seat because Miss Minter's nightgown was the one that had been found at Mr. Taylor's house the day he died.

Miss Minter's *alleged* nightgown.

Aurelia wasn't the only person in Hollywood who was muttering rude things about Miss Minter, but after what he'd learned about the studios and the press, Robbie had serious doubts about the truth of anything anymore. Although, maddeningly, the stories that Leo had fed to the fan magazines about Robbie's background had been true.

It figured that the one time Robbie would have appreciated a little prevaricating or at least coyness on the studio's part, they'd decided to tell all. *Or almost all.*

So this premiere promised to be far more stressful. He was escorting Aurelia again, but without her mother, thank goodness. Leo had made sure their limousine was one of the last in line, which put Aurelia in a better mood—she dearly loved to make an entrance.

But that wasn't the only difference tonight. Tonight Robbie wasn't just a spectator, one of the interchangeable men in evening dress who escorted actresses to Hollywood events. Tonight he couldn't be invisible, because he was one of the stars.

Yes, tonight was the Los Angeles premiere of *The California Trail*, and Robbie's stomach hadn't stopped doing the Charleston since he got in the automobile. Tonight he'd face the full onslaught of fans and press and studio expectations.

Tonight, I'll see Martin again.

"Robbie, are you *listening* to me?"

He tore his gaze from the window and faced Aurelia. Her little bow mouth was drawn up as though she'd just eaten a lemon like the one Robbie had choked down on his first day in Hollywood. He almost wished he'd cadged a lift all the way to

Mexico instead of hiding out in that shed and then having breakfast with Pops the next day. He could have avoided tonight's three-ring circus.

But I wouldn't have met Martin.

"I'm sorry. What did you say?"

"Oh, never mind." She flounced around in the seat and took a compact out of her handbag. She studied herself in the little mirror, angling her head and practicing different expressions. "I hope they sit us next to Mr. Brentwood."

Robbie clutched his knees, crumpling the smooth wool of his tuxedo trousers. "What? Why?" *She can't know. Nobody knows. Martin and I haven't even spoken for over two months.*

"Because," she said, her voice dripping scorn, "at least *he's* enough of a gentleman to pay attention to me." She tilted her chin up and smiled into the mirror. "And without my mother along tonight, there won't be anything to stop him."

Robbie's jaw sagged. "You think Martin wants to... to...."

"Oh, please." She snapped the compact shut. "It's *obvious* he's crazy about me. Even someone as stupid as you should have seen how careful he was on the set. He *never* did anything to make my mother suspicious, because he *knows* what she can be like. But tonight, she's not here. We'll be able to be together. He can escort me to the reception and to Mr. Schlossberg's party afterward." She looked down her nose at him. "So *you* needn't bother."

Robbie blinked at her. *And I thought I was oblivious.* Thank goodness he'd won the argument with Leo about transportation. Although he and Aurelia would arrive together, Robbie had insisted on meeting the studio limousine a few blocks away after parking his own new Nash roadster. He hadn't wanted to be trapped at the parties, which he would have been if he depended on studio drivers. He couldn't face being in the same room, the same crowd, the same *photographs* as Martin-the-motion-picture-star. Not when he'd seen the real

Martin. Not when the real Martin might be forever out of his reach.

When they reached the curb in front of the Million Dollar Theater, it was just as bad as Robbie expected—flashes and shouts and Aurelia hanging on his arm, holding him to a crawl when all he wanted was to get inside the theater and take his seat. Once the lights went down, he'd be all right. Once the lights went down, he could hide.

Except once the lights went down, he'd be watching himself on the screen.

Oh God.

When they reached the lobby at last, Ira Schlossberg was standing next to the stairs to the mezzanine. "Robbie! Aurelia! The cast seats are this way. Leo will meet you at the top of the stairs. But first—" He held out his arm, and Aurelia let go of Robbie to slip her hand in the crook of his elbow. He beckoned to Robbie to take his place on his other side. Then he angled them all to face a nest of photographers.

"Smile," Mr. Ira growled out of the side of his mouth.

So Robbie smiled as flash after flash burst like a string of firecrackers. When Mr. Ira finally pushed them up the stairs, Robbie couldn't see the carpet for the spots dancing in front of his eyes. He was still blinking, trying to clear his vision, when they reached the mezzanine.

"Here you are." Leo shooed them down a wide aisle toward a group of people in evening clothes. As Robbie got near enough to recognize them through the fading spots, his belly jolted again.

Martin.

His mouth dried, and he couldn't have said anything if he'd tried. Which he didn't, because once again, his brain was nothing but snow. Martin looked... *Jehoshaphat. So beautiful.* Robbie had always been a sucker for Martin in formal wear, and apparently he still was. Miss Trent was at his side, her gown sparkly enough that for a moment Robbie thought his flash powder spots had returned full-force.

"Rob!" Dottie hurried toward him. "Isn't this great? I'm so excited!"

He smiled down at her, his vision clear enough to see that instead of an evening gown, she was wearing what looked like a white tuxedo. It suited her. "Your first picture. But not your last."

"Nope." Her brow wrinkled. "Where's—Oh."

He followed the direction of her gaze to where Aurelia was hanging on to Martin's arm, gazing up at him and fluttering her eyelashes. "Do you suppose she's got something in her eye?"

"No. But she's got something in her mind, and we need to scuttle it pretty darned quick. Come on." She grabbed his elbow and towed him down the aisle.

And then there he was, face to face with Martin.

Dottie had been right, all those weeks ago. Robbie needed practice to be with Martin in public, because right now? He couldn't do anything but stare.

"Robbie, how lovely to see you." Miss Trent leaned over and pressed her cheek to his. "You're looking quite dashing this evening."

"Th-thank you, Miss Trent."

"Come now. I'm your on-screen sister. Surely you can call me Evelyn."

He smiled shakily. "Of course. Evelyn."

"There now, that wasn't so hard." She gazed at something past his shoulder. "Oh, dear. From the face Leo is making, he either needs to find the men's room or it's time for us to take our seats. Here. This is our row."

She ushered them out of the aisle and somehow managed to arrange it so that Aurelia went first, and when they'd all been seated, Robbie had Aurelia on his right and Martin on his left. Evelyn was on Martin's left and Dottie beyond her. Aurelia, with Otis on her other side, was fuming.

Robbie was just trying to breathe.

"It's good to see you, Rob," Martin murmured as the lights dimmed and music swelled from the theater's massive pipe organ.

"Y-you too." His earlier mortification about watching himself on the screen vanished because he was pretty sure he wouldn't be able to focus on anything. The scent of Martin's almond shaving soap, the occasional brush of his trousers against Robbie's, the heat from where their thighs nearly touched at the edge of the plush seats sent his head reeling.

Then the first title cards appeared, and though Robbie never lost awareness of Martin at his side, he got caught up in the picture too. The story, the way Boyd had staged the shots, the way Howard had photographed them—by the time Robbie appeared on-screen, he didn't register himself as *himself*. He was watching Moses Schallenberger, his family, and his friends as they endured the grueling trek to their new home.

When the final shot faded to the accompaniment of a triumphant organ chord, the audience erupted in cheers and applause that went on for minutes.

Leo appeared in the aisle between them and the screen. "Stand up. Take a bow. Then follow me."

Still under the spell of the picture, Robbie struggled out of his seat. He bowed as ordered, then filed out of the row in Martin's wake, all of them following Leo into a cloakroom off the mezzanine stairs.

Once they were inside, he turned to them. "Wait here. Once the crowd's thinned out to press and VIPs, I'll come back to take you down to the reception." He paused, one hand on the door handle. "And congratulations, everyone. It's a hit." His grin was the first truly satisfied smile Robbie had ever seen on him. "This picture is gonna make more money than *Four Horsemen* and *The Kid* put together!"

CHAPTER TWENTY-FIVE

Damn it, how did I let myself get cornered like this?

Strike that. Martin knew exactly how he'd gotten himself flanked by Aurelia Arthur on one side, clinging to him like a limpet in lavender chiffon, and a reporter from the *Examiner* on the other, his photographer lurking behind him with a seemingly endless supply of film and flash powder.

Robbie. That's how. He'd been so busy trying to avoid the man, keeping a minimum safe distance between them so he wouldn't be able to *smell* him the way he had throughout the screening, that he'd forgotten that Robbie wasn't the only danger.

"Mr. Brentwood," Aurelia cooed, pressing her bosom against his arm, "I've been meaning to ask. Don't you think—"

"How much does he really weigh?" the reporter barked.

"—if an older man, a *sophisticated* man—"

"You think he's a pervert?"

"—cared for a younger woman—"

"Heard he's got a gold-leafed bathtub."

"—he shouldn't worry about what anyone—"

"LA Athletic Club voted him out."

"—for instance, her mother—"

"Wasn't he a dope fiend back in '16?"

"—might say about it. Do you?"

"Lotta people think he should hang."

Martin threw up one hand to stop the double onslaught of absurdity. "Mister… whoever you are, this is no longer a story. The jury acquitted Roscoe in *six minutes*, five of which were spent writing a formal *apology* to him."

The reporter cracked his gum. "Yeah, but do you think he did it?"

Martin's vision started to go black around the edges. He pried Aurelia's claws off his arm. "Pardon me. I'm suddenly feeling quite ill."

He strode across the lobby and up the stairs to the cloakroom on the mezzanine where Leo had hidden them all after the screening. He slapped the wall with both palms, leaned into it, and took in huge lungfuls of air.

The door clicked open behind him. *Damn it, if Aurelia had followed him—*

"Martin?" Robbie's tentative voice arrowed straight to Martin's heart.

He wanted to fall into Robbie's embrace at the same time he wanted to order him far, far away, out of the reach of importunate Hearst reporters and scheming, adolescent would-be starlets.

"Miss Trent, I mean Evelyn, was worried about you. She sent me to find you."

Martin closed his eyes, fingers curling into fists against the wall. *Damn you for trying to* help, *Evie.*

He dropped his arms, and because it would be ridiculous to hold a conversation with his back to Robbie, he turned around. And then regretted it, because the concern on Robbie's beautiful face made his knees buckle and tears prickle his eyes. *Brace up, Gottschalk. At least you can't* smell *him from over here.*

"Rob. Thank you, but I'm perfectly fine."

"Are you sure?" Robbie took two steps forward. *Damn it, now I can smell him.* Robbie had been so thrilled to discover that orange-scented shaving soap. He'd confided in Martin that something about it reminded him of the day he arrived in Hollywood.

"Absolutely." Martin tugged the hem of his jacket. "I'm… glad to have an opportunity to talk to you, though."

"Really?" Robbie's mouth tilted in a doubtful smile. "That must be why you've been avoiding me all evening, not to mention for the last two months."

The worst two months of my life. But Martin refused to admit it, to open the door on that conversation, because once opened, he wasn't sure what would burst out. "Your performance in this picture was nothing short of a miracle. Didn't I tell you audiences would go wild for you?"

"You told me a lot of things, Martin." Robbie advanced another two steps, causing Martin to retreat until his back was against the wall. "I'm not sure what I should believe anymore."

"You can believe that. I'd think that the way the press swarmed around you, the fans clamoring for autographs, Ira and Jacob bracketing you like wide and narrow bookends should tell you the truth about your success."

Robbie waved his hand as though brushing away a persistent fly. "Success. That's such a… what did Ma call it? A subjective thing. For Robinson Crusoe, success was making a calendar out of wood. Harvesting his first crop. Taming a parrot." Robbie was barely a handspan away, and Martin couldn't call his expression anything other than *predatory.* "Finding a friend and lifelong companion."

"Rob—"

"Now, I'm not sure about the calendar and the parrot, but I agree with him about the friend. I thought I'd found one myself." Hurt and anger chased across his face. "You said you loved me, Martin. Why did you run?"

Something roiled in Martin's belly. Guilt? Anger at the world's unfairness? Pure, unadulterated terror? "Robbie, somebody *killed* Bill Taylor."

"I know." Robbie's voice was soft. "He was your friend. Did you think I wouldn't understand your need to grieve for him?"

"If that's what you believe, then you *don't* understand."

"Then what?"

Martin swallowed against the constriction of his collar and tie. "What if the killer acted because of not *who* Bill was but *what* he was?"

"You mean like us? In the life?"

Martin nodded.

"Were you afraid that the killer might strike again? That next time it would be you?"

"Me?" Martin choked on a laugh. "No. I was afraid it would be *you*."

Robbie's breath caught. "Martin—"

The door banged open, and Leo barged in. "What are you doing up here? The party's really getting started now. *Valentino* is here. Pickford and Fairbanks. Chaplin."

Martin gritted his teeth. "We'll be right there, Leo."

"All right. But hurry." He grinned at them, rubbing his hands together. "You don't want to miss the buffet, and I don't want to miss the chance to gloat!" He bustled out, leaving the door hanging open.

Martin cursed under his breath and then crossed to close the door. He faced Robbie and returned to the center of the room, keeping his hands resolutely behind his back. "I won't put you in danger, Rob. I can't. If keeping you safe means never seeing you again, then—"

"Bullshit, Martin." Robbie's voice held an edge Martin had never heard in it before, and his blue eyes narrowed.

"But the killer's still out there."

Robbie shrugged. "Maybe. Or maybe he's halfway to the Yukon by now. But we don't know who he—or she—is or why they killed Mr. Taylor. I've heard the rumors, same as you have. It was a disgruntled drug dealer who took exception to Mr. Taylor's lectures against doping. It was that shady secretary who robbed him and wrecked his car. It was Mary Miles Minter. It was Mary Miles Minter's *mother*, who, if she's anything like Mrs. Arthur, I could actually believe. But whoever it was, I don't see why I should hide under the bed in case they might come for me someday. Because chances are they never will. And then how many years will we have wasted?"

"But there are other dangers—the laws, the press, the morality watchdogs."

"You know what? I don't care. We'd only be unsafe if we're *stupid*. But I'm not stupid. Neither are you." He stepped closer. "So what do you say?"

The puff of Robbie's breath on his jaw pushed Martin to do something he'd been resisting for weeks.

He touched Robinson Crusoe Goodman. *Oh God, how have I lived without this?*

Martin gripped Robbie's arms, although he resisted pulling him closer. "It's not *our* stupidity that's the problem. It's the stupidity and malice of—"

The door flew open again. "So *this* is what's going on." Aurelia Arthur stood in the doorway, all blonde ringlets, chiffon draperies, and scorned outrage.

Martin let his arms drop. "Oh God. Can this evening get any worse?"

"This is *so* like you, Robbie."

Robbie cast a panicked glance at Martin. "Me?"

"Yes, you. Delaying Mr. Brentwood when I *told* you he'd rather escort me." Aurelia raised a trembling hand to her mouth, leading with her wrist—a gesture she'd copied from Louise Brooks. But before she could launch into a truly convincing fit of hysterics, Evelyn appeared at her shoulder.

"*Here* you are, Aurelia. You'll never guess who's finally arrived." Evelyn turned and smiled at somebody out of sight. "Yes, Dottie. Here she is. Bring Mrs. Arthur up."

Aurelia dropped any pretense of fragility. "My *mother*? What the *fuck* is she doing here?"

Evelyn smiled brightly. "I invited her, of course. Sadly, my driver didn't pick her up in time to catch the picture." She shook her head mournfully. "Los Angeles traffic really is a scandal, isn't it?"

"You!" Aurelia's eyes fairly blazed. "You've always been jealous of me. You… you… you *hag*."

"*Aurelia!*" Mrs. Arthur loomed behind Evelyn, the ostrich plumes in her enormous hat quivering in time with her jowls. "Such language is extremely unbecoming to a young girl. Beg Miss Trent's pardon *at once*."

Aurelia's chin took on a mulish cast, but she muttered, "Sorry," before her mother towed her out of sight by her elbow.

Evelyn, Dottie at her side, waggled her fingers at Martin and Robbie and then pulled the door closed softly.

After a moment Robbie huffed out a breath. "Well. That was…."

"Typical," Martin said, his tone laced with resignation.

Robbie glanced at him. Their gazes locked, and then they both dissolved into laughter.

"So…." Robbie gasped. "…ridiculous."

Martin leaned against the wall, slid all the way down to sit on his arse and try to get his breath back. "Next time… maybe… Howard can… film the whole thing. And Leo can alert the reporters."

That set Robbie off again. "Jehoshaphat, Martin. Don't p-p-put *ideas* into their heads."

When they finally sobered, Robbie held out a hand to help Martin stand, but he didn't release his grip when Martin was on his feet. "Martin, we're constantly interrupted by other people's opinions and agendas. Aren't you tired of that?"

Martin gazed at their joined hands. *This is right—right for me, right for him. Why is anyone entitled to say it's not?* "You were wonderful tonight. In the picture. You're going to be a big star."

"You know, I get lectures from Leo—*daily* lectures—about what I need to do if I expect to be a star." He let go of Martin's hand and held out his arms. "No more dungarees and collarless shirts for me. I have to wear custom-tailored suits." He leaned forward and whispered conspiratorially, his breath warm against Martin's cheek. "I have *three* tuxedos. One of 'em's... what did you call it? A thirteen-and-the-odd?"

"Your tailor deserves a medal, then, because you look incredible."

"Although I have a bone to pick with you, Martin."

Now he'll read me the riot act for betraying him. For walking away from my promises. For being a bloody coward. Martin nodded, ready to take what was coming to him. He deserved it, after all. "Yes?"

Robbie's eyes widened in mock outrage. "Why didn't you warn me that these things are so dang uncomfortable?"

Martin's laugh surprised him. He hadn't imagined he'd be able to laugh again in the face of Robbie's anger. *But apparently that's not to come.* "Ah, the cost of fame."

"And that's not all. To be a star, apparently I have to *act* like one. I have to go out to see and be seen at the Cocoanut Grove, the Alexandria Hotel, the Writer's Cramp ball. I have to jockey for invitations to parties at producers' Beverly Hills mansions. I have to buy my *own* mansion and host parties myself. Leo gave me the names of several respectable bootleggers to guarantee the parties would be successful—and not in the least memorable the next morning for anybody who attended."

"That's the customary procedure, yes. *Hollywood's* ideas aren't quite as subjective as Mr. Crusoe's. Ostentation is the only absolute proof of success."

"I want to show you my mansion, Martin. I bought it with you in mind. Will you come with me to see it?"

Robbie's eyes had never been so blue. *God, if pictures were in color, everybody in the audience—man or woman—would come in their seats.*

"All right."

Robbie grinned and reached out as though to take Martin's hand. His grin faded a fraction as he dropped his arm. "Come on. We can go out the back way."

Outside the cloakroom, the stairwell was deserted, although from the sound of overloud conversation and the clink of silver against china, the reception was still going strong in the lobby. Robbie led Martin across the empty theater and down behind the stage that fronted the screen, to a door that opened onto the sidewalk behind the building.

"This way." He crossed the street, ignoring the stares from passersby, and turned down a deserted side street. He stopped next to a Nash roadster, its canvas roof white in the darkness and streetlights sparkling on its hood.

He opened the door. "Won't you get in, Mr. Brentwood?"

Martin approached slowly. "This isn't a studio automobile."

"No, it's not. It's mine. Bought it with the first paycheck on my new contract and had some left over. Sid really knows how to work a deal."

"The studio lets you drive yourself?" Martin smiled ruefully as he climbed into the passenger seat. "Of course you've never wrecked anything, but the Schlossbergs do like to protect their assets."

Robbie ducked his head to look inside. "They paid me for driving other people around. They can hardly claim I'm incapable now." He shut the door and trotted around the front of the car, just as he had the first day they'd met.

As Robbie pulled away from the curb, Martin tried—unsuccessfully—to dampen the anticipation that sang along his bones. *Soon. Soon we'll be alone again. I can touch him again. Love him again.* For fear he might disgrace himself in his tuxedo trousers, he distracted himself by gazing at Robbie's profile as it was lit and shadowed by passing automobiles and streetlights.

But as the traffic thinned to nothing and the streetlights grew more sparse and then disappeared as well, he shifted his attention to the passing scenery.

"Where are you taking me?"

"I told you. My mansion."

Martin peered at the hill rising above them. "Your mansion is in Griffith Park?"

Robbie chuckled as he turned off Highland. "No. Close, though. Up on Ivarene. You'll see."

But after following the road into the Cahuenga Hills, and then up a winding driveway, Robbie pulled to a stop in front of a house that was nobody's idea of a mansion. It was lovely—a two-story Craftsman-style bungalow set against the hillside, with single story wings stretching out on either end to embrace a grassy courtyard.

"A mansion, Rob?"

Robbie shrugged and turned off the engine. "Mansions are subjective too, I guess."

"Does... does Frank live here with you?"

Robbie glanced sharply at him. "You know about Frank?"

"Sid told me."

With a sigh, Robbie leaned back against the seat. "Sid was wonderful. He found Frank for me, you know. Arranged for him to come to California. He even went out to the farm and browbeat my pa. Took Ma back to her sisters in Oregon."

"Have you seen her?"

"Not yet." Robbie smiled a little sadly. "I've written to her. She might write back someday, when she's better."

"What about your father? Will he cause trouble?"

"Pa?" This time, Robbie's laugh rivaled Martin's for cynicism. "Once he found out what I was doing for a living, he washed his hands of me, which suits me down to the ground."

"So *is* Frank here?"

"No. He says he's developed an aversion to hills or mountains of any kind. He's got a place by the ocean, down the coast a ways. Balboa, it's called."

"Yes. I've heard of it. But isn't that a little far to drive every day for gardening jobs in Hollywood?"

"Who told you we're just *gardeners*?" Robbie raised his chin and put his nose in the air. "I'll have you know we are *landscape artistes*. Although—" He grinned as he opened the door. "I'd like to see the person who can keep me from grubbing about in the dirt when I feel like it." His smile turned shy, and the sweetness, the *hope* in his face, melted Martin's heart. "Will you come inside?"

"My dear, I would like nothing better."

Robbie's hand was so sweaty that it slipped on the doorknob. He tried to remember if he'd washed the dishes before he left home this morning. If his socks were strewn across the bedroom floor. If the bed was made.

If I'd known I had a chance of bringing Martin home tonight, maybe I'd have made more of an effort.

On the other hand, he and Martin had been happy in a drafty cabin in the Sierras in the middle of a blizzard, so surely this house, with its lovely lines and gorgeous woodwork and furniture chosen for both comfort and style wouldn't disappoint. The only thing that the house had lacked was Martin.

And now he was here.

Robbie led him into the living room, with its bank of windows, its french doors facing the patio, the yard, and beyond it, the terraced hillside that someday would showcase the gardens Robbie had been dreaming of since his days resisting Pa's demands for straight rows and lack of ornamentation.

He turned to face Martin. "Wh-what do you think?"

"Beautiful," Martin murmured, and Robbie warmed from his belly to his toes.

"I hoped you'd like it. It's private too. The nearest neighbors are—"

"I wasn't talking about the house." Martin closed the distance between them and cupped Robbie's face between his hands. "Although I suppose it's nice too. I'll tell you later."

Then Martin was kissing him, and Robbie was kissing him back, and *oh*, it was just as glorious as Robbie remembered. And when they shed their tuxedos and lay skin to skin in bed, *that* was even better. But when dawn peeked in the windows and Robbie woke up with Martin still next to him, that was the best yet.

He slipped out of bed. He wasn't due on set until ten. Boyd had wanted to give everyone the day off after the premiere, but Mr. Jacob was keen to get the picture wrapped as soon as possible. While Robbie was anxious to finish shooting and be one step closer to being done with acting, he wished he'd insisted on the day off.

Because as wonderful as the night had been, he wanted to show Martin exactly how wonderful their days could be if they spent them here. Together.

He ran downstairs to do some quick breakfast preparation. Then he took a shower and dressed in one of the suits he'd complained to Martin about last night. The Schlossbergs might allow him to drive himself in his own car, but they insisted that he not look like a chauffeur—or worse, a hick from Idaho— while he was doing it.

When he crept back into the bedroom, Martin was still asleep. Robbie stood at the foot of the bed for a few minutes, captivated as always by Martin's incredible good looks. His hair was tousled, his lashes dark fans against his cheeks. But the hollows under his cheekbones were more pronounced than Robbie remembered. *He hasn't been eating right. He needs someone to look after him.*

He moved to the bedside and dropped a kiss on Martin's jaw. "Good morning," he murmured.

"Mmmm." Martin opened his eyes. "Is it morning?" He blinked at the sun streaming in through the windows. "Unless you've installed a klieg light in your backyard, I suppose it must be."

"I'm sorry to wake you, but I've got to be in Santa Monica by ten. I thought you might like a ride home, as well as a bit of breakfast."

Martin stretched. Then he hooked a finger in Robbie's vest pocket and drew him down for a more thorough kiss. "I'd rather have you for breakfast."

Robbie returned the kiss, but then he reluctantly disengaged Martin's finger and stood up. "I'd like that, but this is Dottie's picture, remember? She'd send the posse up after me if I wasn't there on time. Come on. I squeezed some orange juice for you with my own hands."

"How can I pass that up?"

"I'll set us up out on the patio. Come out when you're ready."

Robbie trotted downstairs, humming as he positioned the Adirondack chairs just *so* next to the round cedar table on the patio. He brought out plates, napkins, glassware, and coffee mugs. And doughnuts, of course. He was setting the coffeepot next to the juice pitcher when Martin spoke from the doorway behind him.

"You look… contented, Rob."

Robbie shot Martin a grin as he filled the juice glasses. "You have something to do with that."

Martin blushed. He actually blushed. Robbie had never seen him blush before, and it was oddly arousing. *You'd think I couldn't manage another hard-on after last night.* Apparently Robbie's pecker was made of stern stuff. *Or else Martin is that irresistible.*

Martin stepped onto the patio and sat down. "This is lovely—the house, the yard, the hills."

"It'll be nicer once the plants are established, but it's not bad now." Robbie poured coffee for both of them and flushed a bit when Martin chuckled over the doughnuts.

For a little while, they ate in contented silence—or at least it was contented on Robbie's side. *This is what I want. Nothing glamorous or adventuresome. Just this. Just life.*

"I understand you're doing an excellent job as Billy the Kid."

Robbie glanced at Martin over the rim of his coffee cup. "Who told you that? Dottie? She's partial."

"Oddly, no. Apparently it's the sentiment of the cowboys who are working on the picture with you."

"They're only being nice." Robbie toyed with his second doughnut and then set it back on the plate. "They'd say that about anybody who helped muck out the horses' stalls."

Martin laughed. "Do you?"

"Sure. Somebody has to do it."

"Yes, but you're the star of the picture. I understand they're putting your name above the title."

Robbie rolled his eyes. "Jehoshaphat, Martin, they're paying me half a million bucks to do this picture. That's good for more than a shovel or two of horse manure."

Martin whistled. "What did I tell you? Sid *is* good. Are you getting the same for the next picture too?" Robbie nodded. "Do you know what it is yet?"

He nodded again, wiping doughnut icing off his fingers with his napkin. "You'll laugh."

"If I do, it won't be at your expense, I promise."

Robbie sighed and met Martin's inquiring gaze. "It's *Robinson Crusoe*."

Martin didn't laugh, but he did grin. "Did Dottie write the scenario?"

"Of course. She tried to talk me into doing one more picture with Citadel after that because they're finally going to let her direct."

"Good for her." But despite the satisfaction in his tone, Martin's eyebrows pinched together. "Did you agree to do it?"

Robbie shook his head. "Not even for Dottie. I told Sid two pictures, and two pictures is all I'm going to do. After that, I'll be a gardener for the rest of my life."

"Gardener?" Martin smirked at him. "But I thought you were a landscape artiste."

"You know what I mean. After...." Robbie licked his lips, his belly swooping like a trapeze. "After that, would you... I mean, I know you said *you* wanted to buy a house, but you don't need to now. Could you.... You could move in here. With me."

Oh God. Martin covered his face with his hands. "Rob. You know that's—"

"Don't say no. Not yet. Think about it, all right? I—I still love you."

The sincerity in Robbie's tone gutted Martin, absolutely filleted him like a trout. *God, if only it were that simple.* "Love was never the question."

"So you still love me too?"

Martin huffed a laugh. "I don't think I'll ever stop."

"Then why not?"

"You *know* why. The press dearly loves a juicy scandal."

Robbie's eyes took on a steely glint. "The press doesn't care about gardeners, Martin."

Martin opened his mouth to retort, but then.... *Why not?* Robbie was right. Gardeners, even landscape artistes, weren't normally fodder for Hearst and his jackals. It might work, especially if Martin were to step out of the limelight as well.

"Two pictures, Martin. Two pictures and I'm done." Robbie gestured at the secluded yard, the lovely house behind them. "I told you we're private here. I own the lots on both sides and above us. It's not like we're the kind of folks to throw big Hollywood parties. Please, Martin." He reached across the table, palm up. "Please say yes."

Martin gazed into Robbie's pleading blue eyes. *How can I say no?* For that matter, why would he want to? Living with Robbie, coming home to him every night, waking with him every morning, with nobody poking their noses into what they did in between? Even if they couldn't reveal their relationship in public, it sounded a lot like heaven. *And someday, maybe things will change and we won't have to hide anymore.*

He placed his hand in Robbie's and laced their fingers together. "Yes. Yes, my dear. Yes, yes, yes."

Robbie's grin could have lit an entire shooting stage. "You won't be sorry. I promise. I'll—"

A telephone bell shrilled from inside, making Martin flinch. "God. If that's Dottie, tell her she's at least an hour too early."

Robbie squeezed Martin's hand. Then he rose and circled the table to drop a lingering kiss on Martin's mouth. "I will."

As Robbie disappeared inside, leaving the french doors open, Martin called, "And tell her Evelyn needs to step up her game if Dottie's able to put two thoughts together this morning." *Because God knows I can't.*

So while birds chirped in the trees, he sat on the patio, coffee cup in hand, and gazed at the hillside that would someday burst with Robbie's flowers. Even after less than twelve hours, it felt like home. *Of course, anywhere with Robbie would feel that way.*

"He did what?"

Robbie's half shout propelled Martin to his feet. He set his cup down on the table and walked to the door, although he didn't step inside. Robbie was half-turned away from him, his shoulders hunched forward as though trying to shield the telephone from Martin's eyes.

Martin reached out blindly for the door. *Oh God. What now? Did that reporter follow us after all? Is even this privacy an illusion?*

"No. That's all right, Sid. I'll tell him. Sure. Yes. One o'clock. Got it. Goodbye."

Robbie hung up and set the telephone back in its niche, moving like an old man. Martin let go of the door and took two strides into the room, but the expression on Robbie's face—devastation, defeat, fear—stopped him.

"Rob? What is it? What's wrong?"

"That was Sid. He said...." Robbie passed a hand over his eyes. "Will Hays just banned all of Roscoe's pictures."

Martin's knees gave out and he dropped onto the davenport. *Hays. Hollywood's handpicked moral watchdog.* Why should it be surprising when he showed his teeth?

Robbie stumbled over to sit beside him. "Roscoe was acquitted. The jury *apologized*. Why would Mr. Hays do this? It doesn't make sense."

Martin remembered the reporter's questions from last night, as much as he'd prefer to forget them. "I've heard Hays doesn't have a backbone unless somebody else forcibly inserts it. In this case it's probably Hearst. He's not going to let this go. He'll stir the coals and keep the public in an uproar because it sells newspapers. Hell, Roscoe's trials were a windfall for him. He doesn't care about the truth, justice, or anybody's livelihood but his own."

Robbie's breath hitched, and he slid a little closer, until they were hip to hip. "Sid.... Sid knew you were here."

"Yes, I imagine he did." Martin stroked Robbie's cheek. "But you needn't worry. It doesn't make any difference to him."

"He wants you to meet him at his office at one o'clock. Something about putting your plans in motion?"

"Ah."

"Martin?" The uncertainty in Robbie's voice brought Martin's head up with a jerk.

"What is it, my dear?"

"You're not going to run again, are you?"

Martin closed his eyes for an instant, as contempt for his past behavior swamped him. *It's a fair question.*

"No. I won't run, but perhaps we should reconsider. If Hays can ban Roscoe's pictures after his ordeal is supposedly over, then he could ban others as well. He could ban yours. He could ban mine. And in our cases, we would actually be guilty." Martin threaded his fingers through Robbie's hair because he still could. "Or at least guilty according to the letter of the law and therefore at the mercy of the press."

"Then we need to be so boring we're not worth the ink."

"You don't know reporters. If they can't find news, they create it. It's far easier. Look what they've done with Bill's case."

Robbie grimaced. "All right. Boring, but not *too* boring."

"Moderately boring, then. Who knows? Perhaps I'll become a gardener too."

"Martin. Do you know the difference between a rhododendron and an oleander?"

"No. But I can learn."

Robbie smiled sadly. "But you wouldn't love it, not like I do. You deserve to do something you love."

"Fine. I won't be a star, then. I'll just be an actor. I expect to discuss that with Sid today at one. And if that doesn't work, I'll find something else. Hell, maybe I'll be a tailor again."

Robbie leaned into him and rested his head against Martin's. "I don't know. I thought your seams were barely passable."

"True. But something that isn't simply *passable* is how I feel about you." Martin stood and pulled Robbie to his feet. "It seems as if every time we find a way forward, something arises to threaten us. Yet every time, we bounce back and find another way to persevere. So I'm determined, Rob."

"Determined?"

"Yes. You. Me. Our best life. No matter what they throw at us, we'll find a way. And maybe that will make things easier for everyone who comes after us."

"You promise?"

"No more running. No more pretending, not with you. I promise." And Martin sealed the promise with a kiss, with Robbie's enthusiastic cooperation.

CHAPTER TWENTY-SIX

March 2, 1944

Martin turned sideways to study his reflection in the full-length mirror. Maybe he wasn't able to fit in the same tux he'd worn to *The California Trail* premiere, but he didn't look too bad for a man pushing fifty.

These days, he didn't have many opportunities to wear a tuxedo. Homebody vocal coaches didn't, as a rule, and Martin didn't regret that fact any more than he regretted giving up his days in front of the camera.

Not when it had gotten him so much more.

He chuckled as he straightened his tie. He wasn't the only one—or even the most notable one—who'd given up his career for a love that dare not speak its name. Billy Haines had been a much bigger star—in the top five for several years, something Martin had never come close to achieving—when he refused L.B. Mayer's demand that he give up his lover, Jimmie. Billy had famously agreed to do so, as soon as Mayer gave up his wife, and Mayer's power was such that Billy had been virtually wiped from Hollywood history.

Although that hadn't bothered Billy. He'd become one of the most sought-after interior designers in town, and he and Jimmie were still together.

Just as Martin and Robbie were.

Downstairs, a door slammed. "Martin?" Robbie called.

"Up here, my dear. In the dressing room."

From the sound of it, Robbie was taking the stairs two at a time, as usual. "Sorry I'm so late. The clients wanted to chat about the next phase." Footsteps pounded across the bedroom, muffled somewhat by the new Persian rug Billy had found for them only last week.

"I hope you took your boots off downstairs," Martin said.

Robbie appeared in the doorway, looking down in dismay at his feet—still in their boots. "Dang. I forgot. Billy's gonna kill me."

If Martin didn't look bad for fifty, Robbie looked even better at forty-three than he had at twenty-two. His skin was browner and his hair bleached blonder from all the time he spent in the sun. Yes, the laugh lines at the corners of his eyes were deeper, but his body was toned by the physical labor he could never leave entirely to his crews, and his almost perpetual smile was just as bright and ingenuous as ever.

"I won't tell him if you don't."

Robbie looked up. "Wow." The admiration in his eyes never failed to bolster Martin's ego. "You look so handsome." He grinned. "But then, you always do."

"You flatter me, my dear." Martin strolled toward Robbie. "But then, you always do."

Robbie held up his hands. "Don't get too close. I'm all sweaty. I'll grab a shower and meet you downstairs. Ten minutes, tops, I swear."

Martin followed as Robbie raced across the rug—still in his boots, of course. Martin made a mental note to let the housekeeper know to take special care when he came on

Tuesday. "You don't have to hurry quite so desperately. We still have time."

"I don't want to miss anything, though," Robbie called from bathroom, the shower half-drowning his voice. "It's so exciting. George is nominated for *two* art direction awards. Two!"

"It should have been three." Martin ducked into the bathroom to retrieve Robbie's dirty clothes and make sure he'd remembered a towel. "He ought to have been nominated for *Casablanca* too, but mark my words, it's going to win Best Picture, so at least he can bask in that glory." But even if George didn't win tonight, he would someday. He was just that good.

"I wish Dottie and Evelyn could be there."

"They wanted to, but it wasn't possible. Not with Evie still playing in *The Cherry Orchard* at the National and Dottie filming those safety training films for women in the aircraft factories. They sent a telegram." He chuckled. "In fact, they sent three—one from each of them individually, and one from both together."

Martin closed the bathroom door behind him on Robbie's off-key rendition of Cole's "You'd Be So Nice to Come Home To"—also nominated for an award.

Yes, it's a good night for our friends.

Martin tossed Robbie's clothes in the hamper and walked downstairs. They still lived in Robbie's "mansion" and probably always would. Its grace, comfort, and privacy suited both of them perfectly. They both kept offices, of course—Martin in a cozy sound studio in Hollywood and Robbie next to the nursery he owned in Santa Monica, near the old Inceville site.

The Depression hadn't hit them as hard as some, primarily because neither one of them had anything invested in the stock market in '29. Martin had cashed out his portfolio when his acting income fell off, and Robbie claimed he didn't believe in stocks. He said he wanted to put his money into something he could see, so he'd gone in for land, preferably land with well-established vegetation. By 1930, he owned half the orange groves in Orange County.

But then, with the advent of sound, Martin's income had picked up again in a very unexpected way. All the tricks he'd learned about vocal production back in vaudeville were suddenly in demand. In fact, two of his students were nominated for awards tonight too.

Robbie clattered down the stairs, his wet hair slicked back against his head, his bow tie hanging loose around his neck. "Ready. Or mostly. At least I managed to scrub the dirt out from under my fingernails."

"Come here, you nut." Martin beckoned Robbie over and tied his bow tie. "There." He smoothed Robbie's lapels and dropped a kiss on his lips. "*Now* you're ready."

Robbie toyed with one of Martin's shirt studs, not meeting his gaze. "Are you ever sorry? That you left acting? That you'll never be up there on that stage?"

"Darling, I'd never have been up there even if I *had* continued acting. I was never that good. I simply looked the part. You, on the other hand—"

"Oh no." Laughing, Robbie held up his hands, palms out, the calluses at the base of his fingers clearly visible. The feel of those calluses on his skin still set Martin aflame. "I never wanted to be an actor anyway. I just wanted a good life. And my ideas of a good life aren't that fancy. A home. A garden. Decent work. Friends." He pulled Martin closer. "Someone to love. That's all I ever wanted."

"Isn't it lucky, then, that you've got them?" Martin kissed him, and it may not have been as electric as the first time, but it was better. Warm. Comforting. *Home*. "Come now. We mustn't be late letting our friends celebrate our success."

Robbie laughed, but didn't resist as Martin led him out the front door. "Don't you mean *we're* helping *them* celebrate?"

Martin stopped on the porch of the home they'd shared for the last twenty years. "No, my darling. Because in my opinion, I've won the greatest award of all. My life with you."

Dear Reader,

Thank you so much for reading *Silent Sin*, my first ever historical novel! I had a wonderful adventure writing it and hope you had an equally lovely journey reading it.

Did I mention that this is my first historical? My other books range from paranormal romantic comedy (*Cutie and the Beast*) to supernatural romantic suspense (*Stumptown Spirits*) to contemporary romantic comedy (*Clickbait*). You can see all my books on my website, https://ejrussell.com, or on my Amazon author page here: https://www.amazon.com/author/ej_russell. Most are also available at Apple, Kobo, and Barnes and Noble.

Would you like exclusive content and ARC giveaways, not to mention gratuitous dance videos? Then I'd love for you to join me in Reality Optional, my Facebook fan group (https://facebook.com/groups/reality.optional). My newsletter is the place to get the latest dish on new releases, sales, and more. I promise I only send one out when I've got…well…news. You can subscribe here: https://ejrussell.com/newsletter.

All my best,
—E

ACKNOWLEDGEMENTS

This book would not exist without the support and assistance of so many people. I'm forever grateful to them all.

If Suzanne Brockmann hadn't written a play called *Looking for Billy Haines*—and later graciously shared it with me—I might never have discovered the truth of an open, enduring gay relationship smack in the middle of Hollywood's golden age, Hays Code be damned. Thank you, Suzanne!

If Barbara Hambly hadn't written *Bride of the Rat God*, with its wonderful and evocative picture of silent movie-making (flavored with a little supernatural menace), I might not have fallen so happily down the Hollywood research rabbit hole. Thank you, Barbara! (I placed Robbie's house on Ivarene Street as an homage—I imagine him as one of Chrysanda Flamande's neighbors, perhaps farther down the street, past the Sabsung Institute for the Well-Being of Souls.)

If the lovely Kelly Jensen hadn't offered me support and encouragement with her beta read, I might have retreated in panic, because me? Writing a historical romance? How could I be so presumptuous? Thank you, Kelly, for your reassurance and suggestions!

Special thanks to Natasha Snow for the gorgeous cover; to Liz Fitzgerald and Andrea Zimmerman for editing and enthusiasm; to Amelia Vaughn, self-proclaimed soulless marketing hack, who's a constant source of comfort and championship. You all rock!

I can't forget the family—Jim, Hana, Nick, Ross, and Billy—who put up with my constant anecdotes about how things were done in early Hollywood. You're the stars in my life, and I love you all.

And of course, my readers. Thank you so much for accompanying my characters on their journeys!

AUTHOR'S NOTE

Try to imagine a world without movies. Without the cult of celebrity. Without *Hollywood.*

The film industry and its connection to Hollywood are so entrenched in our culture now, in our consciousness, in our daily lives, that it's somehow shocking to realize how very young it is, barely over a century old. The first film studio wasn't built in Hollywood until 1911.

In its early days, many were convinced that it would never last, and in those early days, dismantling it would have been far simpler than it would be today. Nobody was more terrified of an industry collapse than the studio heads themselves. When scandals rocked the town—not only the Taylor and Arbuckle cases, but the deaths of actors Olive Thomas and Wallace Reid, and producer Thomas Ince among others—they were ready to sacrifice almost anything to protect themselves and their budding empire.

What did it matter if a few stars' careers were destroyed (especially if they were expensive ones like Arbuckle) as long as the industry itself endured and as long as the producers' control over their world remained inviolate?

When it appeared that motion pictures would be subjected to government censorship, they invited in their own watchdog—Will Hays, former Postmaster General, and the progenitor of the infamous Production Code that would shape what appeared on-screen for decades.

It's ironic in a way—the producers thought they were protecting themselves from strict oversight, yet they had introduced a censor they couldn't escape because they'd invited him in and willingly subjected themselves to his authority.

Nevertheless, the studio system and its stranglehold on its *assets*—performers who were forced to toe the line if they expected to work in films—was so great that it kept actors like Cary Grant, Randolph Scott, Gary Cooper, and Ramón Novarro in the closet for their entire careers, sometimes for their entire lives. Louis B. Mayer was able to essentially erase William Haines from history. Haines had been the top box office draw for several years in the late twenties and early thirties, including making the transition from silent films to talkies. But Haines refused Mayer's order to abandon his lover, Jimmie Shields, and marry a woman. His studio contract and acting assignments suffered, but rather than repine, Haines quit acting and became one of the most successful interior decorators in Hollywood. Joan Crawford, a lifelong friend, was one of his first clients.

If the Taylor murder and the Arbuckle case gave me the framework to hang my story on, Billy Haines and Jimmie Shields (who were together until Billy's death in 1973) supplied the inspiration for Martin and Robbie's romance. Two men could build a rich and happy life in Hollywood by evading (and ignoring) the studios' hold.

William Desmond Taylor's murder has never been solved. Given the corruption in the police department at the time and the hopelessly compromised crime scene, it's unlikely that it will ever be. That doesn't stop people from speculating. King Vidor was convinced Charlotte Shelby, controlling stage mother of starlet Mary Miles Minter, was the guilty party. Some believe Mary Miles Minter herself, who was romantically obsessed with Taylor despite being thirty years his junior, pulled the trigger. On her deathbed in 1964, Margaret Gibson, another actress who had fallen on difficult times back in 1922, reportedly confessed to killing Taylor. There were other suspects, none of whom ever panned out. Speculation is all we'll ever have.

A note about timelines....

The documentation for some events in those early days can be a bit sketchy. Whenever possible, I used the first-person accounts of those who worked in silent films (historian Kevin Brownlow's excellent *The Parade's Gone By* includes many such anecdotes). My primary source of the sequence of events in February of 1922 is King Vidor's account of his own investigation into the murder, as related by Sidney Kirkpatrick in *A Cast of Killers*. Vidor was actively working in Hollywood during the silent era and knew many of the principals in the case. *A Cast of Killers* includes Vidor's story of filming scenes from *Sky Pilot* in the Sierras, getting caught in a blizzard, and walking into Truckee to be greeted by his father with the news of Taylor's death.

I've taken some liberties about where certain premieres might have taken place, but you know, this is fiction. I can do that!

But the story of the Stephens-Townsend-Murphy party's trip to California, including Moses Schallenberger's ordeal and subsequent rescue by Dennis Martin? That's all true. Members of the Donner party sheltered in Moses's still-standing cabin during their later (and vastly less successful) trip. If you visit the Donner Memorial today, you can see a commemorative plaque on the site.

BIBLIOGRAPHY

William Desmond Taylor sources:
- *A Cast of Killers* by Sidney Kirkpatrick
- *Murder in Hollywood* by Charles Higham
- *Famous Players* by Rick Geary
- *Tinseltown* by William J. Mann

Roscoe "Fatty" Arbuckle sources:
- *Room 1219* by Greg Merritt
- *Frame Up!* by Andy Edmonds
- Numerous contemporary articles from *The New York Times* archives

The queer experience in Hollywood:
- *Behind the Screen: How Gays and Lesbians Shaped Hollywood 1910 - 1969* by William J. Mann
- *Gay Hollywood: The Last Taboo* (documentary, available on YouTube)
- *Wisecracker: The Life and Times of William Haines, Hollywood's First Openly Gay Star* by William J. Mann

Silent film sources:
- *The Parade's Gone By* by Kevin Brownlow
- *The War, the West, and the Wilderness* by Kevin Brownlow
- *The Hollywood Posse* by Diana Serra Cary
- *Spellbound in Darkness* by George C. Pratt
- *Silent Lives* by Lon Davis
- *Silent Stars* by Jeanne Basinger
- *A Girl Like I* by Anita Loos

- *Hollywood: The Pioneers* (video series narrated by James Mason; multiple episodes available online)

Early Hollywood (general):
- *The Story of Hollywood: An Illustrated History* by Gregory Paul Williams
- *The Hollywood Story* by Joel W. Finler

ALSO BY
E.J. RUSSELL

Paranormal Romance
Mythmatched Universe
Fae Out of Water Trilogy
Cutie and the Beast
The Druid Next Door
Bad Boy's Bard

Supernatural Selection Trilogy
Single White Incubus
Vampire With Benefits
Demon on the Down-Low

Howling on Hold
Possession in Session

Art Medium Series
The Artist's Touch
Tested in Fire
Art Medium: The Complete Collection (omnibus edition)

Legend Tripping Series
Stumptown Spirits
Wolf's Clothing

Enchanted Occasions Series
Nudging Fate
Devouring Flame

Monster Till Midnight

Contemporary Romance
Mystic Man
The Probability of Mistletoe
An Everyday Hero
A Swants Soiree
For a Good Time, Call… (A Bluewater Bay novel, with Anne
Tenino)

Geeklandia Series
The Boyfriend Algorithm (M/F)
Clickbait

ABOUT THE
AUTHOR

E.J. Russell–grace, mother of three, recovering actor–writes romance in a rainbow of flavors. Count on high snark, low angst and happy endings.

Reality? Eh, not so much.

She's married to Curmudgeonly Husband, a man who cares even less about sports than she does. Luckily, C.H. also loves to cook, or all three of their children (Lovely Daughter and Darling Sons A and B) would have survived on nothing but Cheerios, beef jerky, and Satsuma mandarins (the extent of E.J.'s culinary skill set).

E.J. lives in rural Oregon, enjoys visits from her wonderful adult children, and indulges in good books, red wine, and the occasional hyperbole.

News & Social Media:
Website: https://ejrussell.com
Newsletter: https://ejrussell.com/newsletter
Facebook Reader Group: https://www.facebook.com/groups/reality.optional
Amazon: https://amazon.com/author/ej_russell
BookBub: https://www.bookbub.com/authors/e-j-russell
Facebook: https://facebook.com/E.J.Russell.author
Twitter: @EJ_Russell

CPSIA information can be obtained
at www.ICGtesting.com
Printed in the USA
LVHW110257250220
648043LV00003B/52